THE
SILENT
ONES

Elisabeth Ogilvie

THE
SILENT
ONES

Amereon House

TO THE READER
It is our pleasure to keep available uncommon
titles. To this end, at the time of pubication, we
have used the best available sources. To aid
catalogers and collectors, this title is printed in
an edition limited to 300 copies. *-- ENJOY!*

To order contact
AMEREON HOUSE, the publishing division of
Amereon LTD.
Post Box 1200
Mattituck, New York 11952-9500

LIBRARY OF CONGRESS CATALOGING IN PUBLICATION DATA

Ogilvie, Elisabeth, 1917-
The silent ones.
I. Title.
PS3529.G39S5   813'.52   81-3723

Manufactured in the United States of America

To Flora Macdonald of Aignish,
Isle of Lewis

Prologue

HERE AT THE STONES the Priest-King had walked in his cloak of feathers, with wrens flying about him, so long ago that he was only a dream, a myth, to the first Celtic and Pictish Christians who built their chapels and beehive cells on Leodhas: a dream, a myth, but they still called the place pagan and accursed, believing the turf to have been nourished by the blood of human sacrifice.

The Viking raiders went wide of the place, believing that if they could not see the Stones, the Stones could not see them, and thus they would be spared the awful magic of unknown gods from whom even Thor could not protect them.

Over the centuries the peat built up around the Stones but their power never lessened. For they could hide themselves from those who had no right to see them; sometimes they spoke. They saw the Beltane fires each May, and at the Midsummer sunrise the Shining One walked the avenue, proclaimed by the cuckoo's call.

The peat was cleared away. The scholars came and went as they will always come and go. And the Stones will stand, impervious to interpretation; all their successive mysteries will never be told. Those who believe they feel the emanation of mystic forces here are like the child who holds a shell to his ear and believes he hears the sea; it is the salt tide of his own blood that echoes there.

1

DREAM OF THE DEAD and hear from the living, that's how the saying went. Who would be writing to her, Alison asked in cynical amusement, after dreaming all the way across the Atlantic of her father, her mother, and the brother whom she had never known.

She'd given no one an address. She'd said, "I'll be in touch when I know where I am," and thought, Don't hold your breath.

She had put her lawyer's name in her passport as the person to notify in case she was found dead somewhere, but he didn't know it. The last time she'd seen him had been two years ago, when they were settling her father's small estate.

Aboard the *Queen Elizabeth 2* she had a table to herself in the dining room, by request. It was not that she was antisocial. She enjoyed researching and teaching her subject, and working with enthusiastic students, but whenever she was tired it was of people. There'd been times during the last few weeks when she'd ached with a positive lust for solitude. And now weeks of marvelously private days were tossed down before her like gems.

This was the last part of the year's leave of absence she'd taken to write the final draft of *Folklore in Fact, Legend, and the Human Psyche*. She had worked at home, surrounded by her own books and close to the college library, respectfully left alone by the rest of the academic community except for occasional but fairly insistent questions from colleagues about what she was going to do for a rest and a change when the book was finished. When she gave only vague or provoking answers like, "I guess I'll clean my flat," the questions turned to earnest advice for her own good.

"You should do something different," her department head told her. "You need to move around. Even the best of us can go stale. I know you think it can't happen to you, but that's only the overweening confidence of the young."

Alison laughed. "Overweening; conceited, presumptuous, brash, arrogant. That's me all over."

"Don't nit-pick. You know what I mean."

His wife said maternally, "But you *are* young, Alison. Too young to be so circumscribed, or do I mean circumspect?"

"Oh, Alison is always *that*," said her husband, with nuances of either pity or disapproval.

She was harangued by a friend who was a biologist in the science department. "Don't you ever want to see *anything* outside this town?" she demanded. "Oh, I know you make those working trips out into the hinterlands, but don't you want to go somewhere just for the sheer fun and adventure of it? Be a *tourist*? My God, I'd go like a shot. Anywhere! San Francisco. Mexico. The Caribbean. Even a budget tour of Europe on a bus."

Alison said modestly, "Well, I might look up some distant relatives in Wisconsin."

Her friend groaned. "I give up. You're impossible."

But when the book went into page proofs, Lynn began again. "You've got five months from now until September." She sighed with longing; she'd be teaching summer courses. "If I were as free as you—" A bit of complacency there. She had a lover, and sometimes attempted to analyze Alison's reasons for not having one.

Alison was going somewhere, and the phrase "distant relatives" contained a literal truth. She had made her plans back in the winter and now, reluctantly, she told people she was sailing on the QE 2 in mid-April. She was reluctant because, once they knew, it was no longer her own, and also because she was afraid of jinxing the trip by talking about it. Her superstition amused her but she couldn't help respecting it. A lifetime of losses had made her as wary as a cat, though no one would have suspected her of it.

Everybody was astonished by her news, delighted, claimed to be envious, and gave her a party. She'd been to enough of these for other people to wryly appreciate being the star herself, and she was touched by the good will.

"What are you going to do over there?" she was asked from all sides.

"I'm going to investigate ancient fertility cults still flourishing in the heart of London," she said. "Did you know that the Playboy Club there is built on the site of a Roman temple to the little-known but powerful goddess Coniglia, whose symbol is a rabbit?"

After that, nobody got back to asking her questions, but she was given plenty of advice on what she mustn't miss. She accepted it all with grace, as she'd received the useful gifts.

"And Alison, have fun," her boss commanded. "I know you've got something in mind, you'll come back with a book, but all work and no play, you know. To coin a phrase."

The genuine affection and concern both embarrassed and touched her. She was glad to get away. And then in her cabin there was the huge basket of fruit from the librarians, and that started the prickle of tears in her eyes and nose.

"Smashing, isn't it, love?" asked her stewardess.

"Yes," said Alison, bemused with love for them all now that she was at a safe distance. "Help yourself, will you? I mean it. I can't possibly eat it all."

Now she felt guilty for not telling them her destination after Southampton. Maybe there was such a thing as being too
secretive, and what harm would it have done? But she hadn't
wanted to be questioned about her choice, which was certainly
one the others had never suggested or even dreamed of, supposing they knew where it was.

She shrugged off her doubts. She'd send notes and postcards all around later on, from spots like London, Glasgow,
Edinburgh. Why quibble about keeping minor secrets when
the big one would have really knocked the wind out of them?

They all knew her professional writing, which brought her
more respect and reputation than money. If any of them knew,
or would admit to knowing, the sexy thrillers by Mariana
Grange, they would never have suspected any relationship.
Whenever Alison saw Mariana's latest in the hands of a student, or being frantically stuffed into a faculty wife's shopping
bag away from Alison's supposed intellectual contempt, she
had a delightful vision of her increasing royalty account.

"Oh, what's that?" she would say. "Colorful cover, isn't it?"

"It belongs to my daughter." Or, "I picked it up for my
mother, she dotes on the stuff. *I* can't stand it!"

"But she's really very good," Alison would say. "Don't go
by the cover. At least her historical backgrounds are authen-
tic."

"*You* read them?"

"Now and then. Actually I find them very relaxing."

Once it occurred to her that the recipient of this blessing
probably went away thinking that Alison Barbour must find
all her romance in paperback Gothics, and what a shame for
such a good-looking girl.

Mariana Grange had been named for Tennyson's famous
maiden, with whom Alison had identified when she was a
child missing her mother and longing for the brother who had
died as a little boy before she could ever know him. She had
imagined him all through her childhood, giving him a life her
parents never suspected. But by adolescence a dream brother

had gone with all the others that she dreamed no longer, like the Shetland pony under the Christmas tree, and the miraculous return of pets that had died.

Growing unhappily and gawkily into her teens with an uncommunicative father, she saw herself as the maiden waiting wearily for one who cometh not; the lost brother, the lost mother, the old dog and cat, the puppy and kittens whose lives had been cut as brutally short as her brother's had. The pony had never existed in the flesh, but she had dreamed of him so often that even now she still lumped him in with all the lost loves.

Her first Mariana Grange book, when she was twenty, had been a *cri du coeur*. It embarrassed her now with its passion and hyperbole, its auburn-haired heroine was so clearly herself. At the time she'd been immensely proud, excited by the sale itself and then by the increasing royalties as the book sold and sold. She'd been happy to keep her secret, rather than present it to her father like a particularly robust but illegitimate grandchild.

She had quickly become adept at weaving tight, cliffhanger plots against sound historical backgrounds. She was a best seller in supermarkets and drugstores, while her professional publications were esteemed by a small, choice audience.

Aboard the ship, crossing moderately calm seas, she had plenty of time to contemplate her double life. Sitting in a lounge, facing the water, a notebook open on her knee and a pen in her hand so she would look thoughtfully busy and not inclined to conversation, she reflected that it would not be absolutely wrong to say she lived vicariously through paperback adventures. The writing of them was pure escapism. Well-paying escapism, though. That made it respectable.

She knew it was her own fault that no lovers came across the moat into her life. She reasoned that it was logical for her to grow up with a wary attitude toward males, considering that her father hardly ever talked to her and her brother had deserted her. Learnedly she called *deserted* a Freudian slip, a holdover from her early conviction that the missing boy had really run away from home because he resented the new baby sister instead of realizing how much she would need a big brother.

Alison might have lived surrounded by a moat, with the drawbridge up and the portcullis permanently down in case anyone intrepidly swam the moat, but her heroines had marvelous lovers. They never began their affairs with rape, for instance. Rape was *out*. Her present hero was a magnificent Highlander who was offering to marry the lass he'd stolen and locked up in his remote mountain keep, hoping to start a healthy dynasty to inherit all the lands he was accumulating by fire and sword. Given the ethics and manners of his period, he was showing an unaccountable reluctance to take his woman by force or even to bring in a tame clergyman to marry them without her consent. So the stalemate had lasted for some time, during which he argued with her over the wine glasses in lovable frustration when he wasn't satisfying his honor with bloody forays down the glen.

As for the victim, between her plucky attempts to escape she often saw him being kind to a child or a dog or some tottering old clansman, and heard talks of his deprived youth from the old woman who'd been his foster mother and nursed him at her own breast. This all showed her how sensitive and poetic the Highlander really was, and so lonely too, even though that was because he'd killed off all his relatives. Under extenuating circumstances, as his foster mother explained; they'd stood between him and the title.

Alison's Scotland so far was a feat of her imagination and her reading, but she expected to get back to gallant Alasdair and brave Catriona once she was on their native turf. They would pay for the trip. But the reason for the journey was not the novel; she could write about almost any setting without ever having been there, as long as she had maps, guide books, and a comprehensive history of the region and the period.

"Distant relatives," she had said to Lynn, and she hadn't been lying. The relatives were so distant they had died long ago, and she knew the name of only one of them. But that one had been a fixed point in her life since she was a child, remaining when all the others vanished. Paradoxically this figure never appeared in her dreams. She was simply *there*, a permanent spark like a distant lighthouse in Alison's consciousness.

As a child Alison hated her looks, especially the red hair about which the other children teased her and well-meaning adults made quips; she didn't like the color of her eyes, she resented her sharp cheekbones and she used to think glumly, I look like no one else in the world. So little did she resemble her parents that she believed for a long time she'd been adopted.

Then one day her father said, unexpectedly, because he was not given to making personal remarks, "You put me in mind of my father's mother. You look like her. Her hair was red too, I believe."

She had been tremendously excited, exploding with questions, but she got very little more except that he'd never known his grandmother, he'd seen her picture just once, and Alison looked like the picture. He didn't know where the picture was; he'd lost track of it years ago.

He said no more. Her mother couldn't help; he had never talked to her about his people. "But his feelings run very deep," she said. "I'm sure he hasn't talked about his family because he never really got over losing his parents when he was young." They'd died suddenly in the big influenza epidemic in 1918.

He was never at a loss for words in his teaching or in his books, but he had been almost inarticulate in his love for his wife and child. Alison used to wonder if the lost boy would have made a difference; he could have completely changed all their lives. She never had the courage to ask if *he'd* had red hair.

After her mother died suddenly from pneumonia, as his parents had died of the flu, he became even more silent, though Alison never doubted his affection. But in her adolescent desolation she had thought angrily, Some people talk more to their plants than he does to me!

One thing she was glad about now was that she had finally told him about Mariana Grange. He had been incredulous at first, then burst out laughing and slapped his desk and said he couldn't wait until he'd read one. She saw then the man her mother had married.

Afterward he'd congratulated her and read the others. Whenever she remembered this she couldn't help smiling. It was *something*, this good feeling they'd had at the end of things, the shared joke on everybody else. Better than never having had it at all. But she'd not been able to ask him about his grandmother; she was still inhibited about personal questions.

But just that one remark of his so long ago, coming apparently from nowhere and never followed up, had had its effects. The mysterious great-grandmother whom she resembled had become a valid presence in her existence. The child accepted herself, if not with grace, at least with a sense of continuity.

The adult Alison knew her hair to be not just red, but a true, rich, dark copper, and was grateful for its not being a gaudy orangey-red. Her face was strong across the cheekbones, narrowing down to the cleft chin. The brown eyes were delicately hollowed. She had grown up to her nose, as her mother had promised her when she was still glooming around about tip-tilted noses and violet eyes.

She carried her height well and wore that glowing hair in a short, neat, modified page-boy style, and dressed to complement it. She had enough vanity to want to look well when she stood before a roomful of students not too much younger than herself. She liked matching coppers, bronzes, old golds, peach and apricot shades, subtle greens, warm browns; she wore silk shirts and scarves, fine tweeds and cashmeres. Mariana Grange's heroines bounced from bed to bed to pay the clothing bills.

This elegantly turned-out young woman gazing at the Atlantic from aboard the *QE 2* was seeing, instead of ocean, the collection of cartons and trunks which had been stored in the basement of the apartment building when she and her father moved there from the house. After he died she had gone to them with a kind of savage, teeth-gritting opposition to the idea of sorting and probably discarding ancient things her parents had saved for their private reasons. What if there were a little boy's clothes and toys?

She went through everything with a grim dedication to the job, and found no relics of the dead boy. On the whole it wasn't too harrowing—it was even absorbing sometimes.

Then, inside an old Bible with molding leather binding she found a photograph mounted on heavy cardboard, and there was her own face between the roguishly tipped chip bonnet and the narrow ruching and bow at the throat.

It was a little broader and a little younger, but the cheekbones were the same, and so were the delicately hollowed eyes, though they were widened with the sober intensity of the gaze she had fixed on the camera. The faintly smiling mouth was serene above a round young chin in which the dent clearly showed, and made Alison instinctively put a finger to her own chin.

The girl sat in a low chair, one arm in its ornate sleeve resting on a small table with the hand elegantly drooping, the other hand in her lap. She'd been carefully posed to make the most of her dress, probably she'd never had such a dress before. It was a marvel of puffs, pleats, bows, shirred overskirt and striped underskirt. The chip bonnet had a plume and a flower. Her thick hair seemed to be caught in a snood at the back of her neck.

The background was an artificial forest glade, and the photographer had a Boston address. On the back was written in a thin clear brown handwriting, elegantly drawn out with large elaborate capitals, "Christina MacLeod. Born in eighteen-hundred and forty-nine, at Torsaig, Isle of Lewis. Outer Hebrides, Scotland."

2

SHE CARRIED her grandfather Barbour's Bible upstairs and gave first aid to the leather. The photograph went on the night table beside her bed.

The Outer Hebrides would have been outer space to her if she hadn't read about the Standing Stones. But it had always been a superficial mention; Stonehenge and Carnac were the stars. Now, in the space of a half hour on a Saturday morning, the name Lewis became as personal to her as her own.

She looked up everything she could find about the island, which wasn't much except that flat Lewis and mountainous Harris formed one long island, the Viking chessmen had been found there, and Harris tweeds were woven mostly on Lewis. There was an old road map of England among her parents' things—they'd driven around England on their honeymoon—and she wrote to the mapmakers, hoping they were still in existence. They were, and would send her what she required upon receipt of an international money order.

The map of the Long Island was extraordinarily detailed. For a place with so many open spaces and so few roads, it was as spangled with names as the Milky Way with stars. Every stream, every loch, every hill, cove, headland, islet, and ledge, had its name. She tried to make her search systematic, but she was continually diverted by the riches spread out before her. She went to bed with names ringing in her head like poetry; Valtos, Kirkibost, Barvas, Tolsta. Bernera, Breasclete. Aignish, Swordale. She woke with them in the morning.

She worked on her books during the days. (Professionally on weekdays, as Mariana Grange on weekends.) She spent most of her evenings with the map spread out on the floor before the fireplace while she wandered happily across the heathery barrens searching for Torsaig, but enjoying the distractions along the way.

One night she found Torsaig on the western side of the island, on the shore of a sea loch only a few miles away from the Standing Stones at Callanish. She looked at it for a long time through a magnifiying glass, at the name itself and the black dots for houses, as if she would see people, cottages, even sheep if she could only get close enough.

A curious quiet settled over her, as if she had been traveling a long time through tumultuous noise and motion, and suddenly it had all ceased.

That night she dreamed of the Callanish Stones. The dreams kept shifting like a series of camera images dissolving into one another. Once she saw a figure moving at a distance among the Stones, and she thought, That's Christina! But when she reached it, it was one of the Stones and there was nothing but herself and the avenue of silent upright slabs in a light that was both bright and dark. Then she could see the figure moving again, somewhere else, and again she tried to reach it, running with the painfully impeded motion of dreams, and her own hard breathing woke her up.

The next day she addressed a letter to Tourist Information at Stornaway, the major town of the Isles, enclosing international reply coupons for return postage. In a week she received by airmail some material on the Isles, a register of tourist accommodations, and a handwritten note warning her that the weather in the Outer Hebrides wasn't always as sunny as the publicity photographs showed. The writer was a Mairi MacLeod.

"Thank you, cousin," Alison said aloud. Through the accommodations register she rented a cottage at Aignish for April and May. She decided to sail instead of fly to England because she didn't like planes, and Mariana Grange had done well enough with her last book to pay the ship fare.

She went to Boston for her passport and travel arrangements. Her secrets were easy to keep. I must take after my father, she thought. He could have had a succession of mistresses and never given himself away once.

One day when she took a professional magazine from its wrapper its cover photograph showed the Callanish Stones, taken late one autumn day. She had an immediate sensation of *déjà vu*. It wasn't because she had seen the picture before, but it was as if she had been there herself among the Stones in this late silence after the day's wind had died down. The very way the light slanted along the Stones and brushed the turf was dizzyingly familiar. And so were the shapes of the low hills in the background.

She remembered the dream, but it was different from that. She put the magazine down and went to the window, needing to sight-touch familiar landmarks. Behind her the magazine waited; extraordinary how a piece of paper could be so pervasive, it had a life of its own that clamored in the room.

Once she read the article inside and became lost in the usual morass of astronomical calculations that made the builders out to be only slightly less brilliant than Einstein, she would have gained control over the Stones.

"That's a weird thing to say," she remarked aloud. "If anybody else knew about this they'd be calling me more than set in my ways. Poor Alison, she's heading for the funny farm."

She watched the traffic under the bare elms, and children

climbing on the tops of dirty snowdrifts. She had no sense of dread connected with the Stones, and there'd been none in the dream, just that incredible familiarity potent enough to shake her.

This has happened to a good many people, she thought. They write about it with pride. It makes them unique, they think. It gives them one more dimension than the ordinary human being has. They think they're absolutely fascinating when the simple truth is it's all due to a romantic imagination, and I have one, or I wouldn't be Mariana Grange. And I don't think I'm fascinating. Just lucky.

On a mild windy afternoon a week or so before she was to leave, she was walking across the campus, away from the library where the staff had been wishing her a good trip. One of them had cheerily hoped there wouldn't be a violent gale like the one which had severely damaged the *QE 2* in the autumn. She gave an enthusiastic account of a friend's seasickness, terror, and bruises, while Alison maintained an expression of polite interest.

She'd escaped finally, wanting to laugh, but as she joined the foot traffic she thought, What if it does happen again, only worse? Nobody expected it that time. And what about icebergs? Who mentioned *that*? Oh God, Alison, you're turning into a ditherer. Ditherer: ancient musical instrument. Wind or stringed? Early zither? Maybe somebody had a speech impediment, like that King of Castile who lisped. . . .

"Have a great trip, Dr. Barbour," someone called to her.

"Thank you!" She walked on. She was passing the chapel when a man spoke to her. She turned and the stranger was smiling timidly and taking off his hat.

"I beg your pardon for this liberty, Dr. Barbour, but I just wanted to tell you how much I enjoyed *The Mythology of the Hudson River Valley*."

"Well, thank you. That's nice to hear."

He kept smiling with shy pleasure. He was a stocky, tidy man in a Balmacaan topcoat, with graying hair cut short and heavy rimmed glasses. His mustache was as neat as his hair.

"I knew this was your college, but I didn't think I'd be lucky enough to meet you. One of the librarians pointed you out. Oh!" He looked worried. "I'd better introduce myself. My name is Harold Marshall." It fitted him exactly.

"I'm a dealer of rare books, but your field is my avocation, you might say. I'm strictly an amateur, but sometimes an old book comes into my hands that carries some very exciting stuff." He ducked his head bashfully. "Exciting to me, that is. You'd probably know it already. I imagine there isn't much that's new to you."

"What I don't know would fill quite a few libraries. How do you do, Mr. Marshall?" She put out her hand and he took it in both of his and shook it fervently.

"I can't *tell* you what this means to me. When I call my sister tonight and say I've met you, she'll flip, as the youngsters say."

"I'm flattered," said Alison. "But how do you happen to be here? If you're local I should know you."

He still had her hand in an ardent grip. "I'm not, I'm from upper New York state, on my way to Boston to fly to England tomorrow. I planned to leave from there instead of New York just so I could visit Hazlehurst and take a look at the library, primarily the Eccles Collection. And I've found a few of your things I hadn't seen before. Oh, excuse me!" He dropped her hand, blushing. "I didn't mean to wring your fingers off."

"They're still attached, see?" She flexed them.

"I'm relieved. Anyway, one of the librarians told me I could get copies at the campus bookshop, so I'll stop here on my way home to pick them up. Could I—if you have the time and it wouldn't be an imposition—could I buy you a drink or a cup of coffee?"

There was something so ingenuous about his eagerness, she

couldn't shoot it down. "You can buy me a cup of tea about one block from here."

"Thank you. I feel as if you'd just given me an auto-graphed first edition of William Blake."

At Barney's, student noise swirled around their booth like hurricane clouds as photographed by a satellite. Tolerantly they smiled at each other across the table.

"Could you possibly call this riot 'youth's sweet-scented manuscript'?" Alison asked. "Never mind, that's rhetorical. So you're a dealer of rare books and an amateur folklorist. You have the best of both worlds."

"Sometimes I think so. Right now I'm on a buying trip to England, a country I love. I'll have only a few weeks this time, and I'll be going to some sales, but I hope to visit some corners where the very air of centuries seems undisturbed. Until," he added, "the local motorbike club roars by on the remains of a Roman road."

"Maybe they're descendants of the Romans who worked on that road."

"I'll try to remember that next time. But I don't want to talk about myself. I'm so honored to be sitting here drinking tea with Dr. Alison Barbour." He colored up again like a boy.

"But I'm interested in what you do in those remote corners," she insisted.

"I look up the local clergy, there's always one who's happy to talk to an interested visitor. The doctor, if he's been there long enough, and he can always point out some old story-teller—well, you know how it goes. And of course if there's a library, I never miss that. I ask about old books, old manuscripts in the neighborhood, just for a chance to handle and read them, make notes, take photographs. I might make an offer on behalf of a client, without pushing it, you understand. The sale could put a decent bathroom into an old house, give it a new roof, revamp the heating. I leave my address so they can get in touch after they've thought about it. . . . But for myself—" His eyes gleamed. "Ah, that's *my* luxury! To look up collections of legends, myths, superstitions, or what were genuine beliefs when they were set down."

She listened with respect. Intelligent and curious amateurs often turned up rich nuggets.

"There are some things I've heard about," he said, "that I'd give anything to lay eyes on. The Book of St. Neacal, for instance. You quoted that in your last article in *North American Folklore*. The childbirth bit you found surviving almost intact in the back woods of Maine."

"But I've never seen it, and I know practically nothing about it. I quoted somebody else's reference, if you remember. Martin Landelius writing in the sixteenth century about childbirth superstitions."

He looked disappointed. "I thought that in your travels as a bona-fide expert you'd have had the chance to see that book."

"It was in Norway when Landelius saw it—he was a Norwegian—and I've never been across the Atlantic. I'm going next week for the first time in my life, by the way." She sounded much more blasé about it than she felt; with the time so close, the words gave her a jolt in the midriff. "I hope you don't mind if I don't say anything more than that, because I'm not sure what I'll do or where I'll go."

"I understand," he eagerly assured her. "And I hope it's all that you want it to be and more. Well, I mustn't keep you. But I was wondering—" He turned diffident again. "Could I see you tonight before I drive on to Boston? Just for an hour? There's something I'd like to show you. Unless you're all tied up for the evening, of course. You probably are."

It would have been simple to take this way out, and she was tempted, but his pale blue eyes were brightly hopeful behind his glasses.

"My flat's in the Bullard Building, just two blocks away from the west gate. 3-D. Come around seven."

"You won't be sorry," he told her. When they left Barney's he headed back to the library.

She thought of him at random intervals during the day, and saw her charitable impulse as a nuisance. But even if she'd known where to reach him and tell him that something urgent had gotten in the way, she wouldn't have done it; she'd been brought up in a strict ritual of courtesy and truth. One hour of her time wouldn't hurt.

It did occur to her at supper that she should mention him to someone, just in case he turned out to be a Jack-the-Ripper type. But she hadn't felt anything like that about him. Don't be so naïve, she warned herself. Many a victim hasn't felt *anything like that* about her murderer when she invited him in, and you're no psychic.

She told the people in the next flat that she was expecting a business caller and the man was a stranger.

"We'll keep our ears glued to the wall," the girl promised. "One move on his part and you scream bloody murder."

"And if you give him a drink," the husband added, "don't give him a chance to drop anything in yours. You wouldn't want to wake up in a bordello in Buenos Aires."

"Oh, I don't know," said Alison. "I might get a book out of it. Quaint Folkways of the Argentine."

He appeared promptly at seven, smiling broadly, carrying an attaché case. He checked his watch with the mantel clock. "On the stroke of eight I go, leaving not a glass slipper behind me, but this." He opened the case and took out a flat package wrapped in white tissue paper. "I was going to leave it at the library for you. I'd never dreamed of actually meeting you."

It was a small old leather-bound book, the pages still whole, the print eye-achingly tiny but clear. The name on the binding was indistinct, but the title was on the fly-leaf; *"The Witches of the Doune Valley,* by George Ringrose, Esquire." It had been printed in 1833.

Marshall was watching her without speaking. She took a long breath. "You shouldn't."

"I wanted you to have it. I was pretty sure you'd never heard of it, because you didn't mention it in your piece on early American witches in *Horizon* last year."

"I'm flabbergasted," she said. He was delighted. "Sit down," she urged, "and tell me about it, where you got it, unless that's a secret."

"Not at all. I acquired it quite openly and honestly. Last year I was buying books from the Ringrose heirs for a client, and they gave me a full day in the library. I saw this, and I offered to buy it, but they gave it to me, they were so happy to be getting a good price for the annotated Poe and a couple of other things they wanted to sell."

"I'll have to do a whole new study on witchcraft now," said Alison.

"Wait till you read the foreword. George Ringrose's mother came from this famous clan of so-called witches, who'd brought their knowledge over from England. He wrote up the facts to vindicate a brilliant family of natural healers, self-taught botanists, and zoologists. George gives many examples of the wild yarns told about them, and you can still hear traces of these stories today in the Doune Valley."

"What can I do to thank you for this?"

"You've already done enough. No matter what else happens on this trip, you'll have made it one of the high points of my life."

"You're making me blush. Let's have some wine and drink to successful journeys for each of us."

She brought in a bottle of Moselle and glasses. She lifted hers to him and said, "Good hunting."

"Many happy discoveries," he responded. "Wait until I tell my sister about this!"

"Tell me more about St. Neacal. Landelius simply quoted him without any details, except to say he'd read the book in the library of a Norwegian nobleman."

At once Marshall put down his glass and sat forward, his hands on his knees, obviously pleased to be able to instruct her. "Neacal was a Celtic monk of the seventh century. I don't know who canonized him, maybe the title is one of respect for his memory. He belonged to a monastery somewhere in the north of Scotland, and he transcribed this mass of material collected from the other monks, the villagers, and people he'd met in his travels. He seems to have been enormously interested in people not just as vessels to receive the gospels, but in all the other signs and symbols by which they lived. Their charms, spells, good and evil spirits, their word-of-mouth histories and legends."

He held out his hands, open and upward as if to receive. "Besides all these riches, the book was a jewel; all these sheets of vellum so beautifully illuminated. A monk who survived the destruction of the monastery by the Vikings in 1017 wrote as a very old man that the Book of St. Neacal was one of the lost treasures of their library."

He drank his wine quickly, as if overcome either by the story or by talking so much all at once.

"So some raider took it home and sold it," Alison said. "Wouldn't it be awful if it survived those raids only to be destroyed in another way? The house burning down, or something? I wonder if the Nazis could have swiped it when they were occupying Norway?"

Marshall looked so pale and quenched she wished she hadn't mentioned that.

"But a lot of these things have been recovered," she said. "I hope you find out something. If you're lucky, let me know. I'll be back in September."

"Then I haven't bored you with my enthusiasm. My sister says I go overboard."

"If you can't go overboard about something now and then, what's life?"

"That's what I say. I tell Rita she should be grateful my obsession isn't liquor or gambling or women." He stood up, looking around for his coat. "Well, I must be off to Boston and my hotel."

"Thank you for my book." She touched it gently. "I hope you have a great flight tomorrow and that your stay in England will be exciting and rewarding."

"That's so very kind of you, and you'll be hearing from me eventually about our elusive saint."

She smiled and put out her hand. He held it for a moment without speaking, looking down at it. Then his head came up and he said abruptly, "I wanted to meet you because of your work. But I never expected you to be young and beautiful."

He went alarmingly scarlet, blinked his eyes fast as if they were watering, and left, so embarrassed he couldn't look directly at her again. She called after him, "Your case!"

He grabbed it blindly and hurried toward the stairs.

She waited to see if he looked back, but he didn't. The neighbors came out into the hall, grinning impishly. "I just happened to remember," said the husband, "that Jack-the-Ripper killed only prostitutes. Could this be a type that looks for academic ladies?"

"Oh God, what a dreary phrase," said his wife.

Alison laughed. "He turned out to be a perfectly nice man who loves old books and manuscripts, and look what he gave me."

3

THIRTEEN DAYS LATER, up forward on the boat deck watching the tugs take the ship into the port of Cherbourg, she wondered where in England Harold Marshall was now, and if he'd discovered any traces of his elusive saint. She thought of him with mild affection and wished him well. He was likely to turn up at Hazlehurst again some time; well, he'd earned it, with his little book on the Doune witches. Mariana Grange would profit from that book, as well as Doctor Barbour.

It was Good Friday, and summer-warm after a cold, cloudy week. There was just enough breeze to blow small sailboats like gull feathers out across the pastel-blue water toward the fortifications the Germans had built.

Once the ship had docked, Alison stayed out for a little while to see what she could of France from up here, but it wasn't much. The men in the tugs had been more of the essence of France to her than this city stretching away in the sunshine. She walked aft past other viewers, and went inside for tea in the Double Room, taking a seat by the windows so she could look down on the pier.

The usual crowd hadn't gathered for tea. Many had left the ship, and most of those remaining were outside in the rare sunshine, or in their cabins packing.

That's really France out there, she told herself, her gaze traveling across the city toward the horizon. Already people are on their way to Paris. It's there, beyond the hills. But she could hardly make it credible, as long as she didn't step foot on French soil, walk on a French street, and speak with a French person. It remained a gauzy backdrop for her real journey. Again she felt that jolt in the midriff, without pain, only a fearful shaking-up, like being knocked around in one's private earthquake.

What am I building myself up for? she thought. Rain and peat bogs, that's what, and not even a trace of Christina MacLeod among the thousands of MacLeods who have come and gone for centuries.

"May I join you for tea?"

She hadn't seen him approaching, but now he was standing behind the chair across the small table from her. He was a tall, fair-haired man, probably in his mid-thirties. At a distance he would always look younger than he was. "I've wanted to speak to you from the start of the trip, but—" Rueful shrug.

"What the mind doesn't know the heart doesn't grieve for," she said dryly. "I think that's how it goes."

"Well, may I? You won't be committed. It's the end of the voyage and we all go our separate ways."

He waited, hands in his pockets. She had seen him often all the way across the Atlantic, always with the same woman holding his arm. Where could she be now? Alison had named her "Boots" because she always wore them, different colors for different outfits.

"I really can't keep you from sitting anywhere you like," Alison said, wishing she'd brought her notebook.

"Thank you." He dropped into the chair, rather than sat; he had a loosely youthful way of moving, without being awkward. He was gray-eyed, conventionally handsome in the style of the old Arrow Collar ads, and his short hair contributed to the effect. But his smile changed the standard good looks to something else. He was so benignly pleased with himself for accomplishing this meeting, one smiled back without intending to.

"Isn't this nice?" he said.

Feeling as if she'd fallen for an April Fool's trick, Alison said, "Where's your friend?"

"On the boat train to Paris, I hope. Where's some wood to knock on? Oh, well." He held up his hands with crossed fingers on each. A waitress who had not noticed Alison up to now was homing in on them like a carrier pigeon. Alison had observed this phenomenon all week; so had his woman friend, who had been openly amused at them at times and annoyed at others, usually when signs of high life the night before were showing through her meticulous make-up.

The waitress set out the tea things. "Thank you, dear," he said, and received a radiant smile. "Do we have any of those delicious little éclairs today?"

She called to a boy waiter who was just approaching a group of women. Instantly he swerved off course and came with his untouched tray of pastries. The waitress left reluctantly with her tray of teapots. Alison took an éclair, giving the waiter a special smile and thanks just to show that all the sex appeal wasn't across the table from her. The boy's response proved that the effort was worthwhile.

The man took three éclairs. The waiter said to Alison alone, "I'll be back. You might like something more. Those little round things are smashing."

"And today's my last chance, isn't it? I'd better take one now." He was pleased, and said "Cheery-bye!" to her when he left them.

"Will you pour?" the man asked. He took his cup and lay back in the deep chair, stretching out his long legs. "You're a professional woman, aren't you? Doctor, lawyer, physicist, systems analyst—though I've never quite understood them. How about architect? Editor?"

"Teacher." She thought of adding, "Kindergarten."

"Oh?" He was good; he looked convincingly interested. "What's your subject?"

"I'm in the English department at a small New England college, and my specialty is folklore and all that involves. Legends, traditions, maxims, superstitions."

He contrived to look charmingly amazed; rather overdoing it, she thought. "I'd have thought the subject was pretty well mined out by now."

"You wanted to knock on wood, didn't you? And you crossed your fingers."

"Touché." He waved an éclair at her, then ate it in two bites. "I suppose you must know all the things about red hair. You probably learned them very young. I love red hair, and yours is glorious. My God, is it real?"

"I came by it honestly. It's a family hand-me-down."

"Where are you going?" he asked. "Isn't it too early for the festivals, the Morris dances and the old fertility rites all gussied up for the tourists?" He leaned forward and whispered theatrically, "Are you going on a flying tour of the covens?"

She had to laugh. "Oh, gosh, I never thought of it, so I left my broomstick home."

"A pity. It's the only way to travel. But where *are* you going?"

She gazed at him as if in wonder and he grinned. "You don't have to answer. I'm known as Nosy Norris to my intimates, and they aren't a bit polite about it."

"What do *you* do?" she asked.

"I make bum investments."

"That's no profession."

"I seem to have made it mine."

She was suddenly tired of him and wanted to be alone with her anticipation, not wasting an hour of it in boredom. He did nothing, he was nothing; she had no patience with such people. She drank the last of her tea. The sun over the dock area was in her eyes and she turned to look across the dance floor, where the children were playing on and under the curving staircase.

"I take it you have no use for gamblers," he said.

"Do you mean that literally or figuratively?" she asked. "In the sense that I'd have no use for one as I don't need a posthole digger, or an orrery?"

"A *what*?"

A passing couple were startled into stopping. The woman laughed. "Hello!" she said. "I suppose we've missed tea." She was plaintive about it; she was a small, brightly dressed woman.

Norris slowly unfolded and stood up. "I'm afraid so. They seem to be tidying up."

"My, you *are* a tall one," she said with awe.

"And the bar's not open," the man said, not so much plaintive as dismal. "I don't see why at the price this business costs they shut everything up for the afternoon."

"Or they could at least have let us go ashore and walk around on French soil for an hour." She giggled. "Listen to us! As if we won't be coming over to France later anyway, and as if the bar won't be open by and by!" She had one of those emphatic, cheerful, Midwestern voices. She hugged the man's arm. "Honey, think how much better your drink will taste when you do get it. Don't carry on now, or these people will think you're a lush."

He remained gloomily inscrutable behind his sunglasses.

"Oh, sit down again, please!" she said to Norris. She took the third chair at the table. "Jake, bring over another one," she ordered. Jake obeyed, ungraciously. He was dark, gaunt, hollow of cheek, and paunchy. Both he and his wife (they had matching wedding rings, very wide, ornate, and unavoidable) were much dressier than Alison and Norris. Alison had seen them before, usually in the vicinity of one bar or another. Jake

was always saturnine and his wife was always unrelentingly sociable with anyone within earshot.

"We're Jake and Terry Danforth," she announced.

"Norris Elliot," he said, indulgently. He and Jake shook
hands, not with noticeable fervor on either side. Terry looked
at Alison as expectantly as a hungry young bird. She was not
young, but she had a bright, beaky, eager face, oddly attractive
in comparison with Jake's thirsty gloom.

Alison identified herself, leaving off the "Doctor" as she
usually did. Norris had sunk back in his chair again with one
long leg slung over the arm and his fingers tented before his
face.

"What a pretty name!" Terry cried. "I've been admiring
your hair all week. Mine's just hair-colored when I leave it
alone." With its shiny brown swirls it looked as if it had never
been left alone in its life. "Just think, we could have all got to
know each other earlier, but you always looked so *remote*," she
said to Alison, "and *you*—" to Norris—"were otherwise engaged."

"Not engaged, please," said Norris, and she giggled again.

"You're wise," Jake said to him. Norris opened the fingertip arch, regarded Alison, then closed the arch again.

"Not that we haven't met a lot of nice people and taken
down a lot of addresses," Terry ran on, "but I don't suppose
we'll ever look them up. I mean, the ship's a special world of
its own. Once you've left it, it's gone. Still, it's fun, and we've a
lot of pictures to remind us. Jake's got his Polaroid with him.
He took some beauts at the Twenties dance last night. I saw
you and your lady there," she told Norris. "She looked simply
out of this world in that flapper outfit. All that fringe."

Alison wondered if his lady had taken off her boots for the
occasion. He smiled remotely behind his tent of hands.

"How come we never saw you at any of the evening events,
Alison?" Terry demanded. "You wouldn't have been left alone
for a minute. Of course *this* one—" she gave Norris a roguish

glance—"couldn't have done much, but there are plenty of unattached men aboard."

Jake said unexpectedly, from somewhere down by his paunch, "She's probably met up with enough of a sampling to make her prefer her own company."

"But what about that Arab prince who's been losing thousands every night in the casino?" said Terry. "If he ever got a look at that gorgeous hair—"

"What makes you think a one hundred percent American girl would look back at him?" Jake growled. He offered Norris a cigar, was refused, and lit one for himself, glaring at the sunlit scene outside. If he was really suffering for want of a drink, this inane conversation must be driving him up the wall, Alison thought in sympathy. Terry's voice had a penetrating quality.

"Well, I think I'll go down and finish my packing," she said pleasantly. "I might as well get my bags out into the corridor early." She already had them all out but one.

"Oh Lord, yes!" said Terry. "I'd better attend to ours, if I can get Papa Bear here to decide what he wants for the night. Besides his bottle, of course." She patted Papa Bear's thigh. He sighed with frustration, not lust, Alison was sure.

"Look, why don't we all meet for drinks before dinner tonight?" Terry said. "It's the last night, so it won't be a case of 'Oh God, what've I got myself tied up with, and three thousand miles to go!' "

Alison and Norris both laughed. Why not, Alison thought, with a little wave of intuition; Terry desperately wanted to be seen having drinks with *somebody* on her last night aboard ship. Maybe she'd get someone to photograph them with Jake's Polaroid. "All right," she said. "Where and when?"

"Six-thirty, Queen's Grill Bar," said Terry happily. "And by then Jake will be his own sweet self, won't you honey?"

Norris stood up. "I'll walk you to the elevator," he said.

As they strolled through the lounge Alison met face-on

some amused and curious glances; for five days all these people had seen her alone, and Norris with the short-thatched blonde in the high-fashion outfits and boots. Some of them were now thinking that either he or Alison was a very fast worker.

"I can hardly wait to see Jake being his own sweet self," said Norris. "I wish we could have dinner together. I mean you and I, not you and I and the Gold-dust Twins."

"Where do you get that?"

"They glitter with it. I think he's one of these new quick millionaires. A fortune in real estate, computers, or a motel chain. I don't mind, I'm very democratic about those things. What bothers me is that your waiter and mine won't let us get together for dinner in one restaurant or the other."

"I feel deprived already," said Alison. They were at the elevators. "Don't press the button. I'd rather walk down."

"You wouldn't settle for coffee and sandwiches in seclusion, would you?"

She smiled and shook her head, and started down the stairs. She had a feeling he was waiting for her to look back, but she didn't.

Her packing was all done, except for a few last details. You kept out what you wanted for the night and the morning, anything that you could carry yourself, and you wouldn't see the rest until you left the ship in the morning.

In the morning. In the morning she would be in England. In two days she would be in Scotland. It was so tremendous a concept, after so long a wait, that the effect was dazing rather than exhilarating; one was grateful for all the chores that had to be done.

She had changed money earlier, and put tips into separate envelopes. She changed into the soft gray flannel suit and paisley silk shirt she'd wear for traveling the next day.

By now the ship was subtly vibrating and she put on her trenchcoat and went up to the boat deck to watch the tugs take them out of the harbor. She wished now she hadn't accepted the drink invitation. She'd rather stay outside as the ship began her passage across the English Channel in the soft, dimming light. Only a stone-headed dolt could not be moved by the enormity of this adventure, unless the rest had all done it so often that it was nothing to them now.

But none of them are me, she thought fiercely; and it's my first time and I deserve to have it to myself.

Finally she went inside, feeling extremely ungracious. Jake, mellowed by the opening of the bar, actually stood up when Norris did, and even smiled at her. "I've decided Jake has a secret thing about redheads," Terry said. "He couldn't really see you clearly this afternoon, but look at him now."

"She'd be surprised how many secrets I have," said Jake, winking at Alison. The phenomenon was startling, and Norris was quietly entertained by it. Alison thought it best not to let him catch her eye. Jake had also found his tongue. He gave them the details of the letter he was going to write to Cunard, suggesting improvements.

"It's a good thing he wasn't allowed up on the bridge," said Terry fondly, "or he'd be redesigning that and the Captain both."

"I can't find fault with a thing," Alison said.

"Neither can I," said Norris.

"You're awfully sunny, considering that everything came unglued for you on this trip," said Terry, piercingly.

"Good God's sake, woman!" Jake protested.

"Well, honey, those two were an item for five days—you couldn't miss it—closer than some honeymooners I've seen. Never even danced with anyone else except when she danced with the Captain one night, remember? And now she's suddenly gone and he's all bright-eyed and bushy-tailed." Her drink was all going to her tongue; she leaned chummily toward Norris, chin in her hand. "So I'm *positive* he doesn't mind if we mention the subject, do you, Norris?"

"Maybe he's being very brave about it all," Alison suggested demurely. "Stiff upper lip and so forth. Grieving behind a smiling mask."

"Or I could really be twitching with nerves," said Norris, "because I did her up in a tight little bundle and pushed her out a porthole this afternoon. Just before the pilot came out to meet us."

Terry let out a screech that brought heads around. "Norris! What a *sick* sense of humor! How can you say such a thing and sit there *smiling*?"

"Well, a man can smile and smile, and be a villain still," said Norris.

"But you're just *awful*!" She sounded delighted. "What if somebody took you *seriously*?"

"Terry, will you shut the hell up?" said Jake. "There is plenty more to talk about than this guy's busted love affair. Like what's ahead on this so-called pleasure trip. We could run into an epidemic of these damned strikes. Anybody thought of that?"

"Jake always looks on the dark side," Terry explained to Alison. "He always expects the worst."

"Because it always happens." He signaled a waiter and ordered more drinks. "I'm telling you we're heading for a hotbed of disasters."

"Like bombs in the Tower of London and all that cheerful stuff," said Norris.

"Well, if you're going to worry about *risks*," said Terry, "you might as well stay home in bed for the rest of your life."

Alison gave Terry five minutes more to think about taking pictures. When the time was up she was still trying to argue Jake out of his pessimism. Alison arose and said firmly, "Thank you for the drink. I'm going to dinner now. If I don't see you in the morning, goodbye, have a great trip. All of you." She didn't single Norris out, and he seemed bemused anyway, staring into his drink. She walked quickly away with Terry calling rather forlornly after her. Norris didn't catch up with her; she had successfully discouraged him at last.

She reached her table with a sense of homecoming, and even a twinge of nostalgia. When she tipped the waiter at the end of the meal, she said she hoped she could have the same table on her return trip and that he'd still be there.

"I hope so too, Madam," he told her. "It's been a pleasure to serve you." He was very young, with a curly head and a little gold ring in one ear, and had told her once that it was his ambition to own a pub in Cornwall.

She went outside again to watch the far-off lights and try to think coherently about these historic waters. She supposed that a psychic would be tuning in on all kinds of craft coursing about the ship, sailing forever on voyages of escape, exploration, and war. But for Alison it was almost too much and she concentrated on Lewis, the lodestone.

She had to go there before she could stop to look at, or even think about, anything else, and why? To establish a kind of identity for herself because the girl in the picture had her face? Because the discovery of the picture had unsealed a spring of ancestral memory in her?

The imaginary psychic who was always barging in these days would say that Alison had taken on Christina's homesickness for her island, an ache of longing that had never deserted her even though she'd made a new life and raised an American family.

What if, until now, none of them had ever taken Christina's blood and genes back home? What if this journey now was not even Alison's own idea, but Christina's, spun from secret anguish so strong that it had lived on after death?

It would help to explain Alison's father. It would help explain *me*, Alison thought. She wondered what Christina's son had been like. Astonishing that the girl in her chip bonnet and new frock had ever been old enough to have a grown son who would be Alison's grandfather.

It was tempting to lean luxuriously into the supernatural cushion, like one of Mariana Grange's haunted heroines. Being Alison Barbour, she couldn't do it. But there was no reason why she had to rationalize everything down to a page in a psychologist's notebook. You have to have an Unknown in your life. Planets for some; for others, the Unknown lay clouded in a universe contained inside their skulls, and the possibilities were infinite.

The night chill drove her in at last. She skirted quickly around the nighttime life of the ship and walked down to her deck, where she had a last chat with her steward and stewardess and tipped them. She went to bed and read a paperback by one of Mariana Grange's competitors, picked up in the drugstore above the Double Room. She was alternately critical and admiring; "not bad" was the extent of the admiration.

At midnight she watched what she could see of the docking procedures in Southampton, lucky enough to have a big tug nosing at the hull just outside of her porthole.

Later she slept in short naps and was wide awake early. When the night steward brought her coffee for the last time she tipped him and said her thanks and goodbyes. At breakfast she repeated this with her alternate waiter. He was an older man from Portsmouth with teen-age children, and he and Alison had talked a good deal.

"You'll have a fine trip to London," he told her. "The countryside will look lovely in this sunshine. You've brought the good weather with you."

"I'm glad you're giving me the proper credit. Nobody else would believe I've done it all myself."

"Ah, but I know what red hair means, you see," he said solemnly. "I'm married to a red-haired woman. So if old England has a foul summer I'll know whom to blame."

"But you won't tell?"

"And see you burned at the stake? Never, Madam!"

From breakfast it seemed a very short time before all the landing procedures were carried out, according to the printed slips distributed the day before, and she could queue up to disembark and be reunited with her luggage.

She didn't see Norris anywhere, but people who could manage their own luggage had left the ship at eight, so perhaps he'd gone then. The Danforths, being first-class passengers, had evidently been processed at a different place on the ship, and would also be gone already.

She could land alone on English soil, and hail her first English porter, who whisked her around Customs and settled her in a first-class coach aboard her first English train. She had a few minutes alone to sit in utter stillness, thinking, I am here. I am on my way to London, and then to Lewis. I will travel from the very bottom of the map to the top. She was light-headed, but that could be from lack of sleep.

Then some other passengers came in, and there was no risk now of her having to listen to the Danforths or to Norris Elliot all the way to London.

4

THAT AFTERNOON she walked over a good part of London. The city was luminous, green, and warm on the day before Easter; the north in her mind's eye and in her bones was never the sunny purple hills and sapphire lochs of the calenders but a region veiled in cold mists. True, Brave Catriona met up with sunshine now and then, but otherwise she'd have been an unappetizing mess of chilblains and sniffles, the kind of realism which could sink a Mariana Grange book without a trace.

Not having slept much her last night on the ship, she expected that after an afternoon on foot she'd sleep heavily in London, but even when she did drop off she dreamed she was awake and walking, and then she'd return to full consciousness again. I want to stay, she mourned. She ached to give in. It would be cold in Lewis. Rainy. At least if it was rainy in London there was still everything to see and do. Mrs. MacBain had sent her telephone number, and it would be simple to call in the morning and put off her arrival for a couple of weeks.

Turning, stretching, wishing she had a fifth side to lie on for a while, out of bed and looking down at a street just quieting at three in the morning, she knew she was helpless in the power of the enchanter.

She shivered and plunged back into bed, curling up as if she'd never get warm. Yet it wasn't dread she felt, she was sure, but a kind of battle fatigue from being on edge with anticipation for so long, lack of sleep, and too much coming at her from all sides. About twenty-four hours of coma would cure it. One's brain shouted Enough, enough! Muffle the ears and cover the eyes and turn off the communications system.

I'll be back, she promised herself and London. Then she fell asleep quite suddenly, and was awakened by her call from the switchboard. Her continental breakfast arrived a few minutes later. Church bells were ringing, and she wanted to get out into the parks. But tonight she would sleep in Scotland.

She left from Euston for Glasgow. There was no chance of napping on the train, not with England outside the windows and then the borders and lowlands of Scotland, still in sunshine and looking like the calendars after all. She'd been booked into the North British Hotel in Glasgow, adjoining Queen Street Station. Her room overlooked George Square, which was full of hyacinths and monuments; she identified each statue and was charmed by Haig's lions.

She went into the station and bought a first-class ticket for Mallaig, not from snobbery but so she could put her feet up. A busy railroad station was a novelty for the average American these days. She enjoyed it.

The food in the hotel was good, and her bed was comfortable, but again she didn't sleep much, mostly because there seemed to be an all-night party going on in George Square, and she was anticipating this morning. The train for Mallaig left at six, and her breakfast was to come up at five. She had ordered a packed lunch for the train, and it was waiting for her on the hall porter's desk when she and the boy came down with her luggage. The porter wished her a good holiday and so did the boy when he left her in her compartment. The morning was gray and cold, but her first Scottish contacts had turned off any residual pining for London.

It was approximately six hours to Mallaig, and she was alone in her compartment. She should have been able to sleep, like the Australians who'd been on the train from London, dropping off with enviable ease and not caring what they missed. She could not. The train wound slowly into the mountains, stopping at small stations to let off backpackers, people with bicycles, or travelers getting home. Alison checked each name on her map, stared out with eyes that felt like two burnt holes in a blanket; she saw snowy peaks, white waterfalls; sheep, shaggy cattle, one roe deer. When she visited the buffet car several times for reviving infusions of fresh tea she talked with people who were marvelously matter-of-fact about living in a country that was so spectacular. They seemed much more interested in her, and their accents were both musical and kindly to her ears.

They crossed Rannoch Moor and passed the Braes o' Lochaber, turned down to Fort William, and then went westward toward the sea. She was in the buffet again when they passed Glenfinnan, and a couple wearing climbing clothes and slung with binoculars pointed out the monument marking the place where the clans had rallied to Prince Charlie.

She felt as if she were functioning on three levels. At the deepest, she stood in a dazed silence before the fact that she was *here*. The second level was the head-swimming stage of pure fatigue. She thought she was losing her coordination, though she managed the trips through the other coaches to hers without falling into empty seats or passengers' laps, and she remembered reading somewhere that a drunk could keep his balance on a heaving deck when a sober man couldn't. If the Minck was rough today she could put that theory to a test.

The top level was the light dancing on the water; the placenames; the little roe deer; the soft voices. Someone had thought, until she spoke, that she was going home, and then had said smilingly, "But you'll *feel* at home on Lewis, with all the redheads there!"

At Mallaig the sun flickered out to enhance the charm of a small railroad station at the sea, with gulls flying over it. There weren't many passengers left by then, and they all knew where they were going and disappeared while Alison was making her second trip out with luggage.

There were no porters. She stood on the deserted platform in the uncertain sunshine and salt wind, wondering where the ferry left for Armadale on Skye and how she would get everything to it; with the restful resignation of exhaustion she believed it was even now preparing to leave while she stood here in befuddlement.

Befuddlement. New name for Mallaig, she thought. Named for Fred the Fudd, one of the more stupid Vikings, who raided this area under the impression it was France. Boy, was he ever surprised!—If the ferry goes without me, I'll have to find a room till tomorrow, and it's the Easter holiday and there won't be a place empty. Maybe the police station will take me in. I could give myself up.

There were other people in sight, happy souls going about their daily business. She picked up her typewriter, Loden coat, and smaller case. Maybe she could find someone on the street who'd carry the big bag for pay.

She looked around once more, and saw two men coming up the platform behind her, talking. The big one was black-haired and black-browed, wearing a heavy-knit sweater and tweed slacks, a raincoat in a bundle under one arm, a canvas bag slung over the other shoulder. His shorter friend wore a windbreaker and jeans, and a tartan tam cocked forward on his sandy head. When he saw Alison he grinned and sang out something she couldn't understand but took it for a greeting.

"Excuse me," she called back to him. "Will you tell me where the ferry leaves from?"

The dark man looked as if she'd just interrupted the final

computation of the greatest equation of the century. His friend said merrily, "Well, now, we'll take you there, lassie!" He picked up the big case. His friend said curtly, "I'll take that one." He did, and strode off.

The tam-wearer took the other case away from Alison. "Just you follow us," he told her.

Blessing them and her crepe-soled shoes, she kept close behind them past the station and down a short steep street to the ferry landing. The ferry was still there, nobody seemed to be in a hurry, and a few passengers stood around in the sunshine while the freight was being loaded aboard. The two men set her cases down by the other luggage. She thanked them, and the sandy-haired man said, "Ach, it was a pleasure." The s's were very sibilant. His friend nodded absently at her. She had a feeling he didn't even see her, he was so preoccupied with his own thoughts.

The men went back up the street again, two women smiled at her and she smiled back. "I'm going to Lewis," she said, suddenly ready to lift off like a balloon.

"It's good you have your warm coat, then," one of them said. They were talking when the black-haired man came back and went aboard and disappeared.

It was a half-hour ride across the blue Sound of Sleat to Armadale on Skye. The mountains ahead were apparitions in the milky sunlight, and the mainland mountains behind looked like dreamy landscapes in old aquarelles. She stayed aft with the two women, who were from Glasgow, going to visit on Skye. There was a black and white calf neatly done up in a burlap sack like a baby in a bunting, and settled in a sheltered corner. Two children in jeans and anoraks squatted beside it, stroking the broad head and talking to it in hushed voices, their heads bending over it, their eyes concerned and tender.

There was an empty pier at Armadale, except for a couple of men, and a girl meeting the Glasgow women. Most of the other passengers and the calf were going on up the coast. One of the Glasgow women said to her, "The bus is just up the road there."

"Just up the road" was a good walk beyond the long pier. Would it wait for her to make two trips? The man with the black hair appeared at her side like a genie and said curtly, "Will you be taking the bus?"

She had barely time to say yes, he was already going away with her two cases. She said goodbye to the women and went after him, ironically amused that her landing on the island of poetry and song consisted of a fast gallop after her luggage.

He left it at the bus and went on up the road and disappeared. The bus driver had been one of the two men on the pier. He was a small and twinkly man. He stowed her bags away, and told her there'd be a change at Broadford for the bus to Uig. He went off to smoke his pipe with the other man. The Glasgow women passed in a car, waving. She was then alone on Skye, to all intents and purposes. The silence was intense. She walked back to the pier and found there a ladies' room. How lovely of them, she thought dreamily.

A few people now began to materialize around the bus, and she hadn't the slightest idea where they'd come from. The driver returned, and once more she was on her way to Lewis.

Her impression of Skye, after the change into a crowded bus at Broadford, was of hurtling along narrow roads among brown fields and barren mountains, charging at oncoming cars which, by the miraculous intervention of some Celtic saint, went on their way whole after being apparently swamped, trampled, or chewed up by the bus. There was a brief stop at Portree, which to her aching eyes looked like a divine haven of rest, and then they were off again.

They descended out of the fragile sunshine into cold and fog at Uig, rocked around unconcerned black cows in the road, and shot out to the quay where the ferry *Hebrides* waited. Alison's head throbbed in the sudden silence.

Outside, at the back of the bus, the driver rapidly dispensed luggage to its owners. He was a younger version of the small twinkly driver at Armadale; could there be a clan of them? "You can't be carrying that aboard by yourself, lassie," he said to her.

"I could if I had three hands," she said. She felt like giving the big case a hard kick. A burly man with a cap down over his nose took it and headed for the boat. "You'll be fine now," the driver assured her. "Have a good holiday."

When she got her ticket and went aboard, her case was on a shelf among the other luggage, and she couldn't see the man to thank him. Finally she sank gratefully into one of the comfortable chairs in the forward lounge, put her head back and shut her eyes, and drifted in a sort of limbo. There'd be three hours crossing what her map poetically called The Sea of the Hebrides, and she didn't have to do a thing for all that time. There was fog outside so she wasn't missing anything. They were under way now, and the gentle vibration and the lulling motion of their progress across calm waters, the voices pleasantly indistinguishable around her, put her to sleep.

She woke up suddenly. Her neck was stiff. She thought, I didn't know Gaelic sounded so much like German. It *was* German. A ruddy-faced man in climbing clothes was reading aloud to a small girl. Behind her somebody was talking in lilting English about going for a cup of tea, and she was suddenly starved in spite of the hearty lunch furnished by the hotel. She located the Ladies', combed her hair and washed her face and hands, and then went to the cafeteria. It was pleasantly uncrowded. She got coffee and two fresh scones and butter, and sat at a table by a window. Outside there was only silver-gray water and fog.

The coffee tasted wonderful, and when it began to take effect she leaned back and looked around at the other passengers. Suddenly she saw the black-haired man at a table with some other men. He hadn't been on the bus, so he must have crossed Skye by car. She wondered if he was a native of Lewis and what he did for a living. You didn't often see that real crow-black hair, coarse and shiny, with gray glinting through it. With a beard he'd look like Teach the pirate. He had a good strong profile, a great face for a Mariana Grange hero. You could start him off with a beard, which makes him look a lot more savage than he really is, until—

As if he felt her gaze he turned his head and looked across at her. Instinctively she smiled and lifted her hand. He barely nodded, and turned away; also he shifted his chair.

Don't worry, buddy, I'm not trying to pick you up, she thought. He was either very conceited or very shy, or just naturally bad-tempered. Maybe he was xenophobic, and loathed Americans especially. Maybe he was also a Marxist, and hated her on sight because of the Cunard tags on her luggage; everyone back at Hazlehurst seemed to think you were a closet millionaire if you sailed on the *QE 2*.

Now the men were all laughing at something one had said, and it changed him completely. Quite a phenomenon.

She realized it must be Gaelic they were speaking, and that was the language in which the sandy-haired man had greeted her at Mallaig. The most ordinary comments always sound exotic in a language you don't know. The intonations, emphasis, the gestures all seem saturated with conspiracy, as if the speakers are plotting the return of a ruler or the overthrow of one.

. . . A girl is sitting by the fire, not on a MacBrayne ferry, but in an inn somewhere in France, after Prince Charlie's escape to that country. These exiled Jacobites are positive nobody can understand their strange language. Little do they know that the demure English miss, traveling with her maid, has been reared by a Highland nurse, and spoke Gaelic before she knew a word of English. . . .

Alison took her notebook from her bag and began making notes. The ideas proliferated from all sides of the seed, as if she were high on no-sleep, and she forgot to watch the men, and was only interrupted by their passing her table on their way out. He didn't look in her direction. She made quick notes on

each man, which would save having to think up what the con-
spirators looked like. Now all she needed was a fresh new way
to throw hero and heroine together. He's not going to like it,
she thought happily. He's going to fight like mad. He thinks he
hates women. He's the absolute opposite of that wild Alasdair
who carried Catriona into captivity.

She could now see gulls outside, and black humps and
peaks of rock. They were on their way up through East Loch
Tarbert. She went back up to the lounge.

In the material sent her about the Western Isles, a photograph of Tarbert in Harris showed a sunlit village cozily settled at the foot of mountains in sharp detail against a blue
summer sky. Today it was a huddle of wet roofs cowering below indistinct and thus even more menacing hills of barren
rock.

But tonight I'll sleep on Lewis, she thought. And the sun
has to come out sometime.

Standing at the lounge windows, watching the cheerful ac-
tivity on the pier below as the *Hebrides* docked with elephan-
tine grace, she saw Norris Elliot standing at the corner of a
building, and Boots was with him.

Norris was looking up and she could have sworn that he
gazed directly into her face. That was doubtful, with so many
others at the windows too, and some of them redheads, and the
glass streaked and steamy.

She blinked her eyes to clear them, and in that interval the
two had vanished. Yet she retained the images in diamond-
sharp detail. His thin height, his fair head, the very way he
stood. Boots' hair, the white trenchcoat she'd worn on deck,
even the big soft bow of her tri-colored scarf.

Alison moved around trying to see different sections of the
pier, but they had vanished like a hallucination. The two
people hadn't been imaginary, of course, but men with fair
short hair and women in white trenchcoats weren't all that uncommon. It was coincidence. She'd see them again when she
was ashore, and realize just how much her tired brain and eyes
had tricked her.

5

THE GANGPLANK was maneuvered into place, and the black-haired man was almost the first one down, raincoat still an untidy bundle under his arm. He was met by a thin, very straight man with thick white hair and mustache, and a border collie that went mad with joy at the sight of him. They left the pier, the dog properly at heel but the tail was still in motion. They disappeared beyond the buildings.

Alison went to get her luggage, intending to take the big bag ashore and come back for the smaller gear, but a boy getting himself harnessed into his backpack said something she couldn't understand, expecting it to be Gaelic; it turned out to be French, and he was offering to carry the large case for her.

On the pier she thanked him, and he gave her a smile and a little bow and went away. She sat peacefully on the case, holding her Loden coat, waiting. Everyone else seemed to be arriving home or to visit relatives. The backpacking boy and the German father and daughter knew exactly where they were going. She had reached a mellow passivity in which she felt she could have sat forever watching the faces and hearing the voices of other people, looking up at the gulls now and then, occasionally yawning so that she saw everything through a blur. If she had landed on Venus she could not have had a more potent sense of dissociation from the world as she had known it until she sailed eight days ago.

Who at home could possibly imagine her now? She was having a hard time of it herself. She remembered—yawning helplessly again—times when as a child she used to think (usually in a boring classroom), Supposing I'm really dreaming all this. How would I know?

"Would you be Miss Barbour?" It was a gentle voice to come from a thickset man in tweed, turtleneck sweater, and cap. He had a broad face and a once-broken nose. His eyes were extremely blue under bristly eyebrows. "Mrs. MacBain sent me. She has some trouble with her car. My name is Donald MacLeod."

She was awake, all right. She stood up, delighted with this stranger. "How do you do?" They shook hands.

"Welcome to the Western Isles," he said, smiling. "Is this all you have?"

"Yes, and already I'm ashamed of that big case."

"Oh, it's nothing."

On the way to his car she saw a tall fair-haired man who was not Norris Elliot but who looked like him from the back. From the car she saw a young girl wearing a white raincoat which could have passed for a trenchcoat if that was what she expected to see. She was satisfied.

She rode in front with Donald MacLeod. He apologized for the weather, but she told him she was from New England where the weather was unpredictable.

"But you see our weather *is* predictable," he said. "We know it will rain. We are famous for our rain."

"Well, I've got enough Scottish blood so I won't throw fits about it," she assured him. "A little from my mother, a lot from my father."

"Yes, Barbour is Scots, and Mrs. MacBain was saying your great-grandmother was a Lewis woman."

"Christina MacLeod, and she went from Lewis to Quebec, and she ended up in Massachusetts marrying my great-grand-father."

"Then welcome again," he said. "You're one of the family and have the hair to prove it."

"At home I'm almost the only redhead I know, and over here in two days I've seen more red hair than I've seen in my life."

They both laughed. "What part of Lewis?" he asked.

"Torsaig. I know I didn't say it right."

He repeated it. The difference was indefinable, but there. She tried it and was frustrated.

"You did very well," he told her kindly.

"Does the village still exist? It's on my map, but what's there?"

"A handful of cottages. There's no minister now, and the children go to school somewhere else. But it's a great place for the old folk. They say it's the pure western air over there." He laughed. "Years ago they used to say it was their own whiskey before they had to give up making it. We're passing Loch Erisort now."

They had been driving through the mist-blurred mountains and now the land was gradually flattening out. The water gleamed with a cold pallor in the dark and drenched terrain. Sheep grazed at the sides of the road unconcerned by the car. When another car was seen approaching, the driver who was nearest to a pulling-off place did so until the other car passed, usually with a courteous signal of thanks.

"Mrs. MacBain is a nice woman," Donald MacLeod said. "A very nice woman. You'll have a fine holiday here if you don't need excitement."

"It's enough excitement just to be here, first on Scottish soil and now on Lewis."

"I'm glad you separated us. The Isles are a country apart." He chuckled, but she felt that he meant what he said.

The lowering light affected her eyelids, the warmth and comfort inside the car turned her torpid and heavy. It was a long way to Stornoway, and Aignish was beyond that. She thought of bed, of a long and sodden sleep. She would wake up refreshed in the morning, make her coffee, and sip slowly, dreamily, collecting herself.

Coffee! She roused up. "Is there any place open where I can get a few groceries?"

"Mrs. MacBain says you're not to be anxious. She's expecting to give you your tea tonight, and she's put in something for your breakfast. I'll be out in the morning to drive her into Stornoway to get her car, and you'll come along and visit the shops then."

"Oh, good." Marvelous to be so taken care of. She sagged back and fell asleep. She snapped wide awake after what seemed an hour and asked, "Are we near Stornoway yet?"

"We're through it."

"I missed it!" she mourned. "How could I?"

"I hadn't the heart to wake you. It'll be there tomorrow. It's already been there a long time. We're on the Braighe now, crossing to Aignish, with the North Minch on our right and Broad Bay out there on our left, all lost in the fog tonight."

There was considerable and fast traffic on this much-wider road. The inevitable sheep, some with lambs, grazed or lay on the grass verges. "Are they lost?" she asked, worried.

"Oh no! They know the way home. But if there's a way to get off the croft they'll find it."

Fog was drifting across from one body of water to the other, increasingly opaque, so that what lay along either side of the road beyond the insouciant sheep was hidden. The road climbed gradually up from the Braighe, the car made a sudden sharp left turn off the main road and went a little distance along a short street, and stopped by a gate on the left.

"We're here," said Donald MacLeod. "Some say the word Aignish means 'we're at it now,' and so we are."

The front door of the cottage opened, and a woman waited

in the lighted doorway. Donald MacLeod carried in the luggage, refused a tip, and said he'd see them tomorrow. The cottage was warm with electric fires. Mrs. MacBain, in a rosy wool dress, had curly dark hair cut short; she had strong features and a fresh youthful coloring, and a most attractive accent. She showed Alison where everything was, and how to deal with the electric fires and teakettle, and told her to come across to the house next door when she was ready.

Left alone, Alison felt she could have sunk into the deep chair before the living room hearth, and fallen asleep as the dusk came on. Outside the garden wall the cries of the lambs belonging to Mrs. MacBain's ten ewes were the contented night-sounds of any infants. She could barely make them out from the big window, the fog was now so thick.

Sleep, she thought lustfully. Deep, stuporous, comatose. . . . She yawned till her jaws hurt, and washed in cold water in an effort to wake up. It helped a little. She thriftily turned off the electric fires but left one light on to welcome her back again, and remembered to put the key in her coat pocket.

As she walked along the wall to the gate into Mrs. MacBain's garden, some of the black-faced eyes bunched up expectantly in the corner, one of them clearly asserting rank by thrusting her horned head at the others and getting closest to the gate.

"No hand-outs," Alison said. "I'm not your mother." They stared up at her with wary curiosity, the little ones nosing around their flanks, enchanting woolly toys with black noses or black ears, dancing on minuscule hooves. She wished she could lift one and hug it, but all those maternal horns precluded that.

The tea turned out to be a substantial meal. It was wonderful reviving, especially with the prospects of bed only a short time away. Mrs. MacBain's husband was at sea, like many Lewis men; he was the master of a container vessel. Their children, all adult now, lived and worked on the mainland.

It was still not quite dark when she walked back to the cottage in the heavy fog scented by the fields and the sea. The sheep were quiet now. She stood with her hand on the cold wet gate, thinking, *I am here.* She stood there until the chill was penetrating her clothes, just listening, and hearing nothing at all. Then she went inside with her armful of borrowed books about Lewis.

She switched on the electric blanket, and got ready for bed. To start reading any of the Lewis books tonight would be a mistake—she'd never get settled down. She got out a paperback Ngaio Marsh she'd bought in the hotel at Glasgow.

Warm in a very comfortable bed, she wasn't able to stay awake for long. She put off her light, turned over, falling head-first into a wave of drowsy happiness straight out of her child-hood. *When I wake up it will be Christmas Day.*

6

$\mathcal{S}$HE DREAMED of the Shetland pony. It was the old dream that he was in the living room nibbling at the Christmas tree while he waited for her; a dream so heartbreakingly beautiful that she'd never told it, but had never forgotten it either. Her Rob Roy. She found him now, and it was just the same, the way his tousled mane felt under her hand as she lovingly brushed it with her best hairbrush, the dark luster of his big eyes rolling around at her, the soft snort of warm breath through his nostrils, the solidity of his little body. They knew each other well at their first meeting; she could have climbed on his bare back, the walls would melt away, and she'd ride off with him like the wind, as the fairy tales said—

"They're going all the way to Scotland!" someone cried, and already the voice was faint with distance.

And that's what we did. We're *here*, and he's out there with the sheep. What do they think of him? Wait till I tell Mama and Papa.

From there she was on the train again, winding slowly along a mountainside, and there was a large gathering down at the monument at Glenfinnan. She thought with great joy, The Clans are meeting. The prince must be there!

But the train went relentlessly on. Before she could recover from that disappointment she was no longer on the train. The black and white collie from the pier at Tarbert came up to her, his dark amber eyes fixed intently on hers as if he were about to speak, and she expected him to. She put out her hand to him and he disappeared.

"Oh, come back!" she called, grieved. Behind her someone was weeping. She looked around in distress and there was Christina in her new dress and chip bonnet, with the tears running down her face and her fist at her mouth to thrust back the sobs, while a man talked and talked. But Alison couldn't understand the words, only the intonations, and she hated them. She couldn't stop the voice and she began to cry herself, and woke up with the sobs wrenching their way out of her throat, and her fist at her mouth to hold them in.

"Oh, good God," she murmured, struggling to orient herself in a strange room dimly pink from the light coming through drawn salmon-colored drapes. A ewe called imperiously and was answered by a pair of infant voices.

The sorrow of the dream left her as quickly as the black and white dog had vanished. Her face was still wet, her throat slightly ached. Christina must have wept often, knowing when she went away that she'd probably never come back. And of course in the dream she'd be wearing the clothes of the photograph because that was the only way Alison had ever seen her.

She opened the curtains and looked out on treeless fields lighted with sunrise, stretching away from the garden walls in partitioned pastures to a distant line of houses parallel with the shore of Broad Bay. Blackfaced lambs energetically bunted their mothers' udders to make the milk come, tails waggling as they suckled. The ewes nonchalantly walked away when they were tired of feeding the young, and grazed on the new green grass. Their fleeces were thick and ropy, their horns looked dangerous. The lambs jumped and ran and squared off at each other like children. Gulls walked among them all, picking at something on the ground.

But my Rob Roy isn't there, she thought tenderly.

Muffled in her wool robe and wearing fleece-lined slippers, she switched on the heat in the living room and kitchen, and a few minutes later carried a mug of coffee, a plate of fresh rolls and butter into the living room, and ate looking out over the fields to the deepening blue of Broad Bay. Beyond the yellow sands and houses of its opposite shore, mountains showed like apparitions, to disappear if she looked away for a moment.

Her journey to the Western Isles had been a business of almost mystical disclosures and disappearances, and illusions like the one at Tarbert yesterday. It was a wonder those two hadn't turned up in her dream, but her brain must have had the good sense to discard them as worthless.

She wanted to do everything at once, but she wouldn't be going to Stornoway until ten, and she couldn't stand to stay inside and unpack. She dressed in her lined jeans, hiking boots, sweater and Loden coat, and went for a walk. Outside the gate she met some children going toward the main road and school. They'd been playing as they went, all over the road and in and out of the ditches, but when she spoke they were struck dumb and motionless. Then one little girl answered. This broke the spell and they scampered off like the lambs.

The small cottages of the past were used for outbuildings now, and the modern cement-block houses had big windows to make the most of the sun. The dooryard gardens were walled off from the crofts, and they all had daffodils and small shrubs; young trees were lovingly cherished and encouraged here. Some kitchen gardens had rhubarb already showing. There was a rounded stack of peat behind or beside each house, and she realized that the astringent tang in the cold bright air was the scent of peat smoke.

Mannerly dogs observed her quietly from behind gates.

One had blue eyes. "Hello, Blue-eyes," she said. He didn't wag his tail, bark, or curl back a hostile lip. He simply gazed at her with a silent, intense curiosity.

"Good morning!" a woman called to her from where she was hanging out clothes. A tiny lamb bumbled around her legs like a puppy; an orphan, Alison guessed.

"Good morning!" she called back. This was as good as Christmas morning ever was. A blackbird was singing from a ridge pole, the British blackbird who seems part thrush and part robin. Gulls floated overhead. Enormous clouds billowed up in the northwest. Without trees the sense of space was liberating and exhilarating.

She went on until another road crossed hers. To the right it went up a moderate hill to join the main road that ran the length of the Eye peninsula to Tiumpan Head. On her left it went down to the machair and the shore. For next time, she thought contentedly. At sunset tonight, perhaps.

When she went back to get ready for town, from behind the cottage there rose a frantic clamor of lambs, and she hurried around back to see what was wrong. The nine were crowding at the door of a small shed, inside which their mothers were jostling each other and Mrs. MacBain to get at the food she was putting in the manger.

She picked her way out past their rumps, laughing. She was wearing knee-high rubber boots and an old jacket. "Special feed for nursing mothers," she explained. She put down her bucket and caught a lamb and brought him over to the garden wall. His frightened eyes were like gems in his black face. The two women talked softly to him, and Alison scratched behind his ears.

"He's Angus, Annie's lamb. She was an orphan I took from my neighbor across the road, and raised her myself four years ago. She has a daughter and twin grandchildren, this year. You're young to be an uncle, aren't you, dearie?" She put Angus down and he ran off crying and flung himself at his mother as she pushed belligerently through the crowd.

"She bullies them all," said Mrs. MacBain, "and me too, if I let her."

On the way to town Donald MacLeod and Mrs. MacBain discussed Alison's Lewis connections. Donald MacLeod said gallantly he was proud to claim her for a cousin. When he left them off at the garage he said, "Charlie Macaulay is the man to talk to in Torsaig. He knows everything that's happened for the past five hundred years, and he'll give you chapter and verse."

Mrs. MacBain parked her car at the Cromwell Street pier, where the Victorian battlements of the Castle showed over the trees across the water. She took Alison first to her bank to cash some traveler's checks. Then they visited the grocery stores, the butcher's, and the greengrocer's. They put their supplies in the car and separated with a set time for meeting again.

Stornoway looked to be the sort of town where one could wander happily for a couple of hours, at the same time enforcing a rigid self-control toward Harris tweeds and handknit sweaters; uninhibited impulse buying could lead to bankruptcy in no time at all. But Alison could never pass a bookstore, and this time, like a drunk promising himself just a quick one, she went inside. She was to meet Mrs. MacBain in about fifteen minutes, so she was safe from committing any massive self-indulgence. In happy despair she scanned the wall of books on Scotland, with a whole section on the Isles. Finally she took a locally printed paperback about the Standing Stones. On her way to the desk she saw some Mariana Grange books in a rack of Gothics and mysteries.

When she paid for her book she told the proprietor she'd be back. "Indeed you will," he said. "I can always tell."

She was back at the car first, glad of a few minutes in which to stand and stare. A man and woman came to the next car and stowed parcels away, speaking in Gaelic; she was hearing as much Gaelic as English in the streets, whose signs were in both languages. Then there was the red hair. A small child in a stroller with curls like copper silk; a gingery tangle on a youth in tight jeans and leather jacket, a rich curly mane on a very tall girl. And these were only three out of many.

A man walked by with a West Highland white terrier on a leash and she watched them out of sight, remembering her old Scottie. When she turned back, she saw the black-haired man and the older man who'd met him at Tarbert. They stopped just across the sidewalk from the car park, waiting for a break in the traffic flowing around the curve. He hadn't even glanced in her direction, otherwise he couldn't have missed her; she was standing at the front of the car where it nosed toward the sidewalk.

They must be discussing a pretty engrossing subject, she thought, shamelessly trying to catch a word. The gestures made it even more intriguing.

There was a gap between cars and they went across the street. The black-haired man looked back over his shoulder but not at her.

"What are you watching?" Mrs. MacBain asked from behind her.

"Those two men. They're just going into that restaurant. The black-haired one and a friend helped me with my bags at Mallaig, and then he unloaded them at Armadale."

"I'm sure he was happy to."

Alison laughed. "He wasn't! Far from it. Later I saw him on the ferry, when I nodded the response was more than cold. It was glacial. And this morning I was just part of the neighboring telephone booth."

"He'd be having something weighty on his mind. That's Ewen Chisholm."

"What does he do? Is he a crofter, a weaver, a fisherman, a professional man? Merchant marine, home on leave?"

"I'll tell you all I know over a cup of coffee later. It's not the sort of thing to be narrated in an instant."

"It gets better and better. I can keep guessing."

They were disappointed at the car-hire office. Mr. MacNeil had been obliged to fly to North Uist, but he'd be back in the late afternoon. "We'll come then," said Mrs. MacBain. When they left the office she said, "We can go home and put away our supplies, and this afternoon I'll drive you across to Torsaig and we'll look up Charlie Macaulay."

Alison made a token protest about being a bother, but was gently silenced. "I'd love to do it, and besides, you need to be shown the way. If you went alone you could take a wrong turning and be lost on the moors forever."

"Adding a new ghost to the local collection. All right. I'm relieved. I'm bashful about knocking on strange doors and saying is this where Mr. Charlie Macaulay lives?"

"Even if it wasn't, they'd ask you in for a cup of tea."

7

WHEN THEY STARTED OUT in the afternoon Mrs.
MacBain said, "I've rung up Charlie Macau-
lay's number, and his daughter said to come along. Charlie's
only too happy to have someone to tell the old stories to."

"Tell me a story now," said Alison. "About Ewen
Chisholm, or do we have to wait for that cup of coffee?"

"Oh dear no. And it's not that long a story after all, I suppose. You asked what he is, what he does. He has a fine educa-
tion in Celtic studies and could be teaching now at Edinburgh,
but here he is, raising sheep with Murdo Morrison, his
mother's cousin, at Callanish, and obsessed with the Stones, as
if they hadn't been studied to death already. The dear knows
what more he hopes to discover about them."

"I would be very interested in that, if he'd talk to me." Her
mind alternated rapidly between an academic paper and a
Gothic heroine dodging around the Stones in moonlight or fog.
Intense shadows and a full moon were great, but invisibility
could be spookier.

"He's not the most sociable man in the world," Mrs. Mac-
Bain said, "as you've doubtless guessed."

"Maybe I can convince him I didn't come to Lewis with

the sole idea of seducing Ewen Chisholm. That's not a Lewis name, is it?"

"No. His mother was a Lewis girl who met Colin Chisholm when she was working in Inverness. He was in the Merchant Navy then, and kept on with it until after Ewen was born, and then they came back here to be with her father. So Ewen grew up on the island."

"Are his parents still living?"

"His father is dead, but his mother is married again, and living in Morayshire these days. She owned land on Great Bernera and turned it over to Ewen. But there's no fit house yet, so they're renting at Callanish, close by the Stones. His aunt told me he was engaged to a brilliant girl in Edinburgh, an advocate's daughter, but she washed her hands of him when he took it into his head to come back to Lewis."

"Maybe that's his story," said Alison, "but he really came back here *because* of the break-up, and he's never going to trust a woman again."

Mrs. MacBain laughed. "You could be right. But there's at least one lass who's not going to give up. She followed him from Edinburgh, his aunt says, always adding a few words about brazen besoms. But she's a nurse, and she arrived when they happened to be short-handed at Lewis Hospital and they were happy to have her. She's very good, I understand, so she's been here ever since."

"Maybe *she* was the reason for the break-up with the brilliant girl," Alison suggested. A blatant live-in arrangement wouldn't be countenanced here, but there were ways of managing.

The sun had begun to dim soon after they left Stornoway. The narrow road across the moors seemed to go on and on, up and down, around hairpin turns, past hills of rock, down to narrow bridges over shallow streams. Sometimes they passed long rows of freshly cut, chocolate-brown peats, and there were always the sheep.

Fog was appearing, and Alison was disappointed but tried

not to show it. "We have all kinds of weather at once on Lewis," Mrs. MacBain said.

"So do we in New England. I don't mind." But she did. She wanted to see Torsaig for the first time laid out clear and entire before her, with the sea loch at its feet.

The signpost stood out sharply before them like a shouting man. They went abruptly to the left, up a hill where sheep cropped among the rocks, and down the other side. East Loch Roag was unseen in the fog, but the sea scent came strongly into the car. At the bottom of the hill the road turned right and became the village street, with the loch on one side and a row of cottages on the other.

"Second one in," Mrs. MacBain murmured. "Blue door and blue around the windows. Next after the pink. There it is. My, that *is* pink, isn't it? Maybe it will fade in time," she said encouragingly. They passed a fenced field where two goats watched them through the wire, and came to the house with the blue door.

Behind the gate a black and white dog pointed his nose to the sky and hallooed. A stout woman in an apron over her long-sleeved sweater and skirt came quickly out the door and called to the dog in Gaelic. He ran to her wagging his tail, but hurried back barking as they entered the gate.

"He's not cross!" she reassured them.

"We can see he's a lovely dog," Mrs. MacBain said. "He's a fine boy, aren't you?" He was civil to her but went out around her to Alison. She thought, This is the dog in my dream. It wasn't that other dog at all.

She put out her hand and this time he did not disappear. He smelled it carefully, then looked into her eyes, started toward the cottage, glanced back, saw that she was following, and hurried ahead to be welcoming on the doorstep.

Before the door shut behind them Alison heard the swash and gurgle of the water around the rocks across the road.

The bald old man smelling pungently of tobacco and peat

smoke looked for a long time at the picture of Christina, whispering to himself and sometimes shaking his head. His glasses were far down his nose and askew. He seemed lost in senile revery. Mrs. MacBain watched, serenely. Mrs. Martin, the stout, high-colored daughter waited. The clock on the mantel ticked loudly and the dog shifted his position on the hearth rug with a groan, and sank back into sleep again.

Alison was depressed. There was more fog about than what had come in from the sea; the old man probably had good days and bad days, and this was a poor one.

Suddenly he spoke to his daughter in the hushed, breathy Gaelic.

"Yes," she said in English, nodding at Alison. "You do."

"Yes, yes," her father repeated sibilantly. "You're very like. The living image." He smiled at Alison and won her with that and his blue eyes. He was very far from senile. "Even the hair. It's like a miracle! They heard that Cairistiona died over there, you see, before she could ever marry. It was a great relief always in my father's life. He talked about it when he was old."

"Did he *know* her?" Alison's voice came scraped and small.

"*A Dhia!* Yes! He was heartbroken when she went away. He'd been in love with her. A wee lad of twelve or so. He worshipped from afar." He studied the picture again, smiling tenderly at it. "She sent him one like this, you see. She was working in a mill then, in the States. He still had it when he married my mother. By then he thought Cairistiona was dead. He kept the picture a secret from my mother, and I don't know how, the tigress that she was."

He chuckled. "When I left home to work in Aberdeen, he gave it to me for safe-keeping. Whenever I came back I brought it so he could see it. And the day we buried him, I burned it. But I never forgot her, mind you. The way it was, I might have known her myself."

"It's fine that my own mother didn't know it," said his daughter. "Poor soul, she'd have been that jealous even of a ghost." She had a robust laugh. "But you understand, it was always a struggle for her. Not that this man led the lassies on, but he couldn't help the spark in his eye."

Charlie hushed her in Gaelic but he was obviously delighted. "I can well believe it," said Mrs. MacBain. "I can't resist it now."

"If he wasn't lame he'd be leaping about the hillsides like a young ram," said Mrs. Martin.

"The yellow-haired lad I was in those days," Charlie said, ruefully rubbing his bald head. "But not like the one in the poem." He chanted a long elegiac phrase that gave Alison gooseflesh.

"What is that?" she said quickly.

"Just a sad story from a sad past," he said.

"Would you be willing to say it all for me on tape, then afterward explain it in English? I could play it again at home, and always remember this day."

"Certainly," he said with grace. "But there are pleasanter things than that to remember, surely."

"Oh, I expect you to be saying all sorts of charming things on that tape. But if you don't want to, I shan't mind," she assured him quickly.

"Oh, he'll want to," said Mrs. Martin. "You won't be the first one. He should have been an actor. He'd be on the telly now."

"With a fan club," said Mrs. MacBain. Charlie basked, still unquenchably the yellow-haired lad.

"Did Christina leave parents behind her, or brothers and sisters?" Alison asked him.

"They're all up there in their graves on the hill," he said. "Her father was Tormod MacLeod, seven feet high, with arms like an eagle's wingspread. He could carry a ram under one arm and a ewe under the other with no trouble whatever. And he had hair like the Burning Bush, it was so red."

"Is the house still standing?" Alison asked. "Does someone live in it now?" She got up and went to the front window to look out past the plants, but the fog was still there.

"It was away up the glen, but it burned long ago," Mrs. Martin said. "There's only the old walls left."

"But I'd like to see them. Only I'd probably get lost in the fog today, so I'll wait."

"We'll have a cup of tea now," Mrs. Martin said. She went across the hall to the kitchen, and the dog arose and followed her.

Alison remained by the window, looking at the flowering plants, thinking, I have plenty of time. Why do I feel as if I'm running? *Must* run?

Charlie Macauley spoke in Gaelic to Mrs. MacBain and she answered him in kind, but with a question. Alison caught the name *Cairistiona*.

She was too excited, she wanted to go out in the soaking fog and cross to the shore, even if she couldn't find her way up the glen to the ruins. She could at least be walking where Christina must have run barefoot as a child.

Suddenly the other two ceased their dialogue in a language which couldn't help sounding secretive, and turned solicitous faces toward her. They were too concerned. By now one of Mariana Grange's heroines would be having premonitions like mad.

"I love the sound of Gaelic," she said.

"And why wouldn't you?" Charlie asked blandly. "Isn't it the language of the Garden of Eden?"

"How do you suppose it got way over here?"

"Why, lassie, after the Lord drove Adam and Eve out they came here, of course. For their sins. He told them they would work hard all the days of their lives, and what better place than Leodhas for that?"

He burst into laughter. Mrs. Martin came in with a loaded tray, and Alison and Mrs. MacBain moved papers and magazines out of the way to make room for it on the table. Their tea was poured into bone china cups. Charlie's went into an outsized model labeled "Father" in gold. The cakes were still warm, fresh for the occasion, Alison thought. She settled back into a comfortable slow bake of pleasure. The dog settled hopefully on the hearth rug, staring at her.

Charlie asked her what her work was, and seemed impressed because she taught in a college.

"But it's a very small college," she protested.

"She's modest," said Mrs. MacBain. "She writes books too, keeping alive the old songs and stories."

"Ach, I have plenty of those for you," Charlie said, the true performer.

"And old beliefs, too, I hope," said Alison. "Myths and legends? You must know some about the Callanish Stones, for instance."

"We all have those," he said with a duck of his head and a mischievous sidewise look over his glasses. "But it's Ewen Chisholm you should be talking to for the true facts. He's in communication with the *Fir Bhreige,* you know. They talk to him when the moon's full."

"Father!"

He braced back and gazed innocently at her. "Well, Peigi *mo ghaoil,* will you tell me what a man's doing there when he's been educated as that lad has, and could be teaching in University now, respected for his learning?"

"Maybe he's taking a year's leave of absence to write a book," Alison said. "Like me. We have to publish now and then, you know. Our colleges expect it of us."

"That's sure to be it, Father," said Mrs. Martin. "Have some more tea."

"You know," Alison said, "some of the old stories may not seem very important today, in this world of North Sea oil and atomic power and space flight, but we are what we are because of our past, and if we ignore that, we're people without a country."

"You're right," he said solemnly. "Well, there's many a strange thing said about the Stones."

"If you walk there with a lad," Peigi said, "you might come away engaged. That happened to me."

Her father looked at her over his glasses. "You'd better keep your youngest girl away from there this summer," he said. "By luck you got a good enough lad, but they're a different lot these days."

"Can you walk to the Stones from here?" Alison asked Peigi.

"Oh yes, it's no walk at all. Only three miles and a bit more by the footpath around the shore."

"No walk at all," said Alison wryly.

"Enough to keep them out all night going and returning," said Charlie.

"How many times did you walk a girl to the Stones?" Mrs. MacBain asked him. He shook a finger at her.

"It's not me we're discussing," he said, "but the younger generation."

"But isn't that you?" asked Peigi. She shook with laughter. They all caught it. In the middle of the uproar the dog pressed his chin warmly and firmly on Alison's knee, and she slipped him a scrap of cake without being seen, she hoped.

Charlie wiped his eyes and whispered, "Oh dear, oh, dear, it's just like yesterday sometimes. Those Stones, now. My father could remember when certain people went to the Stones in secret on certain days. Their families had always been *of* the Stones, you see, and so they went, so as not to neglect them. It nearly drove the ministers wild trying to put a stop to it." His mouth quirked up. "Whenever one of them tried to go to the Stones to catch these pagans, you see, the mists came up so thick the minister was all but blinded by it and lost his way."

"The Stones look after their own, it seems," said Alison.

"They do, and Ewen Chisholm's training them to do even more. He'll be having a Gaelic choir next, or swear he has. It's a good thing Murdo Morrison's there, in case he goes altogether daft. . . . Murdo's dog is a sister to Peadar here."

"Peadar's a great dog," Alison said. "He's trying to hypnotize me."

"Ach, the beggar," said the old man fondly. "He's a good

worker. My nephew owns the mother. There was never a better bitch than Shona, and her children all take after her."

They left soon, escorted to the gate by the dog. The two women were quiet, driving back across the island. Alison was trying to keep everything sharp in her mind so she could set it down as soon as she got home. Mrs. MacBain hummed softly to herself.

"When I was standing at the window," Alison remembered aloud, "you and Mr. Macaulay were talking in Gaelic, and I had the strongest feeling it was about Christina. Is there something I shouldn't know?"

Mrs. MacBain didn't answer at once. After a moment she said, "He's a man of great delicacy and tact. She seems to have left in some disgrace, and he didn't know if he should tell you."

"But I wouldn't be shocked! I always thought she left because life was so hard here, but if something else drove her away, I could only be sorry for her, whatever it was."

"Of course you'd feel that way. But he couldn't know."

"I've had this strong feeling that she wept a good many tears over leaving. I hope her new life was worth it."

"If she hadn't gone to America, where would you be?"

"That's the kind of question that could drive anyone clean out of her mind. What *would* this *I* be seeing with my eyes and hearing with my ears at this very moment? Who'd be my parents? Now you get into Karma, and reincarnation—oh, Lord!"

They both laughed. A few minutes later Mrs. MacBain had to navigate with great daring and technical skill around a drunken driver who was concentrating on getting home fast in a world with no one but himself in it.

"If I happen to see that beat-up maroon Cortina when I'm driving out here," said Alison, "I'll crawl out into the heather and let him have it all to himself. I've another thing to ask you. That long lovely statement that Mr. Macaulay recited. Is that as poetic and romantic as it sounded?"

THE SILENT ONES / 67

Her landlady gave her a sidewise glance. "It's poetic," she said, "but hardly romantic. It means, 'By the ledges of the headlands was the yellow-haired lad murdered.'"

8

AT STORNOWAY the sun was out and the streets crowded with cars and people. Gulls were screaming and circling as two boats unloaded fish at a place on the pier Mrs. MacBain called Lazy Corner. This busy, sunlit, noisy afternoon was as far removed from the fogbound silence of Torsaig as anything could be.

Mr. MacNeil was back from North Uist, and Mrs. Mac-Bain left Alison with him. He was a kindly and portly young man who made her feel like an adolescent niece when he took her on a test drive in a little Ford Escort around quiet residential streets. She had to cope with the stick shift, right-hand drive, and left-hand side of the road, but her coordination and reflexes were good, and she needed only to stay with the traffic. On the narrower and emptier roads over the moors the thing was to remember to pull over into the left-hand passing places to allow someone else by.

She went cautiously out of town, but once she saw the road ahead of her straight to the Braighe she felt like singing in exultation. However, she decided she'd better keep her mind rigidly on the traffic and, after she crossed the Braighe, on the non-conformist sheep. There was a thrilling encounter with three cows taking up the middle of the road. Traffic on both sides edged politely around them. The cows were imperturbable, as if they often strolled out like this. They probably did.

She thought smugly that somebody in Aignish wasn't as careful about shutting gates as she, the outsider, was.

She went up past the school on her right, and her turn came on the left, but at the last moment she decided to go straight on up the hill. She didn't take any of the enticing side roads, she didn't have to rush to see everything on her first day. It was enough for now to be driving along this height of land in the magnificent light, with Broad Bay off to her left and far across the water to the east the spectral mountains of Wester Ross.

It was only a five-mile drive to the end of the Eye peninsula, and she would save Tiumpan for another day. She turned the car around in a driveway at Portnaguiran and started back. Now it seemed as if all Lewis lay before her, and the Harris hills beyond. She sang Scots songs all the way back, waving at other drivers who usually grinned and waved back. A bus driver even sounded his horn. Maybe they think I'm a happy drunk, she thought. Well, I am.

Mrs. MacBain came around the house when she was shutting the driveway gate. The sheep were an offstage chorus. "Now that's a bonny wee thing," she said, looking at the car.

"Isn't she? And she's bonny to handle too. I've been singing like a blackbird. *My* blackbird." He was at it again, from the top of a utility pole outside the wall.

"I've heard from another charmer this afternoon," said Mrs. MacBain. "A young man rang up. He'd like to get in touch with you."

Alison said blankly, "I don't know any young man over here, except—it wasn't Mr. MacNeil, was it? No, you'd know him." She had faint squirmings of uneasiness. "No one at home knows where I am."

"This one was calling from Stornoway. Perhaps he saw you on the street, like Dante seeing Beatrice, and fell madly in love with you."

"I *knew* I was getting too high to be healthy," said Alison. "Did he leave a name?"

"Oh yes. I said I couldn't pass on his message without a name. Norris Elliot, and he's staying at the Caberfeidh."

Alison looked off across the fields. She *had* seen him then at Tarbert, and he had seen her. Boots hadn't been an illusion either. She must have come straight back from France, and whatever the two were doing up here Alison didn't care and didn't want to know.

"I met him on the ship," she said finally. "He could be a nuisance, but I don't intend to let him be. Thank you for telling me about it, and I'm sorry he bothered you."

"It was no trouble. As I told you, he was charming."

"I think charming is the thing he does best."

"Oh well, folk like him add a few light touches to a sometimes dreary world," said Mrs. MacBain. "Like the blackbird."

"The blackbird minds his own business," said Alison. "I don't know if I thanked you properly for taking me to Torsaig this afternoon. But no matter what I said, I can't thank you enough."

"It was a treat for me too. And speaking of charmers, what about Charlie Macaulay?"

"He could run rings around Norris Elliot. Come in and have a cup of coffee with me?" Mrs. MacBain was a dedicated coffee-drinker.

"No, dear, I've things to do. I'll be off early tomorrow morning to spend the day with my sister-in-law over in Uig." The choir invisible rose to a crescendo, with one voice dominant.

"Hear that Annie," Mrs. MacBain said lovingly.

Alison left Norris Elliot outside the door. There were some

things that *would* vanish if ignored. She started a small pot roast with carrots and onions for her dinner, fixed a mug of coffee, and began to write down her account of the Torsaig visit. She put in everything, down to the peat fire in the miniature fireplace, the pattern on the tea cups, the framed photographs of grandchildren and great-grandchildren in their school uniforms and graduation robes. The dog. The wet daffodils edging the walk from the gate to the blue door. Peigi Martin's humor, and her baking.

Charlie's father knew Christina. If she had long ceased to be merely a figure mounted on stiff cardboard, she now became flesh and blood, and within someone's living memory. She had been kind enough to send her picture to the boy who'd worshipped her from afar. He had been in love with her all his life, and even now, pushing ninety, his son spoke reverently of her.

By the time Alison finished writing, her dinner was ready. She was too tired to walk down to the shore tonight, even in a sunset over Broad Bay made even more dramatic by long skeins of geese flying across it.

If she dreamed that night, it was nothing to remember. She woke up early to the gulls and lambs, thinking the word *Callanish*, and fell asleep again. Next time she was both hungry and eager. It was sunny again; all the signs and portents were on her side.

After breakfast she buttered rolls and filled them with slices of cold pot roast, and made a thermos of coffee. She hung her shoulder bag in the closet; she was sure that no one in Aignish was lying in wait behind the clump of gorse outside her gate to break in and steal her traveler's checks. She took her driver's license, and put some pound notes and a collection of loose change in the inside pocket of her Loden coat.

The sun was strong but those great clouds kept rolling up over, and the air was cold. She put on her lined jeans and a heavy white sweater, and her hiking boots; she stowed her key, the book on the Stones, small notebook and pen, and little camera, in her outside pockets. Lumpy but efficient, she thought.

When she went out to start the car, the children had already gone by to school, and the men had gone to their work. But some sheep belonging to the house across the road gathered at the fence to watch her, and she waved to them. When the car was running she went back in to be sure she had shut off the heaters, and she saw her binoculars and took them.

When she opened the door this time, Norris Elliot stepped nimbly inside and shut the door behind him. He salaamed.

"Good morning, Mohammed, the mountain salutes you."

He raised his eyebrows at her expression. "I see your landlady didn't give you my message. She must have disapproved of me."

"She told me you were here and offered the use of her telephone."

"Perhaps I should be calling on her this morning. It's frosty here. Very."

"I'm on my way out," she said brusquely. "What are you doing here?"

"Taking a look at Lewis before the tourist season, which I understand is heavy here, though personally I find that hard to believe."

"Well, I'm here to work," she said, "and I'm awfully busy this morning." She started for the door but he remained in her way, hands in his pockets, head cocked. A whimsical smile, and calculated, she was sure. "I saw you skulking around the pier at Tarbert," she said.

"I never skulk. If I'd been there I'd have greeted you like a French mayor with a buss on each cheek."

"I can't imagine why you're here instead of going to Paris for your girl."

He shrugged, looking as guileless as a setter pup. "She ran away. Let her run back."

She wished she had the brashness to tell him to his face he was a liar. "If you can't see anything good about the island, why don't you go away and look after your bum investments?"

"They're taking care of themselves and doing very well, strange to say. Redheads must bring luck. Dear Dr. Alison," he said winningly, "my being here at the same time as you is pure coincidence, if you don't want to call it my luck, as I do. In London I was talking to a stockbroker who comes here every year for the salmon-fishing, and he was so lyrical about the place that I took the next plane out. I'm impulsive."

"So I see. Now if you'll let me leave—" she reached around him for the doorknob and he moved slightly, but stayed close to her.

"And the place does have something very remarkable to recommend it," he said. "You. Where are you bound now?"

"Nowhere you'd be interested in." She opened the door and he had to move then or be squeezed between it and the wall.

"How do you know I wouldn't be interested?" he asked, following her out. "Try me."

"You're as persistent as a flea, or should I say sheep tick around here?"

"Persistence is the secret of my success, or lack of it. I persist in believing in lost causes."

"Is that a poetic name for bum investments, or me, or both? May I shut my door now?" He was holding it open behind him.

"Have you got your key?" he asked solicitously.

"Yes!" she snapped. But out of habit she rummaged in her pocket until she found the wooden tag. She shifted it into the deep inside pocket with her license and money. When she looked up she surprised an expression of serious concern, as if he too had been in suspense about the key. It changed at once to a smile so attractive and so ingenuous in its vanity that she felt like laughing, but didn't.

"I'm going to Callanish, to see the Standing Stones," she said severely. "I have a professional interest. You wouldn't have."

"Happy Stones, to see you." He shut the door behind them. "Why wouldn't I be interested? After all, there's not much else to see around here, besides you. Let me drive you."

"I'd rather drive myself, thank you." She went toward her car. His was a red Capri parked in the road.

"Then I'll follow you. Do you mind?"

It seemed there was no getting rid of him without being absolutely nasty, and even if it worked she would be upset for the day. She'd always considered this failing of hers very unfair, but there it was. She didn't want him following her, either; it would make her nervous and affect her driving. In the meantime this sunshine was too precious to waste, and there was one way of ignoring him.

"You can go with me," she said shortly, going around the car to the driver's seat.

"I'll take care of the gate," he said happily. He opened it, and gave her a radiant smile and salute as she backed out, then shut it again. Then he locked his car, and got in beside her. "Isn't this nice?"

"Smashing," she said cynically. She could go back to the Stones alone, later. Don't worry, Boots, she thought, he's safe with me. When we come back here he doesn't get one toe of his fancy loafers inside my door.

She was prepared to coldly repel any frivolous conversation but he surprised her by keeping silent, or whistling softly but on key, for which she was grateful; she shared an office with a compulsive under-breath whistler who was tone-deaf.

The sky began to cloud over when they weren't far out of Stornoway, and she was not surprised. Things evened up; there'd surely be times when she'd leave the dark weather behind on the east coast and head into sunshine.

Elliot stopped whistling. After a moment he said casually, "Do you want to be driving out here in rain or fog?"

"I was over this road in fog yesterday," she said.

"This is a lightweight car," he said, still offhand. "A strong wind could pick it up and toss it into the nearest peat bog."

"If you're nervous, I'll let you out here and you can hitch a ride back to town."

"You aren't getting rid of me, my girl. I felt an obligation to point out the risks, that's all."

"Kind of you," she said acidly.

"We could even get a freak snowstorm. It feels cold enough."

"Well, it's not." She concentrated on Mariana Grange. These moors called for a good pursuit scene. She didn't know about any castle on Lewis except the nineteenth century one which housed the technical college, but there had to be a mansion somewhere she could use. Girl taken from mother and reared on remote island. Girl taken from *father* and so forth. Girl growing up on remote island with no idea who she is. *No.* Spirited woman centuries ahead of her time marries big landlord and fights him for the good of his tenants. *No.* That's been done to death.

"Are you praying?" Norris asked. "Your lips are moving. Of course you could be cursing me. Or the fog. See it?" he said with gloomy triumph. "I knew it. My tennis elbow told me."

"It's not too late for you. Hop out and flag this van." She pulled into the nearest passing place. The van went by. Someone waved, Alison waved back. Norris didn't move.

"Too late," she said. "You could be on your way back to home and mother."

"I would no more leave you alone out here, merely for the sake of my creature comforts, than I'd leave Mother."

"Oh good God!" said Alison, putting the car violently into gear. Norris laughed.

"You shouldn't have invited me in, you see. In my own car I might have chickened out at first wisp of fog and turned back."

"I know now. I just didn't want you tailgating me. I

thought you'd be less of a nuisance this way, but I was wrong."

"Nuisance is one of my pet names, besides Nosey. Sometimes I use a French pronunciation, for variety's sake. Gives it class, too." He demonstrated. "And how about Enni Nuisance, the great French actor? All his mistresses spoke of him fondly as a pestilential bore."

"I always thought he was a writer of maxims," said Alison. "The one whose wife finally had him poisoned because she was so tired of his always coming up with a witty little epigram for every occasion, like a plague or a massacre."

"First cousin, same family," he said. "They all ended up violently dead, by the way. And richly deserved it."

Laughter was better than the corrosive annoyance. She would come back alone tomorrow.

9

THE PENINSULA of the Standing Stones was deep in East Loch Roag. The fog came on rapidly, as it had yesterday, and by the time the first of the Stones was in sight, the village had almost disappeared behind the car.

Alison parked at the side of the road by the north gate. The Stones stood up against the mist as if they were on a headland hanging out over open seas.

Elliot was unusually quiet. With a little lift of hope, she thought he might be uninterested enough to let her go alone. She opened her door and started to slide out, saying, "Why don't you stay here while I take a look around? It's pretty damp and raw, but I'm dressed for it, and you aren't."

"Nothing like Stonehenge, is it?" he said grimly.

"You must have seen pictures of this place."

"They used trick photography, then. Crazy angles. And the sun was shining." He got out on the other side. "You don't want to walk up there alone."

"That's just what I want." She tried not to be vehement about it.

"One of those slabs could fall on you."

"They've been standing for four thousand years. I don't

think one's suddenly going to attack me." She went to read the explanatory plaque on a post near the gate. The houses down the road didn't exist, as long as a rooster didn't crow, or a dog didn't bark, or nobody started up a car. The random voices of unseen sheep didn't count as interference. They belonged, enhancing the sense of time isolation.

Norris turned up the collar of his bush jacket and put his hands in his pockets. "It looks as if you picked the wrong time," he said in a low voice. "Or else the Stones don't want you here." He gave her a faint grin.

"Maybe it's you they resent," she retorted. "I have roots here. I have ancestors who knew this place well."

"She said nastily. Or smugly." He opened the gate for her and she walked through quickly, but he caught up and lightly held her elbow. The touch was not offensive, except that she strongly resented his being here at all.

As they walked up the avenue the fog gave the more distant stones the shapes of motionless figures wrapped tightly in cloaks. The *Fir Bhreige*, Charlie Macaulay called them, The False Men, and she could see why. They'd once been described as men turned to stone by an enchanter. From the corner of the eye you were tricked into suspecting flickers of movement here and there, making you want to swing around fast and confront—what?

Norris's whole hand cupped her elbow now. *Gripped* was more like it. She freed it by suddenly stiffening her arm.

"Come on back to town and I'll buy you a hot toddy," he said. "This weather's brutal."

Without looking around she said, "For a Canadian you're not much like the Young Man from Quebec."

"He did admit he was friz, even if he qualified it."

"If you're so uncomfortable, go on back to the car and wait."

"I couldn't find my way! I'm sticking with you for my own protection as well as yours." His fair head was darkened with the damp. "We could be lost for hours out here."

That was too ridiculous to answer. Then, looking at her, he almost walked into a stone, and swore softly. "What in hell are they for, anyway?"

"Nobody really knows. There are all kinds of theories. That's what fascinates me." She took out the booklet and opened it to the diagram showing the lay-out.

"Look, if you can't see anything, why not leave and come back when it's clear? Listen to those lambs," he said unhappily. "They're lost. They sound like babies, damn it. What a place!"

"They're not lost. They're with their mothers. Hear the ewes answering? . . . Look, the fog doesn't bother me. Sure, I'd love sunshine or at least no fog, so I could orient myself by the plan, and get some pictures, but if that isn't possible today I can just stand here letting the atmosphere take over." She dropped her voice lower. "We're in the circle now, and this is either the Stone of Sacrifice or the burial cairn."

He stood with his hands in his pockets, his shoulders hunched. There was a pinched look around his mouth. "You know, in your own way you're as nutty as the characters who stuck those stones up and worshipped them."

"Thanks," she said, "and I mean it."

Ahead of them a stone moved. Norris took a hissing breath. For one chaotic moment she watched with awe too great for terror. The stone turned out to be Ewen Chisholm coming toward them, his sweater misted by the wet. His face was all harsh angles in the colorless light; the gray showed up strongly in his hair.

"Christ, man!" Norris said. "Why didn't you whistle and let us know you were around? I thought it was a stone walking."

"It's not here that the stones go down to the stream to drink," he said coldly. "You'd not have heard me, anyway, you were blethering so loud." He turned to Alison. "He's right, it's no day to be here."

"The sun was shining when we started out," she protested.

His hostility shocked her. "My great-grandmother came from Torsaig," she said. There wasn't a spark of interest, and she'd already become accustomed to a far different reaction from Lewis people. She blushed with anger at herself for saying it.

He nodded at Elliot. "As you said, they don't make everybody welcome."

Norris grinned. "How close were you lurking to hear that? Seems to me I heard some crack earlier about 'skulking'. . . . Well, I suppose I'm the outsider, the evil influence, I've got the wrong blood, Elliot's so Lowland I'm practically a Sassenach." He lifted his face, shut his eyes, and called, "Strike this alien dead, whatever is here. I dare you!"

The other two watched him in silence. Then he opened his eyes and shrugged, spreading out his hands. "See? I'm still here."

"But not for long," said Alison. She could harly wait to get away. She had seen the granitic set of Chisholm's face and the cold sparkle under his lids. "Come on, I'm chilled to the bone."

"Be sure to shut the gate," Chisholm said.

"I shall be very sure." She turned so quickly she tripped on a rock fragment and bumped into Norris, who caught her in an unnecessarily snug embrace. She freed herself, but he held her arm in an intimate grip as they went back toward the gate. The other man's disapproval of them fairly scalded her back through the heavy jacket and sweater. She could understand his distaste for Norris's foolishness, which must have seemed irreverent, but she resented being included. After all, if he'd heard the "blethering" he should have realized her attitude was not Norris's.

She couldn't resist looking back once, but he had already vanished in the fog. "Come on," said Norris, "do you want to turn into a pillar of salt?" She tried to get her arm free but this time Norris pulled it through the crook of his elbow and held onto her hand.

"I can walk better alone," she said crossly.

"Who is he, anyway? Hamlet in modern dress? The resident spook? Reincarnation of one of the priests who ripped out the living heart of some poor bastard on the stone of sacrifice? I can imagine him doing it, you know."

"You're thinking about the Aztecs."

"I know I'm thinking about things I don't like." His fingers laced through hers in a painful grip. "I may be getting pneumonia."

"It's your own fault." She shut and latched the gate behind them. She was disturbed by the faintly bluish tinge to his lips. "The heater will warm you up, if I can find it. You don't have a heart condition, do you?"

"No. I'm just bloody cold. I've found the heater.... You turn this car like a racing driver. You're so damn-all efficient, nothing daunts you."

"*He* did," said Alison. "He's making a study of the Stones and I guess he thinks they're his."

"He's welcome to them. They should all be great company for each other. What is there to study? Rows of rocks, and that's it."

"Even you must have heard about the supposed astronomical aspects of Stonehenge."

"Snide, that 'even you.' I'm not quite a moron. It's when they talk about running stuff through computers that I'm lost, and glad to be."

"The computer business doesn't enthrall me, either. But every succeeding civilization has had its own explanations of these sites. I'm interested in what's been passed on, and what possible meanings these neolithic monuments could have in today's world." She hoped she sounded pedantic enough to discourage him, but at the same time she was thinking something very different and provocative.

Supposing it isn't today's world at all at the Stones, but their world. Somewhere you step over an invisible boundary, and Chisholm's looking for it.

The heat was felt now. Norris relaxed enough to light a

cigarette. "Why does it have to be anything but an art form?" he asked. "Those people must have reached a time when they had the leisure to put up their great monuments. They didn't have to spend all their waking hours getting food, and there weren't enough other human beings in the world so they had to keep fighting for survival. So why couldn't this Standing Stone business be a community way of celebrating their existence?"

"You could be right," she said. "In fact, the astronomical data always throws me. I get to feeling that somebody's hypnotizing himself with equations. Making what's there fit his theories. But whatever the original reason for those huge slabs being put there in just that order, successive peoples have used them for their own purposes, and religion certainly comes into it . . . whether it was with blood sacrifice, or fire or sun worship."

"They couldn't have held many services for *that*."

She laughed. "But it used to be a lot warmer and probably sunnier. The climate deteriorated around four thousand years ago, and some say that's when the forest ended, and the peat build-up began. Those stones were up to their shoulders in peat after a while."

"My, you certainly are a fund of information, Dr. Barbour."

"If you hadn't barged in this morning you wouldn't have to be listening now."

He didn't answer and she sneaked a look at him. He was slouched in his seat, head back, eyes closed. He won't be in a hurry to subject himself to another lecture, she thought happily.

"A word of advice," he said suddenly, without opening his eyes. "Don't let yon Highlander know what your field is. He's likely to set his tame fogs on you every time you step foot in the place." His voice shook suddenly on the last words as if a violent chill had seized him.

"Good Lord, are you all right?" she asked him. "Are you

still *cold*?" The heater was almost too much for her.

"Don't worry, I'm not coming down with something contagious." He shivered again. "It's just one of my things. I have charm, certain talents, I'm a great dancer, and I have an allergy. Probably to what I had for breakfast."

"Do you have anything to take for it?"

"Not with me on Lewis. It's one thing I forgot."

"I have a non-prescription antihistamine I keep on hand for sniffles. You could take a couple of those and I'll give you a cup of hot coffee or tea."

"Thanks. I feel like an utter fool." He lapsed into a silence that made her uncomfortable because he was. She could no longer say or even think in self-satisfaction, It serves you right.

Back at the cottage he took the two tablets with water and refused a hot drink.

"Not that it doesn't break my heart to leave you, but I'd better get back to the hotel and try to sleep this off."

Besides, Boots will be up by now and wondering where Rover Boy has strayed, she thought.

"And I'll remember not to eat eggs tomorrow morning," he went on. "But I'm glad I went with you, and I'm still going to take you out for a drink."

"I don't drink," she said, "and I'm going to be very busy. Goodbye, Mr. Elliot." She shut the door behind him before he was off the doorstep. Then she checked from the kitchen window to be sure he fastened the gate behind him. He didn't look back at the cottage but walked swiftly to his car with his head bent and his shoulders hunched, though the noon sun was warm here. He drove off without a glance toward the house.

She sat down to eat the lunch she had taken with her.

It was the last time he'd destroy her plans; she hadn't come this far, keeping everyone in ignorance at home, to have her privacy mauled by a stranger. She should have challenged him about Boots. That would have taken care of everything.

They must have been driving around for something to do

that day and stopped at Tarbert to watch the ferry come in. Though it was hard to imagine why anyone would want to drive all the way through mountains for fun in such gray weather. Especially after the way he'd fussed today about possible strong winds and snow. Maybe Boots was the intrepid one.

Boots had obviously *not* left him at Cherbourg, but had been sulking in her cabin after a row. So they'd made up, and for some freakish reason had come to Stornoway. Boots was likely buying tweeds. Why not? Maybe she had a tweed shop back in Canada, so this was a business trip for her. But if they'd had a row and made up, and then he saw Alison of all people aboard the *Hebrides*, he surely wasn't going to rush forward with glad cries when she came down the gangplank.

Having it all worked out to her satisfaction, she wished Boots joy of her lover, and enjoyed her lunch. The she wrote a description of Ewen Chisholm in a Mariana Grange notebook. There was no doubt that he was a perfect hero. She had only to invent the sinister secret or unspeakable tragedy.

10

AFTER LUNCH she'd have liked to go back to Torsaig and find the ruins of Christina's home, but it was a long drive across the island to make twice in one day, with the prospect of fog again at the end. Unless the fog at the Stones had been raised just for the occasion by Ewen Chisholm. She grinned. . . . The orphan girl, or ill-treated ward, is fleeing across the moors, fording icy salmon streams and dragging yards of drenched dress, unless some dog-faithful lad in her guardian's house has thoughtfully provided her with boy's clothes. Anyway, she escapes a dangerous bog, and one could throw in a lecherous peat-cutter for titillation. She either outruns him, or is rescued by a harsh dark man who is the demonic custodian of the Standing Stones. The world sees him as a mild, reclusive scholar, but Fiona or Flora, or whatever her name is, sees with increasing horror that he is *mad*, and she is his prisoner!

And how about a genuine touch of the supernatural, anyway? With midnight rites at the Stone of Sacrifice? Magnificent!

After a half-hour of happy scribbling (Mariana Grange's notebooks were never as neat as Dr. Barbour's) she was ready to go out and use the rest of a fine day. At least it was fine on this side of Lewis. She took her camera and drove northeast toward Tiumpan Head.

This time she turned off to her right and drove slowly down to the shore of Lower Bayble and across to Upper Bayble, then back to the main road again. In one settlement all the dogs seemed to belong to the same demented family or else had formed a vigilante force to keep out strange cars. In a yelping pack they saw her to the nearest crossroads, and then all shut up at once and watched her drive away.

There were no other çars out at the lighthouse. She turned hers around, sweating a little as she imagined the gears and brakes suddenly failing and the car rolling backward over the cliff. It made it even worse that nobody was there to know what happened to her. Nothing failed, but she was as relieved as if she'd actually been in danger of death. She parked on the flat, heading out, then left the car and walked in the solitude shared only by the birds and some distant sheep. There was a thin overcast now but the sun shone warmly through it and the wind was light. The sound of breakers below came up to her in long sighs.

In the northeast she could just make out a ship on the horizon, perhaps heading for some Baltic port. In the east the mountains of Wester Ross were no longer there. She walked along the road away from the lighthouse, glad her soles made no sound to disturb the stillness. On the left, the water side, peats lay in long dark rows. The land surged away from her in tawny swells whose sides and hollows sometimes glimmered into greens as light and tenuous as the bloom on taffeta, and as swiftly changing. She took some pictures but at best they could only remind her of how it had been.

The rams were so quiet they'd been a part of the inanimate foreground until one turned his head to watch her. The movement stopped her, and there they were and here *she* was, about fifteen feet away. Seven of them lay in a group at the side of the road, all watching her. She was unprepared for their size, and the horns massively magnificent in size and curl. One big ram alone would have been a sight, but seven constituted a spectacle, and there was not another human being in sight.

Oh, well, she thought with giddy apprehension. Make the best of it. She snapped a couple of pictures while they gazed at her with superb indifference.

She backed away, and they still didn't move; she was nothing to them. Finally she turned around and walked back to the car.

When she drove up to them a few minutes later she slowed the car and spoke to them out the window. "The Los Angeles Rams aren't in it with you, in spite of their fancy helmets."

She had gone on a little beyond them when she saw a Mercedes coming toward her, and she was glad she'd had her time alone out here. She pulled over to the side of the road as far as she could but, instead of squeezing past, the other car stopped.

"Alison Barbour, is that *you*?" a woman's voice cried. A man's gaunt dark face appeared out the driver's side, he waved a hand holding a cigar, and said, "It may not be. If you've seen one redhead you've seen them all." He gave Alison a sour grin.

"*Jake!*" Terry shrieked. She got out and ran around the car to Alison's. "For heaven's sake! Of all the people in the world!"

"I could say the same thing," said Alison faintly. Terry held onto the car, giving a high-speed travelogue of which Alison could make no sense and didn't want to. Terry was wearing a bright red pantsuit and a pink turtleneck, her hair so perfectly done it looked like a wig.

Jake got out of the car like a man who has had enough, and came across the road, flicking cigar ashes. "Any place to turn around at the lighthouse?" he asked Alison.

"Yes, but it's on a cliff, so be careful."

"Thanks," he said sardonically. "Back to the car, Terry. You wanted to see the sights, such as they are, and this is one of them."

"But I want to talk to Alison too." She giggled. "Isn't it

funny, we only met that last day on the ship, but when we meet again it's like old friends and relations because we're in a foreign country."

It may be like old friends and relations to you, thought Alison, but it sure as hell isn't to *me*. She hoped her smile looked like one and not like a grimace. Jake put out a big hand on Terry's shoulder and propelled her toward the car. She cried back to Alison, "Where are you staying? So we can stop in?"

"Aignish!" Alison called back.

"*What?*"

So it sounded like gibberish to her. Good. Alison waved her hand, and skinned by the Mercedes before Jake started it again.

Once out on the main road past Portnaguiran, she was frantic to get back and flood the moat and lower the portcullis, to say nothing of boiling up a pot of lead. They might find Aignish if there was a map in the car, or they might ask someone. She would lock up and pretend she'd gone for a walk. No, she'd really go for a walk.

Coming toward her, a battered car wavered back and forth across the road, and she slowed down to watch in horrified anticipation as he missed sheep on one side and almost tipped into the ditch on the other side, which at least would have immobilized the menace. He was either sick or drunk. The car lurched back onto the road and wobbled in her direction, and she froze, wondering whether to keep still, try scooting past him, or leave the car and go over the fence into the nearest pasture.

The car inched abreast of her and she looked into the stupefied eyes of the drunkest driver she had ever seen. His lips moved without sound. His window was down and so was hers, and the fumes that were wafted across the narrow gap were strong enough to make her blink.

She said inanely, "Be careful," and accelerated. A safe distance away she looked for him in her mirror and saw him still on the hard surface but creeping along the wrong side.

She stopped at the Aignish corner for the children coming across from the school. The three cows were out again, and an infant about three feet high and a small shaggy brown-patched terrier were driving them toward a field beyond the school, opposite the Aignish side.

She left the car outside her gate and started down the road on foot, but before she reached the next house a horn brayed a salute behind her, and there was the Mercedes pulling in behind her car.

"Oh damn damn *damn!*" she swore, wishing she had something to throw. Terry was waving and shouting, "Hallo there! We found you!"

"Oh God, don't I know it," Alison muttered. She walked back slowly, trying to get herself into a decent mood.

There was no chance of a dooryard visit. Terry wanted to use the bathroom. Jake stood looking over the fields toward Broad Bay, finishing up a cigar, his heavy dark face rather melancholy.

Terry marveled about the comfort of the cottage, used the bathroom, and cooed over the lambs outside the garden wall. Jake's silence was so martyred that Alison told him to smoke if he wanted to, she didn't mind.

"Thanks," he said flatly. He lit a fresh cigar and picked up one of the books she'd borrowed.

Alison, for something to do, gave them tea and shortbread. "Isn't that stuff out of this world?" said Terry. "I'm going to look like a barrel in no time—I just can't resist it. . . . How did you ever find this place?"

"Well—"

"Isn't it the weirdest coincidence? Meeting you on the ship and then coming to the ends of the earth—it *feels* like it anyway—and meeting you again!"

Not to mention Boots and Bubbles, Alison thought, but preferred not to bring them into it.

"We came out on the morning ferry, from Ullapool," said Terry. "Actually we're on the way to Aberdeen, so Jake can see what's being done with some of his investments. He's very heavily into oil, you know. But we bought the car in London, and we're making a good tour, and when we reached Inverness we thought—"

"*You* thought," said Jake.

"Yes, darling. *I* thought we really should take a look at these western isles we kept hearing about. And maybe I could get some fantastic bargains in Harris tweeds. Well, Alison, they're really not all that cheap, even here right on the *spot*, but they're still fabulous. And we really love this place, don't we, Jake?"

"You love it," he said morosely. "And it loves you. In two hours off the boat you've already boosted the economy by buying half the tweeds and sweaters in sight. Three more days and I'll be having to sell the car and go to the nearest American consul for our fare home." He gave Alison that long, glum look. "I'm not crazy about miles of peat bog, and I saw a dead sheep on the road this morning and it's put my stomach out for the day. I just hope it died quickly, that's all."

"Me too," said Alison. "I hope I don't see one. I did meet an awfully drunk driver on the way back here."

"Christ," said Jake, "he nearly put us in the ditch and didn't even know it."

"We weren't far behind you," Terry explained. "We turned around quick at the lighthouse and didn't stay, because Jake's not into lighthouses, and we hurried to catch up with you but wow, this man looked like a *zombie*—" She laughed and reached over to pat Jake's arm. "Jake almost swallowed his cigar."

"Too bad somebody couldn't knock him off instead of innocent sheep," said Jake. "He's a threat to society if I ever saw one. He could wipe out a carful of kids, for God's sake."

"Keep calm, dear," Terry told him. "Probably everybody knows who he is and keep an eye out for him, like J. D. Weaber back home. Alison, don't you wish you had one of those darling peat fires instead of that make-believe electric fireplace?"

"Managing a peat fire probably calls for a set of special skills," said Alison. "As an amateur I'd probably smoke myself like a kipper or a ham."

Jake sighed. "I'm ready to go back on the first ferry tomorrow."

"Jake!" cried Terry. We haven't seen anything but Tiumpan Head yet, and that doesn't count because we didn't even stop."

"We've seen every store in Stornoway."

"I mean the sights." She took a familiar booklet out of her handbag. "These fabulous sands at Bosta. The Pictish Broch. The Standing Stones. I'll bet you've been there already," she said to Alison.

"Just to the Stones, but there was thick fog. I saw practically nothing."

"See?" said Jake. "I'm not driving these roads in the fog, old lady. Between the sheep, and the natives driving like bats out of hell on the wrong side of the road when they're drunk. Good God!"

Alison smiled at him with so much compassion she was afraid she'd overdone it. With any luck she wouldn't be bothered by them much longer. When Jake finally got Terry moving toward the door, she wanted to make a dinner date. But Alison got out of that by saying she was very tired, as she wasn't used to her new bed yet. Jake gloomily sympathized, he was having the same trouble at the Caberfeidh.

"But we'll get together *sometime* before Jake drags me off this island," Terry insisted.

When they had really gone, Alison poured a fresh hot cup of tea and stood at the sitting room window to drink it. In a few minutes she recognized the green Mercedes going toward the Braigh and expected that Terry would go back to the shops while Jake headed for a bar. They were likely to see Norris and Boots at the hotel before the day was out, and Terry could concentrate on them and forget Alison.

She got her walk to the shore finally. When she came back,

she took her tape recorder out to try to get the blackbird and the lambs, and Annie's peremptory bawling for a handout. She knew that to play these tapes back in Hazlehurst would cause the kind of homesickness she had never known before.

11

SHE LEFT EARLY in another clear morning for Callanish. Fog or not when she got there, she intended to stay as long as she pleased. Mrs. MacBain's garage was closed, so she'd come home from Uig in the evening, and was probably sleeping late this morning.

The sunshine held all the way across the island, but she abstained superstitiously from gloating. When the houses were behind her and only the Stones ahead, it was like driving over a threshold into another age. There they stood with their shadows at their feet as they must have looked at the beginning, on the first morning after the design was completed some four thousand years ago.

She walked up the avenue. A rooster crowed back in the village; the sound carried across time rather than space. She thought, All I need now is a cuckoo to sing from the tallest stone in the circle, and I'll be really spooked. She turned slowly in an arc of her own, using herself as a camera to take in the circling hills, moorlands, and waters.

"Good morning."

She gasped, her hands flew up and out in reflex, the blood beat in her throat. She turned toward him, letting her breath go loudly, shaking her head. Ewen Chisholm.

"I'm sorry," he said but with a slight smile as if her start had amused him. He stood in the stone circle and she thought he must have been behind one of the stones the whole time, watching her approach and her dreamy turning-in-place. It angered her.

"Good morning," she said. "I was listening for a cuckoo, but it's probably too early. Do they really come here first?"

He shrugged. "I don't know. The cuckoo was never a favorite of mine. Some of its habits are reprehensible." In this light the faded scar across his chin showed clearly, and there was another on a cheekbone, going back into his hair. His expression was neutral, as if he were simply waiting for her to leave. She wondered how it would change if she gurgled at him, "I *love* the way you say 'reprehensible!' "

He was safe from that experiment, but she wasn't leaving. "Well, if there's no cuckoo, at least there's no fog," she said. "Was it foggy before I arrived yesterday, or did it come with us?"

"You *have* been reading up on the Stones, haven't you?" He nodded at the booklet in her hand.

"Yes, and I could almost believe the Stones whipped up the fog yesterday to discourage the man who was with me. Which it did."

"Yes, your friend was uncomfortable." If a smile ever did break through, it would be like the ice going out in spring. *The Demonic Master of the Stones. Merlin on the Moors.*

"He's not my friend. He's a shipboard acquaintance, and from the last day only." Saying too much again. "Whatever possessed him to turn up here I don't know." She walked away from him. "Do you mind if I walk around and look and absorb?"

"Why should I mind? They're not mine. I happen to live just below here, that's all."

She opened the booklet for something to do with her new awkwardness. He said suddenly, "What's your name?"

"Alison Barbour."

"Ewen Chisholm," he said. "I saw you in Stornoway two days ago. You were standing near the telephone on Cromwell Street."

She looked up from the book. "I saw *you*. I didn't speak because when I tried to on the ferry you didn't want me to." She was astonished by what she was hearing.

"I beg your pardon." Color stood out on his cheekbones. "I meant no disrespect. But I'm not easy with women."

"It's past now," she said graciously, or almost. "Where is this?" She pointed on the map to the name *Cnoc an Tursa*.

"To the south there." He pointed. "The rocky outcrop."

"And it means Hill of—?"

"Some say Pilgrimage, others say Mourning. You didn't get a proper look at the burial cairn yesterday. Come and see it," he said. "It's not as impressive as it sounds, though it was when it was first excavated in 1857. I wish they'd filled it in again. Too many thousands of feet have walked through here since then, and for ninety-nine percent of the crowd it means nothing at all. Simply one of the sights to stare at without wonder."

"Well, it's more than a mere sight to me," she said. "My great-grandmother might have heard the cuckoo here." She laughed. "Or come up here on a May day morning or Midsummer's Day with a boy."

"What was her name?"

"It's a common enough one. Christina MacLeod. She lived in Torsaig."

"You said that yesterday." He looked at her without expression. He was either thoughtful or bored, or he had nothing more to say and was uneasy again. Maybe the girl in Edinburgh had given him up because a man who is still awkward with women in his late thirties is a lost cause; except to the pursuing Female, who probably had her own reasons for liking shy men. They'd make a lovely couple.

Consider me just a person and relax, she felt like saying. She wasn't letting him go until she was ready. "Do you know who or what is the Shining One?"

"I can't tell you that because I don't know."

"Did anyone ever see the Shining One walk down the avenue at Midsummer sunrise?"

"I don't know," he repeated. "The story persisted a long time, and no one knows where it began." He walked around the circle as he talked, now and then putting his hand on a stone, looking closely at a fleck in the texture of one, then resuming his pace. "People create their gods, and the Shining One may have been born of a great yearning. The Stones have always been seen as a place of worship. You must know that early Christian temples have been built on Roman temple sites, and the Roman ones on primitive sacred spots, and those on earlier ones still. I'll leave you to yourself now." He turned to walk away.

"No, wait!" she said involuntarily. He stopped and looked back, still unsmiling but with a difference, invisible but perceptible; a sharpening, a tuning?

"Where is the Stone of Sacrifice?" she asked inanely.

"There," he said, "if you want to believe in it."

"I don't particularly, but it's a part of the mythology. I like the Shining One better, and the Beltane fires."

"You've a good many myths to pick and choose from. And a good many other stones and circles on Lewis besides this place."

He nodded at her and left the circle, walking south toward the *Cnoc an Tursa.*

The silence was no longer the same. He had been an intrusion and she supposed she was the same for him. Instead of brushing against the centuries in a timeless hush, she had his after-image to contend with even when he had gone out of sight. Interference. Jamming. A little breeze sprang up among the Stones as if he'd sent it, and the loch darkened. She walked around and took some pictures but any large sense of leisure was gone.

She drove over to Torsaig. When she went down the hill the loch was whipped to silver in the sun's track, a deep bold blue elsewhere. Small waves broke over the sands and against the rocks across the road from the cottages. Charlie's house looked shut up, with no dog in the front garden. Beside the house with the pink trim, a gaunt white-haired woman wearing a serviceable old coat, a knitted cap, and Wellingtons, was hoeing her fenced-off garden, watched by the two goats.

The woman looked severe, but when she glanced up and saw Alison watching her from outside the wall, her hair blowing in the wind, she smiled and came down to her. "Good morning," she said. "That's Leodhas hair."

"Good morning, and thank you. I'm looking for the remains of my great-grandmother's house. It's in ruins up the glen, Mr. Macaulay told me, but—"

"Yes, you would be the lass Tearlach told me about. All the way from America. Now tell me, it's not often they see hair like that on the streets of America, is it?"

Alison laughed. "Not as often as I see it on Lewis. Could you tell me how to find what's left of the cottage?"

"Aye, but there's more than one, you see. The old village was all up there once. What was your great-granny's name?"

"Christina MacLeod."

"Oh." Her face lengthened out. "Tearlach didn't tell me that. He told me no name at all. I thought it was a Matheson or a MacIver you'd be wanting."

"Is there anything wrong with wanting a MacLeod?" Alison asked humorously.

"Och, no!" She was flustered. "It's just the surprise of it, you see."

A surprise, with roughly half the population named MacLeod? "Mr. Macaulay did tell me everybody thought Christina had died young in America and left no family."

"That would be it," the woman said quickly. "Peigi Martin and her father are off to Valtos for the day to Calum Macaulay's, taking the dog to help with Calum's sheep. If you just follow the road past Tearlach's gate and go on past the cottages and the postoffice, you'll come to the glen, with the manse and the kirk on one hand and the old schoolhouse on the other. The place you want is the last one up, it's just across the track from the cemetery. Not a soul will stop you."

Alison thanked her and left the car outside Charlie's. Beyond his field there was a row of attached cottages, their white walls blinding in the sun, gardens in every dooryard, most chimneys puffing peat smoke. There was a pram in the lee of a wall, a few cats on sunny doorsteps and window sills. A stout old dog watched her placidly from the last gate in the row. A couple of women talked in the doorway of the combined shop and postoffice. They called a greeting when she waved.

The land rose abruptly behind the postoffice and a brook plunged noisily down the hill in its deep narrow channel, rushing through a stone arch under the road and spilling out in small streams cut through the sands, and into the surf. Just over the bridge the track left the road to go up the glen. The Victorian-looking manse stood almost at its entrance, and on the steep ground above that rose the small stone church, which the driver Donald MacLeod had said was no longer used for worship.

She turned up the double-rutted track; evidently it could be driven over and probably was, if the cemetery was still in use. Across the church was the old schoolhouse, its stone dignity spoiled, or enhanced, by the line of washing snapping in the wind. A terrier barked from behind the gate, but not with any great passion.

The stream poured down the hill between the schoolhouse and the track, and its sound blended with the swash from the shore. The wind was soon cut off here and the sun was warm. She passed the roofless remains of the old "black houses"; the space between their double walls was grass-grown. Sometimes there was a small rectangle or open circle of stone wall; and traces of outbuildings. At the top of the short glen the land flattened to her left, and there was the walled cemetery. At her right, on a little slope, stood what was left of her ancestors' home, and the hill rose in a green knob behind it.

There was no clear path now but she took the natural way up to it, across the short greening turf among the gorse showing its first yellow blossoms on prickly stems. She crossed the stream by balancing on big stones around which the water flowed. On the other side it seemed that her feet could feel the old path. Any path worn deep by so many years of use would have to be there yet.

She went in through the vacant doorway to rubble and plants pushing up to fill the corners. The chimney had fallen in, and anything movable, like cupboards or beds, had been taken away. She knelt to touch the hearthstone. It was very warm inside the enclosure, with the sun coming down on her. She wondered if the roof had been a thatched one when Christina lived there. Probably. She went back onto the sunken threshold. What lay out here—the slope to the stream and then to the track, the cemetery across the way, the church steeple down below, had been what the girl Christina saw when she came out in the morning to fetch in peats or water. She had run down the track barefoot to go to school, and walked it in her best clothes and boots to go to the kirk.

From this height, which set her family apart from the others, she could look over the cemetery to the dance and shimmer of the sea opening up around the long point that made Torsaig; she could see, between folds of land, that bit of the western horizon which to the child Christina must have seemed the very edge of the world. She'd have known there was land beyond it, with Lewis men going away there always, so some Torsaig men must have gone, and some came back. But the child living up here had probably expected to live out her life in Torsaig or not far from it, and to be buried inside the walls across the road.

Maybe, if she'd been a spirited child, she longed for something else. But how, back then, did you find it, unless someone else found it for you? A good many people had been forcibly dislocated in those days; whole villages were either resettled elsewhere on the island or shipped out to the Eastern Settlements in Canada, some against their will, some choosing to go because there was nothing left at home. But Torsaig's only move seemed to have been from the glen down to the flat and the shore.

The sound of the wind was faint up here, and the stream quieter. "Oh, Christina, Christina," she murmured. "Why can't I know? Why is there just nothing here?"

She went back down the old path and across the stepping stones to the track. From there she looked back. The round hill rose high behind the cottage, and she was positive that Christina must have climbed to the top many times. Any child would. She'd have been all over the place either at play or to help with the lambs, or to bring home the cow, one of those endearing red shaggy creatures. She must have gone down to the shore to gather winkles and dulse, and when she was old enough she'd have carried a creel of dried peats home on her back. She wouldn't have gone much around the cemetery, even in summer with the birds singing; she'd have watched too many funerals there (only the men went) and some of the burials would have been family ones.

Christina of the beautiful hair, and her father with hair like a Burning Bush. . . . Alison could imagine just about anything but all she could know was that Christina had gone to America in some disgrace, and Charlie Macauley had been too delicate about it even in Gaelic. The lady next door had reacted, too.

She went into the cemetery. It was large for such a minute village, but apparently many Torsaig people had been brought home for burial. When Christina was dying in America, she might have dreamed of the place that should have been hers up on the hill, with the voice of the stream running by, the lambs' cries and the birds, and the locked silences of winter.

Christina walked along the neat aisles looking for the old part of the cemetery. Maybe Christina had died too quickly for dreaming. Maybe she'd become so completely American that she had never looked back, except as one does with humor and nostalgia on oneself as a child.

"The trouble with being a writer," Alison said aloud, "is that you have to turn everyone into a character. You really don't have to *know*. It's enough that you're here to see where some of your roots are."

In the old part of the cemetery, with the moor just over the wall, she realized there'd be no way of picking out Christina's parents among so many MacLeods. She wandered around reading the stones, not wanting to leave the place. From time to time she looked up at the remains of the cottage, and at the knob of the hill behind it. Birds sang persistently, and she thought absently, I should get a bird book so I'll know their names.

Finally, driven by hunger, she went slowly down the glen. When she passed the manse a chunky young woman in slacks and oversize sweater was just opening the driveway gate. A station wagon stood waiting in the road, with two small children and a golden retriever boiling around inside. "Good morning!" the girl called to Alison. "Were you looking for something or somebody? The museum? I'd love to show it to you."

"I was up in the cemetery. I'd love to see the museum, but I can't today. Can I come back?"

"Fabulous!" She put out her hand. "I'm Morag Murray. Mrs. David." She had round red cheeks that squeezed her small bright humorous eyes under black bangs, a wide mouth that tilted up at the corners like a clown's. The whole effect was of insouçiant and innocent charm.

Alison introduced herself and told where she was staying.

"Oh, I know Mrs. MacBain well!" Morag cried. "So you're the nice tenant she told my mother about. Well, that's Iain—" she pointed "—and Jean, and Neacal the dog, known as Nick."

"For St. Neacal?"

"Don't ask me! He was all christened and answering to it when we took him, but now he likes Nick or Nickie just as well." Nick barked tremendously, the children whooped, and clapped their hands over their ears.

A group of sheep grazing across the road were not upset.

"They're ours," said Morag. "They're used to the noise."

"I'd better be getting on," said Alison, "but I'll be back."

"Ring up first so I'll be sure to be here, and we'll have a cup of tea."

"I'd love that."

Morag wrote her number on the back of her grocery list. "Goodbye!" the children called after Alison, leaning far out the windows, while Nick bayed.

A little red Royal Mail van was in front of the postoffice, otherwise life was pretty quiet by the cottages. No one was home yet at Charlie Macauley's, and the woman next door was not in sight for Alison to thank. She backed to the intersection and drove up the hill. Odd how that name Neacal had come up; she hadn't given Harold Marshall a thought since she'd arrived, and now, through an accidental encounter, he was so fresh in her mind she could hear his precise yet eager voice. What a nice man he was. She hoped his sister appreciated him.

She stopped in Stornoway and left her film at the chemist's, and bought the Stornoway *Gazette* at the news agent's shop next door. She shopped for a few groceries and put them in the car, and then went into the bookshop to buy her own copy of the history of Lewis, and a small Gaelic primer. She didn't intend to send any postcards from here, but she bought some anyway because the photographs were very good. She went into another room to look over the tweeds, and shelves of handknit sweaters; she would probably visit often before she could decide what to buy, they were all so handsome.

In the gift section she picked out a creamer and sugar bowl of native Lewis pottery for her boss's wife, and for him she bought a sgian dubh, the small knife traditionally carried in the Highlander's sock. The sheath was decorated with a silvery metal pressed with a vine and thistle design, and the elaborately molded handle had a big mock topaz set in the end. There was nothing mock about the sharp little steel blade.

While she waited for another customer to pay for her things, she looked out past the window exhibits at the people passing by, counting redheads again, and she saw Norris and Boots come across the street and stop outside. She stood very still, willing them not to be attracted by the window and look in. They did not; they were talking too hard, at least Boots was. Her hair was a paler blonde than Alison remembered from the ship, and her make-up was elegant, as always. She wore a belted coat of creamy-beige leather and a vivid silk scarf at her neck. She looked as artificial as a gardenia in the heather. She was angry.

Norris looked harassed rather than angry. Maybe he hadn't completely recovered from his attack, or his lies weren't coming as easily as they used to. Boots was giving him a hard time. She had him grappled to her by an arm hooked tightly through his. Tucked into an open section of her shoulder bag was a Mariana Grange novel.

Then she pulled Norris around, and they moved on. Alison went to the door to look after them. They walked down the street until they were lost in the crowd and shadows of the pedestrian precinct. She paid for her books, cards, and gifts, and ran across the street to her car.

12

CROSSING THE BRAIGH, she met Mrs. MacBain on her way to town. They waved merrily at each other, and she drove on feeling cheerful. Norris was in Boots' hands now, there'd be no more running away. She wished them joy of each other.

When she got out of the car Annie bleated imperiously through the back gate, while Angus took advantage of her preoccupation to nurse with strenuous enthusiasm. "I haven't a thing you'd like, Annie," Alison said. This was a lie, as Mrs. MacBain had told her that hand-reared sheep would eat anything, and Annie probably knew she was lying about all the goodies in her bag and in the house. "Go find some green grass," she said. Annie's retort sounded annoyed.

She made a large thick sandwich and a salad for her lunch, and read the history of Lewis as she ate. In a translation of place names she read that Torsaig meant "Thor's Bay," and was first settled by Norwegian colonists, not the Viking raiders who came later to destroy. Many Lewis families were of Norse descent and proud of it. She read that the MacLeods were descended from Norse kings, and it seemed to her that anyone with a Highland name could honestly claim a distinguished name-father, even if his distinction lay in the skill and speed with which he'd murdered his brothers and slaughtered their children.

Afterward she took a second cup of coffee into the living room, settled in the big chair with her sock feet on the coffee table, and prepared to write up her log.

The heading *Callanish* transfixed her pen. Ewen Chisholm had not really left her mind all day. He was always there among the changing impressions and images, as hard-edged and immovable as one of the Stones itself. Would she use him as hero or villain? Green eyes were in this year, but his were almost black; a nice variation. His faint but interesting scars could mean a dramatic history. As a character he must be either mad, or tragic; in any case, he should have smoldering depths, uncomfortable as that sounded for the poor man.

In real life he could be, and probably was, dull. He could be, in spite of his voice and the accent, enough of a hide-bound male chauvinist to resent her if he knew she was a professional woman. The phrase, "not easy with women" could mean he hated them. And to think she'd gone all fumble-witted in his presence. . . . The memory was both ludicrous and humiliating.

With any luck she could visit the Stones sometimes without his knowing it. He must have other things to do besides haunting the place.

It was a relief to write up the Torsaig visit. She was glad Charlie hadn't been home; there might never be another such hour in her whole time here. She was still there, contentedly remote, when the knocker sounded. It was a long leap from the Torsaig cemetery to her carpeted living room. She went to the door expecting to see Mrs. MacBain.

It was Norris Elliot. He grinned. "If ever I saw consternation, that's it."

"Annoyance is more like it. What are you doing here?"

"Aren't you going to ask me in?"

"I am not." She tried to shut the door but he braced a hand against it. Two women were coming along by the wall carrying loaded shopping bags; out of sight the bus from Stornoway shifted gears to go up the hill.

"Please!" said Norris loudly. "You've got to give me a chance, you can't shut me out!"

"I can too," said Alison. The women's faces were bright with amused curiosity. She didn't mind giving them something to chuckle over, but there was a way to get rid of Norris once and for all.

She stood back and he cried, "Bless you, my angel, you shan't be sorry!" like a character out of a Mariana Grange book, and bounded in and shut the door behind him.

"I know I won't," said Alison. She went into the living room and he followed. He went directly to the window.

"What a stupendous view you have." He gazed at an incoming airplane approaching the airfield outside Stornoway as if he had never seen such a thing before.

"I'm sure you didn't come to admire the view," said Alison. "So why?"

He turned with that supposedly disarming smile. "To ask you to drive to Harris with me tomorrow afternoon. We can visit the church at Rodel, have dinner at the hotel in Tarbert, and a lovely sunset ride back. I'm sure there'll be a sunset."

"Your girl will be going too, of course."

"My girl?" Very good, the bewildered widening of eyes.

"Boots. The blonde in them. Oh, come off it!" she said in exasperation. "The two of you walked by me today on Cromwell Street. She was with you at Tarbert the other day. I don't know why you decided to come to Lewis, but whatever your reason, why don't you just pursue that and leave me to mine?" She turned toward the hall but he remained motionless in the middle of the room. The amusement was gone, and in the bright afternoon light he had the strained and much older look she'd seen this morning.

"Listen, Alison, will you? For two minutes? *Please.*"

"I can't think why I should. Where was she last Friday afternoon on the ship?"

"She was sleeping. She can sleep all day sometimes. We were at the pier, yes." He sounded desperately anxious to win her belief, his eyes never left hers. "We came because Monique had some bee in her bonnet about the place being romantically isolated and so forth. Well, we'd been driving around Harris that afternoon and went to see the ferry come in. When I saw *you*, I was practically stunned. But I wasn't about to rush up to you like a lovesick youth, with Monique there." He was sweating, and he took out a handkerchief and patted his forehead. "She was in one of her rotten moods because of the weather, and I couldn't trust her not to make something unpleasant out of it."

"I wouldn't blame her," said Alison. "You're incredible. Can't you even *hear* yourself? You're here with your constant companion, as they call it, and giving *me* a big pitch. So long, Norris." She headed for the door again, but he didn't follow.

"I'm a free agent, Alison," he said rapidly. "We're together out of habit, we both know that whatever we once had is about gone. The fact is, she can't stand being alone, she has bouts of depression, she doesn't care what I do as long as I'm there to anchor her."

"But you couldn't trust her not to make a scene at the pier? That doesn't sound as if she doesn't care what you do. But even if you were a free agent, you'd be wasting your time following me around."

"I wanted an intelligent companion to explore the island with. Monique loathed the place on sight, but it was her whim that got us here, so I've insisted that we stay at least a week. She doesn't want to go outside Stornoway, she feels safe only in town among the shops. I'm sorry if you've interpreted my behavior in the wrong way." He was beguilingly dignified, and his smile was so patient and charming that she admired it as a work of art, and smiled back.

"Then I apologize. But I have work to do here, my time is tightly organized, so—" She had her hand on the front doorknob. He came a few steps after her into the hall.

"I've underestimated you," he said. "Monique was right when she said you were no fool."

Both the statement and the absolute change in tone and manner were so startling that she was thrown off balance, and he seized the advantage.

"Would you sit down with me and let me tell you? You've nothing to lose."

Her curiosity was always there, as self-willed as a cat. "Can it be said in ten minutes?"

"In less, if I ruthlessly edit myself."

They went back into the living room and she nodded at the sofa. She took the big chair. "Begin."

"I feel as if I'd been sent to the headmaster's office." The familiar grin flickered. "I spent at least half my youth there."

"You're using up minutes."

"So I am. I'm here on business too, not a holiday. I'm looking for a book, or rather its owner. The book shouldn't be here; it's in an air-conditioned bank vault somewhere, I hope. But the owner could be on the island, and it's within my power to make him a rich man, or at least a comfortable one."

"You disappoint me, coming up with a yarn like that."

"It's no yarn." He lit a cigarette as if for something to do with his hands. "Have you heard of the Book of St. Neacal?"

It was one of those moments where the most astonishing element is the *déjà vu* reaction.

She didn't show it, she hoped. "Yes. Is that the book?"

He nodded. He *was* different, tightened in every gesture.

"But it may not even exist now," she said.

"Oh, it exists all right, and you know it. It's had quite a history which I won't go into now, because I'm sure you know that too, but it's back in Scotland, and—"

"You're sure I know that too," she finished. "What do you smoke, to produce fantasies like this one?"

He waved the cigarette at her. "Bensen and Hedges, not Acapulco Gold. Go ahead and laugh." He sounded good-natured, even happy. "It's no fantasy. I told you I made a career out of bum investments. That's not quite true. I have another profession at which I'm very good."

"Let me guess. It's not mind-reading, that's for sure."

"I represent a client who can make the owner of this book a rich man."

"You're in the wrong country. The last I knew, it was in Norway."

He shook his head reproachfully. "You know better, Alison. It came back to Scotland sometime in the 1700's. An heiress of this Norwegian family married a son of the family who owned the land where St. Neacal's monastery once stood, and his Book came with her."

Poor Harold, wondering if the Book had survived the Nazis. She hoped he'd found out by now that it was safely back home, and where it was, and if he could see it. Maybe he was somewhere in Scotland right now, feasting his eyes and his soul. She imagined his eyes blinking and shining ingenuously behind his glasses, his prim face transformed with pleasure.

"Well, Alison? You're smiling to yourself."

"It's a nice story. Very romantic."

"It's true, damn it!" He ground out his cigarette in the ash tray. "But the hell of it is, I don't know the name of the family."

"Didn't that come along with your other information? There must be a branch of the government that keeps track of these things, or some big university library would know. Why are you out here? Why not in Edinburgh?"

He was in good temper again. Expansive. "Reason one: the information came third or fourth hand by an underground source, so it's not complete. Reason two: any inquiries in official places could bring government interference in a private business matter, they're so damned suspicious. Reason three: I'm sure the clues are here on Lewis."

"Why?"

"Because *you're* here. Grandmamma, what big eyes you have."

"I'm in shock," said Alison. "You get crazier and crazier. Am I to infer that you and Boots are here simply because *I* am, and I'm here because of this phantom book?"

"I'd love to see Monique if I started calling her Boots. The word has a treacherous attraction. One of those things you can't get out of your mind, like a soft drink commercial. Yes, we're here because you're here, because he's here—how does that song go?" He started to sing it.

She stood up. She thought she had never been so angry in her adult life. It was too much for noise, so it was not hard to speak quietly. "How did you know I was coming here? I know I told no one on the ship or even at home where I was going from Southampton. Don't bother to think up another lie. While you chatted over the teacups your friend was going through my cabin. It would have been simple, one key fits all, and the staff were all busy. She found my timetables and reservations and my confirmation from Mrs. MacBain."

And thank God the Mariana Grange material was locked away in one of the cases set out already in the corridor, she thought. So Boots hadn't much to go through, but that didn't make her disgust and rage any less.

"The ten minutes are up. Will you go now, please?"

He stretched out his legs and tipped his head against the back of the sofa, and smiled up at her. "You're carrying an offer, probably to Ewen Chisholm. But whatever your principal is offering, mine will double it, and you'll get a nice commission as well."

"Are you *demented?*"

"Far from it. I don't know what and who your principal is, but I can assure you that mine isn't a rich Mafioso, so you wouldn't be doing business with organized crime. He wants the Book of St. Neacal because to him it would be like possessing the Mona Lisa." He spoke with an almost religious fervor. "It's a treasure, it's old, it's beautiful, and the owner's a poor man except for that book. But it's not for sale as far as the public knows."

She sat down again. He was either insane or it was all a huge Norris Elliot practical joke just to win him time with her, and once she got him out of the house she'd call Boots and tell her to put a leash on him. She said, "Has your client ever seen it?"

"No."

"Then why does he want it?"

"I just told you. Besides, somebody else wants it. As the scraps of rumor get around more people will want it. Museums, collectors, and other men like my client, who's an extremely private collector. You may not know that there's a complex underground in the art world."

"I can believe it," she said. "I'm looking at one branch of it. How does Ewen Chisholm come into this? Was his name one of those scraps of rumor?"

"No, love. I told you I have no names, and we don't go making public inquiries. We're really operating on very little sound information. But I have a gut feeling when something's right, and I've learned to trust it. I'm probably psychic," he said complacently. "That's what makes me so good in my business."

"Then why don't you talk to him yourself if you're so sure?"

"Not until I know what the other offer is. The protocol is so delicate, a transaction could be ruined by a false move. If I know something, I have the advantage." He picked up the sgian dubh, and pulled it from the scabbard. "Attractive little thing, isn't it? But deadly." The sun flashed from the mock topaz in the hilt and off the polished blade. He replaced it and stood up. When he looked down at her from his height he was no longer complacent.

"What I didn't count on in all this was falling in love with you."

"Oh, my God!" she exploded. "This is so *corny!*"

"It is, isn't it?" he agreed soberly. "I'm nosey, I'm a nuisance, and what's worse, I'm banal. I'd intended to tell you the truth about myself when we came back from those damned Stones the other day, but I felt so sick I knew I couldn't make sense of it."

"If you think you're making sense now, you have to be completely out of touch with reality. I want to know where you ever got this pipe dream about my carrying an offer to anyone."

He put his hand lightly on her shoulder. "Look, have you talked with Chisholm since that morning? Even if you have, it's not too late."

She moved out from under his touch, and he murmured, "Sorry. This thing would be a hell of a lot easier if I weren't emotionally involved. If it's not Chisholm, who is it? My hunch says it *is* Chisholm, but your influence on me could be messing up the signals."

"Why don't you drop that line?" she said. "It doesn't flatter me, it just convinces me you're not playing with a full deck." She moved out of his reach, over to the window and looked out at Annie and Angus. Annie stared back, then bellowed.

"Are you going to answer my question?" she asked.

"With one of my own," he said behind her. "What about the offer Harold Marshall was carrying, and never got to deliver?"

She continued to stare out at the sheep but she barely saw them. When she thought her face was composed enough she turned around. She felt like exclaiming "Who the hell is Harold Marshall?" but she was never a good liar. She wrinkled her forehead.

"What was that again?"

"He spent the last evening of his life with you, my dove."

The line between lucidity and incoherence had gotten blurred, but she knew she wasn't dreaming. "What do you mean by that?"

"His car was totaled and he was killed on the way to Logan

the next morning. Struck by a drunken driver."

She went back to her chair and sat down, rubbing her chilled arms. That nice enthusiastic little man with his love of old books, shyly presenting his gift and blushing like a boy, was dead like a fly caught on a window pane. And all this time she'd thought of him alive and hunting in old green corners of England.

Norris was leaning over her, a hand on each arm of the chair. "Are you all right? You look white. Shall I make you a cup of tea?"

"No. Sit down, please. What about Harold Marshall?"

"I'd swear you really didn't know he was dead." He sat forward on the edge of the couch, playing with the sgian dubh but looking at her. "You must have known something was wrong when you couldn't get in touch with him, or was there an agreement not to do that until the mission was accomplished?"

"What mission?" she asked wearily. "There was just a visit because he admired my work. *All right!*" she said. "Enough! I don't have to tell you anything, but you owe me some explanations, and then an apology, and then a rapid departure."

He dropped the knife. "Harold and I were in the same business. We knew of each other without having ever met. He was—and I am—a go-between in these silent deals. We do the bargaining and the buying. We arrange the shipping. There's quite a talent to getting something like that out of one country and into another so the income-tax vultures don't grab either seller or buyer."

He was like any businessman now, crisply describing how insulation was made and installed, or how a new machine would be marketed. "Harold Marshall, on his way to the U.K. to make an offer for the Book of St. Neacal—"

"One of your precious scraps of rumor."

"Fact, in this case. There's always somebody to pass along anything like this, for a fee. . . . Harold is a specialist in rare books, so when he projects a trip, and plans to fly from Boston so he can spend a day at a small college in western Massachusetts, it becomes very significant to me."

The scale was tipping toward plausibility. The man had been genuinely excited about the book, he'd wanted to talk about it, but he hadn't gone too far. He had looked stricken at the mere idea of its destruction, and that could have been an honest reaction. But what if he'd known all the time that it was safe?

"After his day at the college he called his sister from the hotel that night," Norris was saying.

"How did you know all that?" she broke in. "What about this *accident*?"

"It was an accident, all right. Or highway murder, if you will. Violence isn't my thing. And what would it serve? All I wanted was to find out where he was going, and outbid him, not kill him." He spread his hands in token of his innocence. "I'd been waiting for him to make his move, and when I got the word, it was with the news of his death. I called on his sister, said I was a former associate of his, and offered my condolences. I thought I could get his itinerary over the coffee cups."

The sister hadn't had a chance, Alison thought, with Norris being so compassionate, and good-looking too. "To her it was a routine buying trip and a chance to chase up his hobby. She wasn't sure where he'd been going besides the sales in London and some auctions at country houses. And then—" he smiled tenderly at Alison—"she told me how happy he'd been when he called the night before, because he'd met this nice young woman, and she'd hoped it meant something, because she hated to have him settle down as a bachelor in love with moldy old books. And she loved your name. It had class. Dr. Alison Barbour, of Hazlehurst."

He beamed. *And what a good boy am I!* Little Jack Horner had really pulled out a plum. "And you were going to England too. That would have been so nice for Harold."

"So you looked me up." She sounded reflective. "Why do you think he told me anything?"

"He could have done what I might have done, knowing somebody was probably on my trail. He could have made it worth your while to deliver a note to someone in the depths— or heights—of Scotland while I, and maybe a couple of other scouts, were keeping our eyes on him and each other. While we were following him, a young woman completely unknown to us does the errand, the seller gets in touch with Harold by safe Royal Mail, they make their arrangements, and you go along with your sabbatical, with part if not all of your expenses paid. Which is a nice deal for anyone, especially a teacher who wants to travel on the *QE 2*."

He almost took a bow. All that was lacking was a girl in tights to hold the props, including the rabbit. Throwing the lamp at him would only amuse him, if it didn't kill him and thus create more complications than he'd already caused.

"So you weren't on the tour, as you told me. How did you manage to get on the ship at such short notice? I had my reservations nine weeks ahead."

He nodded graciously. "If you say so."

"The trouble with being a liar," she remarked, "is that you never know whom to believe."

"How true. . . . You saw that the ship wasn't filled to capacity. It was simple to get our tickets. Simple for you too."

"And how did you know I was sailing, and not flying?"

"I had a researcher. An eager bird dog of a kid. Not a real kid, you understand, but he looks it. He blended nicely into the campus mix. He took a chance and asked a young library assistant when you were leaving, and she was bubbling with joy about your wonderful ocean voyage and how poetic for you to be in England on Easter Sunday."

"Another question. Why did you wait until the last day to start working on me? You might just possibly have found out enough so Boots needn't have gone through my things to discover where I was going. Or do you prefer the sneak-thief approach?"

He reddened. "Nothing was stolen."

"We differ on that. My privacy was stolen."

He ran his hand through his hair and rubbed the back of his neck. "Monique turned difficult when we got our first look at you. But by Friday she knew we had to get to work before we lost you."

"I could say I don't believe this, but I'm tired of clichés," she said. "I'm shocked that the man died like that. He wanted to talk to me about my work, he understood it, and I liked him for that. Maybe he was what you say he was, but it never entered into our conversation."

"Then maybe you received a phone call or a personal visit from a stranger within the next few days, asking you to carry a letter, offering you very good pay for it?"

"No. It's really none of your business, but I don't have to depend on my salary for my living, so I could make quite a few transatlantic trips aboard the *Queen* each year, and take a world cruise without any difficulty. And I wouldn't do an errand for a total stranger who approached me out of the blue. You know," she said conversationally, "you're immoral. Don't look smug. When I call anyone immoral it's not a term of endearment like 'you little rascal, you!' The other morning when you made such a thing of shutting the door behind me when we started for Callanish—did you leave it unlocked so Boots could go through everything again, just in case? Mrs. MacBain was gone for the day, this road is very quiet, anyone passing by and seeing a car, and Boots going in or out, would think she was a tenant."

He had listened in pained patience. Now he said, "My dear Alison, what do you take me for?"

"What you are, and you know best about that, don't you?"

"I suppose I am immoral," he said modestly, "but is it immoral to give a poor man a chance to improve his situation considerably?"

"Oh, get out," she said, "and take this for your parting thought. If I did have a letter for Ewen Chisholm I'd have had it with me that morning, so Boots couldn't find it. And I spent an hour with him this morning, so now you don't know what to think, do you?"

He turned appealingly to her in the doorway, his hand out.

"*Good*bye, Mr. Elliot."

13

AFTERWARD SHE had to get out of the house. She left the windows open so the wind could blow through, and walked rapidly down the road to the shore. There was no one around at the moment. The blue-eyed dog hurried to his gate to watch her and she spoke absently to him.

She let herself through the gate to the shore and walked on the sandy road among the sheep until she reached the last house on the lower road. Under a freshening wind the seas were making up, breaking along the stony beach, sliding back each time with a rattling roar. The clouds blowing over the sun were edged blindingly with light. She turned and tramped back. Her fury was now concentrated on the worst outrage of all. For anyone to paw through her notebooks was even more indefensible than going through her underwear or her handbag. And Norris hadn't denied her accusation about leaving the door unlocked when they went to Callanish.

If Mariana Grange was known, how could she bear this shattering of her most private life? She would have to take a different name, and to do away with Mariana Grange would be like doing away with a sister, a twin. The new name would belong to a stranger. She might not even be able to live and write with it.

Oh, listen to yourself, she thought in a rage, you'll be going on about numerology and the zodiac next.

The house was well-aired. She shut the windows, and emptied his filtertips in the outside trash bin, and scrubbed the ashtray clean. She prepared a good dinner and tried to draw out the eating process, she washed up the dishes afterward and went over her floors with the carpet sweeper, but she still felt ready to walk five miles before she could calm down.

She was considering it when Mrs. MacBain came to the door and invited her to watch a film on television. Mrs. Mac-Bain was not one to retire early, and they were eating crackers and cheese and drinking hot chocolate at midnight.

Speaking about one of her sons, Mrs. MacBain was suddenly reminded of something else. "I met your young man driving away just as I reached home this afternoon. He was preoccupied."

"He had good reason to be," said Alison. "He's the world's worst pest and I told him so. He's traveling with his woman, and he keeps running away from her and bothering me. Tell me some more about Duncan at St. Andrews'."

By the time she went to bed Norris and Boots no longer loomed up larger than life in the foreground of hers, taking up all available space. But just as she was ready to drop off she saw Harold Marshall hurrying away from her toward the stairs, coat flying, attaché case swinging. Hurrying to die. She hoped he'd never had a chance to know what was happening to him.

If Norris was telling the truth, Marshall was a negotiator of illicit deals. But that side of him had nothing to do with the way he had appeared to her, and the way she would probably always remember him. She was very sorry he was dead; and on the practical side she was even sorrier that he'd told his sister about spending the evening with her.

She wondered just where the famous book was. After all this, she'd like to get a look at it herself. Maybe she could use the search in a novel, she thought drowsily. Her panic and rage on the shore now seemed shamefully theatrical. If Mariana had to retire, all right. Back to Tennyson. . . . *Come into the garden, Maud. I am here at the gate alone.* Maud *what*? It would be distinctive. She yawned.

In the morning she woke up to the rain blowing against the windows. Maud Garrett. Maud Garland. Maud Gallant. Ask Ewen Chisholm about the Book of St. Neacal. He should know! He's an expert in Celtic studies. You don't have to tell him the whole insane story. He needn't know that according to Norris's psychic gifts and gut reactions he's IT.

The idea of having a good legitimate question to ask Ewen was cheering and stimulating. It reminded her of the crush she'd had on her American history teacher in high school. There'd also been a college love affair with a music major, which she'd launched by asking the right questions until he took affirmative action. Probably to shut me up, she thought now. Anyway, I'm not having a crush or trying to start something; I just want to talk to him again, and I don't have to explain that to anyone, even me.

She put her typewriter on the coffee table before the living room fire, and spread out the stalled story of the Highland chief and the girl he was trying to wed, and went to work. It rained all day, brightening and darkening as the clouds rolled endlessly across the sky. The great seas of silver and emerald rushed into Broad Bay, piled onto the sands, exploded on the ledges. The sheep were not in sight, they'd be in the lee of the rough shelters set up for them.

There were two days of rain and wind. On the afternoon of the second day Mrs. MacBain ran over during a short let-up with some fresh scones, and Alison made coffee. She was glad to come back to Lewis for a while. By now Norris's story had grown so thin it had almost disappeared; maybe she'd been right the first time about its being an elaborate put-on, or a

Walter Mitty fantasy to gain her attention. Anyway, this weather ought to send him and Boots off the island fast.

On Sunday the rain turned to snow, and that stopped in the late afternoon, leaving a silent, whitened scene; the adult sheep looked dirty against the snow. She hoped Norris and Boots were all packed and ready for the first plane out the next day. Mrs MacBain had lent her a transistor radio and she listened to good music and a mystery play.

In her book a stranger had ridden up to the castle and proclaimed himself the true heir, and Alasdair illegitimate. Alasdair was so stunned by his father's marital thimblerigging that Catriona was sorry for him. The newcomer had been reared a Sassenach, too; anathema! With flawless chivalry he was offering to escort the Lady Catriona back to her home. So she had a terrible decision to make, and so did the author. There hadn't been any blood shed for at least twenty pages.

The newcomer looked rather like Norris Elliot, who was lean and elegant in the costume of the time, and had a great seat on a horse, and a frivolous line of chatter. Killing him off seemed a drastic way of wiping Norris off her slate, but he'd probably turn out to be one of those balletic fencers who are sometimes becomingly nicked, but never messily skewered.

She couldn't let Alasdair be killed. It would have to be worked out somehow, and Catriona would have to stop whiffling around like a weather vane.

On Monday morning the hills vanished as the sun melted the snow, the racing lambs shook diamonds from their tiny hooves. The blackbird was back, and collared doves walked sleekly among the grazing ewes.

Alison packed a lunch, took her camera and tape recorder, and set off for Torsaig. She stopped in Stornoway for gas. She found that she was watching for Norris or Boots on the sidewalks, but she didn't see them, or the Danforths. Of course it was far too early for them all.

Peigi Martin had a washing in the machine, and was giving the house a vigorous shaking-up after a family gathering on

Sunday afternoon. Charlie was glad to get out. He called Alison his darling girl in Gaelic. "And you've brought your little machine with you," he said. "Good, good! Those things hold no terrors for me."

"What would frighten you, if anything does? Which I doubt."

"Ach, I could tell you stories to put the fear on you."

"That's what I want. Not the fear, but the stories."

They drove to the manse, with Peadar the dog running behind them, and she parked at the side of the road. They walked up the glen. Charlie was good on his feet and his two canes. He came up here often, he said. Peadar proudly escorted them, ignoring the sheep who scattered before him. "He's so *pleased*," Charlie said affectionately.

Charlie identified birds for her, first by their Gaelic names and then in English, and told her who had once lived in the old cottages and how long ago, and how the village had gradually moved to the shore. At the cemetery he led Alison to Christina's family graves. Her father had dropped dead in his fishing boat before Christina left. She went away soon afterward, but the mother, Eilidh, stayed behind with the younger children.

"She was old when she died, for a Leodhas woman of that time," said Charlie. "If they escaped the consumption, something else carried them off long before they reached their three score and ten. Not like today." He thumped his broad chest and laughed like youth triumphant among all these who hadn't made it. Christina had seen a little brother and baby sister laid away here, and her father, only thirty-nine years old. Another sister had died at sixteen, probably tubercular, after Christina left. The latest family grave was that of a brother, who had survived toughly until 1931.

"My great-great-uncle Angus," Alison said softly. "His life and my father's overlapped, but neither knew the other existed. It's a terrible waste."

"That it is," Charlie agreed. "Old Angus was a proud and

lonely man. He was the last to live in the cottage there, and he died in it." They looked up at it on the side of the hill, a stone shell roofless and windowless. A sheep stood in the doorway. "I mind him well. He had the height and the red hair, and they said—"

He stopped and began prodding the turf with his stick. Alison sat on the wall beside him. "What did they say?"

"He was disappointed in love," said Charlie with relief. "That was it. Disappointed in love! And I would think, Who could love such a bodach? I couldn't believe he'd ever been young, you see." He shook his head regretfully. "My mother sent me up every night with the milk, and sometimes in the day with a strupak for him. A snack, you would call it. One warm day—it was noon, in summer, and I was a wee lad, eight or so—the door stood open and I saw an adder sunning itself on the threshold. I put the bannocks down on the path, and shouted his name as loud as I could, and I ran off down the patch thinking the adder was after me to grab me by the heel. And I crashed into the minister."

He rocked back and forth on the wall laughing, tears in his eyes. "The poor man thought he was killed, I was bawling like a calf for its mother, and him on the ground with no wind left in his lungs. From that time on he thought I was a very dangerous character. Oh, dear, dear!" He was helpless with laughter again.

She was glad to have all this on tape, but now she was nervous about adders.

"We're safe enough here," he said nonchalantly. "Look over there—" he pointed toward the sparkling V of water—"do you see what looks like a big rock in the heather? There's a ewe with twins standing by it. It's a part of a cell where one of those monks lived. Before the Norsemen came and named the place Thor's Bay." He gave her a sly poke of his elbow. "Our ancestors. It's the mix that makes Lewis men like none others on this earth."

"Starting with Adam and Eve," she reminded him.

"That's right, that's right!"

They didn't get back to Christina or her family, and she was sure he was keeping away from them on purpose, not just because there was no more to tell. But he was a great raconteur. She heard of folk heroes both fleshly and supernatural: of the local Fairy Hill, and a solitary standing stone farther out on the moors which spoke to passersby. "If they were drunk enough," Charlie added.

He was a library of the old stories of people stolen away by the fairies, of seals transforming themselves into human beings, of rare attractions, and of the deadly waterhorse. But when she tried to turn him onto witchcraft, the casting of spells good and bad, runes, charms, blessings—even simple cures for warts and rashes—he was charmingly elusive. He would come up with some new and delightful tale, and she suspected him of creating it on the spot.

Maybe witchcraft was something he still took seriously. She didn't push for more than he was willing to give.

When they went back down the glen Charlie took her across the road to the lochside and pointed out the place where the tide had brought and left Tormod MacLeod's boat, "With him dead in it, laid out among the mackerel and staring at the sky, and the gulls screaming over him. And it was a lovely sunrise too," he added, as if he'd been there.

At home Peigi was breathless but victorious after her confrontation with a willfully untidy house. She had the teakettle on, so Alison sat down with them for what she now knew as a strupak. Mrs. MacArthur from the pink-trimmed house joined them.

"Where is the footpath from here to the Stones?" Alison asked when she got a chance. Everybody answered at once, but Mrs. MacArthur won out.

"It's just where you come to the foot of the hill beyond my house. You'll see the start of it going up again, above the water. It's a short cut right enough, just under three miles."

"Is it the one the ministers patrolled to keep the people from going there in the old days?"

"Yes, and the poor man would be going crazy trying to save souls," said Charlie, "and not just the young ones either."

"The path's still well used," his daughter said. "When there's a full moon, in particular."

Alison looked for the start of the footpath when she left, and knew she would walk it at least once, because Christina had surely walked it. She didn't need a full moon, and she'd wear boots now that Charlie had put adders in her mind.

Christina no longer stood alone; she belonged to a group portrait.

14

AT CALLANISH she sat in the car outside the gate
and ate some of her lunch, not that she was
hungry after the strupak, but she was shy about approaching
Ewen Chisholm with her question. What was natural at sixteen
or nineteen could be ridiculous at twenty-eight. Her shilly-
shallying annoyed her and she left the car and went to the
Stones.

When she reached the circle she heard, like an arcane signal from the supernatural world, the muted hollow bell of a
cuckoo. She looked up and the bird was flying out toward the
loch. It had been just overhead, or perhaps on the tallest stone,
and she'd missed it.

She watched till the winged speck disappeared into the sky.
She could still hear in her mind the hushed melodious call.
With a sigh she lowered her head. Ewen was standing across
the burial cairn from her.

"Do you simply materialize," she asked sharply, "like one
of the resident spirits taking on ectoplasm?"

"I was about to ask you if you were communicating with
them."

"I was watching a cuckoo." She tried to sound dignified, but it was no use. He was entirely different today, and it was unsettling. "Do mediums come here often?"

"There have been some seances, and once a couple sat by the burial cairn all one night, with a ouija board to make it easier for the ghosts, and they nearly scared themselves out of their skins." His mouth twitched. "Or something did. Then there are the ones with the divining rods and the pendulums, and the psychics who say the Stones give off vibrations that tell All, even if they can't tell you what that All is. I hope I'm not treading on your toes. You could be up here waiting for the god to touch you, or putting your ESP to work."

"I don't have a scrap. I get hunches sometimes that work out, and once I followed a lead in a dream, and it was useful, but—" She shook her head. He looked meditatively at her hair.

"What sort of lead, Dr. Barbour?" he asked. He smiled at her expression. "My aunt is a friend of your landlady." Presumably the same aunt who supplied the information about the brilliant girl in Edinburgh and the brazen besom who'd followed him home. If he knew what she'd been telling, he wouldn't be so mellow this morning.

"Well, my dream led me to some valuable old pamphlets in the attic of a little country library, but the idea could have been in my unconscious mind already."

"When Charlie Macaulay was telling you about your ancestors, it's a wonder he didn't say that second sight ran in the family. He's a great one for artistic touches."

"He didn't, but if he had, I'd be sure those special genes all went off on another road before they could reach me. Do *you* believe in second sight?"

"I'm like the man who said he believed in infant baptism because he'd seen it done. Yes, I believe in it, but I don't have it."

"Do you believe it could be inherited?" she persisted.

"I think it could be genetic, there are families recorded

where the trait has appeared in generation after generation. There's been enough said about it both ways, but it's nothing that can be proved or disproved by running facts through a computer. One theory is that it could be a slight malfunction in the brain. Epileptics sometimes experience *déjà vu* before a seizure. There could be a connection. What has Charlie Macaulay told you about your great-grandmother's family?"

"Tormod her father was seven feet tall, with hair like the Burning Bush, and with arms so long and so strong he could carry a ewe under one arm and a ram under the other with no difficulty whatever."

He threw back his head and laughed at that; a bedazzling change, and while she was still wonder-struck he said, "And what else?"

"He started to tell me one thing about her brother Angus and then he changed his mind and told me something else."

"He would. Did he tell you how Tormod died?"

"Oh yes, and the tide brought the boat home and beached her, and how he lay among the mackerel with his eyes open, and the gulls screaming." Chills ran along her arms. "And then Charlie said, 'It was a lovely sunrise, too.' Which brought the whole scene to life right there."

"That's Charlie. Always the master touch. As you've already found out, he needn't be primed with whiskey. A wide-eyed audience is enough to bring him on stage."

"I don't consider myself that much of an innocent," Alison objected. "I've listened to quite a few storytellers who were drawing the long bow, and I knew it."

"I didn't call you an innocent," he said gently, "but a good listener, surely, and you have the wide eyes; you were born with them. It happens to be true about Tormod's boat coming home, though he may have grown some inches in the last hundred years. But he's always described as a very tall man. Did Charlie tell you that someone knew when he died, and cast the spells to bring him and the boat home?"

"No. Is that the rest of the story?"

"I'm surprised he didn't tell you. It's the point of the story, you see."

"I tried to nudge him toward witchcraft, but I couldn't move him. He was so funny about the Speaking Stone and the music under the Fairy Hill that I expected him to be objective about the other things, but he wasn't talking."

"Oh, he had his reasons, no doubt," said Chisholm. "We all have things we feel we're better off not talking about." He looked absently about him; she'd seen him do this before, and expected him to abruptly leave her before she could ask him about St. Neacal.

"Have you been to Dun Carloway yet?" he asked suddenly. "The Broch? Would you like to go now?"

"I haven't been and I'd love to go." She tried not to sound too fervent. For a man who wasn't easy with women he'd been doing well, and she wasn't taking any chances.

"I'll drive you then," he said. No delay, no nonsense.

"I'd better lock up my car, hadn't I?"

"Yes, do that, and I'll meet you there."

They went in opposite directions. She held herself in; she wanted to sprint. She could hardly believe this was happening. She tossed her book on the Stones into the car and slid her camera into her trenchcoat pocket, hung her binoculars around her neck. He came along in a Land Rover, wearing a dark green windbreaker over his sweater, and smoking a pipe. He looked almost too good to be true, and she was reacting exactly like a Mariana Grange heroine, in spirit if not in the same language, and the phenomenon dumfounded her, to use one of Charlie's words.

She saw the Broch for the first time when they left the car at the small area set off for a car park. They had come past a scattering of cottages where small children were playing, and women hanging out clothes, but once they walked away from the car and passed the unobtrusive sign that named the tower and called it an historic monument, she had again the impression of having left all else behind a barrier of time.

The fort stood on a hill, and from the approach it looked almost intact; a round tower of fieldstones. It was reached by a winding, rocky path up through sheep pasture. Below and to the left the road went on to the shore of a small loch. There were cottages set back from the water, and their green or ploughed fields dipped in a broad, shallow, graceful basin to the shore. In this light the loch was a glass reflecting a tenderly dappled sky. The scene was an enclave of gentleness in a volcanic landscape, which itself in this light and mild air became the thickly pelted flanks and shoulders of massive but sleeping beasts, and the huge upheavals of barren rock were turned lion-colored by the sun.

Ewen didn't speak as he led the way up the hill and Alison didn't want to break the silence. It was a primitive hush dense in quality, and rare like something that has been handed down intact from the time of creation. A fossil silence, Alison thought, proud of the metaphor.

At the crest of the hill, the remains of the double-walled drystone tower stood with the same noble indifference as the Stones at Callanish. The rocks had been elegantly laid up with patient skill, and the one side which was almost intact held for Alison the kind of splendor which she found in any beautiful work. She went back around to the broken-away side and read what the plaque said beside the very low door, then ducked into the enclosure.

"No one could possibly attack through that door," Ewen said, "because he had to bend so low to enter."

Some of the inside wall on the high side remained, and she could see the narrow stone staircase rising between the two walls. Ewen left her alone, which was what she liked. She shut her eyes and in the dark she ran her hands over the edges of close-laid slabs of stone and let her mind run free. Men's voices from the shore, someone's burst of laughter, became for her the voices and laughter of the broch builders; they'd had their hours of precarious enjoyment of life when the air wasn't vibrating with shouts and screams.

She opened her eyes and Ewen was watching her. He was neither embarrassed nor apologetic about it. "What were you thinking?" he asked.

"Not so much thinking as feeling and absorbing," she said candidly. "Sometimes I take in more with my eyes shut. The sense of the hands that laid up these walls in the first place, what they looked like, the shape of the thumbs and the finger tips. How were these men dressed? What was their language? Who were they, and what did they watch for up here? I know what the sign says, that it was probably built anywhere between 41 to 400 A.D. But that's just a cold statistic."

"I can't tell you exactly how they were dressed, but they raised crops and animals and they forged iron weapons and tools. If they were Picts, their language wasn't Gaelic but something the experts call P-Celtic. And the Picts were the race which emerged out of successive waves of immigration from the continent, long before the Celts came with their Gaelic. What did they watch for? All their troubles came from the sea, and there have always been raiders and plunderers on these waters, before and after the Romans, and long before the Norsemen took to the sea."

"I always thought of Picts as little naked men painted blue with woad," she said, and he grinned.

"Their ghosts should come in an army and strike you down for that slighting remark. The Romans could never break them. Eventually they held all of Scotland—or Alba—down to the Antonine Wall. They were defeated eventually—it was inevitable—by the invading Scots, in 848 A.D. But Kenneth MacAlpin of the Scots proclaimed himself king because his mother was Pictish royalty, and Scottish kings were then crowned in the sacred place of the Picts, at Scone."

"I know about the Stone of Scone," she said. "It's under the throne in Westminster Abbey when British royalty is crowned, and it was once kidnapped by Scottish nationalists."

"There'll be a good many people tell you it was never the real Stone of Scone which was stolen by the Sassenachs. The real one has never left Scotland, they say."

"Do you believe that? I hope you do," she said fervently. "I want it to be true." He smiled and she said, "What does that smile mean? I wouldn't be surprised if you and Murdo had the Stone of Scone stashed away somewhere yourselves. Buried in a peat bog on Great Bernera, just waiting for The Day."

He burst out laughing, and she was pleased with herself, seeing him as a warm and youthful man. "Well, anyway," she said, "I wish I could pour out a libation of the best Scotch whiskey to the memory of the broch builders. Right here, on this very turf."

"Try that, and the ghosts will spring up like dragon's teeth, all holding cups."

They crawled out through the low door, and he named for her what they could see. They could look over the narrow hilly strip of land beyond the small Loch an Duine to the wider waters of East Loch Roag, with the big island of Great Bernera, and the high Uig Peninsula blue-hazed with distance to the southwest across the other arm of Loch Roag.

"It's a perfect place for a look-out," she said. "The Norsemen were a terror for centuries, weren't they? From up there, when it was still forty feet high, you'd have seen far over the ledges and the islets out to sea, and there'd be the longships coming." She shuddered. "Oh God, what a sight that must have been! And what did they do? What *could* they do?"

"There were survivors, though it's hard to believe. The Celts had come, the Picts as a separate people had disappeared or been assimilated, and after years of invasion and colonization by the Scandinavians, a new race evolved. The Gall-Gaidheil, a ferocious blend of Norse and Celt who became our ancestors."

"I don't know if I'm proud of it or not when I read about their goings-on. But I guess I admire their ability to survive, and yes, I do admire what they became. And if it weren't for them I wouldn't be here at this minute." She smiled at him out of pure content.

"Do you ever admit to yourself in so many words that you're happy?" he asked.

"I'm happy right now," she said. "I'm not always happy because I'm not an idiot. But there are moments when I am, without feeling guilty about it, and this is one of them. What about you?"

"Like you, I have my moments. I can remember a time associated with this spot when I was very happy. 'Remember' isn't quite the word, it sounds too much like the past. I live with this experience as if it's still new with me. Everything about it is as fresh as today."

"Tell me," she said. They leaned against the wall, and Ewen took out his pipe and tobacco pouch. The sun was warm on their heads. A man and a black and white collie walked down across a field to the water, and birds were singing.

Having got his pipe going, Ewen said, "First I must tell you about a great folk hero of ours, Donald Cam Macaulay from Uig. He lived in the early 1600's. There's many a story about him, but my favorite was always the one in which he climbed the outer wall of this Broch using two dirks for steps, and slaughtered the enemies he'd trapped inside."

"A Macaulay hero? Why hasn't Charlie told me about him?"

"He will. He's no doubt saving it, and he'll give you chapter and verse to prove himself a direct descendant of Donald Cam, and by God he may be right. Well, I always wanted to know just how Donald Cam managed those two dirks, so I climbed the wall myself."

"With two dirks?"

"Aye, from my uncle's collection of old weapons, and he never knew." He took his pipe out of his mouth and smiled at it in fond recollection of something else. "I was thirteen, and visiting him at Breasclete. I biked over here just before daylight one summer morning. The climb was like going up the steep face of a mountain, which I've done since then, but never had before. I made it over the top, stopping to take in the view, of course, and the most magnificent sunrise of my life. Then, all jubilant, I went down inside the walls on what was left of the steps, and when I came out the door here on my hands and knees someone seized me by the scruff of the neck and shook me witless."

"A Pict or a Norseman?"

"Believe me, I wouldn't have been surprised at either, I was that terrified. It was a shepherd who'd come out early to train a dog and saw me climbing. By the time he'd reached the Broch I was on my way down inside, but he had to give me a scare to make up for the one I'd given him."

"But you didn't scare, did you? After you stopped being frightened. You'd done it, and nobody could take that away from you."

"To this day," he said, "I never drive between here and Breasclete without remembering how I felt on that morning. The stones were cold and wet with dew, the dirk hilts went slippery under my feet, and my hands turned numb and clumsy, but I was Donald Cam, and I knew I was going to make it, and I did. Of course I skidded on the steps inside, and could have broken a leg or my neck, but all that befell me was the hard hand of an enraged MacSween. After I got my wind and my wits back, and apologized in Gaelic, and gave him my genealogy on my mother's side, I then told him I'd never seen a better-looking dog than his, and I was allowed to set off for Breasclete. One boy on a bicycle, alone with his shadow, the sheep, and the birds, but I'd taken a fortress single-handed. So I went home like an army with banners."

"I don't blame you!" Alison cried. "I'm excited just listening. And envious. My God, am I envious! I loved to climb, but I was never lucky enough to have a real tower. I had to make do with trees."

"Shall we come over some moonlight night and try it?" Ewen suggested. They laughed. "So you were a skinny little red-headed imp climbing trees. Big trees?"

"The bigger the better. That was my Tarzan phase. I'd

give the yell now except that it would shatter this blessed peace."

"They'd think the Vikings were back."

"What kind of little boy were you? I can't imagine you."

"I wasn't really born six feet tall and going gray," he said patiently.

"I mean, were you smallish and slight, or did you grow tall early? Did you have chums, or were you solitary?"

"Let's say I was an average child, and like any average child I had, and kept my secrets. In this case Lachy MacSween never told my uncle, so I remember him with affection. Now he's dead, so you're the only other person besides me who knows."

"And I won't tell," she promised. "Scout's honor. And thank you for telling me."

Clouds like gauze had been moving across the sun, and a small wind sprang up, lifting her hair around her ears. She turned up her collar.

"The wind's not just a force of nature here," she said. "It's an entity, a presence. The wind of Lewis, blowing out of the past across the centuries to us. *They* knew this wind." She thought there was a narrowing around his eyes like a hint of ironic amusement and she said defensively, "Romantic babble, I know."

"I was remembering," he protested. "Who has seen the wind? Neither you nor I—"

"But when the trees bow down their heads, the wind is passing by,'" they finished together, and looked at each other with serene satisfaction in the accomplishment.

Suddenly the day shifted from dull to dark under low heavy clouds driving in fast from the sea. The small loch went lead-gray, with silvery catspaws skittering across it. Far out in the sea loch the water was gunmetal streaked with icy greens and speckled with whitecaps. Gulls rode the wind, and rain rode it too.

"Come along!" said Ewen, reaching for her hand.

"Damn it, I haven't taken any pictures!"

"And you won't be taking any now. You can come again for that."

The rain was beating at their backs by the time they reached the Land Rover. They drove back to Callanish without speaking in the hard noisy rain. His silences disconcerted her, coming always just as she felt the easiest with him. It was almost as if he did it with intent to keep her off balance, so she wouldn't take anything for granted.

Back at Callanish he drove past her car without explanation and around the road below the Stones to his house. It stood alone down here, very suitable for him, she thought. He jumped out and opened the gate, drove in, closed the gate, then came to her door. "You need a good cup of tea," he told her calmly. He put his arm tightly around her waist and ran her through the rain to the door, which opened before they reached it.

15

THE DOG BOUNDED OUT, and the white-haired man stood in the doorway.

"I have the kettle on already," he said. "Give me your coat, I'll put it by the fire." She handed it to him, saying thank-you and getting a smile back. His eyes were a light, bright blue under bristling white eyebrows. Without speaking Ewen steered her into the sitting room and left her. A peat fire burned in the grate at the far end and she went straight for it, knelt on the sheepskin hearth rug and held her hands out to the flames, thinking in naïve delight, I am warming my hands at a peat fire on the Isle of Lewis.

She saw Hazlehurst, the college community and town, like tiny reflections in a soap bubble. Suddenly the bubble burst; the dog was there, all wriggle from stem to stern, and trying to kiss her ear. "Maili, behave!" one of the men called from the kitchen. Maili looked in that general direction, then at Alison who grinned and put her finger to her lips. She stood up, and the dog got into one of the two big chairs by the fireplace, curled around, and rested her chin on the arm, watching Alison.

In the kitchen dishes clinked, and the men's voices were quiet enough so that a sudden fierce burst of rain on the front windows drowned them out. A large work table stood against the front windows, cluttered with books and papers around an aged portable typewriter and a serviceable lamp with the dented shade askcw. The whole room was cluttered, it had the stamp of people to whom order is less necessary than having everything handy. There was no television, but a small radio on one of the bookshelves that filled the inner wall and were themselves filled with books and periodicals. An old sofa faced the fireplace; the two chairs had reading lamps convenient to them, and a stand beside one of them held a couple of pipes in a pottery saucer, and journals on sheepraising and farming. Two books lay on the floor beside the other chair, from which Maili watched Alison.

An oil painting hung above the crowded mantel. It showed the Stones after one of those dense storms when everything is plastered with wet snow. The snow had stopped, the sky was broken but still dark. The Stones stood weirdly wrapped in white; shrouded and faceless figures waiting for Apocalypse.

She imagined the earth cracking and heaving, and the Stones tumbling over in slow motion, tossed like chips on a wave, shattering, disappearing into the smoking cauldron of the earth's core; gone after thousands of years, with no one knowing—or left to wonder—what they had really meant.

She turned away toward the bookshelves with a sense of temporary sanctuary like some medieval fugitive hiding in a church. She wished she'd come to the books first, so as to have more time with them; what a gourmet's feast it would be, an hour or two left alone in this room with the rain on the windows, the fire, the dog, and the books.

Celtic Saints. Small and drab, it still leaped to her eye. She opened to the index and began searching for St. Neacal.

As if on cue the men came across the hall. Murdo carried a big tray with a teapot and cups. He was saying something in Gaelic but stopped as he crossed the threshold, and smiled at her. "Are you parched?"

"I'm getting there," she said.

Ewen cleared the stand of pipes and papers, and moved it to a place before the sofa, and Murdo set the tray on it. He spoke to the dog, who with a sigh got out of the chair and lay on the hearth rug. Ewen went back to the kitchen and returned with a plate of shortbread.

"I haven't even introduced you," he said. "Miss Barbour, this is Murdo Morrison." They shook hands. Murdo was courtly. "It is a pleasure to have such Leodhas hair in this house."

"Her great-granny was a Torsaig MacLeod," Ewen said. "Daughter of Tormod."

"Is that so, now?" Murdo said softly, nodding at her.

"The daughter who went to the Eastern Settlements," Ewen went on. He picked up the books from the floor.

"Ach, yes, I remember."

"Surely you don't remember Christina," said Alison, "unless you're very well preserved."

He laughed, and at the sound the dog went over to him and put her paws up on him. He took her head in his hands and murmured to her.

"Will you pour, Miss Barbour?" Ewen asked formally.

"Yes, but I see only two cups."

"I've just had a cup," Murdo said.

"He swigs it all day," said Ewen. "If it were whiskey he'd spend his life unconscious under the kitchen table."

"Or I'd be the terror of the roads, putting everyone else in the ditch when I wasn't there myself. They'd have to keep a constable at Callanish just for me."

"You sound wistful," said Alison, sitting down on the sofa behind the tea tray. "Well, it's nice to know you're protecting the community from yourself. Milk?" she asked Ewen.

"Yes, and two sugars." He stood before the fireplace with his hands behind his back, watching her. "Be sure to try the shortbread," said Murdo. "It's fresh-baked by one of the kind neighbors. You just missed her. A pity."

The cups were thin china with a heather pattern, the silver

spoons were soft and old. Ewen received his cup from her and sat down. Alison tasted her tea, said, "Ah, good," and took a wedge of shortbread. She wondered how many women liked to bake for Ewen, or if the shortbread were an offering to Murdo. She could understand that.

"Well, I must be off to attend to my patient," Murdo said. "She was a poor wee shilpit thing to bear twins, and she's been struggling ever since."

"She was better this morning," Ewen said. "She's not failing, is she?"

"No, but she likes the attention. It's half the cure." He went out, the dog with him.

"Did the lambs survive?" Alison asked.

"Yes, and they think Murdo's their mother, and Maili's their aunt. They spent their first two weeks in the kitchen, and he still brings them in at night."

"I love the lambs," Alison said. "They're one of the great pleasures of Lewis for me. . . . This shortbread *is* good." She held the plate out to him but he shook his head. Regretfully she didn't take more, so as not to appear greedy. "I was looking up a particular saint in one of your books, but I didn't get that far in the index. St. Neacal." No detectable response. "The one who wrote the famous Book," she added.

"Oh, that one."

"Would you know where the Book is?"

"I'm not sure." He sounded indifferent. *Evasive* was more like it. Good Lord, I've caught something from Norris, she thought.

"In the last few weeks two people have mentioned St. Neacal to me, one of them especially because of my interest in Lewis." This representation was not quite a lie. "He thinks St. Neacal's territory might be here and wanted me to find out." It was rather easy once you got going. She could almost see how Norris did it. "This morning Charlie Macaulay pointed out the ruins of a cell beyond the cemetery at Torsaig, and that put St. Neacal into my mind. No harm in asking, is there?"

"None at all." He handed his cup over to her for more tea.

"Have you ever seen it?" she persisted.

The dog began to bark outside, then there were voices and confusion in the kitchen. Murdo was hushing the dog and saying, obviously not to the dog, "Go in, go in! I'll bring another cup. No, leave me your coat."

Ewen stood up, with a curiously stolid expression on his face, as if he were bracing himself. Someone came swiftly across the hall and stopped in the doorway, her hands in the pockets of her full tartan skirt. She wore a skin-tight dark red jersey and a silk scarf in matching tartan knotted around her neck. She had thick curly brown hair to her shoulders, held back with combs; she was good-looking in a long-faced, aquiline way, spoiled by what seemed to be a chronic discontent or vexation.

"Come in, Kay," Ewen said in a pleasant neutral tone.

She came forward to the fireplace, perfume with her, and the lithe vision of long legs in sheers and high-heeled sandals. Alison had seen enough of this in Stornoway not to be surprised at the dressy elegance, but her own boots, lined jeans, and turtleneck suddenly felt very awkward and inappropriate behind the tea tray, even if the sofa was old and shabby.

"I see you're enjoying the shortbread," Kay said gruffly.

So Kay was the baker; and Kay must have passed them in the rain when she'd just left here; and Kay was upset. Ewen was *not*, at least on the surface.

"Kay Blair, Alison Barbour," he said.

"Hello, Kay," Alison said. "I'm glad to meet you." She decided not to say that the shortbread was delicious.

"American, are you? Whatever do they all want over here?" She dismissed Alison and turned back to Ewen as if she couldn't keep her eyes off him. "I thought you'd be here when I came earlier. There was something I wanted to tell you."

Her voice sounded half-stifled. She's mad about him, thought Alison, and she's sick with it. Sometimes a Mariana Grange heroine had the same complaint, but to meet with the real thing was disconcerting. Alison stood up.

"I'm just leaving," she said. Murdo, coming in with a cup and saucer, protested.

"Ah, sit down, sit down, you've only just come."

"No, I must stop in Stornoway on the way home," she lied.

"I'll drive you around to your car," Ewen said.

"American women are so delicate." Kay spared Alison a glance, not quite openly contemptuous. Her eyes were very light bluish-green, like aquamarines; Alison had never seen any others like them. The make-up set them off, but she was sure that the shadows under them were real. "It's hardly raining at all," Kay said.

"No, it isn't," said Alison agreeably, "and I intend to walk through the Stones. There's a gate at this end, isn't there?"

"I'll show you," said Murdo helpfully. He brought her trenchcoat and held it for her. Ewen observed it all with the air of a man who has removed himself in spirit if not in body from the scene. Kay was already settled on the sofa, pouring tea for herself.

"Thank you for everything," Alison said to Ewen. "Including the tea. Nice to have met you, Kay," she said without waiting for an answer that wouldn't come.

Murdo and the dog walked with her past the old cottage used as a barn. The sick ewe's lambs were in another shed. They broke into cries as soon as they saw Murdo. "You'll get no more till tonight," he told them. "They're on the bottle, to give the poor mother a rest. I bring them in at night, to keep them warm. They'd be tyrants already, if I let them." He scooped one up and put it in Alison's arms. She put her face down to a small hard head; the leggy beast was all warm helpless baby.

"The weak always tyrannize over the strong," she said.

"He's very shy, you see," Murdo said.

"*This* one?"

"Ewen. He was pleased to have you here. But he's shy. . . . *She* isn't."

"Well," said Alison, "perhaps she has good reason." She added hurriedly, "A nurse meets all kinds of people, all kinds of situations. It wouldn't do for her to be shy."

Murdo made an ambiguous sound. He was skeptical, or impatient with her innocence.

16

A SHOWER GOT HER half-way through the Stones. When she reached her car she took her camera from her pocket, took off the dripping trenchcoat and threw it into the back seat. She wondered what the scene had been after she and Murdo left. Arctic silence, or had Kay broken into reproaches, imprecations, maledictions, accusations? Had *Ewen*? Hard to imagine. *He's very shy, you see.* But not in everything, apparently. He hadn't been shy once, if you went by the evidence.

She'd had enough of his little trick of turning on and off. It smacked of mischievous or even cruel manipulation. She'd tricked herself like any dim-witted freshman, and it was possible that Kay could have made herself as much a victim as these hysterical girls who ran away from home after rock stars. Ewen could have simply allowed it to happen, either from self-satisfaction, indifference, or hostility to women.

"I live a life of scholastic seclusion," she said aloud. "Well, almost that. I cross the Atlantic to a remote island, and am immediately pursued by a man running out on his live-in lady, and he's a congenital liar besides. And a strange woman hates me on sight and suspects me of trying to seduce her man, which he may or may not be, but I wouldn't be surprised, and I don't—really—give—one—good—*goddam!*"

The shout on the end was a real help. She drove on through the rain, composing.

The heroine escapes the Keeper of the Stones just in time before she can become a sacrifice in the Circle. This foils the Keeper's sultry priestess, who to ordinary eyes is a valuable and trusted citizen. Long ago a soothsayer (how about Murdo for this?) told her she'd be conquered and cast down by a red-haired woman. (Fiona became red-haired on the instant.)

A familiar car was coming toward Alison. The rain was letting up again and she recognized Norris's face behind the windshield. An arm came out and waved urgently. "The wastrel young Laird," she said aloud in disgust.

It was for her to give him room, and she pulled over and willed him to go straight on, but he parked before he came abreast of her, got out, and ran across the road. Reluctantly she rolled down her window. He had on a warm jacket but his head was bare and the wind ruffled his hair. He turned his collar up around his ears. "I swear it's twenty degrees colder on this side of the island."

"Probably it is," she said. "What do you want?"

"I want you to forgive me!" he said violently.

"Did I come three thousand miles for a scene like this out among the peat bogs?" she asked. "No, I did not." She dropped her hand to the gearshift.

"Alison, listen to me, for God's sake!" He gripped the top of the window with both hands. "I know it's too much to ask you to forget what I told you the other day, but if we could just go past it, consider it water over the dam, and go on from there. Yes, I used you, I admit it. But when I said I didn't count on falling in love with you, I meant it."

"Look, it's no occasion for desperation," she said. "These things happen to all of us, old boy. So buck up. Life goes on.

Maybe you need Boots for an anchor as much as she needs you."

"Alison, don't."

The two words were a reproach, and he didn't look well. "If it's any consolation, I wasn't about to fall for you even before I knew what was going on. You're just not the one, Norris." I sound like a Mariana Grange heroine, she thought, but I'll try anything that works. "I don't know if there could ever be anyone for me. Not after—"

She stopped and stared bleakly past him at the long ridges of chocolate-brown peats, and the moors and rock-ridges heaved up to the horizon. He should have gallantly accepted defeat then. Instead he said, "Life goes on. You just spouted that bit of cheer at me."

She tucked her upper lip tightly over her lower, which made her look as if she were trying to keep from crying instead of laughing.

"If you can find it in your heart to forgive me," Norris said, "I can drop out of this business. Nobody has any hold on me. I'm a free agent. I can quit making bum investments too. I can become a nine-to-five man. Solid. Pillar of the community." His grin was a phantom of its usual self. "All I want from you is a chance to show you he wasn't the only man in the world."

"Norris, you're totally unrealistic. You're standing there freezing while you argue for a lost cause. Get back to your car, please, and let this be the end of it."

"I'm on my way to see Chisholm now. I suppose there's a way to get to him without getting close to his damn rocks. And this will be my last job, if you tell me so."

"It's nothing to do with me!" she said angrily. She started to roll up the window but he held it down. He was on the upswing again.

"I talked with my client last night, and he's gathered a few more scraps of information. Chisholm's the name. Isn't it the damndest thing?" He was jubilant. "I told you I had a sixth sense. I may have come here for the wrong reasons, but it's the right place."

But he's never seen it! The protest was instinctive. Then she remembered her new analysis of Ewen. So what she'd taken for lack of interest in the book could have been caution. Harold Marshall's agent might have already approached him, and the delicate and illegal business would be under way.

"This commission will grubstake my new life," Norris was saying. His confidence was genuine. He had found his footing on the high wire. "We're right on target, no matter how we got here. You turned out to be the luckiest wild goose I ever chased, as well as the most beautiful." He touched her nose with his fingertip. "Of course, Harold Marshall's principal is still on target too, because they knew all along, and if you aren't the agent, someone is. If he's already met Chisholm, I'm prepared to top his offer."

He'd messed up her first week in Lewis, and she couldn't forgive it. And every time she thought he'd gone, he showed up again.

"Harold Marshall's replacement," she said cruelly, "is probably across Scotland somewhere talking to the *real* Chisholm."

"What do you mean by the *real* Chisholm?"

"One of the aristocratic branch. This man's mother was a crofter's daughter and his father a merchant seaman."

"Ah, but what kind of home did his father leave to go to sea?" he asked triumphantly. "How much do you know about *him*? His family might not have any titles, but they could be—they *are*—the branch that holds the Book. And now it comes down to your scholarly and spooky friend. He wants to reclaim thirty-odd acres and build a house over in some wilderness called Great Bernera, and how else is he going to do it on what he makes?"

"Where do you get all this fascinating stuff?" she asked. "In the bars?"

He laughed. "Listen, I'm the expert in this. I know the tricks of the trade."

Apparently nothing flattened him but his allergies. She gave up. Let him go along and break up the tea party. She didn't give a damn who was right and who was wrong in this, who had or didn't have the Book of St. Neacal.

"Goodbye, Norris." She switched on the ignition.

He put his head into the car. "Alison," he said appealingly, "don't be too hard on me. I never pretended to be anything much, but what I do I do well, and I've never hurt anyone. And I'm in love with you."

The day was darkening again. "It's going to rain," she said. "You'd better go back to your car before you get drenched. And from now on, stay out of my sight."

She turned her gaze straight ahead. From the corner of her eye she saw him, immobile. Then he made a sudden fast movement forward and kissed her cheek, laughed, and said, "Did you ever see such god-awful weather? Well, at least I won't have to look for him in his petrified forest. He ought to be under cover today!" He turned and ran back to his car. She rolled up the window and waited till he'd gone by, blowing the horn and waving merrily.

The new rain blew across the road like gray rags and sluiced down the windshield almost too fast for the wipers. She had to drive very carefully, which had a calming effect.

Norris would have to go away sooner or later whether or not he found what he was looking for. As far as Ewen Chisholm was concerned she hadn't expected to meet anyone like him, so he was no loss. She could edit him out, make him a minus, and begin again.

What she had come for was still there, all hers; Christina's village, the ruins of the cottage, the graves, the water rushing down the glen, the sands where Tormod's boat had been found beached at sunrise. Nothing—nobody—could change that fact that her eyes and ears had taken in sights and sounds that Christina must have carried with her until she died.

The Stones were the same, too. In four thousand years they had seen so much that in comparison she, Norris, Ewen, *anyone*, were no more than the smallest mites among a bird's feathers.

We were here, said the Stones. *We are here.*

17

WHEN SHE REACHED Stornoway the shower had passed, the harbor was blue, the wet pavements glistened, and everyone looked merry. A parking place opened up to her like a good luck omen; she thought sourly that she was probably a fool to trust it, the way her luck was running these days. She bought a thick steak, and found that the green-grocer next door had fresh mushrooms today. If I'm solacing myself with food, she thought, at least it's not a gallon of ice cream.

As soon as she got home she wrote up her log, to get it over with. To write about Charlie Macaulay was always a delight, but when she reached the Stones the writing became painful and at the Broch it was almost agony. She left Ewen out of it, but she had to literally push her pen to form a stolid para-graph of descriptive facts, and she looked back with a grinding shame on her simple-minded happiness and open confession of it.

As an antidote, or penance, she forced herself to write an objective account of her visit to the house at Callanish; she de-scribed the sitting room like a stage setting, and the characters, including herself, as their playwright saw them. There was a kind of morbid entertainment in this, and the result might come in handy some time. Henry James had said, "Try to be one of those people on whom nothing is lost," and she devoutly followed this advice in both her lives.

Afterward she rewarded herself by playing the tape made with Charlie, and told herself it was worth everything else that had gone rotten today. Mrs. MacBain came in to invite her to dinner the next night to meet some friends, and she was enchanted with the tape. On this second playing Alison heard other voices in Christina's glen; lambs' cries carried on the wind, birds, the faint sound of the rushing stream, the deep barking of the golden retriever down at the Manse. When I play this at home I shall probably bawl my stupid eyes out, she thought.

"I'm going to Harris tomorrow," she told Mrs. MacBain on the spur of the moment. "But I'll be back in time for dinner." Harris was a good safe distance away, and she needed to think of something else besides Ewen Chisholm and Norris Elliot. Perhaps besides Christina too.

She was under way by eight in the morning. The weather was exceptionally mild, open and shut all the way across the Lewis moorland and through the mountains of Harris. The cloudiness had a luminosity as if the sun were shining through translucent shell, and in the clear spaces the sky opened to blue infinity. The watery moors were scattered with broken bits of its reflection, and the long lochs called Leurbost, Erisort, and Seaforth became a true deep azure. At Ardhasig she turned off the main road to drive west and north along the shore of West Loch Tarbert. This arm of the sea glittered on her left almost all the way. She had the road mostly to herself, and anyone she did meet gave her a wave and a smile. She was happy again, but fiercely so; nobody could demolish it this time, it was her own doing and she had a right to it.

She stopped at Loch Leosavay to look at Amhuinnsuidhe Castle from the road, and take some pictures. It was a perfect setting for Mariana Grange; a large, mock-baronial affair, built in the nineteenth century as a hunting lodge. She could set the castle back in time and make it genuinely baronial, or leave it as it was and dress the heroine in hoop skirts. She kept seeing someone like Glencora Palliser, born a captive in the wrong century and knowing it, and never giving up the battle. Between Fiona forever rushing hysterically across the peat moors of Lewis, and Lady Whoever fighting her Victorian prison in Harris, she could make this whole journey pay for itself twice over. Or thrice, if she counted in Alasdair and Catriona in the mainland mountains.

She drove on to Husinish where the road ended, and walked on deserted white sands by a sea of the improbable blue she thought existed only in picture postcards. She ate part of her lunch here in a kind of solemn communion with the unblemished solitude. From here yesterday's wounds were seen as the minor bumps and scrapes on a six-year-old's knee.

On the ride back to Ardhasig other splendors of sea and islands kept opening up before her. She drove slowly through Tarbert, which until now she had seen only in fog and cold when she was exhausted. She crossed the isthmus to South Harris, and followed the secondary road around the eastern shore, suggested by the brochure. It was a meandering drive past deep inlets like fjords, and long white beaches, with the mountains always there to fill up the sky if she looked back or ahead; benevolent presences today, taking the sun into their ancient bones.

She had given up trying to fit words to it all; she simply accepted what came, reverent and grateful.

St. Clement's sixteenth-century church stood at Rodel at the southern tip, and she looked forward to spending some time here. There were a few cottages close by, but as at the Standing Stones and the Broch, nothing could dilute the essence of the central Place. It stood among its treeless broken fields at the edge of the sea, gracing and graced by its isolation.

Gulls drifted over it, gates kept the sheep out. A blackbird sang from the tower. Alison wandered among the old stones in the churchyard, putting off the pleasure that awaited her inside the church, like the three MacLeod knights lying sculptured in black stone on the lids of their tombs.

In the churchyard, there were several relics of aged stone structures, and she was looking into one of these, wondering what it had once been, when a woman's voice splintered the hush, as penetrating as a gull's and far less melodious. It had a horrid familiarity; it was calling her name.

Terry Danforth. Alison would have sworn out loud except that it didn't seem appropriate here. She considered hiding in some nook of the ruined walls, but the only real escape would be instant invisibility. She didn't wait; the thought of this place being violated by Jake's sarcasm and cigars and Terry's squawks was intolerable. She walked briskly across the churchyard to the gate and was through before they could get to it from where they'd parked behind her car.

I'll be back, she promised the church and herself.

"Oh, there you are!" Terry cried. She had on a blue tweed pantsuit and a blazingly turquoise turtleneck. Jake was also in new tweeds and a white sweater, and a cap like the ones so many Lewismen wore, but under its narrow visor his face looked inappropriate. It had a sallow pallor emphasized by the uncorrupted light.

But he smiled when they met. "There was your car, but the place looked so damn empty," he said. "The wife thought you'd fallen into an old tomb or well down there."

"Oh, there's nothing at all like that. Nothing at all, *period*," she lied.

"Then we'll pass it up," said Terry. "I'm sure visiting old graveyards isn't my idea of a vacation, and if I never see a sheep again it'll be too soon."

"If you don't mind my asking, why are you still here, then?"

"That's what I keep asking her," said Jake.

"Jake has no soul. His dream castle is an oil rig in the North Sea." Terry stabbed a forefinger into his paunch. He winced and moved out of reach.

"But I thought it would be romantic out here," she said pathetically to Alison. And I thought those Stones would be something, but they aren't half as impressive as Stonehenge. Just slabs stuck up there, that's all. Anyone can do that."

"Well, they say beauty is in the eye of the beholder," said Alison, "so I guess that's true about the Stones."

"You think they're *beautiful?*"

"Beautiful isn't the word, but—"

Jake winked at her. "Leave it lay, girl. You won't be able to spin a thread."

Terry pouted. "Oh, I know I'm obtuse, but I never pretended to be an intellectual. I belong to the present, I can't see this worshipping the past. I don't think it's *healthy.*"

She took Alison's arm snugly as they walked along. She had a whiskey breath this early; they must have had a flask in the car. "I mean, the sooner they get some big equipment on here and tear up the moors and turn them into housing—well, they need some good old U.S. of A. get-up-and-go to show them how to use this waste space."

"I'm about to get up and get out," said Jake. "Now that she's bought half the tweed stocks and sweaters in Stornoway."

"Now that," squealed Terry, "is a horse of a different color, or should I say sheep?" She giggled. "Bless their little hearts, I love the woollies, and I'm never going to eat lamb again, I swear it." With a startling strength she gripped Alison's wrist and said, "Come and have lunch with us at the hotel in Tarbert."

"Thanks, but I brought my lunch with me," said Alison. "I'm going to find a place on the shore somewhere, and—"

"*Please.*" Terry was persistently clutching her arm. Since

she'd obviously had a few drinks Alison's tactful objections got nowhere. She gave in finally. Terry let out a shriek of triumph, then insisted they stand by the Mercedes while Jake took their picture.

"Thanks," Jake said quietly to Alison. "This place is really getting to her. But she got it in her head to come here, because none of the gals back home had ever done it on their trips. So I figured I'd let her get a bellyful. Otherwise she'd have kept bugging me. She'll be damn glad to see Aberdeen."

Alison made an ambiguous sound. She dreaded the hours ahead of her so acutely she expected she'd be able to claim violent nausea by the time they reached the hotel, and thus escape. But Terry would probably insist on taking charge of her. Better to go through with it, but what could she have done in a former life to deserve first Norris Elliot and then these two?

They had come by the main road around the western side, and she followed them back that way. At the hotel Terry had two drinks before lunch, and that quieted her considerably. Jake talked about oil exploration and a NATO base as the salvation of the islands and Alison was thankful there was no one near enough to them to think, or maybe even say, the obvious. She wasn't going to take it up with him, she wanted only to get this meal over with as quickly as possible in a place where no one was ever in a hurry. She was hungry and the food was good, so she enjoyed that, looked attentive to Jake's pronunciamentos, and kept her thoughts to herself.

It was after three o'clock when they left the hotel. Terry was yawning uncontrollably and hanging to Jake's arm with both hands. Alison thanked them for lunch and wished them a good trip to Aberdeen. "I'll write you," Terry said sentimentally. "I want your address so we can get together back home." She started pawing through her large shoulder bag for her address book and couldn't find it and seemed about to cry.

"I'll get it to you at your hotel," Alison promised untruthfully.

"Come on, doll." Jake urged Terry over to the car.

"You be sure now," Terry called over her shoulder. "We don't want to lose you!"

"I'll be sure!" Alison answered, taking a ferocious satisfaction in the lie.

She wanted to give them a head start home, so she walked around Tarbert for a half hour, charmed by it in sunshine. When she did start out, she had the fatalistic expectation of seeing the Mercedes in the ditch somewhere and Jake and Terry out on the road flagging her down.

18

Mrs. macbain's guests were a married couple. The man was the manager of a mill that spun and dyed the wool for the looms of the weavers who produced the tweeds, the *Clo-Mor* or "Great Cloth." Their daughter Morag was the young woman who lived in the Manse, and Charlie Macaulay had been a great help in getting the Folk Museum started. Alison told them something of her visit with Charlie that morning at the cemetery.

"Tearlach MacAhmlaidh is a fantastic storyteller," Mrs. Scott said. "Did he show you the grave outside the wall? Morag keeps the stone clear. She's so sorry for him."

"Whose is it?"

"Oh, it's a lovely sad story. A young minister was sent there from the mainland, and he became involved with the wrong woman, poor wee mannie," she said with motherly tenderness. "Innocent as a lamb he must have been, so he took it very hard. And he was so far from home in a place that must have seemed very cruel to a lad from Galloway. Anyway, there was a great disgrace and all, and he drowned himself one night. He must have swum out as far as he could, and then the sea brought him back in and left him on the sands."

Those innocent sands she'd seen shimmering with wet or patterned by gulls' feet; she'd imagined only children playing there. But the Vikings used to gather the stock and the people on the sand for slaughter. How many tides had it taken to wash away all the blood?

"The battle over where to bury him split the congregation," Mrs. Scott said.

"Charlie told me about my great-great-grandfather's boat coming home," Alison said. "With Tormod lying dead in the bottom. It must be the currents there that do it. Charlie probably thought Tormod's story was enough for one session. He wouldn't want to spoil the effect. What about the woman? Was she married? Is that why the disgrace?"

Mr. Scott said dryly, "The lady might have been Episcopalian, or even Roman Catholic. That would have been enough to damn her there."

"Well, it all happened donkey's years ago," said Mrs. MacBain, "and I'm sure God was kinder to his lost lamb than his congregation was." She arose to clear the table for dessert.

"Charlie might know," Alison said. "But it's none of my business," she added. "I wonder about *her* though. Whether she grieved, died young herself, or went away, or—"

"Became solid and respectable," Mrs. Scott carried it on, "and *he* became a Sunday morning memory when she was old. A certain hymn would do it. Let's think of one."

"No, it would be on moonlit nights in summer," her husband said. He quoted unexpectedly:

> *Had we never lov'd sae kindly,*
> *Had we never lov'd sae blindly,*
> *Never met—or never parted,*
> *We had ne'er been broken-hearted.*

"Why, Jamie!" said his wife in surprised pleasure and he nodded modestly.

Went away. Oh, no, it needn't have been. This was not a Mariana Grange novel where such coincidences glued the plot together. Christina's disgrace could have been a too-lively spirit; a dancer who defied the Establishment; a girl who sneaked out to meet a boy at night when she should have been knitting by the fire. She might even have become pregnant by a lover who died before he could marry her, and she had gone away to bear her child in Canada. If she had carried it to term it could have been Alison's grandfather. How had the story got about that she'd died? By the family, to put an end to their shame?

"Come back to us, Alison," Mrs. MacBain teased her.

There was to be a dance in Stornoway Friday night, sponsored by an informal organization formed to help raise money to send performers to the National Mod in October. Alison was urged to come along with Mrs. MacBain; there'd be no lack of partners, Mr. Scott told her; she'd already been noticed.

"I'm outnumbered," she said. "I'd love to go."

She woke up the next day ready to begin living on Lewis free of entanglements. When she was driving toward Stornoway she saw a plane taking off for the mainland and wished that Norris and Boots were aboard it. The Danforths had a car, so they'd have to go by ferry. It was too much to expect she could lose them all in one day, but at least none of them would turn up at Torsaig.

When she passed the turning for Callanish she was forcibly reminded of Ewen, or at least to bring him out into the open; he'd been there right along but in decent obscurity, where he belonged. Face him and get rid of him, she told herself toughly. She couldn't understand the soreness and tenderness around him, as if he were a splinter infecting her finger. There was no logical reason why she should be so disturbed by a man who was a mass of problem inhibitions, had mysteriously left a promising academic career, and was having, or trying to end, an affair with a woman who looked capable of driving a dirk between the ribs of a rival.

The morning was overcast, East Loch Roag was choppy

green and gray, with glints of cold light when the sun almost broke through the shifting layers of cloud. Peat smoke blew down on the wind, but not from Charlie's chimneys. My, what gadabouts, she thought crossly. She felt lonely this morning, it had grown on her since she passed Callanish, and she'd have appreciated a visit beside Charlie's fire.

There were no dogs, prams, or children in sight. She drove on as far as the Manse. Mrs. Scott had urged her to drop in on her daughter any time; Morag was not house-proud and wouldn't care how you caught her. Alison was tempted by the promise of an hour or so with someone near her age, but the garage stood open and empty.

She parked outside the gate and walked up the glen with her hands in her Loden coat pockets and her collar turned up around her ears. There were no sheep for company, the wind rattled in the gorse bushes, the old cottages communicated unspeakable griefs. It was not only blood that had soaked into this ground, but the tears of those leaving and those left behind.

Tears congested her throat now, stuffed her nose and stung her eyes. She saw like a vision of warm light and comfort her safe flat at home in Hazlehurst before Christina came into it. She stood still, transfixed by the desire to be free of the burden under which the other girl had walked down the glen for the last time. Christina couldn't bear to look back, Alison thought; and if she had, she wouldn't have seen a thing through the burning fog of tears.

The moment of anguish passed, leaving her almost dispassionate. There was more to Christina than the agony of parting. Her whole adult life lay before her when she left Torsaig; Tir-nan-Og, the Land of the Forever Young, was only a lovely myth, but America was not. A merry-hearted girl with a will to work and the strength to go with it could do well there.

Christina had sent home a picture to prove it. If the family had received one, had they burned it, or cherished it in secret?

Anyway, Charlie Macaulay's father had been loyal, so Charlie could bring Christina to life now.

Alison visited the family graves, and read all the stones again, then went outside the wall to look for the minister. She found the small stone at the back of the cemetery, on the side toward the monk's cell. His name was Allan Roy Douglas, and he had been twenty-five years old when he died, in 1870.

Hadn't his parents wanted him back? Or perhaps he'd been an orphan. You poor kid, she thought. What a hell of a life it must have been. No wonder you were glad to die.

But whatever Christina had done, *she* wouldn't die for it, she thought proudly. She was too tough. She was a survivor.

When she got back onto the main road she turned left and drove on past Carloway and along up the coast through Dalbeg and Shawbost to Barvas. Here she considered driving on up to the Butt of Lewis, but she didn't have much gas, so she turned right onto a road running beside the River Barvas back across the island, and so returned to Stornoway by a new route. Here she had the tank filled.

When she drove into her driveway, three lambs desperately squeezed under the gate to the croft and rushed crying to their mothers. They'd been eating new leaves on the rosebushes under Alison's living room window. Annie came to the gate and demanded something. "I'll bring you out a strupak if you'll just shut up," said Alison. "I haven't enough for the whole gang."

When she opened the door there was a folded piece of paper on the rug inside. Mrs. MacBain had written, "Ewen Chisholm called. Would like you to ring him back. I'll be home until three."

She leaned against the door, laughing and shaking her head, not knowing why. From outside Annie kept reminding her of the promise. She took out half a roll and Annie chewed while Angus went down on his knees and bunted her udders and nursed. When she finished the roll and saw nothing more in Alison's hand she looked Alison hard in the eye, then walked away, casually shaking off her son.

Alison didn't wish to show unseemly eagerness to return the call, but after she'd exchanged her lined jeans and boots for good slacks and shoes, and brushed her hair, she couldn't think of any more delays, and she didn't want to.

Ewen answered on the second ring. She said neutrally, "This is Alison Barbour."

"There's a concert and dance in Stornoway Friday night," he said. "Some of us will be having dinner first. I would like the pleasure of taking you."

His dry formality was catching. "I'd like very much to go. Thank you." Then she captured her wits before losing them entirely and shouting *Oh damn!* at him. "But I've already been asked," she said with stoic control over her anguish.

The silence at the other end was as profound as if she'd suddenly gone deaf. From behind her the telephone was taken from her hand.

"Are you there, Ewen?" Mrs. MacBain inquired. "I was the one who asked her, but I'm happy to turn her over to you." She waited, received some very short reply, and held the telephone out to Alison, who felt like a wretched wallflower of a high school girl being maneuvered to the spring prom by kindly adults.

Mrs. MacBain went immediately upstairs, singing on the way. "What time shall I be ready?" Alison asked politely.

"I'll call for you at seven. It will be a formal affair."

"I do have something to wear besides boots and jeans."

"I wasn't suggesting otherwise. Goodbye, then."

"Goodbye." She hung up and went into the kitchen and stood looking out across to the Minch. One word from the Demon Lover, and Fiona, the simpleton, is ready to leap out of safety and, if not into his arms, into his immediate vicinity. Well, who wouldn't, when the only other choice is the wastrel young Laird?

Mrs. MacBain came downstairs, singing "Comin' through the Rye."

19

THERE WERE TWO DAYS to live through until Friday night. She could use up Thursday with her drive to the Butt of Lewis, but there'd still be a lot of time left over in which to anticipate the dance, not with unblemished delight but with an apprehension concentrated in the pit of her stomach. It was a familiar sensation both disagreeable and juvenile; it used to be so acute before a date with a new boy that by the time the occasion arrived she was very nearly a wreck. Could they dance together? Could they *talk* together? What if he wanted to leave the dance early and go park somewhere? What would be expected of her, and how could she get out of it? Well, she'd survived, she'd had some good times even if there'd been a few disasters which had looked like the end of the world. She'd recovered from these quickly, astonishing herself.

And here she was, at her age, suffering the symptoms of an old adolescent ailment. She analyzed it and herself with neither kindness nor remorse. From her first meeting with Ewen on the platform at Mallaig, where he had obviously not wanted to become involved with her and her luggage, she'd seen him ever since through a glass wall of untouchability. When he'd surprised her with friendliness, she responded with a puppy's gallumphing enthusiasm and bumped her nose hard on the barrier.

Now, for whatever inexplicable reason of his own, this handsomely packaged mass of contradictions had invited her to a formal dinner and dance. Reflectively she rubbed her nose; she didn't intend to bump it again. If only she could view him objectively as she'd first seen him, a provocative and mystifying man in a romantic novel. But she wasn't objective any more; she couldn't be.

This admission was the climax of the soul-searching hours after the telephone call. She dealt harshly with herself. You cannot be in love, she stated, with a man you've met only a few times and who gives you a negative response sooner or later each time. The phrase *in love with* implies a cooperative venture. It takes two.

You're intrigued. You like his looks. You like his voice and his accent. He's a Scot, which gives him a glamor he probably doesn't deserve. He's part of a country you're emotionally involved with, so you've no chance of seeing him clearly except when he turns you off, and then you can't miss the fact that he's involved with another woman.

Another woman whom he isn't taking to the dance. Instead he has asked you to spend a whole evening with him. Safely in public, I may add, and I do. This does not mean he has been pacing the floor obsessed with your Leodhas hair and your bonny brown e'en, your smile and the dimple in your chin, or even your superb academic brain. You may never know *why* he asked you, but you can be sure it's not that. So make up your mind you're going to have a good time, no matter what, unless Kay shows up with a machine gun. That would be definitely off-putting.

With all this out of the way, she took her two long dresses out of the closet. She chose the less conservative, a high-wasted, square-necked Empire gown of thin silk patterned with pastel field flowers. She would wear an antique gold locket of her mother's and a bracelet of pink and green tourmalines.

She worked on Alasdair and Catriona all evening and went to bed groggy and virtuous, and slept well. A storm blew up in the night, canceling out her trip to the Butt of Lewis. According to radio weather reports, it was snowing around Alasdair's castle in the Highlands; it looked as if May were about to come in like a lion.

From the way the Danforths had talked at Tarbert she thought they must have left by now, and she wondered if they had reached Aberdeen, or had stopped at Inverness and were now waiting out the snow, with Terry madly shopping and Jake talking oil and salvation in the bars.

She worked all morning on the novel. At noon she had a leisurely lunch and gave some thought to Norris Elliot; she'd have loved to have seen his arrival at the farmhouse the other afternoon. Had he walked into a roaring row, thus damping it down to a murderous hush? Could he have charmed Kay out of her sulks? Maybe she was immune to such sunny attractions. Meanwhile Ewen would have gone from one silence into the deeper kind that merited a capital S.

It was a great third act, if you could only decide what the plot was and how it would end. Of course it probably hadn't been that way at all. Kay would have been ladylike behind the teapot, and Ewen frigidly courteous as he told Norris that he was the wrong Chisholm and didn't know anything about the Book of St. Neacal. So by now Norris and Boots had gone, looking for the right Chisholm.

Norris had been so positive with his gut reactions, hunches, and sixth sense, that the defeat must have knocked him flat, yet he'd set himself up for it. His business must be like gambling, he'd won often enough to keep him addicted, even though there had to be times when he was broke and tired and a lot less resilient than he used to be.

There was another possibility. He might have been right, which meant that Ewen had avoided her questions about St. Neacal for signficiant personal reasons.

She went back to work, through with conjecture. The Book

of St. Neacal had caused her enough trouble already. She'd put Ewen Chisholm into proper perspective, so his private life could be left in deepest night as far as she was concerned. She was looking forward to Friday evening, and the only thing to tarnish that was the knowledge that Kay was likely to be very unhappy about it, and she couldn't help being sorry for another woman.

He's very shy, Murdo had said. For a very shy man, Ewen seemed to have made himself a good deal of trouble.

On Friday Alasdair's castle was raided by some distant relatives who'd been plotting in France all this time, where Alasdair couldn't reach them. Alison filled a chapter with flames and blood. To the clash of blades and flash of dirks, to grunts, moans, and shrieks, Alasdair and Catriona were hustled out a secret way by his foster brothers who were resolved to save their chief even if he did want to stay and fight, fearless man that he was. The scene ended with the two huddled under the same plaid in a shepherd's bothy in a hidden glen; Alasdair sunk with shame and grief for his dead clansmen, and Catriona quite overwhelmed by her desire to comfort him in her arms.

It was a good place to leave them for a while. After two days of work Alison was euphoric, and the sky was clearing over Broad Bay. She had coffee and cake with Mrs. MacBain in the afternoon, and taped some of her landlady's stories. As a test of her new detachment she brought up Ewen's name.

"I can't imagine him doing anything as social as dancing, he's so reserved."

"Reserve has nothing to do with it. It's said that the Lewis man may be John Knox on Sunday, but he dances quicker and harder than anyone else. You should see my Rob."

"I'd love to, and I hope to, some day. But I still can't see Ewen kicking up his heels." She laughed. "Maybe because he's not pure Lewis."

"Whatever the blend, he's a Highlander, and dancing's in

the blood." Mrs. MacBain chuckled. "You've no doubt heard that many chiefs have always been called 'The'; it's like saying, 'Wherever The Macgregor sits is the head of the table.' Well, the Chisholms used to claim there were really only three persons in the world entitled to be called 'The.' The King, The Pope, and The Chisholm."

"Oh boy! I'll meet him at the door with a rousing chorus of 'Hail to the Chief.' That should shake him up some."

"You'll shake him up," said Mrs. MacBain, who had seen the dress.

But Alison was the one who was shaken up when Ewen walked into her hall on Friday night looking perfectly self-possessed in Highland evening dress; kilt, black velvet doublet with silver buttons, snowy lace jabot and a silver-mounted sporran.

There was only one possible response to all this glory. Alison whistled. Unflappable, Ewen looked appraisingly at her and then nodded. "You look like spring," he said. "Primavera."

"Thank you. But I don't know if I can live up to *you*. Is that the Chisholm tartan?"

"What else? This is the dress variety. The hunting tartan is a bit quieter." He followed her into the living room. "Where's your wrap?"

"Give me a minute to get the full picture. How do you get those socks to match? I mean hose."

"Woven to order."

"And the sgian dubh in the sock is part of the evening dress too?" He didn't seem to mind her admiring his legs, which were fine for a kilt and tartan hose; bad legs could ruin the whole glorious effect.

"It's always worn with the kilt. It's traditional. For a long time after Culloden it was the only weapon allowed the Highlander, because even the Sassenachs conceded that a man needed some way to cut his meat." He picked up her woolen cape from the sofa. "It's possible to cut a throat with it, or split a gut if there's no fat to go through first. It's a very short blade."

"I'll remember that," she said. "How did the women manage? To cut their meat, I mean. Not split a gut."

"The men did it for them, back in the grand old days."

"You can preen about the grand old days, but it seems to me that the women were forever having to smuggle the men out of prison, or saving the crown jewels, or getting Prince Charlie away."

"I wasn't aware that I was preening," said Ewen with dignity. They began to laugh. She turned for him to put her cape over her shoulders, thinking wryly, I shall cherish the Primavera remark until death as the only pretty speech that ever came in my direction from Ewen Chisholm.

He lifted her hair free of the cape's high collar and she felt an urge to lean her head back against his hand but even if she were that shameless the hand would no longer be there. She almost sighed. Her good resolution to enjoy the evening no matter what, was weak; the phrase "no matter what" could cover a multitude of surprises, and the way she felt right now was one of them.

She moved briskly away from him and took the door key off the mantel, and put it in her bag. They walked out to the Land Rover in a sunny evening.

The local children out playing, running races on the road after their tea, stopped to stare silently at Ewen and Alison; she felt a little like royalty as she spoke to them. She got the usual sparse and bashful answers, but Ewen said something in Gaelic which made them giggle. Annie bellowed from the croft gate.

"You needn't fear for your dress," Ewen said, handing her into the car. "Murdo scrubbed and sweat like an old woman getting ready for the minister, and then he put a warm rug on the seat so you'll not get a chill."

"I couldn't ask for anything more," said Alison.

Under the silent gaze of the children, and while Annie continued to bellow, Ewen saw that all her dress was inside before he shut the door. He was very efficient, as if he'd done it often. When he got in behind the wheel he said, "I never had a nanny until now. He even asked me if I had a clean handkerchief."

It was a great relief to laugh; maybe she'd hold together through the evening after all, though the thought of dancing with him was mind-boggling. She hastily diverted herself from that. "What did you say to them?" she asked as they left the children behind.

"Good evening, young lords and ladies!"

"Say it again," she said. "In Gaelic." He did, and she tried to repeat it.

"Very good," he told her.

"No, it wasn't. I think you must have to be born with a different set of vocal chords to get it right."

"Listen, my girl, the Gaelic's in your genes, the same ones that gave you your red hair. Try again."

It took them all the way into Stornoway, and by the time they walked into the hotel bar she was ready for a drink. Gaelic was a very thirsty language. She and Ewen made up a group of ten; five couples, three of them married. Ewen as a man with friends was a new manifestation. He wasn't loudly convivial, but he was certainly at ease, and his friends accepted Alison with a hospitable and unabashed interest which she could understand, having met Kay.

Three of the other men wore kilts, and one of these was the oldest man in the group. He was stout, white-headed and bearded, and looked like Scott's description of some great patriarchal chief entertaining noble guests. Two of the women wore white gowns, each with a narrow tartan sash draped from a shoulder brooch. One of them was the youngest of the wives, Lillias MacKenzie. She was tall, black-haired and blue-eyed with delicate features and a natural flush in her cheeks; she had what Alison had already begun to call a Highland face.

"Ewen's a beautiful sight," she said in a low voice to Alison when they were going into the dining room. "If my Dougal looked like that in a kilt I'd never let him wear anything else. But he's not got the legs for it, poor laddie." The poor laddie, a skinny and boyish lawyer, looked distinguished in conventional evening dress, and Alison said so.

"And wait till you hear him sing," his wife said proudly.

The food was good and there was plenty of it. Alison was blessed with a hearty appetite, and eating always gave one something to do. Occasionally she was drawn into the conversation but not by Ewen; she had a great view of a black velvet shoulder and his ear, and the way his hair grew around it, his graying temple. He had a rather imposing nose. She'd certainly never heard him laugh that much, but otherwise they could have been strangers. Suddenly she wished viciously that he would spot those pristine lace ruffles with gravy.

He did not, of course. He managed with the finesse of a concert violinist, while talking politics at the same time. He was not only social among his friends, he was ardently political.

"Can you make sense of it all, Miss Barbour?" asked the man on her other side.

"To the point where I know that if I were a Scot I'd be a Scottish Nationalist," she told him.

"And we need you. Do you think we could adopt you?"

"I'm willing," said Alison.

Across the table from her, Lillias MacKenzie said mischievously, "There's the American who thinks a NATO base is going to save our souls."

With a heavy thump in her stomach, as if a stone had just dropped into it from a great height, Alison looked over her shoulder. Jake and Terry Danforth were with two men at a table across the room.

"I thought they'd gone," she said.

Ewen turned his head politely toward her. "I was speaking to Mrs. MacKenzie," she explained.

"Oh." He turned back to the woman on his other side. She was handsome and vigorous; "elderly" was not a word that suited her. She said resonantly, "Independence within the system is no independence at all!"

The patriarch differed, fluently and emphatically, and she told him he was a coward. He laughed, held up his wine glass to her, and spoke in Gaelic. She made an effort not to smile, but she weakened, and that set them all off.

Now that Alison knew the Danforths were still here, she was on edge with expecting Terry to arrive at any moment, screaming, "Alison!" Then she'd say something like, "Don't you men look just darling in your kilties!" It was so horribly possible that the stone in Alison's stomach increased in size and weight. She couldn't resist looking around again; if they'd left, she could relax.

They hadn't. Jake was talking to the other man while energetically shoveling up food. Terry looked subdued. Maybe she'd had enough drinks before dinner to sedate her. Alison hoped so.

Lillias MacKenzie leaned forward. "Are they friends of yours? I was thoughtless—"

"Maybe they're friends of each other, but not of mine. I met them on the ship. The last time I saw them here they were anxious to leave, so I was surprised to see them tonight."

"Maybe she's been ill. She looks a bit under the weather. From what I've seen of her in the shops and at the hairdresser's—I didn't think she could ever be that quiet."

"If it's keeping her anchored to her chair, let's thank heaven for small miracles," said Alison piously.

The next time she looked around was in the interval before the arrival of dessert and coffee. Things were the same at Jake's table, except that one of the other men was having a chance to talk. Terry was listlessly eating.

Alison turned her head the other way to glance around the

rest of the dining room, and she saw Norris. He and Boots were alone at their table, were isolated from one another; the impression strongly reached Alison all the way across the room. Norris was rather pale and unhappily preoccupied. Boots looked like an elegant plastic mannequin folded into her pose by the window dresser in an exclusive Boston shop.

Alison turned back to her own table before Norris could notice her, and was startled to look directly into Ewen's dark eyes. "What's so fascinating?" he asked.

"Not fascinating," she said. "It was just mild curiosity. I thought Norris Elliot and his girl must have gone by now, but there they are." It angered her to feel defensive for no reason. "Did he ever get to talk to you the other afternoon?" she asked. "I met him just a little way from your house."

His expression of courteous blankness exasperated her.

"The day when Kay came in and we were eating her shortbread," she said.

"Oh, that day."

She felt like asking him straight out how Kay felt about not being his partner tonight; that might have jolted him a bit. But if it didn't, she'd be left feeling the fool again. From down the table someone called his name, and he turned away.

She'd been saved from making a fool of herself, but she hadn't found out about *that day*, either.

20

AFTER DINNER the women at the table went in a group to the Ladies'. They didn't pass near the Danforths' table, and Alison hoped cravenly that the others would camouflage her, though she was the only redhead. Norris's table was empty.

The older women left the ladies' room first, and Lillias followed them, to call home and talk with her sitter; one of the children had a cold. Alison was alone. She combed her hair, touched up her lipstick. Well, she thought, we got through dinner. So far, so good. He'll have to dance with me; he can't possibly ignore me then. Oh yes, he *can*. I wouldn't put anything past that man.

She was washing her hands when Boots came in. At the sight of Alison, she turned to leave again, and Alison said involuntarily, "Don't go I'm just leaving." She hurriedly dried her hands. "You'll have the place to yourself."

"Thanks." It was harsh enough to sound sarcastic, but Boots came back without looking directly at Alison. Someone fumbled at the outside of the door, it was thrust open, and Terry Danforth came in. She was so white her lipstick looked purple.

"*Jesus*," she moaned, swaying. Her bag dropped from her hand.

Alison reached for her and Boots caught her from the other side. They lowered her into a chair. She kept moaning, and sweat appeared on her forehead. Boots picked up the handbag and put it by one of the washbowls.

"Do you want to throw up?" Alison asked Terry.

"Uh-uh." She tried to shake her head, and fell over against Alison, who thought, If you heave up over this dress I'll murder you. "Jus' lie down," Terry mumbled. "Thass all. Lie down." The scent of dry hair and a perfumed spray blended with that of liquor and food on her breath into a disagreeable effluvium, and she kept sagging heavier against Alison. Over her head the other two looked at each other; Boots' eyes, bordered with liner and fringed exotically with false eyelashes, were a light yellowish brown. One might call it tawny in a novel.

"Have to lie down," Terry moaned.

"There's no sofa here," Boots said in that harsh, flat voice.

"I want my bed," Terry said pathetically. She lifted her head and then it fell back hard against Alison's breast. It hurt. Alison tightened her lips on the *ouch* and considered disengaging herself and walking out, but heard herself saying, "She should be in her room. They're staying here, aren't they?"

"Oh yes, they're staying here, all right." The tone was ironic; Terry, of course, would have been inescapable once she'd discovered them at the same hotel.

"Let's get her out into a chair in the lobby and let Jake take care of her," Alison suggested.

"I'm for that," said Boots. They hoisted Terry up; she was small and light-boned, and Boots was stronger than she looked.

"Where's my bed?" Terry whined, hanging from their arms.

"All you have to do is walk out this door, Terry," Alison told her, "and Jake can get you up to your nice bed."

Terry said, with surprising spirit, what Jake could do. It was better ignored. She added, "He's gone, goddam him."

"Not far," Alison assured her, knowing nothing of the sort. "Come on, *walk*, Terry." She and Boots shook their heads at each other; they had become for this interval comrades in disgust and resignation. By the time they had maneuvered Terry through the door, it seemed as if her feet were hanging like beanbags off her ankles, she was as limp and slippery in their grasp as boiled lettuce, and the nearest chair was an impossible distance away unless they simply dropped her and dragged her along by her feet. Alison briefly regretted the impossibility. Terry began to slide downward, and Boots and Alison hauled her up again, out of the way of two women who courteously ignored the situation on their way into the Ladies'.

"Oh, hello, sweetie!" Terry said in dazed delight.

Struggling to hold her up, neither Boots nor Alison had seen Norris coming toward them. Without a smile, he scooped Terry up and headed toward the lifts.

"Go get Jake," he said to Boots. She didn't move, and he repeated it over his shoulder. "Go get Jake."

With an almost furtive glance at Alison, Boots went back toward the dining room. Norris went on toward the lift. Alison remembered Terry's bag and retrieved it from the Ladies', where the other two women gave her sympathetic and encouraging smiles.

"She'll sleep it off," one of them said.

Norris was waiting by the lift, with Terry cuddling blissfully against his chest. He looked haggard and uncharacteristically patient. He kept moving his head to escape the tickle of Terry's hair on his chin, but he didn't take his eyes from Alison's face.

"When can we talk?" he asked.

"Upstairs, sweetie," Terry murmured, snuggling deeper.

"We have nothing to talk about," Alison said.

"Yes, we do," he insisted, not raising his voice, and hardly moving his lips.

Alison shook her head. The elevator door opened and a man and woman came out, said "Good evening" as if nothing were out of the ordinary, and went on. Boots came running past them; Norris stepped into the empty lift and Boots slid in past Alison. She was out of breath.

"He's not there."

"Could have told you," Terry giggled. "Talking oil somewhere."

"Here's her bag," said Alison, handing it to Boots.

"Thanks." Boots pressed the button. As the door began to slide shut Norris was still looking at Alison, trying to hold her gaze, and she turned away before the door had closed.

She carried away with her the imprint of his drawn, set face over the lolling head. Oh, that look is part of his act, she thought crossly. It's supposed to make him appealing, and me guilty.

So things hadn't worked out according to his hunches, and along with that disappointment he must be worried about losing his charm, because she was so resistant to it. She wasn't sorry for him any more than she was sorry for the drunken woman in his arms. If she had a trace of pity for anyone, it was for Boots.

The place was busy now with the arrival of people for the dance. She saw Mrs. MacBain and the Scotts coming in with a group. There were scraps of music from the ballroom as the small local orchestra tuned up. She wondered where her party was, and then as a gap opened up in a cluster of talkers ahead of her she saw Ewen standing alone by the reception desk, his hands behind his back, watching her. His impassive face was dark as a gypsy's above the white dazzle of lace. She wondered how long he had been watching, and what he had made of the scene.

When she reached him she said briefly, "A woman was sick in the ladies' room. Her handbag was left behind."

"I see," he said. He crooked his arm for her to take and as she did so, he smiled suddenly, and said, "I like the way you walk."

"Thank you," she said, sounding far more dignified than she felt.

An informal concert preceded the dance. Young girls did Highland dances, accompanied by a boy piper. They were so happy about it and so light on their toes that Alison kept remembering the line, "Dance on the sands, and yet no footing seen."

A lad about fifteen did the sword dance; he was as polished and nimble on his feet as the girls, in a joyously masculine performance of this ancient dance of warriors. An older piper played for him, a retired regimental pipe major superbly turned out, and his music could put the leap upon the lame, as one song had it.

Then Dougal MacKenzie sang. Lillias played the piano for him but her part was quiet and unobtrusive. The songs were all sung in the Gaelic that was now revealed to Alison as the language born to be sung, and Dougal's voice was the right instrument for it. One didn't have to know the language to recognize a lullaby, ribaldry, or a love song. Alison sat beside Ewen hardly knowing he was there, or anyone else for that matter. She shut her eyes and let herself go with the music, until the last one, a great song of reiving and conquest, ended with an exultant shout.

The audience came to its feet, applauding. Dougal, blushing, held out his hand to his wife, who made no attempt to be modest about her pride in him. She curtseyed, laughing, and then embraced and kissed him, and the applause and laughter went on.

And now Alison was going to find out that Mrs. MacBain was right about the Lewis men's dancing, and that Mr. Scott hadn't been lying about partners.

She was guided, spun, swept through country dances in which the white-bearded patriarch was as agile as the boys, and in which Ewen was simply astonishing.

He was tireless. He was having fun, or else he'd become possessed of a demon, or he had a dual personality. There was no chance for consideration of these theories, because when

they stopped for refreshers in the bar, there was always someone else with them. Alison, having no head for liquor, stuck to
ginger ale. The others never showed the effects of their drinks,
they simply danced them off. She had a few words once with
Mrs. MacBain, who said, "No need to ask if you're enjoying
yourself. My, but he's bonny!"

"Isn't he?" Alison agreed; not smugly, she didn't dare to be
that. She was greedily absorbing everything, knowing that once
she left here her life would never be the same again, and nothing was worse than skimpy memories.

After a hilarious and strenuous "Strip the Willow" there
was a waltz, and it was no rest for Alison to be closely held by
Ewen's black velvet arm in an embrace set to music. She lost
any capacity to be objective; it was a great wonder to her that
her feet could behave, though outwardly she seemed to move
in a graceful reflective calm. She found a little relief in petti-
ness, thinking that Ewen was too good a dancer for a man who
was supposed to be shy with women. She'd been skeptical
about his story for some time now, and now he'd wiped out the
last traces of it. For all that the home folks knew of him, he
could be the Playboy of Edinburgh and had come home to rest
up.

It wasn't enough relief; she was glad when the waltz ended,
and at the same time she felt cold and bereft. She tried to tell
herself it was the natural letdown after she'd been so high for
so long. Ewen was standing near her chair, talking with another man; she could have spoken his name and he'd have
turned to her. But already an ocean lay between them. More
than an ocean, a world.

Lillias MacKenzie dropped into the next chair. "Isn't it a
fantastic dance?"

"Fantastic," Alison agreed.

"You and Ewen look so beautiful together," she ran on.
"And he's so proud of you. Anyone can tell just to look at
him."

Alison didn't deprecate; she smiled and said, "Thanks." Lillias was an extremely nice girl and she liked to say nice things. Mrs. MacBain came along and said she and the Scotts were leaving now. "If you leave within the next hour or so, and you see the lights on in my house, come in for a nightcap, if you like."

Alison thanked her, fighting an impulse to rise up and say, "I'll go with you." She wanted to get into her own cottage and into her bed, her cave, her refuge. But she wouldn't sleep, and long ago she'd been forced to learn that you didn't run away no matter how you ached to, you saw the matter to the end, and then when it was over, it was over.

Then Ewen came toward her for the next dance and the woe slipped off like water as she rose to meet him.

The Scotts were still at Mrs. MacBain's after two in the morning, and the nightcap turned out to be substantial; scrambled eggs, bacon, toast, coffee, and talk. Everybody but Alison seemed ready to go on until daylight. Once these Lewis people got started they were indefatigable. She thought it was a good thing she had the table under her elbows to prop her up. She kept missing bits of conversation; how did one get from the Common Market to a salmon stream in one sentence?

"I think I'd better go home while I can still walk," she said, "and the way my feet feel, I'm not even sure of that. I'm not drunk but I feel like it. How often do you people have dances like this?"

"Oh, as often as we think our old bones can take it," said Jamie Scott. "We might as well shake them to bits as sit home and let them slowly crumble."

"Well, I think my bones put a few years' wear on them tonight, and I loved every minute of it." She pushed herself up, and Ewen rose on the other side of the table. Lace and velvet and silver buttons; just like a situation in a Mariana Grange book, a life-and-death confrontation across wine glasses and candles. Catriona must make the right choice or she'll rue this moment for the rest of her life—

"Take her home, Ewen," Mrs. MacBain said, laughing. The others laughed too, kindly; they liked her, they made her feel like a cherished child. It was ridiculous to feel like crying when she hadn't been drinking.

After the warmth and scents of food and tobacco smoke inside the pure chill of the night air came as a salutary shock. Alison was revived at once; she wrapped her cape more tightly about her, and breathed deeply. The stars looked thick and near, as if they clustered together and pressed closely toward the sunless side of earth to examine it while it slept. There was no wind, there were no lambs' voices. There was a pervading scent of damp grass and earth, with a ghostly whiff of the day's peat fires.

Instead of taking the small garden gate they walked up the driveway to the big gate on the road, and out past the Land Rover and the Scotts' car. Aignish windows were dark in all the scattering of houses along the lane, except for Mrs. Mac-Bain's. A pebble rolled under Alison's foot and she stumbled against Ewen.

"Gie us your hand, lassie," Ewen said, and laughed.

"What's funny?" she asked. He took her hand and pulled it through his arm.

"It's a very old joke," he said. "I don't know you well enough yet to tell it."

"Oh well, I can wait." The *yet* had sounded promising.

They walked by her gate, and on down the road. Their footsteps were the only sounds. The blue-eyed dog was inside, and so was the dog on the corner who always barked at her as if he thought she expected it, and he didn't want to disappoint her. The daffodils glimmered in spectral borders from gates to front doors. Ewen's face jabot gave off the gleam of new snow in the starlight.

As they turned down the road to the shore a briny exhalation from the water subtly undermined the essences of the land. It was the same cold saline whiff which had always sped up Alison's heartbeat when she was a small child and driving to the seashore with her parents. Incredible to experience the identical reaction now, at this age, in this place, with this companion; to have this incoherent, greedy, dazzling, assurance that some great treasure or adventure was waiting for her.

She must have tightened her hand involuntarily on Ewen's arm. He said in a low voice, "What is it?"

"I don't know you well enough yet to tell it." The answer came like a reflex action. He laughed.

"Like you, I can wait. Ach, a patient waiter is no loser," he said, sounding like Murdo. They had reached the gate to the shore. "Now if you had decent shoes on, we'd go down to the machair. Loch a Tuath's hardly breathing. We could see the stars in it, I think."

Not to be able to go down to the machair right now with Ewen felt like the bitterest deprivation yet. "I could take off my shoes," she offered.

He ignored that. "Where haven't you been yet on Lewis that you'd like to go?" he asked.

She stammered in her surprise. "Why—well—everywhere, I guess!"

"Give me a starting point," he ordered.

"Well, I'd have gone to the Butt of Lewis yesterday if it hadn't stormed."

"We'll go tomorrow, then. Today, rather. You'd better get some sleep." He swung her around. To head back, she expected; instead, it was into his arms. He kissed her firmly and commandingly. He knew his own mind, and she knew hers; she put her arms hard around him, felt the diamond-shaped buttons pressed through her dress and the jabot tickling her throat. My God, a Highlander! she thought. I hope I haven't invented him and the whole thing's a hallucination.

The kiss was neither thrusting nor arrogant but it was a

long kiss. When it was done, there was no comment; no dazed, heart-struck whisperings. She hoped through her own fog that it was because he was too stunned to speak.

He walked her back to her own gate and escorted her through it. On the doorstep she couldn't find her key. Her fingers rummaged coldly and weakly in her evening bag. She made a smothered sound of despair and Ewen took the bag from her and found the key and opened the door. He propelled her by the arm into the hall and switched on the overhead light.

She wondered if she appeared to him as someone colorless, drooping with fatigue, whom he'd kissed for his own reason—probably curiosity—and already regretted it or had dismissed it. She longed for the brazen power to take his face in her hands and kiss him like a passionate woman of the world. Instead she found herself leaning wearily against the wall. Ewen's silence, which she had been reading as immutable and adamantine, broke up.

"Away to your bed with you," he ordered, "or you'll be fit for nothing today. Come across to Callanish when you wake up, and if it's too late to go to the Butt we'll do something else."

"I never sleep late," she told him proudly, but it was a feeble effort. From a hazy distance she remembered her manners. "Thank you for a wonderful evening. I'll never forget it."

"It was a pleasure for me too. You're a fine dancer. Good night, now. I'll see you later."

He went up the walk to the gate with the quick step that sets a kilt swinging. Through the gate and fastening it, he saw her still in the doorway and lifted his hand. She waved back, but waited until he had gone along the road to the Land Rover before she shut the door.

21

$\mathcal{S}$HE YAWNED all the way through getting ready for sleep. She remembered to wash her face and brush her teeth, but she left her clothes where she stepped out of them, and fell into bed with her legs aching and a familiar sensation of floating, as if the whole house were floating, like an old green sofa which used to sail through her dreams when she was a child, with her aboard, hanging on for dear life with her feet hauled up so nothing could make a snatch at them when she passed overhead.

It had been delightfully scary in its dizzying swoops and soarings. It was delightful now. She was trembling on the edge of some fearful joy. Neither Catriona nor Fiona had been kissed tonight, but Alison Barbour had, and it was Alison Barbour and no one else who had responded with so much enthusiasm.

In the old days she used to be asleep before the sofa glided in for a landing. Tonight she was grounded and awake, suffering her characteristic doubts. She was worse off than before the kiss, because she didn't know how to take it. The indecision was as intimate and painful as walking on blistered feet. One ached to collapse by the road and weep with the pain, while knowing that the real relief and salvation lay ahead if you could just make it. Or rather—it *might* be ahead, and could change your life. But if, after all the agony, it wasn't there—

She wept a little and then, also characteristically, made a decision on which she could go to sleep. She would ask him straight out if he was in love with her. He should appreciate her honesty and respect it by being honest in return.

She did not allow herself to anticipate anything beyond the question.

She woke up a little before nine, and in the morning light her solution appalled her. Imagine cornering a man with a question like that because of one kiss. Her only concern right now was to be with him today, and she could hardly wait to get there and feast her eyes on him. The feast would have to be discreetly managed, while her impeccable conduct assured him she didn't consider herself either compromised or engaged.

The MacBain lambs played follow-the-leader in the lower field, with young Angus at the head of the band in exultant leaps back and forth over a handy ditch. Broad Bay or Loch a Tuath was as blue as cornflowers. Alison was going to see Ewen, and her head was full of music from the night before; she wanted to hear more and more, and to dance again. Who'd ever want to go to a Hazlehurst dance now? God, these people know how to live! she thought.

She didn't stop to make coffee, she drank a glass of orange juice and took two buttered rolls to eat as she drove. Out on the moors beyond Stornoway she passed people cutting peats, those whose jobs took up their weekdays and who made their Saturday peat-cutting a family occasion, with a picnic around the car at the side of the road. It was good driving weather today and she wished them more of it.

Every scrap or expanse of water was porcelain-blue and the treeless land rolling away in great swells, cresting in waves of rock and moor against a silvery horizon, was flooded with a tender light, which was as ephemeral as the gems shaken off the lambs' hooves when they ran and jumped in the dew.

When she reached the Stones she had a whim to walk through them to Ewen, as a sort of ritual to commemorate their other meetings here; and in a morning so full of promises—to the peat-cutters, to the children who waved from the side of the road, to herself—she might hear a cuckoo again. She parked where she'd left the car the day they went to the Broch, and went through the gate, walking slowly to prolong the approach. She was nervous, all at once; she had no guarantee that Ewen would feel the way she did this morning.

She stopped to listen for the subtle, hollow call of a cuckoo, but there was none. The rooster crowed from the cottages back down the road, and ahead of her, high up over the circle, some herring gulls glided in narrowing circles, crying and answering, their voices echoing in space; it was as if they were discussing her, and one banked toward her so she could see its head cocked to look. A pair of gray and black hooded crows swept in at a lower level, just over the top of the tallest stone in the circle, calling out hoarsely. At the sight of Alison, they climbed again, still sounding their rough cries.

Though she saw herring and black-back gulls all the time in Aignish, and the hooded crows often picked around in the fields with the common crow and the uncommon (to her) jackdaw, she had never seen them at the Stones before, and she thought, If I were a bundle of superstitions would I consider them a good omen or a bad one? Now if a raven should appear I'd be convinced Odin had his eye on me; the raven was his. I'll ask Murdo about gulls and hooded crows. They don't shoot an arrow of ice into my heart or freeze my breath in my throat, but then I'm not one of my own heroines. All I've got is the sensation that somebody's tramping around in my belly wearing ski boots, because I don't know how Off-again On-again Gone-again Finnegan is going to greet me this morning.

She reached the circle and looked up at the top edge of the

tallest stone, past which the crows had swooped. How had those men ever struck out these slabs of Lewissian gneiss in the first place, let alone get them up here and then so firmly grounded?

She could see it as a memorial to a dead god-king; first they dug out and lined with rocks the burial chamber, and put him in it, and then they planted their grove of stones over a long period of time, the way cathedrals were built. It was a cathedral of its own kind, it had even been laid out roughly in the form of a Celtic cross thousands of years before the cross became a Christian symbol.

"Now *that's* something!" she said aloud. "I wonder if—"

She looked down at the burial cairn, to better imagine him lying there in his feather cloak; would the wrens have been fluttering all about the place in mourning? Why the tiny wren for a sacred bird, in contrast to Odin's raven?

She saw Norris. He was lying almost at her feet, and his eyes were open. At first she thought he was looking at her, that it was a morbid practical joke and he was going to start laughing in a moment. Then it wás as if a drawn shade had suddenly snapped up in her brain and let in a brutally unsparing light. She saw that the open gray eyes were blind. They were dead eyes. His fair hair was darkened and stiffened with blood. Where the blood had run from his nose and mouth it looked black. The tan trenchcoat was streaked and stained with dirt.

She didn't scream. She heard herself whispering inanely, "Somebody come. Something is terrible." She knelt to touch his cheek, but her fingers knew before the actual contact what they would feel. Something so marble cold, and wet with dew, as if it could never have been human flesh. She wished she could have closed his eyes against whatever it was, the last thing he had seen and recognized as the death of him. She wished it very fervently as she walked away from the circle, and she knew she was clinging to the wish because it kept her from thinking about anything else.

When she went down the slope to the farmhouse, both the men were outside, but they didn't see her coming. Ewen was holding the sick ewe's head while Murdo poured something down her throat. Maili sat by, watching. The twin lambs cried in baby voices from their enclosure. The black-face ewe struggled enough to nearly break out of Ewen's grip, and Murdo said with satisfaction, "She'll do fine, I'm thinking. A week ago she could hardly hold up her head."

They watched her walk away from them and begin to eat grass.

The dog saw Alison and bounded toward her, and the men turned. She'd intended to be calm, but when she opened her mouth to speak her jaw felt unhinged, she was stammering without sound, and she thought in panic that she was about to fly apart like one of her more hysterical heroines. She saw Ewen's expression change to alarm; he started toward her and they came together in a magnetized embrace. He held her as if she weighed no more than a lamb and she clung as if she'd drown or fall off the world if she let go.

"What is it?" he kept asking her. The dog was dancing about them with little nips of frustration, and Murdo came up to them.

"Bring her into the kitchen for a good strong cup of tea," he said. "Or maybe a little whiskey. Come along, Maili." He started for the house.

Alison's jaw felt more secure. "Listen, Ewen," she began. "Listen. It's—"

"Just wait," he hushed her. "Get your breath. Murdo's right."

He walked her to the house and into the kitchen. Murdo was filling the electric teakettle at the sink. Ewen tipped a cat out of a low rocking chair by the hearth.

"It's all right," she said. "I mean, I'm all right. It's N—" Her teeth chattered on his name. "Norris," she got out finally. "He's dead, up in the circle."

"*A Dhia!*" Murdo said, staring at her with the teakettle in his hand. Ewen put his hands on her shoulders and sat her in the chair the cat had left. Still holding her, he looked into her eyes and spoke very distinctly. "Sit still. I'll ring the constable at Carloway."

She nodded meekly at him, and he straightened up and went out into the hall.

"You'll need that tea," Murdo said briskly. "We all will." He plugged in the teakettle and began taking cups from a cupboard. She hunched herself together against a chill that wasn't in the warm room but in herself; she'd have liked to cuddle the displaced tiger cat which sat on the hearth rug looking at her, undisturbed by Maili's waving tail. She took the dog's head in her hands to warm them. The cold of Norris's cheek seemed to have permanently chilled her fingertips. Murdo, moving quickly and quietly around the kitchen, took an old tweed jacket from the back of a chair and draped it around her shoulders. It smelled comfortably of sheep and tobacco.

She could hear Ewen's voice out in the hall, but not his words. The teakettle began to boil. She went on smoothing the sleek hair back on the dog's skull, and the hypnotic motions calmed her; Maili's eyes were liquidly entranced.

Ewen returned from the hall and looked down at her. "You're all right now?"

"Oh yes. I'm sorry if I didn't make much sense." Then she burst out without meaning to, "If only his eyes weren't open!"

"Ach, that's what you can't forget," said Murdo with a sigh. He rinsed the teapot with hot water and measured dry tea into it from a metal caddy ornamented with sheep and thistles, then poured in boiling water.

"We'd best go up there," Ewen said. "Will you mind waiting here or do you want to go?"

"I'll stay here," she said quickly.

"I'll come along when the tea's ready," said Murdo. "If I leave it for her to pour, she'll burn herself. Or she'll never stir out of that chair, and she needs the tea for shock."

Ewen nodded, and went out.

"This will be good in your stomach," Murdo promised Alison. He brought her a large cup of sweet, milky tea and stood over her with the same authority with which he tended the sick ewe.

"Drink it, but be careful. It's hot enough to blister your tongue."

The dog ran to the door with him but he said something to her and she came back to Alison and lay down beside the chair, her head on her paws, facing the door. The kitchen clock became very loud, and the little flames of the peat were sibilantly audible. Murdo was right about the tea. The hot cup warmed her hands and the small cautious sips helped her stomach.

By now Ewen would be at the circle and exchanging stare for stare with Norris.

"Maili," Alison said, to establish contact with something alive, and the dog scrambled up and came eagerly around to put her chin on Alison's knee. The big tiger cat washed behind his ears. "I suppose you understand only Gaelic," Alison said to him. He stopped scrubbing, one paw poised, and gave her a long, unblinking, green-gold gaze.

She drank more tea and tried facing facts. Norris was dead, with the sun in his eyes. The crows and the gulls had seen him, and that accounted for their presence.

The cup shook in her hand and she set it down by the fire. She got up experimentally, like someone who's been bedridden for a long time, but at once she felt in much better control of her reflexes. She walked around the kitchen, concentrating on details. She'd never been in it before, but Kay must have been here many times. Damn Kay. They'd been free of her last night, or had they?

It was a clean kitchen, but lived in only by men, and at least Kay had left no feminine touches. There was another crowded mantel, a variety of calendars much marked up, no bright curtains or plants on window sills. The table and the counters were scrubbed wood. In the corner by the door to the yard there were two shepherd's crooks, one plain, the other with an elaborately carved handle. She picked it up and concentrated on the design, which was full of little surprises if you looked hard enough at the intricate twinings. She wondered if Murdo had carved it. The wood was richly polished with use.

She drank more tea, then accompanied by Maili she looked for and found the bathroom. It was clean, but strictly utilitarian. She tried to imagine Ewen shaving in here each morning, in an undershirt or no shirt at all. Had Kay—*No*. She diverted herself with a vision of Murdo grooming his white mustache. Mustaches were extraordinarily silly, when you came to think of it, but Murdo's was so beautifully kept that it was a work of art.

She looked into the sitting room without crossing the threshold. Papers like manuscript pages were spread untidily around the typewriter. The sgian dubh he'd worn last night lay across the open pages of a book as if to hold them down. Curiosity about Ewen's work blew like a cold and healthful gale through the miasma, but there was such a thing as honor, she thought drearily, going back to the kitchen. It would have been nice to think of something else besides her innocent ramble toward the circle and the discovery.

She sat down and drank the rest of her tea so as to please Murdo. "Well, what do you think, Maili?" she asked the dog, just to assure herself her voice hadn't frozen permanently somewhere down in her larynx. Maili responded as if the question made perfect sense and she'd reply when she had thought out her answer. "And you," Alison said to the cat. "Why aren't you out in the sunshine? I suppose you stay out all night. Then the Stones belong to you."

She shut herself off, biting at her lower lip. Those greengold eyes sleepily watching her could have watched something else last night.

22

OMEBODY OPENED the front door, Maili shot into the hall with a flurry of toenails, and Ewen spoke to her. He came into the kitchen scowling.

"Are you all right?" he asked curtly. "You haven't been nervous alone here?"

"With these two? Of course the cat doesn't have much to say, but you can tell he's a deep thinker."

"So Murdo claims."

"Are the police there?"

"Yes, and an ambulance. The constable called headquarters at Stornoway." He poured a cup of tea and stood on the hearth drinking it. After a few swallows he set it on the mantel and propped his elbow beside it. "I drove your car here," he said, "and on the way I passed a car parked on the side of the road, just back there where it runs along below the Stones to come to this house. It's a red Capri. It might be his."

"That's what he's been driving. It's a rented car, like mine."

"Well, it was there when I came home this morning, around half-past three." He began abruptly to pace between fireplace and sink, his hands in his pockets. "I drove on here, with the intention of walking up to the Stones to see what was going on; we've never had vandalism there but it could happen, I suppose, because anyone can come to the island by plane or ferry."

Back to the fireplace, a turn, and across to the sink again. "But I didn't go. Murdo'd left a note for me under my work lamp and I had to make a call to Perth."

"At *that* hour of the morning?"

"Do you remember the chap who was with me at Mallaig? He turns night into day, and he'd have been waiting for me to reach him. So I did, and it was important to both of us." He came back to the hearth and put another peat on the fire. Sitting on his heels by the fender he looked up at her and said softly, "I didn't go up to the Stones. I didn't give that car another thought. Now I have to live with the premise that he might have still been alive then."

She put her hand out without thinking and took hold of his shoulder. "Ewen, don't," she said. "How could you know? It might have been lovers up there, or—"

"I should have gone," he said stubbornly. He looked older than he had an hour ago; she saw lines she had never seen before. He reached up and lightly touched her hand on his shoulder, then stood and moved to the bench opposite, beside the cat. Maili put her head on his knee and he stroked it, looking into the fire.

"What do you think happened?" Alison asked.

He did her the honor of being blunt. "It looks as if he's been run over. The tire tracks are clear on his coat. He may have been on foot for some reason and been knocked down and run over by a drunk. Then the fool, or fools, dragged him up to the Stones."

"But why go to all that work, when they might have been caught at it?"

"They took a chance, and obviously they weren't caught.

Some drunks have been known to do weird things, as you must know. . . . It might not have been a drunk but somebody driving dangerously. Or drugs could be involved. It happens here. Not often, but—" He shrugged. "However it was, it happened. There's no escaping it. Did you say once his girl was on the island with him?"

"Oh, my God!" Alison exclaimed. "I forgot all about her! Poor Boots!"

"*Boots?*"

"It's really Monique Something or other." She laced her hands tightly together. "I feel as if I ought to do something, but I don't know what. I don't think she'd want any help from me. Maybe the Danforths, if they're in any shape this morning—" She stopped. She saw Norris gazing at her over Terry's wobbling head as the lift door closed. She felt an enormous and angry sadness. She'd silently accused him of pretending to be vulnerable, and all the time he'd been only a few hours from his death; he'd been moving inexorably toward it. Oh, he'd been vulnerable all right, and he hadn't even known it.

She pulled the old tweed coat tighter around her but the inner chill prevailed. An embrace from Ewen would have helped, but he seemed lost in his own regrets.

"What are you thinking?" he asked her suddenly. "The expressions are chasing across your face like showers across the island. It's better to talk about this, you know. So tell me, Alison." The sound of her name in his voice, in this context, was like an unexpected caress.

"There's nothing to say, except—well, I thought I was perfectly justified in behaving toward him as I did, and if I met him alive today I'd probably behave the same way again, but he's gone, and I feel so damn *guilty.*"

"You mean, if you'd known he had such a short time to live you'd have been kinder." Ewen took out his pipe and tobacco pouch.

"Yes. I snubbed him last night, and now I wish I hadn't. I

could have said I'd talk to him today, even if it only turned out to be more of the same, which I'm sure it would have." She watched Ewen filling his pipe. "But like you I have to live with an uncomfortable thought. Whatever he was doing out here in the middle of the night, he just might not have come if I'd agreed to see him today."

"Perhaps it will all straighten out for both of us," he said, trying to get his pipe going. "I suppose that to blame oneself for ignorance in such a situation is self-pitying or egotistic. It's enough to be victimized by the living without worrying about the dead."

There was certainly no trace of last night's dancer or the man who'd kissed her in the road. However, a little strong-arm comfort wouldn't have compromised him. She'd been too quick to say she was all right; she should have clung a bit longer. Right now she was lonelier with him than when she'd been alone with the dog and the cat. He was probably resenting all these trans-oceanic intrusions in his life; she'd be doing them both a favor to get out now. She stood up, dropping the tweed coat. Maili arose hopefully from the hearth rug. Ewen tipped his head back and took his pipe out of his mouth.

"Where are you going?"

"Back to Aignish."

He pointed his pipe stem at her chair. "Sit down again. You can't go yet. They'll be along to get your statement."

She felt rebuffed and foolish; she felt like crying for the first time this morning; and not about Norris. She took a turn around the kitchen, looking out the windows like a prisoner at the sunny sheep-dappled slopes rising to the Stones. She couldn't see them from here, she didn't think she ever wanted to see them again, but it was a fair day out there and there was plenty of escape room away from the Stones if she once got out of here.

The bright scene outside swam glitteringly in her vision. She blinked tears back, something which her heroines were able to do without having their noses stuff up and their eyes go red. She had no hope of being personally successful in this, and did not care. She went back to the hearth rug and Maili met her with as much enthusiasm as if she'd just circumnavigated the globe instead of the kitchen.

"Did he ever get here that afternoon?" Alison asked in a crisp so-what's-new manner. "I asked you about it last night, but you never answered me. You remember the afternoon Kay came in while I was making merry with her shortbread. She hated that, and I would have, too."

It was a successful attack; now he had the swift-passing expressions, and he opened his mouth to speak, but she went on. "How did Kay feel about your taking me to the dance last night? Why didn't you ask her, by the way? Was she on night duty? I hope she realizes she has nothing to fear from me."

She sat down and leaned back in the rocker and stretched out her legs toward the fire. Ewen said, "He's never been here. He rang up several times, but he wouldn't say why. Did he tell you?"

Kay had been superbly ignored. You cold-blooded bastard! The words came out of nowhere, she'd never applied them to anyone in her life in speech or in thought, and she was as shaken as if she'd shouted them at him.

"He thought," she said to the fire, "that you own the Book of St. Neacal."

"The hell he did!"

That had done it, but she couldn't take any satisfaction in it. "You probably know there's a shady side to the art business," she said. "Well, by some kind of grapevine the news got around that this rare old book, something equivalent to the Book of Kells, was for sale, and Norris is—was, I mean—representing a rich client." It was impossible to think of Norris as dead. The picture of him as she'd found him remained only a picture, even though she'd touched him; that hadn't felt real, either, except as cold damp marble was real.

"Was it just a coincidence that you asked me about St. Neacal on the afternoon of the famous shortbread?" he asked sardonically.

"It's a coincidence in this way," she explained to the fire. "Someone was talking to me about St. Neacal just before I left home. Then Nor—he came out with it because he thought—incredibly—that I was here to make a deal for a client." From the corner of her eye she saw Ewen lean forward, but it was easier to talk to the fire than to his face while dealing with this sad, silly, little business of rumors and gambles.

"I got that idea out of his head, but he swore that he was on the right track with you. He said he had a sixth sense about these things. But when I asked you about St. Neacal it was because I'd like to get a look at the book myself. I mean I wanted to see it once, but no more." She couldn't avoid the desolation in her tone. Harold Marshall had also been killed by a car. "Anyway, I met him on the road when I left that day, and he stopped me, and told me he was on his way here."

"If only he'd mentioned it to me in his first telephone call," Ewen said. "I'd have put paid to his theory and he'd be hunting the book elsewhere by now. At least he wouldn't have been run down on a Lewis road last night."

"Could you, or would you, have put him on the right track? His operation involved some illegal fiddlings."

"That sort of thing, was it? Well, I'm not sure myself what the right track would be. I could have made suggestions, that's all. Too bad the grapevine wasn't more exact."

She looked around at him then, raising her eyebrows. "An expert in Celtic studies doesn't know where something like *that* is?"

"Ignorance of the Book's whereabouts has nothing to do with Celtic studies; it's a matter of feuds and alliances. The branch which acquired it through the Norwegian girl so long ago has always been very prolific, as well as secretive, so it's a bit like 'Button, Button, who has the button?' "

He stood up and stretched. The cat jumped down and went to the door, and he let it out. "No, Maili, wait," he said absently to the dog. He came back to Alison.

"By now it's gone, I should imagine. If they did want to sell, someone had all the facts before the grapevine spread the word very far."

Harold Marshall had all the facts, and had probably been replaced by another knowledgeable agent, while Norris was chasing shadows.

"I told him," she said sadly, "that while he was believing his gut reactions here someone was tracking down the right Chisholm, and he admitted it was all gambling, and he liked the excitement. Haven't you ever really seen the Book?"

"Once, when it was behind glass in an exhibit. Oh, I suppose that I could have begun inquiries as a serious scholar and eventually seen and handled the Book, but I never felt the need."

"Couldn't you have just used your name and your right as a Chisholm to see a family treasure? I'm curious, that's all. What about clan ties?"

"My attachment to clan traditions doesn't go beyond wearing the proper tartan and knowing the clan motto. 'Feros Ferio.' "

" 'I am fierce with the fierce,' " she translated. "Well, that's better than being milk-toasty with them."

"My father used to say that. He was very proud of his name. We'd call him An Siosalach to tease him."

"The Chisholm," she said.

He laughed. "Sir Walter Scott wrote this: 'Every Scottish man has a pedigree; it is a national prerogative as inalienable as his pride and his poverty.' I like that. It always makes me laugh, but at the same time it moves me. It's so inescapably true of the Highlander."

"Including you," she said.

"Oh, I admit to the pride and the poverty, and I can't very

well deny the pedigree, if you want to call it that. But the sire of all those lambs out there has a pedigree, and Maili here, and Shonnie the cat; *he* comes of a long line of superlative mousers." He gave her an intent look, then said, "You're feeling better."

"It's from talking about something else besides what's happened," she said. The wave of desolation had drawn back far enough to save her; she hoped it wasn't building up out there to return as a tidal wave. "What are they doing up there, to take so long?"

"Don't you know by now that nobody ever hurries in the Hebrides? I'll make some fresh tea, or would you like coffee? Or a drink. Or food?"

He'd be this polite to anyone. "Nothing, thanks. My stomach's rolling at the prospect of describing it all to the police."

"Ah, you'll find them very easy to talk to."

"Can we go outside to wait?"

"Of course." He led the way through the hall to the front door, and Maili managed to get there first. They went out into the fresh wind and sunshine. Little clouds like bits of lambs' wool blew across a cerulean sky that looked higher than usual.

A blackbird sang from the chimney here as one did in Aignish. The hard road ended outside the gate, and some children came along on bicycles. Maili barked at them through the gate, and when they saw adults beyond the garden wall they stopped and stared.

"Good morning," Ewen said gravely. "Iain, Jessie, Roddie, Mairi."

"Good morning, Ewen," said Jessie, the tallest. She was about twelve. "We're just going down to the water."

"Go along, then."

They didn't hurry. They were taking in everything about Alison, and there was something else besides. Suddenly a small dark boy said in a rush, "What is happening at the Stones? The police are there, and the ambulance is at the gate, and Murdo wouldn't let us in."

"A man was found there who'd been hurt," Ewen said.

"They were bringing him to the gate, and Murdo drove us away," the boy said, aggrieved.

"How was he hurt?" asked Jessie. "Did a stone fall on him, then?"

"A stone wouldn't fall on him," the other boy teased her. He was yellow-haired like her. "It couldn't."

"How do you know, Iain Matheson?" she cried passionately. "After all these years one could be just ready to fall! I never go near the Stones because it could happen any time."

"Ach, it's just waiting for Jessie Matheson!" he said, laughing, but the others looked more impressed with Jessie's theory than Iain's amusement.

She sped off on her bike like a Valkyrie with her hair streaming out behind her. The others followed along the rough track to the shore.

"We'd go down there ourselves if the police weren't on their way here," Ewen said. "I'll have to show you that on another day."

Another day. That was nice, but she was too tired now to feel encouraged. The police car was coming along the road, Norris having begun his ride to Stornoway.

23

Until now the only police Alison had seen on Lewis had been a man-woman team walking along Cromwell Street in Stornoway. She'd expected that the police department was a purely domestic affair like the town and city organizations at home, with a chief appointed by the local governing authority, in this case the Comhairle nan Eilean, a council of representatives from all the islands in the Outer Hebrides.

Instead, the police department resembled the state police, in that it was a branch of the Northern Constabulary, which covered most of the north of Scotland. Sergeant Sinclair was a native of Ellapool on the mainland. He was a slight wiry man with pleasant eyes and a soft Highland voice. The constable driving the police cruiser was a Leodhais, who looked hardly old enough to be out of school. He was solemnly dignified as if he thought someone ought to be rigidly official around here to make up for the sergeant's affable and leisurely way of taking a statement. Alison wondered what he'd do if she winked at him.

Her statement was very short and she confirmed the identification in Norris's billfold, and said he'd been driving a red Capri. Sergeant Sinclair thanked her as if she'd made an immeasurable contribution. She asked him then if the hotel had been notified; Norris was traveling with a friend.

"Yes, she must know now, the poor young lady," he said. "It's very sad, for their holiday to end like this."

Murdo was back, and he and Ewen went out to the car with the officers. They talked by the gate, looking up at the sky and obviously discussing the weather; then sheep dogs came into it, she could feel by the way they contemplated Maili. Even the super-regulation constable was interested in border collies, perhaps because it was impossible to resist Maili once she was convinced you were the most fascinating creature she'd ever come across, and the constable was getting the full treatment. The discussion of dogs led to sheep—yes, Murdo was pointing at a group across the road. From sheep it could go anywhere, like the Lewis men who turned up in almost any unlikely spot on the globe that you could mention.

Now, Alison thought, I can go back to Aignish. Her whole desire was to shut herself up away from both the dead and the living. She would write. Ah, you're always the practical one, Alison, she thought. Escape through liquor costs money and leaves hangovers. Travel with your typewriter through Beautiful Never-Never Land, and be paid for it.

As soon as the police car backed around and drove off, she went out, and met Murdo and Ewen coming in.

"And where would you be going?" Murdo asked her.

"To Aignish on the Machair, as the song goes."

"But you've not had a mouthful of food all this long morning," he protested. "You'll faint with hunger on the way."

"Now, Alison." Ewen was sober but not grim, his voice warmly clasped her as his hand clasped her elbow. "Let's have a bite and then go along to the Butt. It's a grand day for it, and we need something to come between us and what's happened."

"Good, good." Murdo rubbed his hands and went into the kitchen. The telephone rang. Ewen answered it, and Alison heard clearly the woman's voice, though not the words, and she saw Ewen's expression change to none at all. "No," he said. "We're all right here. It was a visitor, a man staying at one of the hotels."

Alison walked rapidly into the kitchen. "How would you like ham and eggs?" Murdo asked. She didn't answer, and as he backed away from the refrigerator with his hands full he heard Ewen in the hall; he cocked his head and said, "Is he on the telephone?"

"Yes," said Alison. "A female caller," she added dryly.

"Ah," said Murdo mysteriously. For an instant everything was static in the kitchen except for the clock and the fire. "It could be his aunt over in Swordale," Murdo suggested.

The name Kay was as blatant in the room as if some great banner had rolled down from the ceiling with the three letters on it, six feet tall. They were all the larger because Alison had completely forgotten her until now.

Ewen came out to the kitchen. "Kay," he said to no one in particular. "They'd heard at the hospital that there was an accident at the Stones. She wondered who and how."

Murdo turned his back on the others and began arranging ham slices in a large skillet. His silence was thunderous. Ewen gazed into space and drummed his fingers on the table. Maili took a long noisy drink, and this aroused Alison from a trance-like state.

"Murdo, will you forgive me if I don't eat?" she asked the back of his neck. "The way I feel, I couldn't even swallow. I just want to go back to Aignish and go to bed."

He turned quickly. "I'm the daft one, for not seeing how tired you are."

"Ewen, will you give me a rain check on the trip to the Butt?" she asked, on the way to the front door. And I don't care if you say No straight out, she thought viciously. *She* pipes the tune you dance to, doesn't she?— Ewen caught up with her.

"Daft isn't the word for it," he said. "I'm damned stupid

not to realize you'd be exhausted by now, meeting all this on only a few hours' sleep. I'm driving you at least as far as Stornoway."

She protested, but he wouldn't listen. "I'll get a ride home with someone. Besides, there's business I should do in Stornoway and this is as good a time as ever."

"All right," she said spinelessly. His kaleidoscopic rearrangements of mood were hard to take when she hadn't the resistance to meet the rapid changes. "Goodbye, Murdo," she called, "and thank you for everything."

He called back something in Gaelic and Ewen said, "That means Haste ye back."

Alison's eyes filled with tears. She turned her face away from Ewen who either didn't notice or pretended not to. He walked her smartly out to her car and put her in the passenger seat.

Even though she suspected that his Stornoway business was to reassure Kay that he was all in one piece, she was glad he'd insisted on driving. The narrow road dazzled and blurred in her vision so she kept blinking; the ups and downs affected her stomach, the sweeping curves made her head light, and the stretches of staightaway glaring in the sun had a hypnotic effect. Even with Ewen driving she felt as if she were trying to balance on a high wire without having been on one before. Any oncoming car seemed to be hurtling toward a head-on collision with hers. She wondered if this was how drunks felt trying to navigate their way home across the moors. She remembered too, as if from a year or so ago, how it had all looked to her in the morning when she drove to Callanish; the exquisite porcelain blue of every little pond, the rough wild beauty of the moorland in sunshine, and her own mood.

Well, the ponds were still blue, the little tufts of clouds still scampered like lambs across the sky, birds rose up singing, the families were still cutting their peats, but everything was most horribly different inside this car.

Ewen spoke now and then. He identified birds for her; he told her about the good fishing in a stream they passed, and explained the certain skills involved in poaching salmon without being caught by game-keepers or their hired watchers. He was amusing about it, she knew that, but the fine points never seemed to get to her past some outer layer of thick insulation.

Suddenly something did get through. "I keep wondering," Ewen said, "what he was doing out there in the middle of the night. I could imagine his simply driving around if he couldn't sleep, but do you think he'd be mad enough to be coming to see me at that hour?"

"I might say he was crazy enough for anything," she said. "But he could have spoken to you at the hotel last night. He knew you were there, he must have seen you in the dining room. Maybe he intended to, before Terry Danforth threw her fit, and then later on he missed out, for some reason or other . . . well, I suppose he could have thought he'd catch you when you came home."

· "The car's tank was empty, Sinclair told me. If Elliot ran out of petrol just where he did, he would have walked on to the house. But he was struck down before he could make it. Poor devil."

"Whatever the explanation is," said Alison, "it's no good, is it? Even if they remember, and they're sick about it, a man's dead. Someone else I know was killed by a drunken driver, just before I left home. He was so full of hopes and happy excitement one day, and the next day he'd ceased to exist except as a memory."

"I'm sorry," Ewen said. "It must make this affair twice as bad for you." His quiet sympathy was very personal, as if he thought she was talking about a close friend or even a lover. She started to correct the impression, then thought, Why bother?

"I'll leave you at the Comhairle nan Eilean building," he said. "I have to battle my way through the jungle of red tape between me and what I want to do with my Bernera property."

"You must feel like Prince Charming trying to find the Sleeping Beauty."

He laughed. "The sword hasn't been forged that could slash away all that bureaucratic verbiage with a couple of good clean strokes. The council building's outside town, on the Braigh side, so you'll have a straight road to Aignish. Are you awake enough?" He sounded so solicitous that it hurt; she was sure he was going to Kay eventually.

"Oh yes, I can keep my eyes open that long," she said. "Thanks for driving me across, though. I could have fallen asleep very easily back there."

At the Comhairle nan Eilean offices, she watched from the car park until he'd disappeared inside the building. Then she swung the car around and drove back across Stornoway to the Caberfeidh Hotel. When she got out of her car she saw Jake Danforth just coming out the front door, and she greeted him with a relief that must have surprised him.

"I want to speak to Monique and I don't know what name to ask for at the desk."

"Fournier." He didn't give it a French pronunciation but Alison guessed at it. "Christ, what a mess," he said. "And they tell me the worst charge is likely to be dangerous driving, they don't like the sound of culpable homicide. So the bastard will lose his license for a few years, pay a fine or do a little time, but he'll still be alive, and a harmless good-hearted guy like Elliot is dead."

Alison winced. "What's her room number?"

He told her. "But she won't let you in. She's—" He fidgeted, he looked at his cigar with distaste. "She's in a terrible state. I don't blame her, but Jesus, I wish some relative would show up to take care of her."

Alison's dread was now so potent she knew it wouldn't take much more to discourage her completely. "Well, I'll try," she said. She went in, bypassing the desk where a family of new-comers were checking in.

She knocked at Monique's door, once softly and then more authoritatively. Monique finally answered in a thick voice, "Who is it?"

"Alison Barbour."

"Go away."

The corridor was helpfully vacant right now. Alison said, "If you don't let me in I'll stand here and keep on knocking until you do." She'd never been very good at threats, at least answerable ones, and the instant she made this one she expected Monqiue to say, "Go ahead, knock all night, what the hell do I care?"

But instead, Monique opened the door. Her blotched, puffy face and swollen, inflamed eyelids made her hardly recognizable. Her hair was a straw-colored tangle. She hadn't dressed, and the delicate blue of the quilted robe made her neck an unhealthy yellow by contrast. It was gaunt, with prominent cords.

"What do *you* want?" Her eyes were streaked with red around the tawny iris.

"Just to see if there's anything I can do." Confronting the mask of tragedy, Alison felt inept and inadequate.

"Haven't you done enough already?" Then Monique said wearily, "Excuse the cliché. It's straight out of soap opera. Come in." She stepped back. She was barefooted. The room was hazed and sour with cigarette smoke, and as if she had just noticed it for the first time she opened the windows and stood looking out, her arms folded.

"Monique, what *can* I do?" Alison asked, not moving from just inside the closed door. "We're both strangers here, and for that reason alone, I—"

"You found him, didn't you?" Monique didn't turn her head.

"Yes." And I hope they closed his eyes before you saw him.

"It seems more horrible that way, where he was, than if

they'd left him in the road," Monique went on tonelessly. "It was like using him to make a sick joke after they killed him. Especially where he—" She took an audible breath and said more strongly, "They've been kind here at the hotel, and the police have been too."

"Have the Danforths been around?"

"*He* has. She was still sick this morning, after last night." Memory caught her by the throat and squeezed. It hit Alison too; could one be haunted, and how long, by an elevator door closing? Monique went on. "He said he'd do anything he could, make calls for me if there was anyone to call, and see me—us—onto the flight home from Prestwick ... *Oh God!*" she wailed suddenly. "I can't believe this!"

Alison went to stand beside her at the window. "Look, you shouldn't be alone. Come home with me for supper, and spend the night if you want." *I* don't want, she thought, but I can't walk out on her.

"I'll be all right. I've got something to make me sleep."

"Then come out with me for a walk or a ride and get some fresh air and some food in your stomach."

"Who do you think you are?" Monique shouted at her. "Coming in here like a bloody nanny and telling me what's good for me? I know what's good for me, and he's dead. He was all I had, and he's dead. I fought with him because of you and that kept me awake all night—I didn't sleep till daylight and then they woke me up to tell me he was *dead*." The word hammered at Alison. "And all the time I thought he was on the other side of that door." She pointed at the connecting door. "But he wasn't. He was *dead!*"

She burst into loud ugly weeping and Alison made an involuntary gesture, then withdrew it. She felt utterly useless and horribly guilty.

But why should I feel guilty? she pondered, driving home, having to concentrate on the traffic, the children walking or biking to the beach at the Braigh, and then the sheep. They conspired to go through my things; they followed me. If they hadn't come here on this insane errand, he wouldn't be dead by now. At least not on Lewis. What right had they to spoil things for me? I'll never be able to forget Norris's eyes. Never.

It was now early afternoon, and the children were out in Aignish, and the man across the road was ploughing up his garden spot. Mrs. MacBain was watching for Alison; she came over and opened the gate for Alison to drive in. "Ewen called me from Stornoway and told me about the accident, and that you were on your way. I rang a friend of mine at Parkend to watch out for you when you didn't come straight along," she said. "I didn't know what could have happened to you in that short distance."

"I'm sorry," Alison said. "But I couldn't come home without saying something to Monique Fournier. She was traveling with him."

"Oh, poor soul. How is she?"

Alison shrugged. "She's so alone, but she wants nothing to do with *me*. I don't blame her for that. And nobody in the world can make up for what she's lost." She yawned on the last word. The ground seemed to heave under her feet like the deck of the *Queen* in rough seas.

"Have yourself a long sleep," Mrs. MacBain said, "and then eat dinner with me tonight. That's what I came to say. Don't worry about the time. We'll eat when you're ready."

"Oh, thank you," said Alison with relief. "You don't know how good that sounds."

She drew her curtains against the afternoon sun, changed into her pajamas, and went to bed. Annie bawled at the garden gate while the other ewes contentedly ate new grass in the lower field. The sound of the tractor came faintly from across the road; children's voices calling like gulls, a dog barking. Alison went to sleep.

She awoke abruptly, with the knowledge that she'd been deeply asleep for a long time. It was quieter now but the sun was still strong, her curtains glowed with it. It was nearly seven o'clock. She felt rested and hungry, even though she remembered at once what had happened, and was in a hurry to get next door before it could swamp her.

After dinner they watched a documentary film. It was well-done, and close enough to Alison's academic field to engross her in spite of herself, and thus acted as a sedative. But the walk home in the sharp-edged air and aureate light of the late sunset of this northern island roused her up again. She wished she had something she could take that would send her to sleep without thinking first, but she had never used anything like that. She took Macdonald's *History of Lewis* to bed with her, thinking grimly that if she had to read all night it couldn't be helped.

She'd already begun reading the history had found it absorbing, but what with her writing and her traveling around the island she hadn't gotten very far in the book. Tonight it was a life-saver. When she reached the chapter on agriculture, the despotic tacksmen of ancient days showed up as good villain material, and she thought she could lull herself to sleep thinking about these new people and ideas. She was already beginning to yawn, sure now of her sedative, when she turned one more page, discovered a poem in Gaelic with its translation below it, and the last line was *By the ledges of the headland was the yellow-haired lad murdered.*

The historical explanation was a brief, brutal tale of greed and murder around 1785. Some men from Uig, on the western shore of Lewis, had sailed to Wester Ross on the mainland for timber. Coming back, they'd been caught in a storm and had gone for refuge into a bay on the southeastern side, and were murdered there for their cargo, timber being precious on a treeless island.

The crime was eventually discovered, and later the wife of one of the murdered men told how he had come to her in a dream. The poem was her account of his death, as he had told it to her.

There was no going to sleep now, and she couldn't concentrate any longer on reading. Norris's death had been a terrible accident, but it could be called a kind of murder; it was all the same for Monique. Now he came between Alison and the page, he filled her tired mind, he stared forever at the sky with the sun in his eyes when they were already blind. She heard him laughing, saw his hands playing with the sgian dubh, and again holding down the car window so she couldn't roll it up; she remembered that last long look before the lift door closed. There was no worst memory, they were all bad.

She got up finally, and turned on the electric fire in the living room, made cocoa, and went to work. She barged in on Alasdair and Catriona in the shepherd's hut, where they'd moved to the bed of dried heather in the corner; she shook them out of each other's arms and told them that no troop of loyal riders was going to descend *ex machina* and get them out of the glen with Alasdair alive and Catriona unviolated. Though after two nights of comforting Alasdair, Catriona was no longer a virgin, and was wishing she'd married him in the first place so as to have a clear conscience now.

I wish you had too, you tiresome little twit, Alison told her. Well, you'll have to bloody well get yourselves out of this mess, the way you got yourselves into it.

She got out her detailed map of the Highlands to plan their escape route and its dangers, and the end of the book. There would be marriage, of course, and a reduction in Alasdair's blood-lust due to Catriona's influence, and a new way of life that wouldn't threaten his Highland pride. Wasn't there some other family castle, abandoned and dilapidated, they could take over and repair with Catriona's money? With her map spread out on the floor and a lamp beside it, she journeyed quite happily for a long time and filled several pages with notes. When she was safely on the edge of stupor, she went back to bed and slept. She just barely remembered to turn off the heat first.

When she woke up it was late Sunday morning and it was raining, steadily but gently, without wind. She felt like a snail in its shell. She had no telephone to bother her, she had work to do and she intended to waste no time brooding over what couldn't be helped.

She prepared a large breakfast that would do for lunch too, took it into the living room before the fire, and began at once to decipher her new notes.

Mrs. MacBain looked in to say she was going to Stornoway for the afternoon and to have dinner with friends. Would Alison like to use the telephone first? Alison wouldn't.

"But you're sure you're all right, now? You wouldn't like to ring Ewen Chisholm?"

"He lost most of yesterday because of everything, and I'm sure he has plenty to do today." She added, "He's probably cursing the evil fairy that dropped this American and those Canadians on his doorstep."

"Somehow I don't think he'd mind this American ringing him up."

But Kay would, Alison answered silently, and she'll be there, I could swear to it. All snuggled in for a long wet cozy day. Murdo disapproves. I wonder what he does when she comes to stay. She shook her head at Mrs. MacBain, smiling.

Mrs. MacBain sighed. "I can't help it if I'm a romantic. I was born on St. Valentine's day." She left. Alison returned to her map. She found a suitable site on high land above the junction of two rivers, only needing a new name. She could create that with the help of the Gaelic place names listed in her primer along with their literal translations. She had just poured a fresh cup of coffee and settled down to this fascinating chore when the knocker sounded.

24

THE SIGHT OF MONIQUE on the porch jolted her like the concussion of an earthquake or a jet breaking the sound barrier directly overhead. She looked blind in immense dark glasses. She was wearing the white raincoat, and an elegant type of sou-wester. A taxi waited in the road, not Donald MacLeod's.

Before Alison could speak, Monique said, "Will you drive me back?"

"Oh sure!" Alison said. Monique waved to the driver, who nodded, and drove off toward the main road. "Well, come in, come in," urged Alison, unnecessarily since Monique was already on her way in. She handed her wet raincoat and hat to Alison, muttering "Thanks," and sat down on the hall chair to take off her boots. Mutely Alison hung the raincoat over the bathtub and brought Monique her fleece-lined slippers.

"Your feet are smaller than mine but these are warm, anyway," she said, incredulous about the whole thing. "Come in to the fire." She went ahead, hurriedly scrabbling up all her papers and taking the half-done sheet out of the typewriter. She bundled them all into the extra room and dropped them onto the bed. When she came back Monique was on the hassock close to the electric fire, holding her hands to it and rubbing them. She was wearing a tweed skirt and a heavy fawn sweater, and no jewelry at all, except for one ring and the tiny stones in her earlobes.

She had taken off the dark glasses. Her short hair gave no quarter to her ravaged face. It wasn't swollen now, but gaunt, and she wore no make-up except lipstick. She looked all eyes and mouth, the thick-rolled collar of her sweater hid her lean throat.

"Thanks for letting me in," she said in a painfully scratchy voice. "I didn't know where else to turn. Terry Danforth's no good, she just cries every time she looks at me, and Jake tries, but he's as uncomfortable as hell around where I am. I know he'll be glad to have me off his hands, but damn it, I don't want to be on anybody's hands! I wish I could tell him to just *git* and forget me, you know?"

"I know," said Alison. "But why can't you go away?"

"Oh, God, I wanted to be off this place today, but they're not through with the police red tape yet. And I couldn't stand that hotel room another minute. Funny, my coming to you. But I'm—well, if I told this to anybody else they'd think I was crazy." A dull color came into her face. "It sounds hysterical even to me. It's just what I *know*."

"Then tell me." The back of Alison's neck felt as if a cold breeze were blowing on it.

"You don't have anything to drink around, have you?"

"I'm sorry, no." It was a lie, but she suspected that Monique would drink down her whole bottle of sherry in an hour and then a very unpleasant genie would follow from the empty bottle. "How about coffee? Or tea?"

"Never mind, I've smoked enough and drunk enough. It's a wonder those pills didn't kill me last night on top of all the booze. I suppose I hoped they would. But no, I had to wake up this noon to the damn rain and the facts of life. Of death, I mean." She grimaced. "Don't worry, I'm not going to cry. There's no tears left. Besides, it's this other thing on my mind now. It never registered with me yesterday, but it still must have without my knowing it, because it was there when I woke up, and it scared me foolish." She hugged herself, rubbing her upper arms hard.

"Tell me," Alison said again, calmly, though she felt like yelling it. Monique took out cigarettes and lighter from her bag, and Alison put an ash tray on the coffee table. Monique blew smoke from her nostrils. She was making an effort to be composed and lucid.

"They said the car was found out of gas somewhere near the Stones, and he must have been walking. But listen!" Her bony face was both anguished and unbelieving. "He would never have gone near that place at night, he couldn't even stand it in the daytime! And he wouldn't tell me why, but maybe he didn't know, and that made it worse. Like wondering if he had some fatal disease, you know?" Alison nodded. Monique said, "I knew he'd be all right once I got him away from here, but *you* know all about why he was here, don't you?"

"Not much," said Alison.

"He got this Chisholm on the telephone and asked him to come to the hotel and talk, or even meet him halfway somewhere, on the road, but that's one stubborn bastard. He wanted to know what it was all about, and of course *he*—" She couldn't say Norris—"wouldn't tell him over the phone. So he got nowhere. Chisholm told him to come there if he had business, or questions, and I said I'd go with him, but he *could not* make himself go anywhere near those damned Stones, and he wouldn't tell me why."

"The tragedy is that what he was looking for isn't here. But he wouldn't believe me," Alison said.

"Oh, he thought you were honest enough, but that you'd been lied to. He knew all about lying. He was a master of the art. But he wasn't lying about the Stones. I wanted to go see them—hell, you have to go see what the place provides, such as it is—but he said I'd have to go alone. . . . No, he'd never have driven over there. We had a row in the Danforths' room after we took Terry up there—Oh God, I have to live with *that*." She was wrong about having no more tears. She put her hands over her face . . . "To part like that, and never see him alive again. Oh, dear Jesus," she whimpered.

Alison didn't move. Her own throat felt swollen.

"It was about you," Monique lifted her wet face. "If only Terry had decently passed out. But no, after she heaved up her dinner and I got her settled in bed, she went on a talking jag and began on you and him. You know, coy, shaking her finger at me, telling me I'd better lock him up, and beware of red-headed women and so forth. I should have ignored the fool but after a while she got to me. So I turned on *him*, instead of her. And after we got into it, she began to cry. I walked out and she was pleading with us not to go, she was afraid of nightmares, she said, and she was hanging onto his hand. Well, it was up to him to shake her off and follow me if he really cared. But he didn't come. I could hear the music downstairs, everybody having a ball. It made me feel worse. I went back in a little while and listened at the door. She was going on and on giving him her autobiography, and half-crying. He's so damn *soft*, except when it came to seeing how *I* was suffering on account of *you*."

Alison decided to ignore that. "It's hard to shake off certain kinds of drunks."

"I know. Maybe if he'd walked out on her she'd have yelled Rape. I went back to my room but he never came, and I don't know when I fell asleep. But when they woke me up, I knew that I'd never be able to take back the last thing I said to him."

"I'm going to make you something hot," said Alison. "How about cocoa?"

"All right." Monique followed her to the kitchen, talking hoarsely above the sound of running water as Alison filled the teakettle. "I swear he wouldn't have headed across the island to those damned Stones. Yet there he was. What could have got him there, and at that time?"

The last words came out in a kind of croaking shout as the water was turned off. Alison plugged in the kettle and set a tray.

"And that's why you're scared," she said. Her hands wanted to tremble.

"Yes. I keep wondering if there was some other reason besides the old book why he wanted to see Chisholm, and Chisholm didn't want to see him. He never told me all his business. I heard about that book only because I had to know what I was looking for in your stuff," she said candidly.

"And you didn't find anything, did you?" Alison asked, remembering as from years ago her fears that Mariana Grange had been discovered. "No letters of introduction, no material about the Book of St. Neacal, no directions."

"Only that you were coming here, and that was enough for him. I'd like you to know," she said with dignity, "that I never looked into your notebooks. I do have some principles."

"I appreciate that," said Alison, "but supposing what you wanted was camouflaged in one of those notebooks."

"I shook them for envelopes, but beyond that—forget it."

Alison measured the chocolate mixture into mugs and poured boiling water over it. "Have you eaten today? How about some cinnamon toast?"

"All *right!*" Monique said, as if to get rid of some trivial annoyance. "You were Chisholm's date that night. Did you know him before you came here?"

"No, but we've become acquainted because our fields are related, you might say." She put thick slices of bread on the grill in the oven. "If I lived here for long, I'd buy a toaster. But how I love that electric teakettle. I'm going to buy one when I get home."

"If Terry hadn't thrown her fit, he could have grabbed

Chisholm in the lounge before the dance. He was going to, he told me at dinner when we saw you two in that party. Then once we got stuck with Terry it was too late. God, there's nothing worse than a female drunk," she said with healthy disgust. "Though she claims now it was all her gallbladder."

Alison turned the toast. Monique leaned on the back of a chair and watched her. "He might have gone over there to see him eventually, if it was his only chance. He'd have had to go, wouldn't he? I mean, it was his job. I'd have driven him, and he could have taken one of my Valiums first. What I'm getting at is, if he had such a hell of a time to get there in broad daylight, he'd never have gone on his own at night. If I could believe he *did* go on his own—because something was so important he couldn't wait till the next day—then I could believe in a couple of drunks panicking, or some weirdo stoned enough to do what they did to him."

"Are you going to tell the police your theory?" Alison turned off the oven and took out the toast.

"They'll say I'm neurotic, or worse. I'm only telling you because I have to talk to somebody, and you haven't told me yet that I'm crazy, but maybe you're thinking it."

"No, I'm not thinking it." Alison spread butter and sprinkled sugar, glad to concentrate on that and not look at Monique. "Norris went with me to Callanish the first time I ever saw the Stones. You should remember; you came here while we were gone. Anyway, Norris took a chill at the Stones and then broke into a sweat."

"I remember! He came back in a bad way." She sounded almost happy in her relief. "Did he say anything about it?"

"Only that it was an allergy." She shook cinnamon.

"He didn't have any allergies."

"Then I met him on the road to Callanish one afternoon last week," Alison said. "He stopped me. He was positive he was onto something good, but he wasn't too keen about driving by the Stones."

"And he *didn't* drive by them. He chickened out. I knew he'd been talking to you—I could always tell. But the other thing—the physical thing—that was the Stones."

"They must have aroused old associations in him, maybe of some childhood terror that he couldn't consciously remember." She picked up the tray.

"Well, it's all academic now, as they say," Monique said bitterly, following her into the living room. "We're talking about him in the past, and I can't—I can't—" She sat down hard and doubled over, convulsively clutching at her flat belly. "What am I going to do without him?"

Alison put her hand on Monique's shoulder and pressed it, repelled and yet moved by the shaking and the ugly sounds of sobs wrenched up from the gut.

After a moment or two Monique went into the bathroom and blew her nose and washed her face. She came back with the shine powdered away, and fresh lipstick. "I don't know myself without my eye make-up," she said in a brittle voice, "but I never know when I'll overflow, and all that stuff running down your face ceases to be a beauty aid. Besides, it hurts when it gets into your eyes." She gulped cocoa thirstily. "I've cried so much I must be dehydrated."

"Have some toast."

"I can't swallow anything solid."

"Yes, you can."

"What do *you* know about it? Did you ever lose a lover?"

"No," said Alison, "but I was thirteen when I lost my mother, and I used to pray every night for weeks to die in my sleep. I was going to starve myself to help speed the process, but my cruel father wouldn't let me. Then one day I took a good look at him and decided we'd better stick together."

"Well, you know something about loss then," Monique conceded. She took a piece of toast. "But the point is, I haven't anyone to stick together with. *He* was the anyone."

"I haven't anyone now. Are your parents dead too?"

"They might as well be. I haven't gone to them for anything since I was about twelve, and my mother wouldn't explain menstruation to me. I moved out as soon as I finished high school. They still live in Quebec, they're Frencher than the European French, and I live in Toronto." Her voice faded. She looked into space. "Or did," she murmured. "I don't know how I can face that flat." Mechanically she began to eat the toast.

"Does—did he have family?"

"A sister who cast him off after he began to live in sin with me. I've let her know," she said drearily. "He'll be hers now. I can take him home, but afterwards—" Her eyes refilled and reddened, she shook her head hard. "No more of that, now."

"Are you going to the police with your theory?"

"I don't know. What if they ask me if I have any ideas? I'd have to tell them about your friend Chisholm. There has to be more to it than an old book, even a valuable one!"

Alison shrugged. "I don't for one minute believe that Ewen Chisholm knocked him down and ran over him—" the brutality of the words hit her—"and then put him in the circle. But if you think there's any chance of foul play the police ought to know."

"Maybe I'll tell them, then." She took another piece of toast, considered it. "But I won't mention Chisholm, though. Not yet."

She was running down now, and in the quiet Alison felt exhaustion taking over like a drug. The last hour had done it. She'd like to sleep again, but she was through with hoping that when she woke up it would have all gone away.

"You know why I could hate you?" Monique asked suddenly. "Not because he fell in love with you, but because you can sit there like a goddam lady saying how awful it is, but never shedding a tear for him. He was *in love* with you and it hasn't even touched you! You don't *care*."

"That's a lie!" Alison snapped at her. She felt the rush of tears like blood breaking loose. It was a horrifying sensation because she knew she couldn't stop it. She jumped up and went into the bathroom and locked the door and cried into a bath towel. At first she wept not so much for Norris as for his thinking he was in love with her and breaking Monique's heart; then she cried for Norris lying dead with his eyes open.

Finally the spasms died down. She bathed her face with cold water, and tidied herself up. When she came into the living room Monique was subdued. She was putting dishes on the tray, and she carried it out to the kitchen. "Thank you for the cocoa and toast. I needed that, as they always say when someone slaps them out of hysterics. Would you drive me back now?"

"Look, Monique," Alison said reluctantly, "if you can't stand your room you're welcome to stay here tonight."

"I can stand it better now, thanks. And I've got to start packing his things before my courage runs out."

Sunday was strictly kept on Lewis, and Stornoway looked completely closed down in the rain. Monique had nothing to say until they were almost at the hotel. Then she said gruffly, "Thanks for listening to me, and I take back calling you a goddam lady."

"You promoted me. Yesterday I was a bloody nanny."

She laughed shakily. "Well, you're neither. I mean, not in a nasty way. I don't know whether to talk to the police and take a chance on being held up on this place, or just get out of here as fast as I can. What would you do?"

"I honestly don't know." Alison swung the car toward the front doors.

"Still, if there's a chance of getting the bastard who did it, I wouldn't mind the risk."

"Whatever you do, wherever you go, I wish you luck," Alison said. "I'm sorry about everything."

Monique was getting out. She stood holding the door open, her head forward, looking in. "Why? None of it was your fault. Thanks for the good wishes." She slammed the door and walked into the hotel without looking back.

25

SHE COULDN'T GET BACK to work after she returned from Stornoway, and she didn't want to stay home. Monique weeping still haunted her living room, like the dripping ghost of the governess in *The Turn of the Screw*. Norris still lay dead in the stone circle with his eyes open. She herself went again into Ewen's arms with a passion that was indefensible when the reason for the embrace was a death; still, standing in her front hall that smelled of Monique's cigarettes, she wanted the embrace now, and her hands remembered the texture of Ewen's sweater when she put her arms around him and the hardness of his body under the coarseknit cables and diamonds. She wanted, in the place of stale cigarette smoke, the whiff from the peat fire, the scent of the wood, and of him. Simultaneously she wished she had never met him.

If it had been fair she'd have gone to Torsaig, even if it was late. Instead she went out for a walk. The rain was lighter now, but blowing in a thick drizzle. She had only gone a little distance, intending to go down to the shore, when a car came toward her from further along the Aignish road, slowing down at sight of her. It was the Land Rover.

"Good!" Ewen called out to her. "I was here a few minutes

ago and you were gone. I was hoping you weren't out for the evening. Get in."

"I'm too wet," she said stiffly. "I'll meet you at the house." She let him drive past her, and followed, feeling edgy and adolescent. He parked outside the wall and waited for her by the gate.

"I've just left Murdo at my aunt's in Swordale," he said. "I have something to tell you." He opened the gate and motioned her through.

"Please excuse the smell," she said in the hall. "Monique's been here, smoking, all afternoon." She propped the door open with the hall chair, and went ahead of him into the living room, more confident now, as if this were actually her own ground. She opened an upper pane in the big window unit to let a breeze sweep through. "There!" she said, turning around to him. "That's better. What did you want to tell me? Have the police found the driver yet?"

"No." He came and stood beside her at the window. The damp wind blew across their heads. "They've questioned everyone within a mile of the Stones. Nobody heard or saw anything, they were all respectably in bed from midnight on except for a couple who were at a dance in Bernera, and spent the night with friends there. On the list of chronic offenders, the types who are back behind the wheel a month after the Sheriff Court forbids them to drive for a year, no car shows any damage. They've had several anonymous phone calls about dangerous drivers that night, and they're checking them out."

He recited all this without expression and while gazing at the fog and drizzle. If he'd come only to give her this list of obvious facts which she didn't want to hear after an afternoon with Monique, and he was so bored with the telling of it, why the hell had he bothered? . . . He went on, still studying the fog outside.

"There's a new development. I imagine they'll be going

over the Capri inch by inch now, and having second thoughts about that empty fuel tank." Now he looked directly at her. "Kay came to tell me something this morning, and she shouldn't have, so please don't mention this to anyone. But I wanted you to hear it from me first." Kay's name was a gratuitous crack to the crazy bone or across the shin; it was ramming the little toe into a chairleg in the dark. It brought her ferociously alive, but cunningly, so that Ewen couldn't guess. She said, "I promise." Had Kay come for Sunday breakfast, or was she already there at breakfast?

Ewen, insultingly (or stupidly) impervious, said, "The undertaker found an injury that didn't seem to fit with the damage done by the car. So the Procurator Fiscal was notified and he ordered a post-mortem. It was done last night by a doctor whose sister talks too much but in this case I'm glad she does."

Kay was dismissed; Kay was nothing compared to what he was going to say, she was sure of it. Her lips felt glued together with dryness. She parted them with difficulty, enough to ask, "What was the injury?"

"A blow to the back of his head which caused a massive skull fracture and brain damage, and must have killed him at once. He was dead before the car ran over him."

She didn't immediately take in the significance of the head wound; her first reaction was relief that he hadn't known about the car. "I'm glad," she exclaimed, then was shocked, and stammered, "I—I didn't mean—"

"I know what you meant. I thought the same thing. If he had to die, at least it was quick. Whether or not I went up to the Stones when I saw his car, it wouldn't have made any difference to him. But we'll be questioned again. I wanted to prepare you for that. Everyone will who had anything at all to do with him."

"Well," she said numbly, "that's to be expected."

"It's a dreadful holiday for you."

"It's a worse one for Norris!" she retorted. She backed off

from him. "Ewen, are we talking about *murder?*"

He nodded. He was somberly compassionate, as if he thought she was too delicate or tender to accept the brutal truth. She could accept it all right; it was the reality of it that was hard to classify.

"I think I can shut things up now," she said. She went to close the front door, while he fastened the window. Walking away from him, performing some ordinary action, helped to adjust focus. At once she saw clearly again, though the curious and insulating sense of unreality remained. When she came back from the hall she said, "I told you Monique was here all afternoon. I stopped at the hotel yesterday, after I left you, and she was hostile. I couldn't blame her for that. Then she showed up here today, wanting someone to talk to. She couldn't have heard about the other injury, but she's very suspicious about his going anywhere near the Stones."

"Why?"

"She said he'd never have gone to them in broad daylight, let alone in the middle of the night. He was scared to death of them, in her words. Scared to death," she repeated. "The way we use terms like that, without even thinking. It makes me cold."

He switched on the electric fire, and motioned her into the big chair. He pulled another one over for himself, and took out his pipe. "Now tell me why he was afraid."

"He never gave any reasons. But the afternoon he was supposed to have gone to your house—the time I asked you about—he chickened out and went back rather than drive past the Stones. So Monique claims. I don't want to sound too credulous, I'm just passing along her story."

There was something peculiarly soothing about watching a man fill his pipe and then get it going. All that austere concentration as if nothing in the world mattered besides the kindling and nurturing of that little fire; as if it were a mystic rite and he was thinking sacred words that must never be said aloud.

"And on my first visit to the Stones," she went on, "when he insisted on going with me, he had chills and looked very bad. He wasn't acting. He couldn't have faked the way he looked."

"So that's why he wouldn't come out to Callanish," Ewen said. "I can believe it, I can even respect it. It gives the poor devil another dimension."

She leaned toward him. "What sort?"

He dismissed it with a wave of his hand. "We can go into it when this business is all over with. What else did she say?"

"When he saw you at dinner in the hotel he thought he could nab you sometime during the evening. But he had to carry Mrs. Danforth up to her room, and he and Monique had a fine old time with her because she was sick and drunk and crying, and Jake had gone somewhere." No need to tell Ewen about why Monique and Norris had quarreled. "She never saw Norris alive again. The next morning the police woke her."

"Poor woman," Ewen said. He sounded as if he meant it.

"She's tormented by questions, as well as the death—and of course when she was here she had no idea of this other wound. But what went on while she was away in her room, sulking and then sleeping, that she could have prevented? What about this whole secret section of his life? She hasn't a clue about it, though she lived with the man. All she knows is that he was found dead in a place he hated."

"And feared," Ewen said softly.

"Yes. She's willing to go along with the theory of the drunk or stoned driver but what was Norris doing anywhere near the Stones in the first place?"

"Does she have any theories of her own about it?"

"Only that if anything in the world could get him out to Callanish on his own, at night, it had to be something else besides an old book. After all, if he missed out on talking with you at the hotel, there was always tomorrow; she could drive him, and give him one of her tranquilizers if she had to."

"Something. else," he repeated, puffing away. "Something between him and me?"

"She didn't say."

"But it makes you uncomfortable, now that I've brought it up."

"Nothing of the sort!" she said with honest indignation. "But now that you've brought it up, I may be able to dream up some sinister connection."

He grinned. "You've got the damndest sense of humor!" she exclaimed crossly.

"At least you'll admit I'm a reasonable possibility. In some circles, if you'll forgive the pun, I'm believed to be edging my inevitable way around the bend."

"I'll admit nothing," she said. *The Demonic Keeper of the Stones.* She was blushing as if he could see the words, the human sacrifice, and all.

"You'll admit the question has been raised, and it will be raised again in official places. Through his play-acting and his fantasies this man has complicated our lives at the expense of his own." He pointed the pipe stem at her. "The tragedy is that if he'd mentioned St. Neacal to me just once on the telephone, I'd have had him off the island fast enough. That is," he added, rather spoiling his effect, "if he could have endured leaving you."

"*Me!*" She erupted out of her chair. "Let me tell *you* something! You don't know just how much of a fantasy this whole thing has been, and what I've had to put up with! I'll tell you why Norris Elliott followed me here in the first place, and if he fancied himself in love with me later, that wasn't what he had in mind when he bought his passage on the *QE 2.*"

Walking back and forth as she talked, letting the words come as they pleased on the fast freshets of passionate indignation, she told him the whole Harold Marshall story. She had his complete attention now, and his pipe went out.

"I've been trying not to be furious ever since I arrived on Lewis," she said at the end. "But I *have* been furious at being used like this, furious because what should be a wonderful experience for me has been tainted by these people. And then there's the confusion. I hated Monique for going through all my things, but I was sorry for her because Norris made her jealous. I despised him for thinking I'd be involved in this stuff, and for being so weightless and witless and amoral, but now I'm furious because he's dead. Quiet sneaky deals to cheat the internal revenue shouldn't be the sort of thing that ends up with a man dead, and a woman completely lost and desolate."

He got up and came to her and wrapped his arms tightly around her in a big hug. "Be furious, *mo chridh*," he murmured. "You have the right." She put her arms around him and her cheek against his chest and shut her eyes. Her outrage had been swept away by the flood; she was very nearly blissful now, even knowing the bliss belonged to the moment only.

"Are you ever furious?" she mumbled into his sweater.

"All the time. Pity poor Murdo."

"Does he allow tantrums? Or does he squelch you with lovely poetic Gaelic versions of 'Somebody got up on the wrong side of the bed,' or 'You could chin yourself on that lower lip?' "

She felt the vibrations of silent laughter in his chest. "He stalks out of the house in terrible dignity, and takes Maili so as to spare her innocent young ears." He held her off from him.

"Come along to my aunt's for tea," he said. She could hardly believe what she was hearing. After the first shock she said, "I'll have to change. Sunday tea on Lewis isn't just ordinary." She hoped this was the aunt who referred to Kay as the brazen besom.

"Get to it, lass," he said benignly. "I'll have another pipe while I wait."

This particular Sunday tea at Mrs. Munro's was attended by most of her family and its connections within walking or driving distance. Seniority went to the two Misses Morrison in their nimble and bi-lingual eighties and their brother, who was a weaver. There were men home from fishing for the weekend and two home on leave from the sea. There were wives, children, girlfriends, an engaged pair subject to a lot of joking. A young crofter couple had a placid red-haired baby which shared pride of place with Mrs. Munro's cairn terrier. Ewen now appeared to Alison in an enthralling new characterization as a family man. If he wasn't right in the middle of everything, he was still very much a part of the scene, smoking his pipe with the weaver and the seamen, while they talked the perennial politics in a way that should have burned off a good many ears in Parliament.

Dropped in to sink or swim, Alison swam well. There couldn't have been a better antidote to Monique and the fresh news about Norris's death. She asked what she could do to help, and felt she had known them all forever, she was so effortlessly absorbed into the group. She sliced bread, counted plates and silver and napkins, set the children's table, was followed around and questioned by a little girl in love with America.

After the meal, a fat man who looked as if he should keep a pub, but who was a bank manager, played the piano for singing. They went from Gaelic to English to Scots, and around again.

"I can't thank you enough," Alison told Ewen when he walked her to her door. "It almost makes up for all the other business."

"I'm glad you enjoyed yourself," he said formally. When he was like this, it discouraged her from being too familiar with him. She wanted to tell him she'd heard him singing, and liked his voice, but his manner kept her at a distance, as if he suspected he'd gone too far. No chance tonight of a farewell hug, or even a chaste and friendly kiss on the cheek. Besides, Murdo was out there in the Land Rover. She sighed.

"Goodnight and thank you again," she said, and reached inside the open door and switched on the hall light.

"Goodnight," he answered. "We'll go to Bernera tomorrow."

"We will?" She managed to contain her pleased surprise. "When should I be at Callanish?"

"Oh, meet me there at two. That'll allow us both time for a good morning's work."

"I'll be there."

"Goodnight, then."

She watched him go to the gate. She preferred not to imagine his reaction to what she was working on. He was probably doing a detailed analysis of some early texts, his pages heavy with learned digressions into the vagaries and nuances of successive translations. There'd be solid banks of footnotes and flocks of *ibids*. Remind me to sound a bit more intellectual now and then, and a little less *gee whiz*, she told herself.

She sat up in bed writing an account of the evening at Mrs. Munro's, describing everyone in detail, even trying to remember the songs, at least the ones in English. All the time she knew she was trying to build a wall between herself and the fact of murder, and that the wall would be breached as soon as she put her light out.

It was. She tried to deal with the invasion being analytical, but there was nothing to analyze. There was simply the fact, massive as the blow which had accomplished it.

She went to sleep finally because she was so tired, dreamed even more surrealistically than what was usual with her, and not enjoyably. She was still tired when she woke up at first light; she knew she had been dreaming of Norris but not how or what she'd dreamed, and she was drearily sardonic about it. He'd been so good at popping up when she least expected or wanted it, why couldn't he pop up in her dreams with some useful clue?

As the yellow-haired lad had appeared to his wife in a dream, she remembered suddenly.

> *My relatives are this year seeking*
> *and searching for me,*

While I lie in Gloomy Bay, on the
bottom of the pool.

He told how the men on shore killed the exhausted crew with their axes; he named his murderer.

Duncan, the mountain wanderer, attended to me;
The world is deceitful, and gold beguiles.
It was while climbing the hillside,
I lost my strength,
By the ledges of the headland was
the yellow-haired lad
murdered.

She wept with pity for Norris, and horror, for the act, and some pity for herself too. As a result, she went to sleep again, deeply for a few hours and woke up rested. The fact was still there but she was better able to get around it.

26

THE BIG ISLAND of Great Bernera, *Eilean Bhearneraidh*, was the land one saw across East Loch Roag from Torsaig. Ewen drove away from Callanish back along the main road to Stornoway, but only for a very short distance, then turned right onto a road new to Alison. When she had first come to Lewis, the aspect of peat bog, moor, pond, loch, stream, and rock, with or without sheep, were the same wherever she went. Now she was aware of subtle but pleasing variations in configuration and in the vistas that opened at each rise in the road or just around each slant or curve of rock.

In the rapidly shifting lights and darks of the open-and-shut day, colors ran through the spectrum like arpeggios on a Steinway. Ewen pointed out a pair of buzzards, drifting, circling, slipping sidewise on an upper wind. A small flock of sheep crossed a steep slope supervised by a dog, a very tall man with a shepherd's crook strode behind them; he was bareheaded, and his red hair flamed against the morning clouds.

It could be Tormod, she thought, and felt her world securely spinning on its private axis. Norris had retreated to another part of the galaxy.

They drove across a bridge over a narrow passage of salt water and were on Bernera. Three standing stones stood on a hill looking down on the approach; they were like guardians in a fairy tale, enchanted stones with powers of keeping out intruders by casting invisible barriers. They were first sunlit against ragged blue and white skies, but in the next moment they appeared almost black in their watchful silhouettes.

The island looked like a petrified upheaval dating from the earth's beginning. The tremendous surge that had become the mountains of Harris had been stopped on Lewis, but the land had been well churned before the rock chilled in place. The stone house on Ewen's property stood with the land rising sheer behind it. In front the terrain dipped away in a broad slope to the shore, speckled white with a neighbor's sheep, gilded by intermittent bursts of sunshine.

Beside the stone house the walls of the original cottage had been roofed over with corrugated iron, to become whatever it was needed for; right now it held Ewen's fourteen-foot boat.

The inside of the dwelling had been almost totally destroyed by fire over a year ago when a small oil heater had exploded. Ewen's tenant and his wife had been outside at the time, and the children in school, so no one had been hurt, but they had lost all their possessions, and Ewen had lost all of his grandfather's house but the shell. Now he had collected the necessary permits for rebuilding.

"We'll put more windows in and a bathroom, pipe in the water from the brook that comes down behind the house, and modernize the heating arrangements," he said.

"But you'll have a place for a peat fire, won't you?" she asked.

"Always. A man has to have a fire to stare at," he said solemnly.

"When do you start the work?"

"It depends." He left it at that. Having often given the same answer herself, she didn't say, "On what?"

"When Lord Leverhulme ran out of money and patience on Lewis," Ewen went on, "and gave the island to the people, not every crofter wanted to own his croft outright; it was cheaper to pay rent than to pay the rates. But my grandfather accepted the gift. He said that to be his own man, to have his own land free and clear, was almost worth what he went through in the French mud from 1914 to 1918, when he used to think he'd never see Lewis again."

"I'm glad he came home safe," she said fervently. Otherwise she wouldn't have been standing here with Ewen right now.

"He was a lucky one. In both wars Lewis lost far more than her share, in proportion to her population. So you'll see the wry smiles when someone says, 'You're so far from the world out here!' Well, it's not Tir-nan-Og, though some of the tourists and Sassenachs think so if they happen to hit here in a spell of fine weather. Let's go down to the water."

Tir-nan-Og, the Land of the Forever Young. Land of Heart's Desire. The Celtic heaven. Walking with him on the shore she thought wildly that it could be true for her but it was not likely to be. Unaware of the turmoil of resentment and longing behind her averted face, he talked of stepping the mast in his boat and sailing on summer afternoons that never seemed to end, and of going out on the loch in the long bright evenings to fish for mackerel. "There's hardly any night here then, you know."

She knew. She nodded and walked away from him. Something felt like a knife in her throat. He caught up with her and turned her around to him. "What's the matter?" he demanded severely.

"I'm homesick for Lewis already, and I'm still here." She made a mask out of a comic grimace.

"Oh, is that it?" His face softened. "What a trouble-borrower you are. You burn your bridges before you come to them."

"Oh, I know," she said with a sigh, still burlesquing it. They began walking again, like lovers with their arms around each other's waists. The sun flashed out again, the loch turned from bleak purple to brilliant cobalt. Across the water, white houses at Breasclete shone all at once among hollows and hillocks washed with green. Farther along that shore to the northwest, Torsaig was illumined by a spotlight and then vanished.

"Must you go back before summer?" Ewen asked suddenly.

"I've taken the cottage only through May," she said. He didn't respond to that and she felt bruised with disappointment. So they come and they go in his life, she thought. All except Kay. I wish I could be a brazen besom.

When they were going up through the field by a different track from the one they'd followed to the shore, they stopped to listen to a skylark. Alison had already heard them in Aignish, but each time it was a fresh and ravishing experience. There was a corncrake in Aignish too, but not many classic poets had written about corncrakes.

Today, listening and watching a skylark in Bernera with Ewen, she thought, Why do we go on storing up miseries for ourselves? I'm glad we don't have this kind of skylark at home.

"This is a genuine Leodhas skylark," Ewen said.

"Is a Leodhas skylark different from a Shelley skylark?"

"Of course," he said solemnly. "It sings in Gaelic."

If I were a brazen besom, she thought, I'd take his face in my hands now and kiss him, right in front of all those sheep, and he'd never forgive me.

"What are you thinking *now*?" he asked her.

"I'll never be able to learn Gaelic, and here's this smart-aleck bird showing off like mad."

He laughed, and they walked on. Did Ewen's arm around your waist or over your shoulders constitute a pass or was it merely comradely, or worse—brotherly? Why the hell couldn't you just *ask* and get it over with?

One thing was certain. She didn't want to go away from this place, even with its painful personal frustrations, back to face the fact that Norris had been murdered. As if Ewen guessed he said, "Murdo expects you for tea."

She didn't want to stop at Callanish either; she didn't intend to get cozily ensconced by the fire and the books and have Kay come in and regard her as The Strange Woman in *Proverbs*.

When they crossed the bridge to leave Bernera, she twisted around in her seat to look back at the three guardian stones. "Why do you think Norris was afraid of the Stones?" she asked.

"What you told Monique was no doubt the truth. An association with some frightening experience, maybe a recurring nightmare. Do you have one?"

"No, but I have a recurring dream that I love. It happens once or twice a year." She told him gladly about Rob Roy, it was such a safe and comfortable dream, and he was much entertained.

"It's a pity you've grown such long legs, you could have your Rob Roy now."

"No other pony could be Rob Roy," she said seriously, "because Rob Roy already *is*."

"Of course. I hope he'll forgive me for forgetting that."

"He forgives you. He has a very nice disposition. Rather like a Labrador's."

They both burst out laughing then; her tension was harmlessly relieved to the extent that she could think, Maybe he likes me because I'm such a restful change from Kay's bitter brooding. Where do you come from? Oh, you wouldn't know, a little hamlet called Bitter Brooding. Colonized by a lot of Ibsen characters who never got into his plays.

"There doesn't have to be any point to his death," Ewen was saying; for an instant of dislocation she heard the statement as a contribution to her own word-play. "It could have been a random attack, like a street crime."

"On *Lewis*?"

"Strangers come to the island all the time, my girl. Supposing he was out driving around after midnight because he couldn't sleep, and he picked up a couple of walkers, thinking they were local lads hiking home from a dance, and they turned out to be something far different."

"Was he robbed, do you know? If they were into drugs they'd take his money."

"Unless they were flying so high that money was no object. But his being left at the burial cairn like that—it's bothered me from the first. We all thought our drunken driver, with a friend, could have taken him up there with some idea that they were hiding the evidence; I've known drunks to come up with some pretty strange reasoning. But there has always been something else about this. Perhaps because I've met some damned odd types at the Stones in broad daylight."

"You mean he would have been a kind of sacrifice?"

He didn't answer, and her stomach began to crawl. Maybe a cup of Murdo's strong tea would be a help after all.

When they reached Callanish a dark green Mini was parked behind Alison's car. She knew it was Kay's, just by the way Ewen looked at it with a stony resignation, like someone in a Le Fanu horror story who knows he will be forever haunted by some nameless sin committed in Paris or Constantinople. Or, as in his case, Edinburgh.

"Look, you have guests," she said cheerily. "I won't stop. Thank you for showing me the croft." She was getting out while she spoke. He got out on his side and met her at the front of her car. "Alison, would you *wait?*"

"Hello!" Kay sang out from the door. Maili bounced out by her and rushed to Alison who cried effusively, "Hello, Maili darling, aren't you a nice girl today!" Then she looked up and said in her most polished classroom manner, "Good afternoon, Kay."

Kay walked by her without a nod. "I thought you'd never get here," she said to Ewen. She began familiarly to pick invisible bits off his sweater. "What *have* you been into, love?" Smiling, she was more than pretty, but there was something so forced and febrile about the smile that it would have made Alison uncomfortable under any circumstances. She opened her car door and slid in behind the wheel. Murdo was crossing the yard now, and she waved and wished him good day in Gaelic.

"That was very fine indeed!" he told her. "But you aren't leaving now, surely?"

"I'm afraid I have to." She spared herself a glimpse of Kay's satisfaction, but its aura was perceptible.

"Ach, now, I was counting on you."

"I'm sorry, I'd love to stay but I can't."

He looked her in the eye. "It's *I* that's sorry," he said with great feeling. A peal of rather theatrical laughter came from Kay.

"Listen to him! You've made a conquest, Alison!"

Without directly staring past Murdo Alison saw the way they stood, Kay's arm through Ewen's. And Ewen motionless; she'd have had to turn her head slightly to see his face and she didn't want to. Neither he nor Kay could see Murdo's face. He was looking her very hard in the eye; the message was plain. She shook her head. "I really must go. I'm sorry," she said again.

His disappointment showed briefly around his eyes and in the thinning of his lips, then he gave her a courteous nod that was almost a bow. He called Maili away from the car and Alison started it. She wanted to say something more to him, and nothing to the other two. But she'd always been mannerly, and manners counted here.

"Thank you again," she called to Ewen. "Goodbye, Kay." She managed it without looking directly at Ewen, and she did not want to look directly at him ever again.

She couldn't blame Kay for staking her claim; she blamed herself for being so gullible. It's that damned voice and accent of his, she thought in a rage, and the place itself. I'm making him into something he isn't because it's not enough for me to be in love with Lewis. Well, from now on it has to be enough, and I'm a damn' sight better off being in love with Lewis than with Kay Blair's wee mannie.

Enough of your idiocy, Dr. Barbour. What do you have in mind for your next book, Miss Grange? It's a pity there's no great spooky old house near the Stones, so why not design your own Hebridean island and your very own personal set of Standing Stones, and then you could incorporate that so-called shooting lodge on Harris—

It was all as strained and feverish as Kay's smile had been. But it beat drinking as a means of escape. The hangover wasn't so bad anyway.

27

WHEN SHE GOT HOME there was a note under her door, asking her to come across to Mrs. MacBain's. She did so, exchanging glare for glare with Annie. "I will not be intimidated by an arrogant sheep," Alison told her. "Kay Blair is enough for one day."

Mrs. MacBain told her that an Inspector Gilchrist had been trying to reach her. He'd left a number to call. "Have a cup of coffee first," she urged. "For all he knows, you might not be home until tonight."

"No, I'd better get it over with," said Alison. "My stomach's queasy enough now."

"This is a horrible business. Why must they keep going on and on about it, I wonder? What could you possibly know about it?"

"Well, I know him—*knew* him," said Alison. "That's the only reason there could be."

"It seems to me they'd be better occupied finding the car that killed the poor man. You look very tired. I hope he doesn't expect you to drive in to Stornoway. I don't know this officer," she said suspiciously. "From his accent I'd say he's from the northeast."

Inspector Gilchrist arrived at Alison's door in a half hour, accompanied by Sergeant Sinclair, who greeted her like a friend. The stolidity of the C.I.D. man seemed to express disapproval of such easy ways. He was a squarely built man with a soldierly bearing and a manner as barrenly official as if he'd been stamped out (in triplicate) by an IBM machine.

"I am conducting an inquiry into the death of Norris Mac-Vicar Elliot," he announced. His attitude was a help to Alison. It requested only the root details, and one felt it would not accept—would severely disapprove of—any lush foliage. It was a relief to discover the body in one brief sentence. The body was not particularly Norris when discussed with Inspector Gilchrist. It was an object, sometimes referred to as The Deceased.

No, she knew of no one with a grudge against The Deceased. He had never told her of anything like that. Her acquaintance with The Deceased was short. She explained how short, in another sentence; a compound one this time. The Inspector consulted his notes, and the natural world began to come back into the room as Annie serenaded the windows.

"It's a fine large voice on that one," Sergeant Sinclair remarked.

"That's Annie," said Alison. "She's hoping for a strupak. She's very tame. She was raised on the bottle."

A creasing at the corners of his eyes suggested an observation which would remain unspoken, at least in the Inspector's presence. Alison's mouth quirked in recognition. It was rather like exchanging signals behind the headmaster's back. When the Inspector cleared his throat she almost jumped.

"Mr. Ambrose Danforth," Gilchrist said, "saw Mr. Elliot at approximately twelve hours on Wednesday last, walking past Stornoway Town Hall with another man. Mr. Danforth had the impression the man had just arrived, either by plane or by ferry. The airline personnel do not recognize the description, and the *Suilven* crew don't remember him, which is not proof that he wasn't aboard. Then again Mr. Danforth might be mistaken in his impression." *Ambrose.* No wonder Jake preferred

Jake. Norris was no longer The Deceased, he had been restored to life; she watched him walking by the Town Hall with the strange man becoming visible in bits and pieces as the Inspector described him.

"He was shorter than Mr. Elliot; 'stocky' in Mr. Danforth's words. He was broad-shouldered; clean-shaven, with average coloring; wearing eyeglasses with heavy dark frames. He wore a tweed hat, a suit of hound's-tooth weave, and he carried a dark blue raincoat, a zippered satchel, and an attaché case."

The trouble was that he had no face. The dark-framed glasses under the jaunty tweed hat fitted over ears with a gruesome blank space between them.

"Miss Barbour, have you ever seen this man with Mr. Elliot?"

"The only person I've seen with him on Lewis is Miss Fournier, and Mrs. Danforth, when she was sick the night of the dance, as I explained."

Without a change of expression the Inspector pounced. "On *Lewis*, you said. You didn't see this man anywhere else with Mr. Elliot? On the ship?"

"He might have been on the ship; there were two thousand passengers and I'm sure I didn't see them all well enough to recognize them later. But I have never seen him with Mr. Elliot, as far as I know."

The Inspector stood up, put away his notebook, and thanked her. He walked out ahead of the sergeant, who gave her an encouraging nod and smile and a soft "Good evening."

So that was over and it hadn't been bad. She wondered if the police would advertise for the stranger if they couldn't locate him otherwise. They'd be bound to, wouldn't they? Just to eliminate him, if he turned out to be simply a new arrival who'd asked Norris for directions, or someone he knew from elsewhere whose presence here was the purest of coincidences. It was possible that he had been on the ship.

If it were something more than an accident, he could be Norris's principal, if a principal existed; or an agent of the same, come to tell him he was on the wrong track. But why go through all that time-and-money-consuming rigamarole when a wire or a telephone call would do? Still, if you judged by Norris's behavior, common sense was too much to ask for; a fine spray of lunacy glittered over the whole business.

Harmless lunacy, she'd thought until now. Sneaky, dishonest, but harmless, if you considered that to cheat the internal revenue was a moral obligation of the free citizen, like that of the Highlander to poach the landlord's salmon.

No. Whatever killed Norris wasn't the search for St. Neacal, she was sure of it. Either Ewen was right about random crime or Monique was right about its being something else which Norris hadn't told her.

But Norris was back in the house with Alison now, playing with the sgian dubh as he talked. She went quickly over to Mrs. MacBain's.

"I might as well tell you," she said. "It looks as if Norris was murdered."

After the first gasp Mrs. MacBain was admirably composed, and made drinks for them, which they sipped while Alison told her about the blow to the head. "I don't know how quiet it's still being kept, so please don't tell anyone about it. You know, while the Inspector was asking me questions, I did all right; he's so impersonal it's catching. . . . Maybe that's why he *is* that way, and he's really human underneath. But after he went it suddenly hit me that I'm involved in a murder."

"Surely not *involved*," Mrs. MacBain protested. "Just knowing the poor soul doesn't involve you."

"I *feel* involved. He's haunting my house right now."

"Oh, my dear child!" said Mrs. MacBain. "Listen, I've a cousin at Leurbost I've been neglecting. Let's drive over there for the evening. I'll ring her up this instant."

If the people at Leurbost had heard of a mysterious death at the Standing Stones, they didn't mention it. They were hospitable and good company, and after they finished exchanging family news with Mrs. MacBain they wanted to talk about America because they had connections there. For Alison they were like the flames of the fire at the mouth of the cave, keeping the wolves away.

She and Mrs. MacBain drove home late in a deep twilight that turned the world into one ordinarily seen only through purple glass. When Alison went to bed, she found pleasure in remembering Bernera. She imagined the clustered or isolated houses huddled comfortably under the violet sky, lighted windows here and there glowing rosily, the sheep quiet as boulders with the lambs tucked in at the ewes' sides; the broad fields going down to the loch, melting into it really, so from the stone house one couldn't tell where the land left off and water began, while across at Breasclete a few lights pierced the thick soft dark like stars.

It'll be like this when I'm old, she thought drowsily. I'll reminisce and imagine, and think how we walked on the lochside like lovers, and listened to a Gaelic skylark.

And came home to Clytemnestra in the dooryard.

She flounced over onto her side and went sternly to sleep.

In the morning she was up early, and working; she had decided to go into Stornoway as soon as the stores were open and look at tweeds and sweaters, and take care of a few more names on her gift list. She'd have lunch there and then drive over to Torsaig. It seemed weeks since she'd been to the village, and the circumstances called for a visit to Charlie Macaulay. If he was gone again, she might catch Morag Murray at home in the Manse, and if that didn't work out, she'd be contented enough to walk up the glen to the cemetery. If Charlie hadn't scared her with his talk of adders, she'd have enjoyed sitting on the stone threshold of the roofless cottage. After all, Torsaig was what she had come for, and the thought of driving down the hill to it was like an exile's dream of returning home.

It was a cold, coruscating day with a spanking east wind. The trees embowering the castle were all in their fresh new greens, and the flag snapped above the battlements. She was lucky enough to find her favorite parking place open, conveniently close to the Ladies' and the restaurant across the street. She returned to the car with her parcels after a couple of hours of browsing and buying, and stowed them away in the back seat; she turned to cross the road for a cup of coffee and nearly walked into Ewen and Murdo.

From their amused lack of surprise she realized they'd been standing there watching her. She was so violently startled to be caught like this, she felt like the victim of a practical joke, and her first reaction was to rage at them for ambushing her. If the unexpected sight of Ewen could do this to her—and it was all for nothing, this adolescent green-sickness—she was indeed in a bad way.

She laughed, but in a proud, angry manner, her face flushing after the first chill. Ewen kept on smiling, faintly but annoyingly. Murdo said soberly, "We thought you saw us."

"How could I? You were invisible, I swear it. You know spells, Murdo. Admit it."

"Here, on Cromwell Street, with a reverend gentleman not three cars away?"

"He's not yours, Murdo," Ewen said.

"Never mind, he wears the collar."

Everything had settled back into place with only a slight jolt. "Come along," Ewen said, taking her arm. "We'll have some coffee." She crossed the street between the two. They found a window booth where they could look out across the pier and see the castle towers above the tossing gold-washed green. Murdo went to get their coffee, and tea for himself. Alison felt embarrassed to be in such close quarters with Ewen, not knowing how she should be with him; she kept looking out the window at the people coming around the corner, and suddenly a man glanced in at her, stopped and nodded, then made gestures toward the door and went on.

It was Jake Danforth. He came in and over directly to their

booth. "Well, how are you?" he asked, surprisingly animated, even hearty. He acted very glad to see her.

"Oh fine," she answered, feeling inane. "How's Terry feeling?"

"Oh, that damn' gallbladder . . . " He thrust out a hand at Ewen. "Jake Danforth. I'm in electrical contracting. Some of my products are involved in getting out your North Sea oil."

Ewen stood up to shake hands with him, civil if not effusive. "Ewen Chisholm."

"I hear you're a professor, like Alison here." He beamed indulgently at her.

"And this is Murdo Morrison," Alison said as Murdo arrived with the tray. "Murdo, this is Jake Danforth."

Murdo set down the tray. More handshakes. "Say," Jake said, "we're all more or less touched by this business about poor Elliot. So do you mind if I crash this kaffee klatsch? I'd like to talk about it with somebody besides the police, if you know what I mean." He didn't wait. "I'll get myself a cup of coffee and be right back."

When he'd gone, Ewen said to Alison, "*Do* you mind?"

"I suppose not. There's no escaping the mess, it seems, and Jake's the one who saw Norris with a strange man."

"Ach yes, the strange man," said Murdo. "Inspector Gilchrist told us about him. But there was nothing that I could recognize about the sound of him." He glanced at Ewen, who shrugged and went on stirring his coffee.

"When did the Inspector come to see you?" Alison asked him.

"Late yesterday. He viewed me with a very cold eye. I expect any time to be mentioned in the Stornoway *Gazette* as 'helping the police with their inquiries.' A fine euphemism that doesn't fool anyone."

"But on what grounds?" Alison asked. Ewen gave her an ironic sidewise glance, and she thought, Oh Lord! Monique's spilled everything she knows, suspects, believes, and imagines.

Her stomach felt very cold and the hot coffee made it feel worse, as if in an instant everything was going to come up like a geyser.

She was casting around in a panic for an escape route before she disgraced herself, when Jake came back with coffee and doughnuts, and squeezed in beside her. "This is one hell of a thing," he said flatly. "There's no doubt about it, somebody had it in for the poor bastard, and dollars to doughnuts it was the man I saw him with, but he's vanished into thin air. They were both riled up, too. I could see it. I told the Inspector."

Ewen looked steadily out the window. Murdo clucked softly, but Alison thought it was in disapproval of Jake's blunt summation. She gave him a small, one-sided smile.

"What's Monique saying?" she asked Jake.

"Nothing to me. Nothing in detail, that is. She sort of smolders, poor kid, and says she has plenty of ideas of her own, but she's telling them only to the police." He leaned back. "Hell, it stands to reason she must know *something* about Elliot, she's been living with him. He could have been mixed up in all kinds of stuff." He said confidentially across the coffee cups, looking from Murdo to Ewen, "It wouldn't surprise me if he made a good living on blackmail. I hope I'm wrong, but when a man has no visible means of support, you always wonder. I've met some strange birds in my lifetime. Used to surprise me, but not now."

"The young man could have belonged to a well-to-do family," Murdo suggested.

"Maybe you're right," Jake conceded. "But where are they?"

"Monique told me there's a sister," said Alison. "She didn't say anything about money, she was only concerned with losing him." She looked down at her cup. Jake sighed.

"Yeah, poor kid. Another thing; nobody knows when he left the hotel that night. Talk about *my* candidate vanishing into thin air, so did Norris till he turned up dead." He dropped his voice tactfully on the last word. "The place was so busy with that dance going on, people coming and going, the hall porter couldn't keep track of anyone."

Alison thought, In just about one minute I'm going to shove him off that seat and tramp over him and go out that door and head for Torsaig. . . . At that moment Ewen's foot touched hers under the table, twice; she knew the second time wasn't a mistake. She glanced at him quickly and caught the ghost of a twinkle in an otherwise impassive face.

His head turned enough toward the window so Jake couldn't have seen. She consciously relaxed her stiffened rib cage, took longer breaths.

"Where does it go from here?" Jake asked. "It looks like a dead end to me. This character I saw could be out of Scotland and back across the Atlantic by now, or over in Zurich counting his money. I keep looking for him, but—" He shrugged.

"It's been only three days," Ewen said. "They've barely begun."

"But will it all be left to this Inspector Gilchrist?" Jake asked. "Don't they call in any big ones?"

"If it's necessary. We have access to the Constabulary Headquarters, in Inverness," said Ewen. "Or even the Big City boys like the Glasgow C.I.D. Forensic scientists are available to all of Scotland."

"What's your equivalent to the D.A. around here?"

"The Procurator Fiscal. He will prepare the case when there's a case to prepare. Murder would be tried in the High Court at Inverness."

Jake shook his head. "Nobody ever hurries around here and you don't have any crime to speak of, so I suppose there's a kind of morbid satisfaction in getting hold of something like this, and they make the most of it. I could see this Gilchrist was feeling a real sense of power. I asked him when we could go, and all I got was a fishy eye. I'd like to get the wife to where she could have that damned gallbladder taken care of."

"It may come as a surprise to you," Murdo said softly, "but

often in Lewis people have their gallbladders removed, and survive."

"I'm not putting the place down," Jake protested. "Oh no, nothing like that! It's just the way the wife is. I tell her she thinks more of her doctor than she does of me. At least she believes every goddam word he says, and that's more respect than I get from her." He laughed. "Well, any minute now there could be a break, huh? Your police must be in contact with the Canadians if they know their business, and I guess they do, all right. . . . Procurator Fiscal," he repeated, as if tasting the words. "Sounds good, doesn't it? A lot more impressive than District Attorney."

He slid out of the booth. "Well, I appreciate rapping with you, as the kids say. I can't talk to the wife because she's just about bawled her eyes out over this thing, and poor Monique's out of bounds. I wish somebody would show up to look out for her—she's going to crack into a thousand pieces one of these days."

He left with a cheerful wave. They said nothing until he was out the door and across the street. Then Murdo sighed. "He's right. With the stranger gone, what have they got?"

"Me," said Ewen pleasantly, "because she will have been telling them that he came to Lewis to see me. I don't know why I thought I wanted this coffee."

"I've tasted better tea," said Murdo.

"I think I'll go back to where I was before you two ambushed me from behind the telephone kiosk," said Alison, "and then I'll decide not to do what I was about to do then."

"Are you deliberately confusing me?" Ewen asked her.

"I didn't think that was possible. I thought you were the expert in misdirection." She smiled at him to make it a joke and headed for the door. He caught up with her as she went out, and held her elbow.

"What did that last remark mean?" he asked close to her ear. It was a very busy corner. Two fishermen coming across from the pier grinned and went out around them, a woman pushing a pram looked at them with smiling and candid interest.

"Nothing. It seemed to fit the moment. You do blow hot and cold, you know," she added boldly.

His fingers tightened. "Where are you going?"

"To get some crackers—biscuits to you—and cheese, and drive to Torsaig."

"I'll go with you."

"Fine," said Murdo encouragingly behind them. "It will take this foolishness off your mind."

A neat small woman with a shopping bag called out to him in a sweet chirp of Gaelic and he turned to answer her. "Come along," said Ewen. "Murdo's in for a good long blether. Have you the keys, Murdo?" he called back.

Murdo nodded and waved them off. "We'll take your car," Ewen said, "but I'll drive. I can't abide having someone else drive me." He was walking her fast across the street. "Where were you thinking of getting your strupak?"

"Whatever I say, you'll say somewhere else is better, so you choose."

"This way, then."

Kay shot out of the chemist's as if she'd been just waiting for the target to move into position. She wore a cape of scarlet wool that suddenly blew out around her in a great shrieking burst of color; that and her voice assailed Alison's eyes and ears simultaneously. She clasped Ewen's arm with both hands. "When will you ever learn?" she asked in a fierce low voice. "Why do you run straight back to them like a dog for more punishment? You're in trouble because of these outsiders. Don't you *realize* that? *Americans!*" she hissed at Alison. "I hate them! They're nothing but trouble wherever they go! And this great fool of mine—" She dug her fingers into Ewen's arm and her tears ran over.

Of mine. These words clanged so loudly through Alison's head that they drove out all the others. Ewen's face was granite, ignoring the girl's frenzy; one felt that if she could have driven her nails through the tweed sleeve and into his flesh to draw blood she would have done so, and still he would have ignored her. He didn't look away from Alison.

Passersby didn't display amusement or interest this time, they walked quickly past, looking straight ahead or into the shop windows. Alison hadn't seen Murdo crossing the street between the cars, but he was all at once there beside Kay, saying, "Now, lassie."

"Don't now lassie me!" she cried, and tried to drive him away with an elbow in his chest. But he got a big arm around her, softly coaxing all the time, and with a sudden shameful surrender she burst into noisy sobbing. Still Ewen didn't look at her, and Alison was repelled by that. Alison turned blindly and stepped off the curb, and heard the violent stop of a car. She waved at it without seeing it. She ran the rest of the way to her own car, back where it all began.

As she was groping in her pocket for her keys, from the corner of her eye she saw Ewen coming past the small cars parked beyond hers. She dived into the ladies' room, and took her time, trying to calm herself down, then went into the waiting room and looked across the street, but the scarlet of Kay's cape was no longer there. She couldn't see Ewen either and wondered quite dispassionately if he'd taken Kay away after all. But when she went outside he was waiting; he'd cleverly stayed out of range of the windows. He took the car keys from her hand, unlocked the car, saw her in, and went around to the driver's side.

"Now," he said grimly, "we are going to have this out."

28

HE DROVE OUT of Stornoway as if toward the Braigh and Aignish, but turned off to the right long before that, and along a narrow side road until they'd left the houses behind, and parked on a track which led down to a small sheltered bay with a high sandbar across it. A fishing boat lay keeled over on the sandbar and some men were working around the rudder. They were far enough away to look very small. Besides them, there were only a few gulls to be alive in the scene.

Alison tried to concentrate on how she would describe the effects of the wind on the water, in the hopes of settling her mind. She hadn't looked once at Ewen since they drove away. She was alternately angry and miserable. I've had enough of this, she kept saying to herself. Damn it—Those sequins run like a school of fish. They shimmer, scatter, and are gone.

"I think you are owed an explanation," Ewen said.

"No. I've had enough of this. I want nothing more."

"Then I am owed the privilege of your attention while I give my explanation."

She sighed to show her martyrdom and continued to stare straight ahead.

"To begin with," Ewen said composedly, "I may be a great fool, but I'm not a great fool of hers. I accomplished it all by myself. She's a nurse, you know. A friend of mine met her while he was in hospital, and afterward they had an affair. I found out about the affair by accident. He was married and I liked his wife very much, and I was their son's godfather. Once I knew what was going on it was difficult to behave with them as if everything was the same, and I was relieved when they told me they were going to New Zealand. The only dreadful thing about it, his wife told me, was leaving their friends behind, especially me. For him, of course, it was far from dreadful. He wanted to be rid of Kay, and he'd begun regarding me as Banquo's ghost."

Alison could well imagine how uncomfortable the friend was under Ewen's cold eye. That was not to say she believed his story; she had the depressing, tiresome sensation of being conned again. The betrayed puppy bruising its nose.

"It was a great relief to me when they left," Ewen continued. "Some others, including students, had seen him with Kay because he'd been so reckless, and it would have been only a matter of time before his wife heard something. I was glad she was spared that. So it was over, and I could stop thinking about them." His words were concise, composed, dry of drama. "In less than a week Kay was on my doorstep, wanting his address. I told her I didn't have it, which at that moment was literally true. Mind you," he said with some warmth, "I wouldn't have given it to her anyway. She was not a young girl who'd been seduced, she knew he was married when they began the affair and that he had no intention of leaving his wife. This doesn't excuse him, but they were equal partners in the venture, and now it was over."

He paused, and something seemed called for. "Mm," said Alison, watching the far-away figures of the men around the boat on the sandbar.

"Still, I was almost sorry for her when she told me she hadn't known he was going; that was true, she was white and shocked when she heard it from me. She'd thought he'd gone to London for a few weeks, and then she heard something about New Zealand but she didn't believe it."

"If she loved him," said Alison, "the pain was pain, even if she'd asked for it. Sometimes you're sure you can handle whatever comes, and then it's so much worse than you expected." She was still gazing ahead, but she knew he was looking at her. Let him infer what he wanted, she thought defiantly.

"She called me the next week to see if I'd heard from him. I told her the best thing she could do was to get on with her life and forget him. The next thing was a telephone call from her, late one night. She'd swallowed an overdose of something or other, had second thoughts, and was frightened out of her wits. I went over there, and called an ambulance; she'd had an abortion in some backstreet manner, had gone home directly afterward, lost a frightful amount of blood, and tried to kill herself."

"Were you blamed for all this?" Alison asked, finding it hard to move her lips and speak in a natural voice.

"I was spared that, because her landlady knew I wasn't the man, and some of the nurses knew, too. They remembered him as a patient and they'd seen the beginning of the affair. During it Kay'd been so carried away with herself that she'd talked about him a good deal. But now that it was over, and she was recovering from that, a botched abortion, and her suicide attempt, she wouldn't go home to her family, and she wouldn't listen to anyone else. So this fool—I told you I was one, didn't I?—had some peculiar delusions about moral duty. Call it conceit if you want to. I thought I might talk her into using common sense. She used to talk so longingly of death—how she wished she'd had the courage not to call me—and I thought that if I turned my back on her, knowing this, that I'd be responsible if she succeeded next time."

Alison forgot to stare bleakly at the outside. She said eagerly, "You couldn't turn your back on her and she knew it. So you got the Old Man of the Sea for your very own."

"Yes, and I hated it. To hell with my moral duty! Given a second chance I could gladly pass by on the other side. I tried to make her loathe the sight of me. I never sympathized; I exhorted her like some grim old Calvinist to mend her life and get on with it, to be useful, to stop being sorry for herself. Good God!" He wiped his forehead.

"And she loved it," said Alison. "She had all your attention. You could have called her a streetwalker, a whore, and she'd have been blissful. She thought you were fighting a powerful attraction, and she was just looking forward to the day when the citadel collapsed and she had you where she wanted you. And you're unmarried, too. And you believe in honor. What a gem!"

He gave her a sardonic grin. "When she was on her feet and fit to work again, I advised her to get away from the city where she'd been so unhappy, find a post in another part of the country, make new friends. I told her, very bluntly, that I had no more time for her, she'd already had far too much of it." He wiped his forehead again. She had never seen him so upset, and it shook her. "I never knew where or when she was going to appear. I forbade her my rooms, and I'd receive parcels through the mail, things she'd bought for me—expensive cufflinks, for one example. I felt like a bloody fool, returning them like some Victorian heroine who refuses to be bought. Then she'd ring me up and reproach me. I'd hang up on her."

"Was she the reason you took this leave of absence?"

He groaned. "Yes, for all the good it did me. She answered an ad in a newspaper and had a position here and a place to live before I knew she was on the island. Then she looked me up."

"What did you say when she appeared?"

"What do you Americans say? Get lost! Or words to that effect. And she said, 'I can kill myself in Lewis as well as in Edinburgh.'"

"Oh, Ewen." She sagged in her seat. "What did you say to that?"

"Not what I thought, which was—I'm ashamed to say—'I hope you do a better job of it this time.' "

"You should be proud of yourself for not saying it. It shows tremendous willpower, because if anybody ever asked for it—do you really believe she could do it?"

"Oh yes," he said matter-of-factly. "I've tried to reason with her, which was probably a mistake. Yet if I told her that whatever she did was of no consequence to me, I'm sure she would be happy to die, just to spite me."

"Knowing it *would* be of consequence to you. You'd feel guilty, and for no valid reason. I feel guilty about Norris, and I'm as innocent as you are about Kay. . . . Monique makes me feel guilty, but she doesn't intend to, and she'll go away eventually. . . . Ewen, is this what you meant when you said one shouldn't be victimized by the dead? That it was enough to be victimized by the living?"

He nodded without speaking. Now he was the one who watched the men by the boat as if his life depended on taking in every detail.

"But good Lord, Ewen, how can you live like this?"

"I don't know," he said. "And now that—" He turned toward her. "Now that you—" Ewen stumbling? "When I came home from the dance Friday night, Kay was what knocked that car out of my mind. Oh, I didn't lie about the telephone. My friend had rung up, right enough. But Kay was there, she'd come directly from night duty and had been waiting. She'd been arguing with Murdo, and she was all ready for me. We had a tremendous row, during which she told me she couldn't live without me and she wouldn't, and that some day I'd give in and I'd never be sorry. Telling you this makes me as much of a fool as the bloody cufflinks did."

"You're blushing," she said. She reached for him as he moved toward her, their hands collided. Laughing weakly they embraced, as if one or the other of them had just pulled the only other survivor onto the raft, or up to the life-saving fire in the freezing forest.

"What are we laughing at?" she mumbled in his neck. "It's not funny."

"What are we going to do with her?"

"I won't deny that several useful ideas have crossed my mind. All of them bordering on criminality." He kissed her temple and then rested his cheek against her head.

"We have to be basic," said Alison. "Get rid of your conscience. I don't mean altogether, but even if in some cultures you're forever responsible for the life you save, it's not so in ours."

"Which I've told myself many times. I've told her too."

"But you think she'd really do it."

"She has me convinced."

"She has you blackmailed. But she's created a scandal, so you're not afraid of that."

"No. Half of Lewis is convinced that she's my mistress and that I've come home in disgrace. Of course a suicide, successful or not, wouldn't improve the picture, but I'm past worrying about that."

"So it's your neurotic, overworked, egotistical conscience. You're almost sinfully proud, you know that, Ewen Chisholm? You think you are singlehandedly keeping her alive. And for what? What good is she? It's so stipulated that she has a presumably immortal soul, so we don't have to go into that. But from the angle of pure objectivity, of what use is Kay Blair?"

"None to me, certainly. But—from an eagle's-eye view of pure objectivity—she is a good nurse. In that phase of her personality she's kind, patient, and gifted, especially with the old and with children. If she ever gave up nursing, it would be the profession's loss."

"So you're saving her for humanity," said Alison.

"Bloody hell!" he said savagely. "Humanity be damned!

The name of the disease is cowardice. I'm afraid to take a chance and have to live with the outcome."

"If she's going to come back and haunt anyone," said Alison, "it should be the chap in New Zealand." She pushed away from him so she could look him in the face. "Why not now? If you have the address, give it to her. She'd be off like a shot."

Slowly he shook his head and she subsided. "You're right. He wouldn't marry her no matter how much hell she raised with his life, but she thinks she can wear you down. Oh, Ewen," she murmured, "we've got to think of a way." He put his hand under her chin and raised her face and kissed her, slowly and abstractedly. Then he said, "Do you still want to go to Torsaig?"

"Not now. I want to stay right here, where no one can find us." The indifference of the gulls and the men working on the sandbar was like a blessing.

"There's something I should do," he said, tightening his embrace as he spoke.

"There's always some *thing* to find us, if not some *one*. What is it, or can't you tell?"

"I'll drive you to Aignish, and take a bus to Stornoway."

She sat up and spoke briskly. "You can get out in Stornoway and I'll drive myself back to Aignish."

"No. I don't want to leave you that soon."

"Then why must you, if you'd been free to go to Torsaig with me?"

"It's something I was putting off." He started the engine.

When they were back in the traffic, she said, "What did Murdo do with her this morning?"

"Took her to her flat, I imagine. Made tea, and talked to her not like a Dutch uncle but a Highland one. He can't put sense in her head but he can calm her down, I've noticed. When I got home from the dance, Murdo went to bed but he got up when the battle had raged for an hour or so, and the first kind word from him she burst into tears. I left them alone in the kitchen and after she'd blubbed for a time with Murdo soothing her in Gaelic, she was in fit condition to drive herself home."

"It's too bad you don't know of someone in her family who can manage her like that," said Alison.

"She's been very canny about keeping her family a secret. They're in a tiny village somewhere in the south, that's all we know."

"Tell me one more thing. Were you engaged to the daughter of an advocate?"

He laughed for the first time. "My dear aunt's favorite fantasy! No, we weren't engaged. We went out together, we liked many of the same things. We were good friends."

"Any carnal impulses?" Alison asked.

"Very. On both sides, and indulged. But I wasn't what she wanted for a husband, and if I'd had any ideas of my own about marriage at that time, she didn't fit them."

She didn't dare ask, *And do you have ideas now?*

She made an omelette and a salad. It was the first meal she had ever served him, and she was surprised that she could put her mind on preparing it. Just having him in the kitchen, smoking his pipe and watching her, made her feel as if she were falling painlessly apart and turning into feathers; fingers, feet, wits, and all.

Ewen was different now. Not more effusive either in language or actions, but as if he had been warmed from the core. Kay was present, but in a new context. Alison kept thinking in the back of her mind, behind and under everything else, that she would wake up early in the morning with the solution, the way she woke up with the solutions to problems in her writing.

While they ate, they talked about themselves, as people do when they want to become better acquainted; saying in effect, *I am like this; are you?* They took a long time with the meal, and neither Norris nor Kay was mentioned. After they ate she spread out her map of Lewis and he pointed out the places they would visit besides the Butt.

When he finally said he must go, and where, it was almost a relief. Inspector Gilchrist wanted to talk with him again. "At my convenience," Ewen said ironically. "Of course I may end up answering the Procurator Fiscal's questions, instead. There's evidence that Elliot was transported in the back seat of his car to the place where the car was left, and the petrol was probably siphoned out to make it appear he'd run dry. It may be up to me to convince everyone that I didn't accomplish all this sleight of hand, with or without Murdo's or Kay's connivance, after I left you that morning."

Alison tried to ignore the claw in her belly. "Murdo will swear to the truth. What about Kay? Do you think she's reliable?"

"I'd prefer not to be indebted to her for anything." He began to laugh. "Oh, Alison, I find it all incredible. Don't you?"

She said somberly, "Kay's right. I've brought you only trouble."

"You've brought me *you*." He took her into his arms and kissed her all over her face. She held onto him with her eyes closed, willing him to stay but finally loosening her embrace in a conscious effort not to cling. He'd had enough of that.

"Let me drive you in," she said. "Oh, I forgot. You do the driving."

"You can walk to the corner and wait for the bus with me." He sounded indulgent, and she hated it, but she accepted. They walked to where the Aignish sign seemed to grow from a lump of blossoming gorse, and crossed the road to wait. The wind had dropped and the mid-afternoon sun was strong; it paled the yellow of the gorse blossoms, and the road coming down the hill had a hard, bluish, steely glare. There was no one else in sight anywhere, only the sheep and the birds. She stood with her hands in her pockets, wanting to put one through his arm so they'd wait for the bus like any courting couple. He looked off across the fields to Broad Bay and said,

"I forgot to mention Tolsta Head. I'll take you there. It's a beautiful color today, isn't it? Like grapes."

"At home I'd say like blueberries," she answered. "Monique is hysterical, you know. Norris told her about the book, but she can't believe that's the only reason he wanted to see you. He must have kept things from her in the past, so she suspects everything now."

"Well, you can't blame her, can you?" he asked mildly.

"What about this Procurator Fiscal? It sounds Roman and deadly, as if you'll end up in an arena with lions."

He smiled. "MacLean's a decent sort. He'll be easier to talk with than Gilchrist, I know. He may decide in time that there's no evidence on which to build a case. And then again, as Danforth says, there could be some news from Canada at any time."

"Or the mysterious stranger has been discovered," said Alison.

"And he's an innocuous little man traveling for a Glasgow firm that makes souvenir tea towels and dolls dressed in kilts. He's never been to Lewis before and was asking for the nearest bar or the cheapest hotel."

It was perverse of him to be so merry when she felt so awful. "Jake said they were both angry," she said resentfully. He shrugged.

"Maybe the man made an improper proposal."

"Oh, *Ewen!*" She turned angrily away from him and he caught her arm and pulled her back. The bus was heard up beyond the brow of the hill. She said, "I've got such a rotten feeling and I don't know why. It's not as if you were Gary Cooper, going out to walk that lonely street in 'High Noon.' "

"Hardly," said Ewen. He kissed her. "Look what you've done to my sense of propriety," he said. The bus driver's smile was broadly obvious behind the windshield. As the door slid open and Ewen swung aboard, she called over the rackety clamor of the engine, "Can I call you tonight?"

"Yes!" he shouted back. The driver said, "Aye, he'll be holding his breath by the telephone." The door shut and the bus charged on; the women on their way to shop looked out smiling, and one waved.

She walked back feeling tired and deflated. Mrs. Mac-Bain's car was gone, it was too early for the children to come from school. She could walk on past her house and probably see some woman working in her garden or taking in the wash, and pass the time of day with her over the gate; she could go down to the shore and sit on a rock and watch the water. She could walk up over the hill. She could get in her car and drive somewhere. She wanted none of it, but at this moment she didn't want Ewen either. She knew she had to reduce the day's happenings to manageable status and deal with her new set of terrors.

When she reached the house Annie, who earlier had been peacefully grazing at the far end of the croft, greedily saluted her, and two whom Alison now knew as Betty and Connie joined in. They'd been named alphabetically as they arrived. These three were the oldest and had an uneasy union because Annie pulled rank on them so often.

Now they jostled each other and tossed their horns recklessly about, all staring hard at Alison. "Oh, go eat grass," she called and went inside. She lay on her bed watching the gulls and trying to think but the process consisted of circles like the gulls' flight, and she relinquished the day with a sigh and fell asleep.

29

S HE WOKE with a start, shooting up out of the dark into a room blindingly full of the westering sun. She had a dreadful belief that she'd missed something of fatal significance, and blundered dizzily off the bed, then remembered she was going to call Ewen and the evening had a long way to go yet. She lay back until she came fully awake, stretching her legs and arms, and wriggling toes and fingers. Then she got up and washed her face and brushed her hair, and went next door.

Mrs. MacBain wasn't back yet. Alison walked up and down the garden path, waiting for her, feeling the pressure mount up until she was ready to drive into Stornoway and use a public telephone, just to be doing something.

Finally she went back into the house, thinking that in five minutes she would take the car and go. Immediately there was an uproar from Annie, which meant that Mrs. MacBain was driving in.

Nobody answered at Callanish. "Oh, it doesn't matter," she said. "I just thought of something I wanted to ask him, about the chapel on St. Flannan's Isle. I was trying to write down everything he told me about the fishermen's traditions, but there was one I couldn't remember."

She suspected she wasn't fooling Mrs. MacBain, who was being extremely busy putting things away in cupboards. "Oh, wait a bit and try again," she said airily. "They're likely just outside. I'm going to make some coffee. My friend, whom I love dearly, simply cannot make good coffee, because she never drinks it. Also, she's starving herself thin like one of those saints on pillars, not for God but because her husband is due home on leave in two weeks. So I'm famished for something sweet."

Alison felt too fidgety to sit, let alone eat and drink, but she played up gracefully, and found that the coffee and tarts helped. At least she could wait twenty minutes without visibly twitching.

Still no answer. Over Broad Bay there was a sunset that called for flights of Valkyries with appropriate music. Mrs. MacBain showed her pictures of a round-the-world voyage she'd made on her husband's ship, with the two younger children. She still made several trips a year with him, though he was now on the less-spectacular Atlantic run. Why did almost everyone's else's life seem infinitely rich compared to her own, Alison wondered feverishly.

Why had she chosen to find her love (to quote Mariana Grange) in the context of a murder and a man and woman obsessed with each other like Sinbad and the Old Man of the Sea?

She tried the number again, and Murdo answered. At once she felt out of breath with relief. "Hello, Murdo," she said in a strained light voice. "It's Alison. Could I speak with Ewen?"

"He's not here, *mo ghaoil.*" Murdo sounded troubled.

A crippling cramp succeeded the breathlessness. "Is he all right? I mean—he's not been arrested or anything like that?"

"Ach, no!" Murdo even laughed. "Nothing like that. But it's just I can't tell you where he is right now. Would you want him to ring you when he comes in?"

"No, it's late now, and I'm at Mrs. MacBain's. I'm going home to bed. But thank you."

"You're very welcome. Say good evening for me to Jean MacBain."

Alison passed on the message. Then she blurted out, "If you heard what I said—about Ewen being arrested—it was sheer idiocy. But they keep questioning him about Norris, because Monique has a bee in her bonnet about him. She's sure there's some mysterious connection."

"But the police and Mr. MacLean will take her state of mind into consideration. The whole thing will be dismissed for lack of evidence, wait and see."

"That's what Ewen says. But I wish I could have talked with him tonight."

"Now don't lie awake worrying," Mrs. MacBain said. "Because it will all be for nothing."

People always said, *Try to relax*, or *Don't lie awake*, as if you had any control over it. Well, perhaps some fortunate souls did have the gift of self-hypnosis. She wasn't one of them. What do you *want*? she demanded of herself. You know about Kay now. But that's *all* you know. She was haunted by the verse Jamie Scott had quoted one night:

> *Had we never wooed sae kindly,*
> *Had we never loved sae blindly;*
> *Never met and never parted,*
> *We would ne'er be broken-hearted.*

In fractured dreams she always came back to the Stones, and Norris and Ewen moved interchangeably among them. There was weeping too, she couldn't tell whether it came from Monique or Kay. The dreams became nightmare when Norris turned on her the face she had seen staring blindly up at the sky. He walked toward her and she woke herself up with her strangled cries. She was out of bed a little after midnight, trying to pick the dreams apart, hoping the horror would grow less. Why was there no stranger in her dreams? There should have been the one or ones who had killed Norris and left him there.

She drank a glass of sherry and it acted quickly on her, as alcohol always did. She went to sleep again, was awakened by the chorus of ewes hailing Mrs. MacBain and their special feed. She had a terrible taste in her mouth, but the last few hours had been sound, unbroken sleep. She thought first of Ewen and then of Torsaig. When she saw Ewen again, if she ever did, maybe she would be rational about him, but away from him she felt as if she'd lost all her bones and turned into a stranded invertebrate. Perhaps Torsaig would give her back her identity.

It was another fine day. Now that the weather had settled, everything else was horribly unsettled, including her stomach. She ate a kind of breakfast and set off for Torsaig. She kept her eyes averted from the Callanish sign, but she was hoping she'd meet the Land Rover.

At Torsaig a covey of small children were kicking a soccer ball around in the road by the loch, refereed by Nick the golden retriever from the Manse, which meant two of the children were Murrays. Nick's decisions were disputed noisily but not savagely by a mongrel collie. Other dogs including Peadar watched excitedly from behind gates. Peadar gave her an hysterical welcome when she stopped the car, and almost at once Charlie was in the front doorway, beckoning her in.

"I was going up to the cemetery first," she said over the gate.

"Ach, don't be worrying about it. It's been there a good many years, and it'll be there tomorrow unless the Last Trumpet sounds tonight."

"I don't know where Christina's buried at home, but at least I can visit her parents' graves for her."

"And Tormod and Eilidh appreciate it, but they wouldn't mind you stopping first. They're not going anywhere. You've never tasted Peigi's oatcakes, have you? Stand back, Peadar, and let the lassie by."

Peadar obeyed, and returned his attention to the football game. Peigi was already filling the teakettle, laughing with welcomes as if Alison had made her day. There was knitting heaped on the kitchen table and when Alison apologized for interrupting work, Peigi shushed her. "I was just wishing for a cup of tea myself. There's no hurry about that, it's for a Sale of Work for the Lewis and Harris Piping Society, over two weeks away."

They had warm oatcakes with butter and cheese, and big cups of tea; Alison was always hungry in this house, even if she'd hardly been able to face food an hour before.

"It was on the radio and in the paper about the poor young man at the Stones," Charlie said.

"You found him, we heard," Peigi said. "Did you know him before that?"

"Only slightly. He was on the ship." Something else about this house; she could speak of Norris as if he and his death were a long way removed from her.

"They gave a description of a strange man," Charlie said, "but I'm thinking it could be anyone. Everyone watches the television now. They know how to commit a crime and to disguise themselves afterward."

"And not leave fingerprints," said Peigi. "Even I could commit a crime and not get caught," she went on complacently, and then added, "I *think*. The police are very clever at finding loose hairs or lost buttons and guessing the whole thing."

Charlie shook his head. "It's a very mysterious tragedy. Whatever was he doing at the Stones at midnight and past?"

"He was brought there, Father," said Peigi. "Isn't that what they think?" she asked Alison.

"Yes. He'd never go there on his own. He hated the Stones from his first sight of them."

"And he was very wise," said Charlie. "For some, the Stones are not a good place to be."

Alison agreed after her nightmare wanderings among the Stones, but on principle she'd never admit it. "I'm still going to walk it from here," she said, "when I can figure out what to do about getting back here for my car."

"You don't want to spend too much time there," said Charlie. "Surely there's much more to see on Leodhas."

"And I want to see it all, but there's something about the Stones that fascinates me. And if Christina walked there from here, that's what I want to do. On the night of a full moon, if possible," she added mischievously. Charlie looked at her over his tilted glasses and shook a thick forefinger at her.

"Ach, it's pagan!"

"Me, or the Stones?" Alison asked, and Peigi laughed, but Charlie sighed at the willfulness of youth.

"If Iain Uilleam was alive now at Callanish he'd have likely seen the death before it happened."

"Do you believe in second sight?" Alison asked him. He brightened.

"I do. Mind you, you don't hear so much of it nowadays. But I remember a family here in Torsaig. They were all a little—" He tapped his temple—"But they were second-sighted."

"Yes, yes," Peigi murmured. She was knitting a child's red pullover.

Charlie gave Alison some examples of the local family's gift: "If gift it was," he added. "Sometimes it was more of a curse. If one of them saw a funeral they'd have half the village in a terrible state of worry."

"Do you know if my MacLeods might have had second sight? Did your father ever mention it?"

"Now that I wouldn't know," he said. By now she thought she could tell when Charlie was being elusive, and Peigi's quick glance up at him from her knitting confirmed it.

"Oh well, it doesn't matter," she said carelessly. "I wasn't about to claim that I had it, or any psychic powers whatever.

But I was wondering whether it was hereditary or not."

"That's what they say," Charlie agreed ambiguously. "Did I ever tell you about Torsaig's own ghostie?" Alison hoped it was going to be the young minister, but it turned out to be a Viking whom she suspected Charlie of inventing on the spur of the moment. The way Peigi kept shaking her head at her knitting needles convinced her. But it was a grand story, and Charlie's telling of it was pure poetry.

He went out to the gate with her when she left. The football game had ended. The dogs had quieted and the children from the Manse and a third child were riding their small-sized bikes on the empty road.

"You look healthier than when you came this morning," Charlie told her. "There's a bloom in your cheeks. It's good to know I can still do it."

"You've put a bloom on the whole day for me," she said. "You and Peigi both."

He looked gratified. "Will you be going away up the glen now?"

"Not today, I think. Not now."

"You'll not be going around by the Stones?" he asked shrewdly. "After your sad experience with the poor young man?"

"That's one reason why," she said honestly. "I had nightmares last night about them, and him. If I stay away, I'll be letting bad dreams control my life, you see."

"Ach yes, and at high noon with sunshine, they can do you no harm," he said grudgingly, "but what would the other reason be?"

She waited, then said, "Ewen Chisholm."

"So that's how it is! Tell me, *mo chridh.*" He lowered his voice, though nothing was nearer than Peadar and Mrs. MacArthur's curious goats. "Have you found out what he's after?"

"Peace and quiet to do some writing," she said. "That's all."

Charlie nodded. "That's what he'd tell you." He could manage to sound as if he was agreeing while strongly doubting. It might be a useful talent if she could cultivate it. But annoying.

"I believe him," she said cheerfully. "And besides—I like him." She winked and Charlie couldn't help laughing.

"*A Dhia*, it's a mystery to me why the lassies choose as they do."

"Well, there's only one yellow-haired lad named Charlie Macaulay and he was taken long ago."

"And more's the pity," Charlie called after her.

At the Stones she parked in her usual spot and walked quickly to the circle before she could lose her courage and her resolution. She stood looking at the spot where Norris had been, and deliberately tried to remember every detail. Up to now the death and her reaction to it had been of far more immediacy to her than the way he died and at whose hands. She had not yet been afraid of the murderer, it was as if he didn't really exist. Standing there in the noon light, with the massive silence emphasized rather than lessened by the long sighs of the wind, she thought, this is where his head was, and here were his feet. Someone left him here, someone with no face or voice I'd recognize, with motives I couldn't possibly guess though I could imagine anything. And we may never know, any more than we know why the Stones are here.

Maybe the killer himself only hazily remembered what he had done. Maybe he was having nightmares that he would never tell.

"*Madainn mhath*," someone said. She jumped as if an elusive cuckoo had spoken. Murdo was standing across the circle from her, leaning on his shepherd's crook. He said regretfully, 'I'm sorry for startling you. I said 'Good morning.' "

"I was thinking about Norris," she said. "Why and how."

"The poor lad," said Murdo. "He meant no harm to anyone, I'm sure. Come down to the house," he urged. "He's been working at his books all day, it's time he left them."

"I'm sure that's when he's happiest. I couldn't interrupt him."

"Ach, he's not that happy."

But she smiled and shook her head. He seemed ill at ease. "It would make *me* very happy if you would come away now."

"Are you like Charlie Macaulay, who thinks there's danger in the attraction of the Stones?"

He smiled at that. "Tearlach MacAmhlaidh is out of his time. He should be bard for some great old chief of our past."

"Did the great Neil MacLeod have a bard?"

"He didn't need one. All the MacLeods were poets themselves. In their own way," he added dryly. "Which might not have been yours and mine, or Tearlach's."

"So I've been reading. Someone was a poet, whoever told first about the Shining One coming up the avenue. And the priest-king in his robe of feathers, with wrens flying about him."

He said somberly, "But we don't know if that was poetry or fact, do we?"

"I'd like to call it fact. An American writer said, 'If we meet no gods, it is because we harbor none.' "

"That is very true. I couldn't have said it better myself."

"Why is the cuckoo the bird of the Stones, instead of the wren?"

Maili hurtled into the circle, gave Murdo her first respectfully joyous greeting, and then rushed to Alison, who went down on her heels to take the dog's head in her hands.

Ewen came behind her. From where Alison crouched he looked very large against the sky. "I was at my work, and suddenly developed a rampant case of second sight," he said. "I saw a red-haired woman walking among ancient stones."

"You didn't!" she said in astonished pleasure.

"Well, to be truthful, I didn't see her until I came through yon gate." He smiled. "But there's no doubt that some powerful influence urged me up and away from my typewriter. Are you and Maili staying down there indefinitely?"

"We're spellbound, that's all." Alison stood up and Ewen reached out unnecessarily to steady her. "Murdo and I were just talking about gods and *you* appear, though without the feather cape and the wrens."

"I use them only on the proper ceremonial occasions, not for noon on a week day."

"He was always a modest laddie," said Murdo. "I'll be leaving now." He did, with Maili overtaking him. Ewen was still holding Alison's arm. He took hold of the other one. "Come away from here," he said softly.

"Yes," she agreed. "I came to exorcise something, but I don't know how well I've done, even with the help of Murdo and Maili."

"It's no spot for a lovers' meeting." He led her away from the circle, out behind the highest stone, and there he took her into his arms. But he kissed her as if his mind was on something else. To focus it on her she said, "I tried to call you last night."

"Murdo told me. I'm sorry I wasn't there."

"I was wondering how your meeting went."

"It was all right. Listen, about second sight. There's something I want to tell you—it's been niggling at me ever since I heard Elliot's full name. Norris MacVicar Elliot."

"What about it?" she asked, perplexed.

"He joked about being a Sassenach, and the Elliots are Lowland, right enough, but MacVicar is a Highland name. Now, love, this is just a fancy of mine, so humor me, and don't stare at me as if I've gone round the bend." He gave her a little squeeze. "When I heard that name MacVicar I knew I'd read something strange about it, somewhere. So I've been hunting up the reference and I've found it. This family long ago was famous for being second-sighted. My source quoted an old manuscript." He took a little notebook from his hip pocket and read out a phrase. " 'The surprising gift of prophecy inherent to that race of the MacVicars for many ages.' This version is spelled with two c's but that doesn't matter."

"I don't know why that quotation makes me feel odd," said Alison, "but it does. What are you getting at?"

"I'm a Highlander. I don't have second sight, but I believe in it. What I am wondering now is if on his first visit to the Stones with you that day he saw himself lying dead in the circle."

30

"OH, EWEN," she said on an outgoing breath. She'd have backed away from him but he held her. "That's a grisly thought."

"Shouldn't I have told you? Does it upset you that much?"

"No, I'm glad you did. There has to be an explanation of the way he felt about the Stones, and that's as good as anything. Right here at the Stones, and on this island, it's very easy to believe. But dear God, I'm glad *I* don't have it!" She laughed shakily. "I asked Charlie Macaulay if Christina's family did and he wouldn't say. Well, if they did, I'm glad those particular genes didn't come down to my father and me."

"And now we might as well forget it," Ewen said. "We have no proof that Norris had the sight, so we can't even use the incident for scientific purposes. Come away from here now, and I'll tell you where I was last night." He walked her toward the gate above the farmhouse.

"Having a social evening with the Procurator Fiscal?" she asked brightly, trying to put Norris out of mind. He laughed.

"That would have been much simpler altogether, even if he'd been asking me to prove I did not kill the man. No. I was with Kay."

Alison was unprepared and her hand tightened on Ewen's arm before she could prevent it. He put his free hand over it. "I took her to dinner and then we drove to the Castle grounds and parked overlooking the harbor, and talked."

They had reached the gate, and stopped. Sheep watched them from the other side; a black lamb was tearing around by himself and soon infected the others with his infant high spirits.

"Or rather *I* talked," Ewen corrected himself. "I told her that she had a life of her own to do as she pleased with, and so did I, and that was how it would be from now on. I have no responsibility for her behavior; if she wants to throw away her life to make a point when so many dying people—and she's known them—would give anything to keep their lives, that's her own business. I have no part in it, and she has no part in mine. I've tried to say something like this God knows how many times before, but somehow it always degenerated into a furious sermon on my part and hysterical threats on hers."

"As we'd say at home, she had you buffaloed. How did you quell her last night, then? By the power of the eye, like a good sheep dog?"

"In a manner of speaking." His mouth twitched. "I threatened her. I said if she opened her mouth once while I was speaking I'd strangle her. I flexed my fingers as I said it. She went white and put herself over as close to the door as she could, and didn't even breathe, as far as I could see. When I finished she said, 'Will you please take me home?' I did. I said 'Goodnight,' but she didn't answer. I expect," he said dryly, "that she's left an incriminating note. I hope you're prepared for it."

"I don't believe she left a note because I don't believe she's killed herself or even faked an attempt. Did you lie awake all night worrying about it?"

"I lay awake," he said, "wishing you were in my arms."

She was so astonished at her reaction to this that she

blushed uncontrollably, and he held her off, laughing at her. "And I thought you were *shy*!" she said accusingly.

"Do you understand now what you've liberated in me?"

"I'm beginning to understand more and more about Highlanders." Between desire and anxiety she was tremulous; she wanted to burst into tears, or hoots of laughter; it was terrible.

The dog barked suddenly down below, as if someone had arrived, but from here they couldn't see if a car was at the front of the house. She could think only of the police. "Maybe they've found Jake's strange man," she said hopefully, over the fright trying to lock her throat. Ewen had a large calm.

"It could be anyone."

"No," she said. She had to feel her throat, it hurt so. "I always knew that when I found someone to be in love with, something would take him away at once. My life has been a series of departures. Other people's."

"No, no, my darling," he said softly, hugging her.

"We have to go down and see," she said. "It's all changed now. He's still here; nothing exorcises him. He'll be here until we *know*."

She was ashamed of herself, burrowing into his coat. He stroked her hair.

"All these months that madwoman has been driving me out of my mind, and then you showed me what an idiot I'd been; because I wanted you, I had to act. Do you think I'd let anything separate us now? We'll go down there and you'll see that it's all right, it's not Inspector Gilchrist to take me in."

"Don't joke about it," she said miserably.

"Who's joking?"

"I didn't mean to fall apart on you."

"I loved it. Come along." He kept an arm around her. He was always propelling her somewhere for her own good. She wondered if the time would ever come when she'd balk. She imagined Highland wrath. *Woman, don't provoke me!* She wanted to giggle.

They met Murdo in the yard, feeding the twins. Even with a bottle in each hand and the two tugging away like sailors pulling for the shore, he was more dignified than usual. He nodded toward the house and said something in Gaelic. It did not sound favorable.

Kay waited for them in the living room, standing by Ewen's work table and holding the sgian dubh. Alison had a sickness in the gut thinking Kay was going to stab herself dramatically before their eyes, but she put the knife down and turned to confront them, staring at Ewen with a wounded longing which seemed both shameless and pitiable.

She said, "I have something private to say to you about that night, Ewen."

Alison's hand twisted in Ewen's with a life of its own but he clamped tightly on it.

"Look at you two!" Kay said. "I saw you coming in, hand in hand like lovers. *Are* you?" Her voice was shaking. "You can't answer that can you? Or won't? And she's a stranger, a foreigner who's brought all this trouble on you and you swallow it like a fool."

"Alison has a right to be here," Ewen said quietly. "There's the grave of more than one Leodhais to prove it. And she didn't bring this death to pass, but through no fault of her own she's been involved in it. So whatever you have to say about that night, let her hear it."

Kay folded her arms tightly across her chest and tucked her shaking hands under her armpits. "I went to the police this morning and I cleared you, Ewen. At least I have if they don't think I'm daft, as you and Murdo do."

"How could you clear me," he asked courteously, "when it's only my word that the car was already there when I came home?"

"When I was waiting for you, Murdo tried everything to get rid of me. He lectured, he scolded, he preached." She laughed scornfully. "I thought he expected you to bring her back with you, and if *she* spent the night with you Murdo the hypocrite would be pleased enough; it wouldn't be sinful for *her* to think of it."

Alison was sweating. Locked in Ewen's hand her fingers were cramped and aching. His face had that granitic look and she was divided between pity for the tormented girl and sympathy for him.

"Get on with it, Kay," he ordered her.

"I walked out on him and I went up to the Stones. I didn't go inside. I leaned on the gate thinking the False Men was a good name. All men are false. I saw a torch in the circle, and at first I couldn't be sure that's what it was, it kept flickering and disappearing as they moved around." Suddenly she was lifted out of her desperation and carried on with her story, giving it quickly and vividly. "I heard something. Not actual voices and words, but the sense of them, you know?" For the first time she took in Alison, who nodded.

"There was movement, and faint sounds. My ears aren't spoiled by all this mad disco and rock noise, and on a quiet night here you can hear the grass growing. . . . Then someone swore, the way they do when they crack a shin or an elbow, but it was cut off quickly. It was lovers out there, I thought, coming up with rugs from the car, to get themselves engaged at the Stones and seal it with a bit more than a kiss. Whoever she is, I thought, the baby'll likely be under the wedding bouquet when she goes down the aisle on her father's arm." She threw up her head. "I wouldn't stay within a mile of such actions! I came away."

Dying of envy, Alison thought. The wedding bouquet, the baby started before or after, it wouldn't matter as long as she had them. Well, she could have them; but not with Ewen.

"And then, when I was halfway back here, I heard a car start up, and drive away."

"If you'd told Murdo about hearing someone at the Stones," Ewen said quietly, "he'd have gone up there to see if there'd been vandalism, and he'd have found the body. If it was there then."

"I wasn't speaking to the *bodach* by that time. Do you doubt me?" she demanded. "Do you think I invented it all for your benefit?"

"No, I believe you, and I appreciate your going to the police."

"They were very polite," she said with a malicious smile. "They must have been humoring me, telling me it was a great help."

"I'm sure they meant it."

"No, they were humoring me. They all think I'm mad. I'm beginning to think so myself."

"Your patients don't. Their doctors don't."

"But *you* do! You've made it very clear! You've left me no more pride than that drunk who used to run about Queen Street Station in Glasgow rummaging through the refuse bins."

"Kay, Kay," he reproached her. Water sparkled in her eyes and she braced her head back as if to keep the water from spilling. She marched out. Ewen looked after her, slowly shaking his head.

"She'll be all right," said Alison with more confidence than she felt. "Oh hell, Ewen, you deserve everything you get if you let her lay that guilt on you." Then as the Mini charged off up the road she went to Ewen and put her arms around him. "I'm sorry, I'm sorry!" she said. "I sounded like the worst kind of bossy, interfering woman."

"You told the truth," he said, "and if I can't take that, how much of a man am I?"

Across the hall the kitchen door opened and Maili bounded into the sitting room. Murdo came more decorously behind her. "I've a Scotch broth simmering that would make your teeth water," he said.

31

THEY SAT at the kitchen table and had bowls of soup with thick slices of bread and butter. Shonnie watched with slumberous eyes from his favorite chair. Maili lay at a polite distance pretending to doze with her head on her paws. Murdo was for frying up a second course of chops and chips, but Alison and Ewen wanted nothing more; the scene with Kay was very much with them, and Alison couldn't help thinking, "What if—" and then bracing up with a deliberately callous, "So what?"

She offered to wash the dishes, but Murdo refused. He stacked everything and went out to work in his garden. Ewen drove Alison around to Uig; they passed the turn-off for Great Bernera and traveled up the western side of the great Loch Roag to visit a friend of Ewen's, a weaver who lived in a small house tucked into the flank of a hill as snugly as a lamb to its mother's side. Outside the mouth of the cove lay the whole western ocean, but inside, and at the very feet of the weaver's house, there was a stretch of sand bank from which he had dug a considerable number of Norse artifacts. The earlier ones had all gone to the government, but he was keeping his latest treasures to admire for a while before turning them in.

Here was yet another world encapsulated in the larger one of Lewis, and the marvel was that twenty-five miles or so of moor and loch could make such a difference. Fingering the long gold pin with its coiled head, the bracelet, and the iron blade whose handle had disappeared, Alison could lose herself in wondering who had worn the ornament and why the blade was with them. Who had last handled them before Ruari found them?

And what about a find as magnificent as the famous ivory chessmen of Lewis? Rivalry—skullduggery—and a heroine smuggling the treasures away in the style of those true Scottish heroines who'd saved the crown jewels from English hands or their husbands from the gallows? She was reluctant to place Fiona at the Stones since Norris's death, so what about this set-up? The weaver was attractive too, a rangy blond with a Nordic sea-going appearance.

Later they went out to the weaving shed, and Ruari showed her how the famous tweed was woven; he was working on a chevron pattern of soft reds and rosy tans. A friend of his drove in and joined them for tea. In fact, she laid it out and did the pouring. She was stout, with black eyes and a high-colored complexion, smiling and at ease in the bachelor's house.

Ewen told the story on the way back to Callanish. "They have been courting for years. But she was left a house in Cliff that she won't give up, and he refuses to leave *his* house, so there they are."

"They seem happy enough."

"By now they'd likely find it hard to endure living together under the same roof."

" 'The very best life that ever was led, is always to court and never to wed,' " said Alison, and then hoped she hadn't thus put any ideas into Ewen's head.

It was nearly seven when they came back to Callanish. Murdo and Maili weren't there. The sheep grazed serenely in the evening sunlight. The twins had evidently been well fed, and Shonnie was absent on his own business. Alison decided not to take it for granted that she would stay in the empty house with Ewen; she wondered if she would ever know him enough to take anything for granted.

"Well, I suppose I'd better head home while the light is still good," she said.

He was supposed to say, "The light will be good for hours yet." Instead he said, "Murdo could be back at any moment now." She was too proud to give him any yearning looks and walked briskly toward the front door. He pulled her back before she could step out and kissed her, murmuring something; she felt tears in her eyes and wanted to hang in his arms forever. "Oh, love," she heard herself whispering. I would take him on any terms, she thought. I have no pride at all.

Outside the gate there was the arrival of a car and the discreet touch on a horn, as if the driver had seen, or guessed, and didn't want to be crass. They went out onto the walk. Donald MacLeod's taxi was parked behind Alison's car. She had seen him several times in Stornoway, and he would always smile and wave, but tonight the smile was worried. Monique was crumpled drunkenly in a corner of the back seat.

"The young lady *would* come here," he said. "At the hotel they told me to take her to hospital, but when we were away from the door she told me to take her to Aignish. She's looking for you," he said to Alison. "She's fairly passing out with whatever she's taken, but she keeps struggling. When you weren't at home, she said you must be here."

Monique looked ghastly. Alison's stomach contracted like a fist. She wet her lips. "What happened?"

"They called me from the hotel to take a guest to hospital. She was very sick, they said. She'd just made it down from her room, and asked them to call someone to take her, she was that frightened. But when they'd put her into the car and we drove away, then she asked me to find you."

Helplessly Alison turned to Ewen. He nodded at her, opened the rear door, and put his head in. "Monique," he said clearly. "Monique Fournier."

Donald MacLeod nervously lit a cigarette. Ewen repeated the name, and Monique finally opened her eyes as if her lids were intolerably heavy, and focused on him. "Where's Alison Barbour?" The words were slurred.

"I'm here, Monique," Alison said, leaning over Ewen's shoulder. Monique rolled her eyes toward her, the lids dropped again.

"Said you'd be here," she muttered.

"Monique, what have you taken?" Ewen asked her. "I don't smell liquor," he said in a lower voice to Alison.

She roused up. "I'm not drunk. It's some damn' stuff of Terry's. Mine weren't working and she came up with this. . . . " She started to sink, but resisted. "Got a hell of a reaction. Empty stomach, maybe. Scared me. . . . Knew I had to get out. They'd gone somewhere, and I didn't want to die alone." She seemed to float off again, then said more strongly, "I guess I'm not dying. But I'm afraid to go back to the hotel. The dreams. If they *were* dreams."

"I can take her home with me, Ewen," Alison said.

"Right." He paid Donald MacLeod, then reached into the car and lifted Monique out. Alison picked up the shoulder bag. There was a ghastly similarity to the night when Terry had been sick; Norris had carried her, and Alison had carried the handbag. She felt shivery with anticipation, but she knew that was all foolishness. Nothing was going to happen to Ewen.

"We'll take her in and see if we can wake her up a bit before you leave," Ewen said to Alison. He went on to the house.

"Thank you," Alison said to Donald MacLeod.

"It doesn't seem that I've done you a favor," he said.

"Oh, well, we can put ourselves out a bit for her. It was her friend who was found dead at the Stones, you know."

His blue eyes opened wider. "No, I didn't know that. The poor young lady. I'm sorry for her trouble."

He turned the car around and drove away. Alison went into the house. Ewen had put Monique on the sofa in the sitting room and was covering her with a blanket. She didn't answer when they spoke to her.

"Brandy? Whiskey?" Alison said. Ewen shook his head.

"She might choke. I'll ring up a doctor to come take a look, just to be sure. There's one from Glasgow on holiday in the village right now. Here for the brown trout fishing."

He went out to the hall. Alison tucked the blanket in closer around Monique's skinny shoulders. Monique looked pathetic and oddly young; her hair was darkened with sweat around her forehead and ears.

"She'll be here in a few minutes," Ewen said. He stood by the fireplace filling his pipe and getting it going. Alison watched from behind the sofa, across Monique, and wondered if they'd ever spend an uninterrupted hour making love.

The doctor arrived by bicycle in ten minutes. She was a lanky woman in jeans and a fisherman's sweater, she had short curly gray hair and a weathered face with high cheekbones, and dark eyes deeply creased at the corners. She slapped Ewen on the shoulder. "What are you up to, you sly dog? Drugging women right under Murdo's pious nose?"

"Hello, Meg." Imperturbably, Ewen introduced Alison. The two women shook hands; Meg's grip didn't surprise Alison. She imagined the doctor jogging or biking every day of her life, in or out of Glasgow.

Meg examined Monique. "Whatever she took, she's in a natural sleep now. It couldn't have been a lethal dose, even if she thought so, but it must have been terrifying. She did well to fight her way out of it."

"What shall we do with her?" Ewen asked.

"Leave her alone. Let her sleep it off." She glanced from him to Alison, and laughed. "Sorry if this spoils anything for you, my dears. After you'd sent Murdo off, too."

Ewen was still unflappable. "It would take much more than this to spoil anything for us, Meg. If one of us dropped dead—yes, that would spoil it. But nothing else."

"Then you're lucky, and I won't say you don't deserve it. But where is your little friend?" Her dark eyes shot toward Alison, who smiled. Enigmatically, she hoped.

"She was never my little friend, Meg."

"Damned if I don't believe you. I wish I'd asked you straight out before this. All along I've been thinking you were several kinds of fool."

"I was, but not the sort you had in mind. Stay and have a drink. Or are the trout waiting?"

"Not the trout tonight, but Roddie Dunlop. We're going to a dance in Barvas. I'm glad to know you," she said to Alison. "We'll meet again, I hope." She dropped her bag into the carrier. "You know how Roddie drives, so say a prayer for me if you have a free moment."

"I'll put Murdo onto it," said Ewen. "He has a direct line."

She laughed, and went up the road like a six-day bike racer.

"She's terrific," said Alison.

"She is, isn't she? I've known her all my life. When she was a handsome woman in her twenties, and I was sixteen, I was mad about her. . . . We had better put this one to bed, and you'll be staying, of course. My room will be best; it's just across the hall, and we can put a cot in there for her, and you can sleep in the bed."

Everything was being arranged. Alison didn't mind. "We'd better put her in the bed," she said. "She might be restless and throw herself around."

"All right. The clean sheets are in the cupboard in the bathroom."

His room was neat and bare, with a good reading lamp and an assortment of books on the stand beside the bed. He took some away and put them on the stairs.

Together they made up his bed. On the surface, it was so matter-of-fact that Alison, thinking about how he said he'd lain awake in this bed wishing she were in his arms, knew she had to do something to keep her mind in a safe channel. "Ever since this afternoon I've had this song running through my mind," she said. "Do you know it? 'The Foggy Foggy Dew.' 'Now I am a bachelor, I live all alone; I work at the weaver's trade—' "

He grinned. "Oh yes. And Ruari knows it well. So does Bellann. I think there's a great deal of foggy foggy dew in that section of Uig."

The subject wasn't such a help after all, especially when you remembered the rest of the words of the song. If the time ever comes, she thought resignedly, I'll probably burn to a crisp at once, and that'll be that.

He carried Monique in and left her, and Alison got her out of her clothes and into one of Murdo's nightshirts. Her feet were cold; Ewen supplied a hot water bottle.

With Monique settled, Alison called Mrs. MacBain to explain briefly why she wouldn't be arriving home tonight. Ewen was building a fire; it could be a splendid evening after all, if Monique slept quietly and Murdo stayed away. There'd been that lovely thing Ewen said to the doctor, about only death spoiling anything for them. Was that a declaration or not? Was this obliqueness a particularly Highland thing, or simply Ewen? Why was she allowed no future past the immediate hour? He needn't worry; his embraces hadn't instantly triggered the nesting impulse in her, with automatic plans for a house, children, and a family dog. But what should she do or say? Was she too passive?

Mariana Grange's heroines never had this problem. They weren't expected to make advances but somehow they always managed to have advances made to them that left no room for doubts.

Ewen sat balanced on his heels before the fireplace, watching the fire take hold of the peats. Ewen, I love you, she said silently. Why the hell am I scared to say it out loud, after all the hugs and kisses?

She went back in to check on Monique—anything to put off the moment of joining him. Monique woke up briefly. "Jake saw the man again."

"Where?"

"Somewhere," she said fuzzily. "Yesterday? Today? I don't remember. . . . He was going to tell what's-his-name." She yawned. "Maybe they have the bas-bastard by now." She fell abruptly asleep again.

Alison hurried back to Ewen. "The mysterious stranger hasn't left the island," she said excitedly. "Oh, I forgot. You don't believe in him."

"I'm afraid to. At the same time I'm hoping. Simplicity is such a lovely thing, but so rarely found." He smiled, and patted the sofa beside him. Simplicity was such a lovely thing, like that gesture. She curled up against him and they watched the fire in silence. "Would you be fishing for trout, if it weren't for this mess?" she asked then.

"*We* will be," he said.

Murdo and Maili came home at dusk. They'd walked four miles to call on a sick relative, who was improving, he said with satisfaction. The cat had come in with him and the dog, and was giving Alison a good deal of attention. She picked him up and he hung onto her shoulder; his purr roared in her ear like a conch shell.

"You're lovely, Shonnie," she told him.

"And intelligent," said Murdo. "If he was as brilliant a lad as he is a cat, I'd be educating him at Lews Castle."

"Alison is staying the night," Ewen told him. "There's a woman sleeping it off in my bed, and we've put a cot in there for Alison. I'll sleep upstairs."

"A woman in your bed," said Murdo gravely. "Indeed."

"He sounds as if it happens all the time," said Alison.

"It's one of Murdo's many principles, to be never surprised." Ewen explained the circumstances, and Murdo made concerned noises. Then he said it was time for tea again, he was that parched. He plugged in the teakettle and brought out a tin of fancy biscuits. Shonnie jumped onto the table to give it a close look and was shooed off by clapped hands and a severe injunction in Gaelic. Maili sat by in conscious virtue, knowing her treat would be forthcoming.

They took the tray in to the fire in the other room. Alison paused at the bedroom door and listened to Monique's breathing. As long as she slept like that all night and had no frightening dreams, Alison would be able to sleep on the cot, even under the same roof with Ewen. She was weary enough.

"I wonder if I should let the Danforths know where she is," she said to the men.

"Drink your tea while it's hot," Murdo commanded. "Then let them know. Have some biscuits. They're not bad, for being English. Ewen's cousin who works in London sent them, as if we're hungry out here."

"Be thankful, Murdo," said Ewen. "We'll be getting no more shortbread, at least from one source."

"That's a blessing," said Murdo. "Though mind you, it was good shortbread. I'll say that much for her."

Maili, who was lying by the fire, suddenly sat up, listening. She growled softly. Murdo, his cup halfway to his mouth, listened also; there was a curious likeness in the way they turned their heads. Then Murdo put his cup back on the table. "A dog barking," he said, standing up. "It'll be that imp of a Westie worrying the sheep again. I'll have more than one word with Coinneach MacNeil tomorrow."

Maili was already on her way to the back door. When they'd gone, Ewen went to one of the windows that looked out back to the slope. "I can't see anything, and I think that barking is a good distance off. If there *is* a dog out there, Maili will run it off. She's a terror in action."

He came back to the fire. "I think Murdo is being kind to the young folk."

"But he'll be tired by now, after walking eight miles tonight," Alison protested. "He shouldn't be out there prowling around."

"Hush," said Ewen, switching off the lamp so that only the firelight remained. He sat down beside her. "Shall we talk? Shall we exchange autobiographies, or tell sad stories of the death of kings?"

"No," said Alison.

"Come here, then." He pulled her over to him.

There was a sweep of light across the front windows and onto the walls; the glare of headlights was broken by the gate, the other cars, and shrubbery. Then they were shut off, and a car door slammed.

"Oh *no*," said Alison, making herself heavy in Ewen's arms. "Maybe they'll go away."

"I have a stronger word for it than *no*, and it's our fate that they'll never go away." Still he didn't move. Lying against him she felt the even rise and fall of his breathing. There were voices outside, and finally the clang of the knocker, insistently repeated.

"Hey, anybody home?" Jake Danforth yelled. "I've got some great news for you!"

Alison sat up. "Maybe they've caught the man and he's admitted everything."

"I suppose we'll have to find out, won't we?" He got up in no hurry, switched on the lamp, and went out into the hall, where he put on another light, and opened the door.

"Hi!" cried Terry. "Did we interrupt something? Oh, gosh, I'll bet we did. I *told* Jake when we saw Alison's car but no lights on in the place that we shouldn't stop, but *he* said that you'd want to know right off what was going on."

"Of course," said Ewen politely. "Come in." He waved them toward the sitting room, where Alison had now moved to a chair by the hearth.

"Alison dear!" Terry hailed her. "Don't you look *natural* there beside that darling peat fire! I wish I had a picture of you. Your hair's so lovely in this light!" She was rubbing her hands as if they were cold, though she was warmly dressed. There was a forced emphasis about her broad toothy smile.

She might have really been uncomfortable about interrupting something. Alison hadn't believed she could be that sensitive.

Jake came in behind her, saying over his shoulder to Ewen, "You got any idea where Monique is?"

"Yes, but what's this great news of yours?"

"Oh—I saw the guy, so he hasn't left the island. I told Gilchrist."

"But have they got him yet?" Alison asked.

Jake shrugged. "Well, I don't know about that yet. We went down to Tarbert and had dinner at the hotel there." He too seemed not quite at ease, hands deep in his carcoat pockets. "Now Monique's missing and considering what shape she was in when we left her—well, let's face it, it's a damn' nuisance but you can't just ignore her."

"She's here," Alison said.

"Oh, thank goodness!" Terry dropped onto the sofa. "Thank *God*, I should say. Oh, my! I've been imagining everything, haven't I, Jake?"

"Get up, girl, we're not staying. If my wife could set down half the stuff she dreams up, she'd have it made as a suspense writer for TV," said Jake. "Trouble is, she's illiterate."

"Oh, honey," Terry pouted, but complacently. "Now, tell us about Monique. How is she? The hotel manager said she felt very sick and they sent her to the hospital, and he told us which one, but she wasn't there so we checked the others, and still no trace. I was *terrified*! I said I just can't sleep tonight, not knowing where she is."

"She had the taxi driver bring her out here," Ewen said. "We've had a doctor to see her, and she's sleeping now, just across the hall."

Terry jumped up from the sofa. "Do you mind if I just take a peek at her so I can satisfy myself?"

"I'll go with you," Alison got up to lead the way.

"Oh, stay there and be comfortable," Terry protested. "I'll just go inside the door. The light from the hall will shine in." But Alison followed her anyway. Ewen was half-sitting on a corner of the work table, one foot dangling, his arms folded. He didn't actually smile at her, but there was an affectionate acknowledgment in his nod that was as good as a touch.

Terry was tiptoeing across the front hall, but suddenly she turned and came back and whispered to Alison, "Can I use the bathroom? I'm just about dying!"

Jake, looking like a cynical martyr, handed her her bag. "Don't forget this."

"He reads my mind," she said.

Alison went into the hall and pointed out the way. "Just down there past the telephone table. The closed door at the very end. The light switch is outside."

"Thanks. You're saving my life."

Alison went back; she listened for an instant at Monique's door and the breathing was still deep and regular. Across the hall Jake was saying, "Low ceilings. Makes it easy to heat. You know, I'm damned impressed by the construction of these places. You folks know how to build for the weather. It must be soundproof too, though you have no close neighbors. . . . Hey, Doc Barbour!" he called.

She went back in. He grinned at her. "I just called you that so I'd get this happy jolt when a good-looking girl comes in-stead of some beat-up old professor."

"Like Ewen," Alison suggested, hoisting herself onto the edge of the table beside Ewen.

"Just goes to show I don't know much about professors, doesn't it? The wife and I were arguing on the way out here. Is it true they have courses in witchcraft in some of these col-leges?"

Alison laughed. "Stories about witchcraft are part of folk-lore, and it also might be included in a study of religions, but I think you'd have to learn how to be a witch from a practi-tioner, if you're interested. Not in a classroom or lecture hall."

"And even then it's no good unless you inherit the gift," Ewen said seriously.

"Well, I've done all right for myself without witchcraft," said Jake. "Though there were times at the beginning when I'd have taken any kind of help I could get, including black magic and voodoo. What do you teach?"

"English," said Alison. "And some courses in folklore, which amount mostly to research and field work." He nodded thoughtfully, looking around the room again at the pictures and books. She expected him now to ask what Ewen taught. Instead he said, "Where's your friend tonight? The shepherd? I was looking forward to meeting that dog of his. Fellow in a bar told me he has a real prize there."

"I'm sorry, but Murdo and the dog have gone to Valtos," said Ewen. "I don't know when they'll be back."

Alison didn't know which was the most amazing; Ewen's straight-faced and inexplicable lie, or the gun, when Jake's right hand came out of his pocket.

Terry trotted briskly into the room, saying in her church-and-grange Midwestern voice, "I've taken care of the telephone, but I can't rouse *her*. She's like a sack of flour."

"Then she'll keep till I take care of these two," said Jake. It was not yet frightening; Alison expected him to say "Gotcha!" and toss the gun at them and they'd see it was a clever fake, and Terry would erupt into geysers of giggles. When Ewen's arm came around her shoulders, the first fear slid into her belly like a carving knife.

"I take it," said Ewen, "that you killed Elliot. Why?"

"My reasons don't concern you."

"If he'd known enough to run over the head," Terry said peevishly, "it could have passed for a hit and run by some crazies, the way it was meant to. I *told* him to run over the head!"

"Shut up," Jake told her, without looking away from Ewen and Alison.

"But I was right," Terry insisted.

Alison realized she was gripping the edge of the table so

hard her fingers were going numb. What would a Mariana Grange heroine have done right now? *She'd have remembered the sgian dubh.*

"You must have helped him, then," she said to Terry, sounding mildly curious. "That must have taken nerve."

"You can say that again. Who'd drive the other car? Jake sure enough wasn't going to have a taxi come for him."

"But you were sick," Alison objected. I can do this, she thought. I can keep them talking. "I know you were, there was no faking it."

"Oh, I got over that quick enough, after I'd heaved up all my dinner and had my little crying jag and a nap." She was relentlessly jolly.

"Listen, Danforth," said Ewen, "what do you have in mind? What do you want?" Alison hitched herself closer to him till their sides were pressing, and she slid her hand out and behind her at the last instant, unnoticed because the light wasn't bright at this end of the room. Her fingers began a cautious reconnoitering over the papers and magazines behind them. Jake was talking all the while.

"Too bad that one across the hall had to come out here to-day instead of staying put where we left her. Otherwise you wouldn't be involved. Tough, huh? Some mad-dog killer made a clean sweep. Dumb-looking little guy. As I told Gilchrist, you'd never guess he was a time bomb."

"He doesn't exist, does he?" Ewen asked. He could tell from the subtle movements of her shoulder what she was doing, she thought. His arm held her tighter and closer.

Jake smiled. At least he showed his teeth.

"I think we have a right to know just why we're dying," Ewen said thoughtfully. Alison's fingers found the knife, walked delicately over it, from the tip of the blade to the gem in the head, and cramped shut on the hilt; she was thankful that Kay had not replaced the sheath.

"It's adding insult to injury," Ewen said, "to wipe us out without a word of explanation. There has to be some point. I won't enjoy it any more for knowing the reason, but at least I'll understand."

"That's fair enough, isn't it, honey?" Terry asked Jake. "After all, they're innocent bystanders."

Jake seemed to consider and for an instant Alison thought Terry was asking for their lives. Then she realized that Terry was merely being literal. They *were* innocent, so it was only fair that they should know why they were being killed. Of course they'd have to die now anyway, because of what they'd just found out. There was a perfect inevitability about it, as if Alison had known from the first that she and Ewen would never be together.

"All you need to know," Jake said finally, "is that Elliot came across something that was none of his business and told his girl." His mouth contorted, viciously chewing his words. "I had him sized up from the first as a smooth bastard who lives by blackmail. I wasn't giving him time to get started on *us*."

"We thought he was the only one we had to get rid of," Terry explained chattily, "and then she said something this morning—just one teeny thing—" She held up thumb and forefinger squeezed together—"and we *knew*. Well! If she'd just stayed in her room and slept today, Jake could have managed it without her knowing a thing about it, and nobody else guessing."

"You're running off at the mouth, girl," Jake told her.

"I don't know how she fought it off," Terry marveled. "I gave her enough to knock her out for a week. She should have been dead to the world when we got back from dinner."

Ewen said, "All she told us was that she was afraid to stay alone; she thought she was dying, so she struggled out. Well, it's all academic now, since we know you murdered Elliot. I suppose you wouldn't like to tell us how you managed it."

"If you're trying to hold this up until your friend comes back," said Jake, "I'll blast him when he comes in the door." Alison felt as if the thin blade in her belly had made a long sidewise gash.

"It's too bad, because I really like you, Alison." Terry could have been expressing regret that they lived too far apart in the States to get together for a cup of coffee.

"Terry," Jake said in that dead voice. "Where's your gun?"

"Do I have to take it out?" She began going through her bag. "I hate the nasty little thing." Her antipathy didn't keep her from bringing it out, a small object very suitable for her short fingers. "I hate guns," she said to Alison.

"Now go take care of her. I'll do these two." When she walked by—if she could be tripped and grabbed somehow, and held with the knife to her throat—

Terry's lipstick stood out as it had the night when she was sick. "I never shot anybody in my life. Why can't we use a pillow, the way you were going to do—"

"Shut up!" Jake snapped. Somehow she'd rattled him.

"*You* go do it then," she defied him, "and I'll watch them."

"Do I have to remind you that you're the reason for this whole goddam mess? You're lucky I didn't crack *your* skull. Now if you want to be going aboard that ferry early tomorrow morning with me and the Mercedes, you'll get in there." He put his forefinger against his temple. "And pull the trigger. This mad-dog killer has no time for faking heart attacks."

Seizing Terry wouldn't have worked anyway. He'd have said, Go ahead, kill her, she's no good to me, and then I'll kill you as I planned.

Terry's eyes were round and glassy; she licked her lips and turned toward the door.

There was a heavy, jarring thud in the kitchen, and Terry yelped, her hands flew up, and the gun sailed out of her fingers. In the instant that Jake was diverted by this, Ewen sprang forward.

"*Run!*" he shouted.

Alison ran, knocking over Terry who was sobbing with nerves and scrambling for her gun, slamming the door shut behind her, and running along the hall to the kitchen, and slamming that door behind her too. Shonnie was braced and glaring with alarm. As she went out the back door she heard a shot, and almost stopped. Ewen was dead, or dying. *My darling,* she cried silently, but kept running. *They won't get away with it.*

At first it seemed blindingly night but as she ran past the glimmering outbuildings and through the yard gate, the dark thinned in her vision to a gauzy duskiness in which boulders moved and became startled sheep bounding away.

She was heading for people and telephones, and the shortest way was through the Stones.

In a moment she knew a man was behind her, and it had to be Jake. Ewen would have called to reassure her, but Ewen was probably dead or dying. She needn't look back to convince herself, she could hear his footfalls, his hard breathing. The ever-present onlooker in her brain observed that he was in better shape than she'd have suspected with that paunch. The onlooker did not allow her to think again of Ewen and thus give up and die with him.

Murdo was out here somewhere; she wanted him, but at the same time she hoped he was a good distance away, so that he would survive if Jake overran her. She reached the gate to the Stones; there was a dreadful moment when her cold hands worked uselessly at it, and she was so sure that in the next second Jake would take her by the throat or shoot her between the shoulder blades that the suspense almost did her in; her whole body was sensitized in expectation. Then the gate swung free and she was through. Now she had four hundred feet to go to the other end, but she knew the Stones and Jake didn't. There were not just the Standing Stones, but the rough terrain and rock outcrops here and there, and in the circle itself there was plenty to fall over, including the burial cairn.

The Stones were a silent, masked, hooded and cloaked crowd in the gloaming. They would hide her, she knew. Maybe she'd lost him already, because he didn't know where the gate was, and while he was looking for it she could be halfway through.

Compulsively she glanced back, and it was fatal; she

stubbed her toe and was thrown violently off balance toward a Stone. Her left elbow struck it, and the pain was enormous down to her wrist and up to her shoulder, and then paralyzing.

Trying to run again, she staggered, lost her bearings, panic began to drown her; she caromed into Jake, who was made enormous by the dusk and her terror. She shot up out of the drowning panic when she realized that she still had the sgian dubh.

She struck like a snake, again and again, not knowing where the blade hit but feeling the contact each time and hearing Jake's grunts. There were no words, only these inhuman grunts and bursts of wordless sibilance. He grabbed for her and one hand thrust by the knife and seized her by the hair. The pain was so intense she couldn't cry out. Her left arm was weak, but she still had the knife, and she stabbed at the pallid distorted shape that was his face. She hit somewhere on it; a sound half croak and half gasp exploded from him, and he loosened his grip just enough so that she wrenched herself free and ran for the Circle, plunging and stumbling, but straight for the jumble of the burial cairn which she could avoid, but hoped he wouldn't.

Almost in her ear there was one sharp piercing yip from Maili. Behind her there was a strangled human yelp and the sound of impact; a *thunk*, not quite hollow, not loud, but solid and rather sickening, and there was no more to the running and hard breathing and cursing.

Maili was all over her in frantic welcome. She threw away the sgian dubh and sank to her knees, hugging the dog, not trying to fend off the kisses. She heard Murdo's voice with the lack of surprise common to dreams.

"*A Dhia*, the poor man stumbled and struck his head," he said softly. "We'll need lights up here, and the police. Are you all right, *mo ghaoil?*"

"Yes," she said. "But I think they've shot Ewen."

There was silence, except for the slow heavy drumming in

her chest and head. Then Murdo lifted her to her feet. "Take my arm. We'll just walk around the poor gentleman."

"What if he comes to, and gets away?"

"He won't," said Murdo. His voice was sere and cold. "Maili, come away from the carrion."

Suddenly they were transfixed by a strong light, and from behind it Ewen called, "It's all right!"

"Oh Murdo!" Alison wailed, and turned her face against his shoulder and wept.

32

TERRY WAS LOCKED in the hall closet, alternately sobbing and pounding on the door. Monique, wrapped in a blanket, was curled up in a chair before the sitting room fire, holding Shonnie like a hot water bottle. It was he who had created the diversion by jumping off the forbidden kitchen table.

In the brief struggle after Ewen crashed into Jake, Jake's gun had gone off; either intentionally or by accident nobody knew, but the typewriter was the only victim. He was able to throw off Ewen by jamming the gun against his ribs; then, with Ewen backed to the table again, he put the gun in Terry's shaky hands and told her to keep it on Ewen or they would be hanged for Norris's murder, and he took off after Alison. The situation had been so suddenly knocked out of his control that he must have turned frantic at last.

But Monique, who had been slowly waking again because of all the voices, had been finally roused by the shot; in Murdo's white gown she had come trailing in like a sleepwalker or a ghost, and Terry—who had been trembling so hard anyway that Ewen expected the gun to go off again at any moment—was so startled by the apparition that Ewen had no trouble in knocking the gun out of her hand. She had fought then, insanely; he had the scratches to show for it. He had dragged her to the closet and locked her in, all the time praying that Alison could outrun Jake and that Murdo hadn't gone too far away.

Now the two guns lay on the work table. Alison said guiltily, "I lost your sgian dubh up there in the Circle."

"The police will take it, and when I get it back I'll enshrine it. It saved you."

Monique stared at the fire as if they weren't there.

"No, the Stones saved me," Alison said seriously. "They tripped him, and—" She stopped. She had just remembered something; Murdo replacing his crook in the corner by the door when they came back into the kitchen. "I'm going to enshrine *you*," she said to Ewen. "When you jumped him you gave us all a chance."

They were on the sofa with their feet to the warmth, their arms around each other. He said, "If we're going to be so meticulous we'd better go back to Shonnie, for getting onto the kitchen table against orders. And Monique for coming in like Lady Macbeth."

Murdo had gone to the kitchen to brew up his universal stimulant, sedative, and cure-all, though in honor of the outstanding circumstances he had allowed himself a small drink when the others had theirs. Terry wailed in the closet. Ewen rose from the sofa, and Maili leaped into his place and leaned heavily against Alison's shoulder.

"I'll go ring up the police now," Ewen said. On her trip back from the bathroom Terry had neatly cut the phone wire with a pocket knife carried in her bag for the occasion.

"Can I make a suggestion?" said Monique. "Once they take her away we'll never get the whole story till it comes out in court, if it gets that far."

"What do you mean—if it gets that far?" Alison asked.

"I have a stinking suspicion that whatever she blabbed about to Norris, they may want her back in the States for, when they hear what it is. Anyway, my idea is to get her out of the closet and let her talk so we'll know something. She's dying to talk. Boy, is she *ever*. While you were all out, she was begging like mad."

Ewen said, "He's up there alone, and I should let the police know at once, tempted as I am."

Murdo was just bringing in the tray with the teapot and cups. "I'll go," he said. "It's a small enough sacrifice to make, I'm so thankful. But mind you remember everything," he said to Ewen.

"What he doesn't remember I shall," said Alison.

"Thank you," Murdo said with great dignity. As he was driving away in the Land Rover, Ewen was unlocking the closet door. Terry was a shocking sight, bedraggled, aged by her terrors and her hysterical weeping, her knuckles red and swollen from her beating against the door. She begged to go to the bathroom. "I mean it this time," she pleaded. Alison went with her to be sure she didn't try to commit sucide with any means found at hand. But it became clear that Terry was concentrating entirely on life—*her* life. There was a strong impression that the only reason she was sorry Jake was dead was that she couldn't have him to fling off the sledge to the wolves, and thus save herself.

"I don't want to be hanged!" she cried to Alison. "Please— *help* me—" She kept rubbing her throat.

Alison brought her to the sitting room and gave her a cup of tea. "They don't hang here anymore," Ewen told her. Otherwise they waited without speaking. When she'd stopped shivering, and the sobs had worn off to occasional gasps and hiccups, she talked eagerly.

Monique's face was like a deathmask as she learned why and how Norris had died. Alison's own face felt chilled and drawn. She sat absently rubbing her bruised crazy bone, as

Terry kept rubbing her throat. Ewen stood before the mantel, with his hands in his pockets, looking as remote as if all his attention and energies were turned inward, but Alison knew better.

None of it was *her* fault, Terry gabbled. Jake started it when he killed off his partner in the business they'd begun in a garage together. He'd wanted the whole firm, and he needed the quarter of a million's worth of insurance there was on Dud. Well, there was the same amount on him, too. They'd set it up that way. . . . Well, Jake had all these *ideas*, he was so smart, he knew what he could do without old Dud to hold him back. He'd also figured out how to get rid of Dud without anyone guessing, but she could tell them exactly how it was done; she'd always had it on her conscience, that's why she was drinking so much. She had nightmares.

"And Jake was right, you know," she assured them. "We did take right off. He's a millionaire now. His systems are all over the place, government contracts, big business and all. But we could lose everything in one fell swoop." She sounded as if it hadn't just happened. "That's what worries me all the time. We can have a good time with the money, we've got nobody to leave it to, so we were just going to bum around on this trip, you know."

Her big toothy smile was a parody of itself. "I'd never even *heard* of the Outer Hebrides till that morning in Southampton, when we were going through all that business before you land, and Monique and Norris were ahead of us in line, and I heard him say something about finding the best and quickest way to get to Lewis. Later I asked the desk clerk at our hotel in Southampton, and he told me." She rolled her eyes. "I wish to God I'd never asked. Never heard the name. All I could think of then was that if I visited a place none of the gals at home had ever seen, maybe I'd be invited to give a talk at the Green Thought Garden Club. They had to let me join, you know," she said confidentially, "because Jake gave them so much money to turn a vacant lot into a park. But if I ever gave a talk—and had all those tweeds and things to show—I'd be *really* in." She took a big gulp of tea, and rushed on.

"I didn't have a thing to do with Dud's death, but I knew about it—he did it with a pillow, and Dud had a heart murmur anyway, so he fooled them—just a hick town police force. But nobody can make a wife testify against her husband especially if he's dead, can they?" she appealed to Ewen.

"I have no idea," he said. "I don't know the American system."

"Besides, I was just his tool. Like with this Norris thing."

From the corner of her eye, Alison saw Monique's hand twitch and then consciously flatten out.

"Yes?" said Ewen judicially. "Would you mind telling us about that?"

"I don't know if I *really* told Norris or dreamed I told him, because I dream about it a lot. But I was so scared of Jake finding out later that I did tell, I wanted to tell him first. Well, he'd just met Norris walking around the car park, smoking. So he made me get up and dress, and we went out. We had to do *something*, you see, because Norris could have drained us dry. Like a vampire." She shuddered.

"And nobody saw you?" asked Ewen.

"There was so much coming and going, with that dance, that we just slipped out. I remember seeing the hall porter busy with some people who'd just come in with all this luggage. Jake had a bottle of Glenfiddich in our car. He got it out and then we went looking for Norris. He was still walking around. I can remember," she said quite cheerfully to Monique, "you and he had a kind of squabble—I guess that was on his mind, but both Jake and I thought something else was too. What I told him. Anyway, first he said I must be feeling a lot better, then he made a little joke about the Glenfiddich, and Jake said he was taking it up to the room. Then he asked Norris the best way to get to some of the other islands, did he have a map of the whole area—which he knew *already* that Norris had, because he'd seen him and Monique looking at it in the lounge."

She drank more tea. She seemed to be taking some satisfaction out of her importance now; she talked expansively, like someone intending to get the most out of a good story, and a captive audience following every word. "We went over to his car. When he leaned in to take the map out of the console, Jake swung on him with the bottle. Then he just tumbled him into the back seat. Oh, the car was a good distance away from the doors, and it was all quiet around there for that few minutes. Jake was lucky again, the way he always is."

"*Was*," Alison heard herself say. She couldn't help it, then was afraid she'd dammed the flow. But it seemed that nothing could. Terry was in full spate, and Jake wasn't there to tell her to knock it off.

"Jake covered him with a blanket from our car. *I* wouldn't drive his car, with him in it," she said like someone proud of her delicacy. "I have a darling little Audi at home," she fondly remembered. "The Mercedes feels so *big*, and that road after dark—Wow! I thought we'd *never* get to Callanish."

"Why Callanish?" asked Ewen. "You could have left him anywhere."

"Well, if you'll excuse me saying so," she said coyly, "he did have something going with you, or wanted to. So Jake thought the police would either think it was some drunk or junkie who dumped him there, *or* you. Even if they couldn't make it stick, it was a damn good distance away from us. I mean, who was going to search *our* car for the gas Jake siphoned out of the Capri, or that whiskey bottle they didn't know anything about? Once we were safe on the mainland again, we could get rid of them in some lonely place and nobody'd ever know anything."

Monique stirred and spoke. She had to clear her throat first. "What did I say this morning that made you want to do away with me the way you did old Dud?"

"*I* didn't have anything to do with Dud, sweetie," said

Terry with ghastly gaiety. "What you said was something like 'life's full of nasty surprises, and if you two don't know that by now, you will before long,' and Jake said the minute we left you, 'That's the seed of blackmail.'" She cocked her head listening. "I never heard him say anything so sort of poetic like that. 'The seed of blackmail.'"

"It beats Shakespeare," said Monique. "But I never saw Norris again after I walked out of your room. I came back and listened once, and you were maundering on, sounding half-asleep, and then I went back to my room. I couldn't have made sense of your mumblings if I'd tried."

"*Oh gosh!*" said Terry. She put her thumb to her mouth and nibbled on her nail. "I wish we'd known. It would have saved a lot of trouble." It was as if they'd made a lengthy trip to a certain store and found it closed.

"What was the plan for tonight, Terry?" Ewen asked her. She was running down a little now; she yawned, and seemed to grope for words.

"Oh—" she waved a hand—"Jake told you. Mad-dog makes a clean sweep. We'd be back at the hotel before midnight and in bed, and taking the early ferry in the morning."

"Didn't it occur to you that somebody might have remembered seeing a Mercedes on the road? There aren't that many on the island, so you would have been examined if only for purposes of elimination."

"Jake said we had to take a chance, and every time that's happened he's been lucky. We'd have been off the island and driving on the mainland before anyone discovered what happened here."

"Unless someone came to the house late tonight, after you'd left, and discovered us dead. The police would be on the job by now, as they are."

"But they still wouldn't have been able to start checking on cars until tomorrow," she argued, "and by that time we'd be over in the mountains somewhere."

Ewen smiled. "The days are past when fugitives can hide out for long in the Highlands. Especially when they're strangers to the place, and are driving a green Mercedes."

She didn't have a ready answer for that. She bit on her thumb nail again. The polish was flaking off, and she had a speck on her lip.

"Anyway," she said finally, "nobody can prove I was anything more than a tool. Anything I did, it was because I was so scared of Jake."

And losing your millions, Alison thought. She would not forget Terry's petulant complaint that Jake should have run over Norris's head to hide the killing blow. Norris had been a good Samaritan when she was sick, and he'd been murdered for it, and the rest of them had come so close to being wiped out that Alison marveled at how the three could have listened to Terry in such stillness.

"Where did you get the firearms?" Ewen asked. "Did you bring them with you from the States? That must have been hard to manage."

"No!" she said indignantly. "We aren't that kind of people! Carrying guns all the time like gangsters! Jake got them after we landed. I don't know how, but he always knows the right people. He just loves guns, you should see his collection! He's got all kinds, but these are some German make he doesn't have, and he was going to get them home somehow—he's so good at managing. Mine's a darling little thing, but I never wanted to use it except for fun."

Potting songbirds? Alison asked silently.

"Can I have some more tea?" Terry asked. She rubbed her throat again. Alison refilled the cup, hoping that Terry was still worried about hanging. She was sorry Jake wasn't alive to contemplate life in either an American prison or a Scottish one.

Murdo came in, and it was the stroke that freed them from the spell. Monique rose up without a word, wrapping her blanket tightly around her, and walked back across the hall to the bedroom. "I will refill your bottle," Murdo said to her. "Your feet must be like ice." She didn't speak. Alison took the hot water bottle from the bed and handed it to Murdo.

When she took the refilled bottle back to Monique, she said, "I'll close the door so you needn't hear anything."

"No, leave it. If I'm shut in here I'll be listening to *her*, over and over." She began to cry, not with passion but with sorrow and weariness. "If he'd come back to me that night, I never would have let him go out again. But I walked out on *him*."

Alison sat in the room with her while Inspector Gilchrist cautioned Terry, who was then taken into custody by a pair of uniformed officers, a man and a woman, and driven away.

Ewen and Murdo took Gilchrist and the rest of the C.I.D. team up to the Stones. Monique wept herself quietly and hopelessly back to sleep. Alison was left alone with the peat fire and Maili. Shonnie had gone out with the men. She wondered if he would follow them up to the Stones, and how many of his nights he spent up there, a cheerful young spirit roaming in the company of the ancient ones. What did Shonnie know without knowing he knew it?

When the men came back Gilchrist took statements from them all except Monique; it was agreed to leave her undisturbed. She could report in the morning. No one questioned the fortuitous accident in the Circle that had saved Alison's life, though the image of Murdo's crook burned so brilliantly in her brain she worked hard to blot it out just in case any of the police were telepathic. Murdo was bland and calm about the whole thing.

"It was a beautiful evening to walk among the Stones and consider the stars, which I was doing when I heard the big car arrive. In a little while I heard the back door shut hard. Maili was for attending to it immediately, but it wasn't until someone came close, running, that I realized it was a desperate situation. Miss Barbour was a very wise young woman to lead him where he would trip and fall as he did."

There had been superficial wounds on Jake's hands and face, and cuts in his clothes; the little knife had bought time for her.

When the police left, Murdo went to bed, and Maili followed him up the stairs. Alison and Ewen said goodnight before the dying fire. It was brief. Now that the longest evening of their lives was over, words were dried up, and emotions were choked out by fatigue like the thick dust of drought.

Alison lay on the cot, trying to relax toe by toe, finger by finger; an exercise demanding such concentration that it left her excruciatingly wide awake, going over everything that had happened. The sound of the one shot echoed again and again in her ears and its impact, the certainty that Ewen was dead, never grew less. He's upstairs in this house, she repeated to herself. Sleeping, or trying to. Yes, he's sleeping; probably he said to himself, "Oh well!" or something salty in Gaelic, and turned over and sank like a stone.

Her scalp was sore at the back of her head where Jake had grabbed her by the hair. He was dead, no doubt of that. Without stirring from their ancient places the Stones had killed him. Her thoughts ran in hazy, floating circles of fantasy like the gulls over Broad Bay, Aignish, and Torsaig, riding the winds. Then she was snapped back to earth where Murdo was putting his crook away in the kitchen corner; she saw them waiting there in the circle listening, the dog crouched in silence, the shepherd leaning on the crook that could draw a lamb to him, or hook a man by the ankle and throw him down.

Mariana Grange had never thought of anything like that, and it wasn't likely that she would ever use the idea, Alison thought sardonically. All that thought expended on Fiona and the Demonic Keeper of the Stones would be for nothing, unless the horror began to fade away in ten years or so.

She dozed off finally but felt as if she were partly awake. They were all up early in a cold, wet, dark gray morning. There was no chance to escape Murdo's big breakfast, but it was surprisingly strengthening. Alison and Ewen had a moment alone together for a quick, fierce embrace.

"I'll see you later," he said to her at the car, too low for anyone else to hear, and she had to be satisfied with that. She drove Monique back to Stornoway. The policewoman had been there to get some things for Terry, so they knew what had happened. Monique was given a kindly, almost tender reception.

Alison drove to Aignish in the dull light and early quiet, her eyelids lined with sticks, her stomach curling up around the edges like a fritter left too long in a frying pan over a hot flame. It was a simile hardly worthy of Mariana Grange or Dr. Barbour, but it was all she could think of at the moment, and it was exact.

33

THE MINCH was gunmetal gray and dead calm when she drove across the Braigh. In Aignish the sheep were up and about, including a batch with blue-daubed rumps, who'd gotten out from somewhere and were joyously eating the lush green grass along the side of the ditches, while their lambs chased each other back and forth across the deserted road. A strong tang of peat came down on the chill damp air; someone was up and had built a fire. Between that and the sheep, the slack hour was given some comforting signs of life. Annie missed her arrival, being busy at the far end of the croft. The birds were beginning to sing as she let herself into the cold house. It felt as if it had been empty for weeks.

She drew the curtains and turned on her electric blanket, undressed and put on pajamas, yawning and shivering. She got into her warm bed and slept dreamlessly, perhaps because it was daylight, and the primitive and innocent unconscious believes some things will never dare appear in daylight.

She was awakened by the persistent tapping of the knocker. It was Mrs. MacBain, apologetic. The time was nearly noon, and Ewen had called to say he was coming to get her at two; they had an appointment with the Procurator Fiscal.

"Let me get my eyes open and I'll tell you all about it," Alison said.

"I'll be back in a half-hour with some hot rolls fresh from the oven," said Mrs. MacBain.

The thing had come down crushingly upon Alison in the moment of waking. But I'm alive alive! her mind caroled to the face in the bathroom mirror, and she was almost overcome by a rush of pure elemental joy. She bathed and washed her hair, and knew she was hungry.

Mrs. MacBain returned with the hot rolls and a little jar of marmalade. Eating them and drinking coffee, Alison gave the story, observing her talent for enjoying food at the same time; she decided she was neither insensitive nor gross (a favorite word on the campus at Hazlehurst) but that her body demanded food. So she couldn't help her appetite.

Trying to remember all the details of the night and keep them straight helped to set the affair in a rather distant perspective, so she could describe it as a scene from a book or a movie. Mrs. MacBain was low-keyed in her reactions, her exclamations very soft, as if she thought Alison's poise was a fragile pretense and might shatter at any moment.

"Listen, I'm fine," Alison said. "In case you're wondering. I'm *alive*, and that's all that matters."

"And it's because you ran to the Stones. Well, I've heard it said they look after their own."

But only if they have Murdo for a back-up, Alison thought. "Wait till I tell Charlie Macaulay," she said. "He'd just been telling me that I shouldn't spend so much time there. I want to walk to the Stones from Torsaig, because Christina did, and Charlie shakes his head ominously, as if I'd awaken strange gods or something."

"I don't know who they'd be," said Mrs. MacBain. "It's not the right territory for Pan. No olive groves to chase the girls in."

"If the Great God Pan ever did put in appearance around

there, Charlie Macaulay would have a few drinks with him," said Alison. They laughed. Mrs. MacBain got up.

"I'll leave you now, with that charming scene intact in our minds. Much nicer than murder."

She was right. While Alison dressed for her meeting with Ewen and the Procurator Fiscal, she thought not of murder but of Charlie's having drinks with Pan while they exchanged joyfully lecherous anecdotes of their youth. She could see blue fire rekindled in Charlie's eyes, and Pan across the table from him, horns burnished, the goatish hindquarters jauntily crossed, one hoof wagging. What would his accent be, or would the two of them perfectly understand each other in a language all their own?

She dressed in the gray flannel suit and paisley silk blouse she'd worn to travel in; it seemed suitable for an appointment with a Procurator Fiscal. When Ewen came he looked formal with a shirt and tie instead of the usual sweater. She was prepared to meet him on the doorstep, ready to go, but he backed her into the hall and took her into his arms.

"Did you sleep?" they murmured to each other. "Have you eaten? Are you all right? Yes, fine, fine. I slept. I ate. I'm all right."

The sun was burning through the cloud ceiling, which was a help. The three beasts were out again, grazing by the Aignish sign; the bus roaring down the hill didn't disturb their dreamy contentment. One of them looked in at Ewen with long-lashed velvety eyes.

"Friend of yours?" asked Ewen.

"I think she'd like to be. Ewen, why did you say last night that Murdo'd gone to Valtos?" She hadn't planned to ask it, but he didn't act surprised.

"I've been thinking about that," he said. "It still puzzles me. I told you I'm not second-sighted, and I don't claim to have E.S.P. I never have lucky hunches. But last night there was an instant—when he asked me where Murdo was—when there was such a stench of genuine evil in the room and such a huge cry of warning in *me*, and then an *of course!* as if I'd just recognized what had come in with them."

"I felt nothing," she said in awe.

"It could have been all intuition, mind you, and what's intuition but the unconscious recognition of subtle clues? Maybe I suspected Jake's affability, or felt the whole scene was false; I might even have seen the shape of the revolver in his pocket. I heard myself lying about Murdo and about one minute later I knew why I'd lied. I didn't want Murdo walking into an ambush, and if there was any chance at all that he was on his way back and just might see something through the windows, because clever Jake forgot to draw the curtains—it meant that even if Jake managed to kill us, he'd never have gotten away with it. The police would have met him on the road back, or at the hotel doors."

" 'If Jake managed to kill us,' " she repeated. "I wonder if I'll ever really warm up again. I know what Emily Dickinson meant by 'zero at the bone.' "

He put his hand over on hers where they tightly gripped her bag. His clasp was large and warm.

"You looked so calm," she said.

"So did you."

"Well, I like to think I was meeting my fate with dignity. In fact I was stupefied. I couldn't have thrown a fit."

"You remembered the sgian dubh."

Ah, but that was Fiona, she thought. "I've often wondered," Ewen went on, "how I'd react with death suddenly looking me in the eye. And this was it. I was sure we didn't have the chance of a snowball in hell. But instead of thinking *My God, I'm going to die*, I wanted only to hold you."

She wanted to say *Oh darling*, but she was afraid her voice would break so she kept it to herself.

Mr. MacLean, the Procurator Fiscal, was not only a decent sort, as Ewen once said, but a charming one. He needed to question them because he was preparing his case for the High

Court. He had already seen Monique and Murdo. Ewen asked him if there was a chance that Terry would be extradited.

"That remains to be seen," he said. "We've notified the proper authorities in the town and county where the Danforths lived in Minnesota, and their legal advisors."

Meanwhile a local lawyer was looking after Mrs. Danforth's interests. She had collapsed and was in hospital under guard. But she had been very forthcoming the night before; her statement was a full one.

"Last night she was afraid of hanging," Ewen said.

Mr. MacLean admitted that the police, the lawyer, and the doctor they'd called for her had had quite a struggle to convince her she wasn't for the long drop.

He thanked them for coming in, and hoped Alison's holiday and the charm of Lewis had not been ruined for her.

"Far from it," she told him. "Lewis means something very special to me."

"Then let's hope that from now on there are no more disasters for you."

"I'll see that there aren't," said Ewen. "We have some trout-fishing to do, and some sea-angling, and an inspection of every ancient site from the Butt to Rodel."

"There's no better way to be private than to make a tour of those," Mr. MacLean said. "At this time of year, before the tourists come. Ah, May," he said lyrically. "It should be three months long. The golf course is in its glory. My wife bird-watches between putts."

When they left him it was with a feeling that the whole episode had been closed; the prospect of a trial in the High Court seemed as insubstantial as the idea that they might be called as witnesses in a Minnesota courthouse one day. At least they needn't brood about it today.

Outside, the sun had conquered; she could echo the Fiscal's wish that May should be three months long. Stornoway and its people basked in gold and heat, the Gaelic and English greetings were called from the heart.

"It's not quite four," said Ewen, "and we have hours of daylight ahead of us. How about that ride to the Butt, and we'll see the restored chapel at Eoropie, and then I'll show you the Eye, where some dimwitted Norsemen of legend cast a line through the hole and tried to drag the island home to Norway."

"That Fred the Fudd certainly got around, didn't he?"

"Fred the *who*?"

"He founded the state of Befuddlement, in which I so often find myself. With a great sense of homecoming, I may add. I'd love to go, but I'd like to see Monique first."

Monique looked very drawn, but she was calm and seemed rested. She was getting ready to deal with Norris's sister and husband, who were on their way to take charge of Norris. The Canadian police had contacted them in their inquiries about his associations at home and this was how they had found out he hadn't died by accident. "They'll blame me for not letting them know," she said. "But between liquor and tranquilizers I've been in limbo. You know, mine were bad enough, but these things Terry came up with—to help me sleep—oh boy! It was very nearly sleep forever."

"If we can offer you any moral support with these people," Ewen began, surprising Alison.

"Thank you. You two are so respectable I could use the back-up. But they can't hurt me. I know I have to hang around here till the law decides it doesn't need me, and then I'm going home. Not to my parents, but I'll make some sort of peace with them, I suppose. . . . Not humbly! I'll never humble myself to them. The life I had with Norris was the only one I had, and I'm not ashamed of it. From now on it'll be existence. I can work; I trained as an accountant," she said with some pride.

"Look at me. I thought I couldn't live a day without him, but it's almost a week later and I'm still here. I can't call it living but it's better than what those two had planned for me. I sweat whenever I think of it. Which means I want to keep breathing, agony and all."

"Would you like to go with us this afternoon?" Alison asked.

"No, thanks. You don't need me, and sight-seeing isn't my thing." She gave them a watery smile. "Bless you, young lovers, wherever you go, or words to that effect."

34

WHEN THEY WERE DRIVING away from town, Alison said, "I wonder if they *will* extradite Terry. What would they try her for? Accessory after the fact of old Dud's murder? I don't know anything about all that legal mish-mash. All I'm reasonably sure of is that she won't be invited to give a talk at the Green Thought Garden Club. . . . Anyway," she added cynically, "she'd probably have lifted it straight from the *National Geographic.*"

"If she's tried here in Scotland for involvement in Elliot's death, with one of our more gifted advocates representing her, she may emerge as a poor defenseless Trilby to Jake's Svengali."

"But if they have an inquiry into Dud's death at home, even if she gets off, Dud may have had people who'll now sue the estate." Suddenly she was enraged all over again. "Norris hasn't been dead a week yet! Jake's death doesn't wipe it out. It doesn't even make the impact less. Norris never hurt anybody, he enjoyed his life, such as it was, and Monique loved him."

"Yes," Ewen said.

"This whole thing was built on a structure of *If's,*" Alison said. "So delicate and so deadly it's frightening. *If* Harold Marshall hadn't admired my work and stopped to see me, he wouldn't have been killed in that place at that time. . . . *If* I hadn't taken off a week later. *If* Terry hadn't heard Norris mention Lewis. *If* she hadn't got drunk and sick, and talked too much, or thought she did. *If—*"

"If Christina hadn't gone to America," said Ewen, "you wouldn't have come back."

"And started a chain of destruction," she said bitterly.

"*No.* Who called me egotistical for fuming about Kay, and added a few more cruel terms to cut me down? Now you're the conceited one, taking credit where none is due."

She gave him a weak smile and looked away.

"If Christina hadn't gone to America," he went on, "the essential you would have existed under another name, in another frame of reference. You wouldn't be Christina's great-granddaughter, and we'd have gone through our lives missing each other and not knowing what was wrong."

"Don't say things like that out in public, Ewen," she said. "I'm feeling very fragile. I could dissolve any moment now. Do you mind if we don't go sight-seeing today? Would you go to Torsaig with me instead?"

"Yes, but why today?"

"I'm going to find out why Christina went to America. It's time for Charlie Macaulay to tell me what he's been hiding from me."

"We'll do whatever you like."

He was so gentle she thought she was being humored, and tried to sound very cold and rational.

"Thank you. I suppose we'll never know who Norris's client was, or Harold Marshall's."

"I'll tell you what we can do. We'll make a tour of the family properties all over Scotland, and see who's putting in new bathrooms or remodeling the east wing. Then we'll know who sold the Book, even if we don't know to whom. I'll give off significant nods and insinuating smiles, and make everyone very uncomfortable, and when we drive away they'll be expecting a visit from Inland Revenue within the week."

"You're a sadist."

"Only when it's called for. Look, I must go to Edinburgh for a few days next week, for some meetings. Will you go with me?"

"Yes." I'll never shilly-shally again, she thought.

"Good," said Ewen. He began to whistle a strathspey tune. He sounded self-satisfied, but she didn't care.

At Torsaig the children were home from school and playing football on the road. The tide was up and the adventure of the game was enhanced by the chance of losing the ball to East Loch Roag. Mrs. MacArthur's goats greeted Alison like a friend when she got out of the Land Rover by Charlie's gate. Charlie sat on a bench under the kitchen window, alone; Peadar was off with the son-in-law, moving sheep, and Peigi had gone to the dentist in Stornoway.

Charlie waved them in with great gestures of hospitality, but he kept his eyes on Ewen. When they shook hands, he said, "So you're living with the Stones." He was unsmiling for once.

"Only until my house on Bernera is ready," said Ewen.

"You're not studying them, then?"

Ewen shook his head. "Well!" said Charlie. "Will you have a seat? This is grand sunshine to be outside in."

Alison sat on the bench beside him and Ewen sat on the step. He took his pipe out, and offered Charlie his tobacco; there was a little discussion here which was lost on Alison, who was not an expert in pipe tobaccos. When finally the two pipes were going and masculine solidarity was assured, Charlie said to Ewen, "Well, I don't mind telling you, this one's stubborn like all red-haired people. I've warned her about the Stones, and now see what's happened there."

"But if she hadn't run to the Stones she'd have died," Ewen said. "They saved her life."

"I can't argue with that," said Charlie graciously to Alison.

"And it's happy I am for it. But you shouldn't be getting any ideas, you know."

"What kind of ideas?"

"That you owe them something. That they expect it. They're only rock, you know. Whatever was there, it went away long ago. Some people wouldn't have it so, and it was to their great cost."

It felt as if the hair was rising on her nape. "Are you talking about Christina?" Then she was afraid such a direct question would end the talk, but Ewen came in smoothly, man to man.

"Mr. Macaulay, if there's something you think she might have inherited, then she should be warned. Or she'll keep going back there trying to find it out."

Charlie sighed. "That's what Peigi tells me, and yet she knows little of it. Very good, then. But you'll not be holding it against me?" he appealed to Alison.

"Never!"

"The MacLeods, your family of them, were always *of* the Stones," he said. "They lived at Callanish once, close to the Stones in a house that's no longer there, and they knew all the old lore. Then Sir James Matheson cleaned the Stones up and the tourists began coming, and Tormod moved here, to the cottage up the glen. They had it from Eilidh's father, all his sons being dead or gone to other countries."

Charlie's voice settled into a hushed and poetic rhythm, as if the story were being told in the Gaelic and she was magically able to understand it. She leaned back against the house wall and fixed her eyes on the sky over the loch, and let herself go with the up and down of the cadences. Ewen was within touch, but she deliberately willed him away. She was alone now except for the voice of the storyteller, because it was her story he was telling.

"Tormod put the Stones behind him in every way, but the lass Cairistiona was always off to them, even when she was a wee thing. She'd go around by the water, following the shore, and she was found there more than once by shepherds or by sightseers, and folk who knew her family. She'd say the Stones were lonely, so she must visit them. When she was older she wasn't the only one; on May Day the young ones would go, or on moonlit nights, and on the walks there and back they had plenty of opportunities for what the minister would be breaking his heart over, and bursting his lungs about from the pulpit every Sunday." Charlie stopped for a few reflective puffs on the pipe.

"Cairistiona was a blithe girl, my father said, always lilting away whether she was herding, or bringing home a creel of peats. All the men watched her, and there were some girls who were jealous and put it about that she was no better than she should be on her visits to the Stones. They claimed she met a lover there, and it could be the one whose name they wouldn't mention for fear of summoning him."

"The Devil," said Ewen. "Did they call her a witch?"

"Very secretly, you understand." Alison felt his blue eyes on her, but she still gazed out over the loch. The children's cries in the road sounded exotic and unintelligible. "The old minister," Charlie went on, "wouldn't allow that sort of talk. He was a scholar, the old minister, and he saw the Stones as an antiquity, you see. It was what the young would be up to there that bothered him, not the Stones themselves. Then he died, and the young one came."

Alison's stomach seemed to jolt convulsively against her lungs and her heart, then subside again.

"He'd never have lasted anyway, my father said. This was no place for a lad like him. Nor was the ministry. He'd never been away from home before. The brutal hard life here shocked him, and the people were strange. But there *she* was, singing her way down the glen, talking to him when he went to the cemetery, coming up to him when he was wandering the hillside and the shores. So he fell in love. Well, how could he help it? And my father—the wee lad—was always watching and listening. He knew when the stories started, not to be held back by fear of the little minister as there'd been with the old one."

Charlie was silent a little while, either to collect his thoughts or to get ready for what was ahead. She knew Ewen was watching her, but she didn't even shift her eyes toward him for fear of losing this precious and absolutely essential detachment.

"She coaxed him to walk to the Stones with her at last, on the eve of the first of May," Charlie said. "Now it might be that they made love on the way there or back. But he came home a sinner, he'd eaten the apple, and like Adam he blamed the woman. He made a great confession in church about how he had almost lost his soul, and he denounced her from the pulpit, and she sitting there by her poor widowed mother and the younger ones. He didn't name her, but everybody knew because he couldn't take his eyes off her. *A Dhia!*, but she was the brave one, my father said. She never took her eyes off *him*, nor lowered her chin, even when he cried that there was a witch among them."

The birds over the Loch were growing blurry, Alison was staring so hard. She laced her fingers tightly and stared at them for a while.

"The sensible folk saw him for what he was, a poor wee mannie disturbed in his mind, but it caused a terrible upset in the village. Her family felt disgraced, and there were all the false stories too, you see; that she'd done strange things at the Stones, or that she was carrying his child. And so—"

The timing of Charlie's pauses was perfect.

"All at once, my father said, she was gone, and the village didn't see her go. But *he* did. Something woke him in the gray of dawn, and he got out of bed and went to the window—upstairs in this very house it was—and he saw her walking along this very street, only it was all mud then. She was wearing her coat and hat and carrying her heavy bag. He dressed and let himself out of the house, in his bare feet, and ran after her, and he carried her bag up the hill. At the top she kissed him and said she'd send him her picture. 'I'll have a grand life in America, Coinneach,' she said. 'You wait and see!'

"She was always like that, with her chin up even with the tears shaking in her eyes like dew in the rowan flowers. And she went off down the road. She got to Stornoway somehow, there was an immigrant ship loading there within the week, and it was then that she sailed. But nobody in Torsaig ever saw her again, and nobody knew, until he told me and now I tell you, that a wee lad was the only one who saw her go and his young heart breaking."

Like mine, Alison thought, the tears were running down her face; she hadn't even felt them gathering.

Ewen gave her his handkerchief. "And the little minister?" he asked.

"When she vanished like that, he knew what he had done. He must have wakened one morning to know it all; how he loved her, the bright bonnie creature she was, and he had driven her away and he would never see her again. My father hated him, as only a child can hate, and he took to watching the man, waiting till he dared to accuse him. But when he saw him wandering on the hilltop above the cemetery, with the white face on him and the mouth working, and the muttering and groans, it frightened the child. It was the next morning they found the poor little man on the sands, drowned."

Alison wiped her eyes again—they kept running over like a never-failing spring—and blew her nose. She sighed and sat up straight. "Thank you, Charlie," she said.

He said delicately, "If she had not been so wild about the Stones, you see. They drew her. So when you came, looking so much like her, and you wouldn't stop asking about the Stones—"

"I understand that, Charlie," she said. "But now I know, and I'm glad of that."

"Then I am." He heaved himself up. "*A Dhia*, I'm stiffer than that gate, and dried out like a peat in the fire. We'll go in and see what we can find for our poor parched throats."

"I'd love something," said Alison, "but do you mind if we go up the glen for a bit and then come back? I'd like to go to the cottage, and sit on the old doorstep for a little while."

"Do you have the Gaelic?" Charlie asked Ewen. He nodded and made an answer in that language. Charlie began to laugh.

"Then he'll have twenty ways to say 'I love you,' " he said to Alison. "And then—watch out!" His laughter followed them to the gate.

They walked around the football game, smiling at the players. "Let's not talk about her now, please," Alison murmured to Ewen. "I have to let it mull. I've just lived through it with her. It's the strangest sensation. It's like being a time traveler."

They crossed the stream and went up by the Manse without being noticed, though the car was there. The church doors were open and they heard voices from inside, but they still could have been invisible; Alison felt as disembodied as if she were Christina's ghost returning. They went to the cemetery first and visited the family graves.

"I hope Eilidh kissed Christina goodbye, Ewen," she said. "Even if she wouldn't walk to the top of the hill to see her off."

"Oh, she might not have been hard on the girl, you know. And what other choice did Christina have, but to run away? What would her future have been? Besides, it was a hard life on Lewis. The people were impoverished and growing more so. No, Christina chose to survive, and perhaps she went with her mother's blessing. Eilidh might not have been able to watch her out of sight, knowing she'd never see her again."

"I didn't think of that. You make me feel ashamed."

They visited the little minister's grave; Morag from the Manse had been there recently and set out a clump of tiny blue flowers. Alison had to blow her nose again. "I never cry at movies or over books," she muttered, "but this is really getting to me."

"I blinked hard a few times myself when Charlie was talking."

"You're just saying that." But she was comforted.

Then they crossed the stream and went to the cottage ruins. She told him about Charlie's adder.

"Did you ask him if he's ever seen an adder since? Come on, sit down, and I'll protect you." Feeling worn out and sorrowful, she leaned into his arm. "Is it true what Charlie said, about twenty ways to say 'I love you' in Gaelic?"

"Murdo said something this morning, too. Between Murdo and Charlie we don't stand a chance, I'm afraid."

"What did he say?"

" 'The husband of the red-headed woman is never a widower.' Which means I'll never have to match up and mend my own socks, for instance."

"You're taking a lot for granted. You haven't begun on those twenty ways yet."

"My dear girl, I've simply been waiting for the perfect ellipse of an uninterrupted interval, and you can't say we've had many of those."

"We're all alone now, and there's no telephone or road, and from my experience there's never much traffic up the glen."

"I'm a methodical man," he said. "There are some things to discuss first. Business before pleasure, to coin a phrase."

"Does that mean you want to know how much of a dowry I'll have?"

"I'm taking you without a dowry. Your pedigree's enough."

"You sound like somebody about to buy a new sheep dog." She moved away from him.

"Are we going to be like Ruari and Bellann?" he asked, "but with three thousand miles of ocean between us instead of half of Uig?"

"Good Lord, no!" she exclaimed fervently. "What's a mere house compared to a sexy blond like Ruari?"

"That wasn't quite the answer I had in mind."

"I love America," she said. "I love Hazlehurst. But where you are is home for me now. I can't help it, Ewen, today I'm vulnerable, I have no defenses. So you get the abject truth—"

She couldn't stop herself. What in hell was pride but a five-letter word? "I'm at your mercy. I'll match and mend socks forever. But *after*."

"After what?"

"After I hear the twenty ways. And then there's that joke."

"What joke?" He was frowning at her, creasing his lower lip as if pondering her mental state.

" 'Gie us you hand, lassie.' "

His laugh echoed off of the walls around them, and he tried to haul her into a bear hug, but she resisted; it was confession time and the last appalling truth had to be gotten over or stumbled around.

"I don't have a male equivalent of Kay in my life, but my life—well—" She blurted out, "It's a double life. I write books beside my professional ones, but not what you'd expect. Nobody at the college knows. It's like having one illegitimate child a year. The one I'm working on now is called *The Prisoner Heart*, and the principal characters are named Alasdair and Catriona." She wanted to look him in the eye but it was he who turned his head so that he was gazing across the cemetery to the little V of scintillating water showing between the hills. She could feel the heat traveling up her body but she pushed wretchedly on. "They're romances. But the history is absolutely correct," she said. "I do a good deal of research."

It sounded pathetic. She thought queasily, for someone like him, it must be like hearing that I write pornography. Finally she said, "Well?"

"My latest bastard son's messing around with Prince Charlie," he said, still staring over the cemetery. "That sounds immoral but I assure you they're neither of them that sort, pretty as the Prince is in his portraits. My pen name is Finlay Gordon."

"Then I saw you on the book racks in London and Glasgow! And in Stornoway! But the jackets were so bloody I wouldn't buy them. Ewen, I can't believe this! Does anybody else know?"

326 / ELISABETH OGILVIE

"Only Murdo." He looked around with a faint and doubtful smile. "Are you as horrified as you sound?"

"No. I'm so happy I could scream, only I haven't the wind. You've knocked it out of me. But if that book is what's on your work table, Kay must know."

"What's spread out there is a serious project. Who knows about you?"

"Only you. My name's Mariana Grange."

"Very good," he said solemnly. Then they began to laugh. In the middle of it he reached for her, and they were abruptly quiet, their faces close.

"Now is the time to begin to tell you the twenty ways," he said, "and this is the place, as you say. Where it began, but not where it will end. And here's another proverb for you. 'The world may come to an end, but music and love will endure.' " Then he spoke to her in the Gaelic, and translated each paragraph afterward.

"My desire and my love is on you from the first time I met those eyes clear as a trout stream in the sunlight."

"That's a lie," said Alison, "because you didn't like me at all. But it sounds nice. Go on."

"Oh, red-haired maiden of the tender mouth, with you beside me I would conquer the seven worlds. An end will come to summer, and the winter winds are cruel, but hot is the fire of the love between us."

"Lovely," she murmured. "Can you really come up with twenty of these?"

"I've only begun, and we have world enough and time." He rested his cheek against her head and began again to speak in the secretive, musical Gaelic. In the middle of a long melodious line he shifted to English. "What did you say about no traffic in the glen?"

She lifted her head reluctantly and looked around. Three children and the dogs Nick and Peadar were on their way up. Peader was on her trail and had almost reached the brook,

Nick was loping in wide ecstatic circles, birds were flying up, and the children waved and shouted, shrill as gulls.

"Charlie says Peigi's home, and come to your tea!"